WILKES
ON TRIAL

Also by Charles Sevilla
Published by Ballantine Books

WILKES: HIS LIFE AND CRIMES

WILKES
ON TRIAL

Charles
Sevilla

BALLANTINE BOOKS
NEW YORK

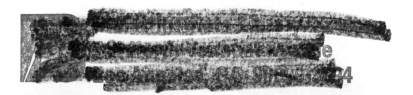

This book's story and characters are fictitious. The setting is New York City, and a number of historical events in the city's colorful history are mentioned, but only as surroundings in which the fictional characters may play. In fact, the author of this novel is but a figment of his own imagination.

Library of Congress Cataloging-in-Publication Data
Sevilla, Charles.
   Wilkes on trial / Charles Sevilla — 1st ed.
     p. cm.
   Sequel to: Wilkes: his life and crimes.
   ISBN: 0-345-37564-5
   1. Lawyers—Fiction. 2. Trials—Fiction. I. Title.
PS3569.C52812W54   1993
813'.54—dc20
                                     92-22113
                                      CIP

Text Design by Mary A. Wirth

Manufactured in the United States of America
First Edition: February 1993
10 9 8 7 6 5 4 3 2 1

Preface

Wilkes on Trial is my second book about John Wilkes. His legal, and sometimes illegal, exploits before the bar of New York City are recorded here by his quiet law partner, Winston Schoonover. Unlike the first book, *Wilkes: His Life and Crimes,* this one has a plot, more or less, as well as a beginning, a middle, and an end. Like the first book, it is a mendaciously accurate depiction of a justice system gone whacko.

The Wilkes saga was first chronicled by your faithful servant—then writing as Winston Schoonover—before, during, and after the always lively court sessions with Mr. Wilkes. For me, the writing has been a kind of self-help therapy, a penned release from a disease known to all court-hardened litigators as Battered Lawyer Syndrome—the mother of all afflictions suffered by the criminal defense bar in the Temple of Doom (otherwise known as the Criminal Courts Building). It is what one gets from daily appearing before the mindless defending the defenseless against the all-powerful.

Wilkes recklessly threw himself in harm's way to defend the citizen-accused in the Temple. He was imprudent, to say the least. He will never be elected President of the United States. Or Judge, although he came close once. But for him, these battles pitted good versus bad, right versus wrong, morality against evil, *People* v. *The Knuckledragger.* Wilkes represented The Knuckledragger. From these bloody battles emerged the smell of Wilkes's legend.

Voyeurs will rejoice that in what follows I have used the correct names of my characters, revealed all of their secrets, exposed attorney-client and work product privileged information (which it was a privilege to reveal), and portrayed the characters in as explicit and as unflattering a manner as possible. Like life, much of what results is in bad taste, but such is the delight of writing fiction.

The reader will also note that while this book is written almost entirely in the voice of Winston Schoonover, occasionally, at certain exquisite moments, I cannot resist jumping into the minds of other characters in order to reveal their sordid perspectives of the revolting developments enveloping them. Forgive me.

Finally, I would like to expose and thank the following people for allowing me this performance: my literary agent, Joseph Vallely of Flaming Star Enterprises; my wonderful editors at Ballantine, Mary South and the late Chris Cox; and my two delightful friends in Los Angeles, Ballantine publicists Liz Williams and Marie Coolman. Also, many thanks and love to my wife Donna, Dad and Jeanne, Michael and Cynthia, Lisa, Laura, and Jessica, Chris and Tim, John and Lew, Bax and Ron, Sloan and Gail, Mike and Terri, Peter, Doris and Mary, Jack and Marilyn, Wilkie and Jimmy, the Eight O'Clock Morning Round Tablers, the Over-the-Mission-Hills-Sunday-Morning-B-Ballers, and to a million bashed lawyers for having to put up with it and enduring you know who.

CMS

WILKES
ON TRIAL

— 1 —

The Field Marshal

*"The acme of judicial distinction means the ability to look
a lawyer straight in the eyes for two hours and not hear a
damned word he says."*
CHIEF JUSTICE JOHN MARSHALL

*"Reel in horror when you draw Judge Knott.
You get more justice from the KGB."*
JOHN WILKES

I love the Woolworth Building. The old Gothic monument at 233 Broadway has the dark traditional beauty of a Flamenco dancer. I like the way she stretches to the heavens some 792 feet above the southern edge of old City Hall Park. I like her elongated pointed archways which hint of medieval spirituality. I like the way her spiraling tower peeks into low-riding clouds. Most of all, I like making big bucks officing in the great lady with my law partner, John Wilkes.

Her height fools you. It pulls your eyes up so you don't notice her lavishly ornamented skirt dressed with lacy carvings. In an era when a 1964 Mustang is deemed a classic of antiquity, this sixty-story building, once the tallest building in the world, is from another age. She was the colossus of her generation. Cass Gilbert designed her, and F. W. Woolworth built her in 1913 with the nickels and dimes he made from a thousand five-and-tens scattered all over America.

Today, she is dwarfed by the high-tech steel and glass monsters that weight down half of Manhattan. She is as out of place as a cocker spaniel in a cockfight. Architecture is like that. It speaks to its time. Modern man has no patience for marveling at the delicate detail of bas relief or the elegance of an elongated arch.

Contemporary buildings must be huge, clean, and efficient. No squandering of effort or material on the cold slab exteriors is permitted. Gargoyles, towers, or windows that open, these are frivolities of the time in which we live.

Intolerance for detail is indicative of our lost capacity for observation. It is why a forgotten beauty like the Woolworth exists invisible in the shadows of her neighboring behemoths. Her sculpted skin and lovely lines go unappreciated by the thousands of New Yorkers who daily dance at her feet.

The Woolworth was the perfect locale for the Law Offices of John Wilkes. We felt comfortable making law there. For more than twenty years my partner and I made monthly donations for the right to do business in the magnificent old temple.

BRENDA

Brenda Van Ark also knew the building. Petite, perky, and smart, she daily made the walk from her small apartment to City Hall Park, usually in the early evening after school at NYU where she studied music. She walked to give her dog, Bertie, a chance to do his business and frolic a bit, a change from his difficult routine of guiding her through the rushing human crush on the sidewalks of New York.

After it happened, I would often think of her in that park at sunset. Wilkes and I always walked through the small park to the office at that hour after our long days in court. In the park, against a backdrop of reddening skies and burnt-orange clouds, the sun shed its golden light and silhouetted our old building's majesty.

Pretty Brenda Van Ark never saw this. She was legally blind. And in the early evening of a cold November 19, as she was walking home from the park on Barclay Street, a fiend came out of an alcove and violently picked her up and pulled her into the shadows of the building. While her seeing-eye dog Bertie stood by quietly (and some would say later, crazily), she resisted him as best she could. She kicked. Her arms flailed. She tried to scream but his big hand covered her mouth and most of her face. So she bit him, and he threw her to the ground like a used Kleenex.

It was then that she felt the pain in her shoulder. The mugger was trying to rip off her purse, but it was attached to her shoulder by a wide leather shoulder strap. On the ground, her hands free, she grabbed the purse and began hollering for help. The man lifted Brenda by the purse strap with one hand while the other made a fist, reached back and came down hard on her temple.

The blow hit her like a bolt of lightning, first the white flash of impact, then the physical sensation of the blunt force of the blow on her head, then the flood of darkness. There was no more resistance in her. She fell limp into the blackness.

Only Bertie witnessed the ugly scene. He calmly sat and watched his mistress beaten and robbed. His head turned slightly when the final blow was struck, as if to say, "That's interesting." But at the time, man's best friend had nothing to say about it.

Brenda, for all her visual limitations, was extraordinarily brave and perceptive during the ordeal. She had fought her unseen attacker, albeit unsuccessfully, but in the struggle, she collected valuable information about him. When the assault was over and she came to, the monster had left her bruised, bleeding, and purseless. She got up woozily, called the onlooking Bertie to her side—he came to her with his tongue out, panting, and eager for a pat on the head. She told him to get to work and she staggered to the phone in the lobby of our building to call the police.

Despite being beaten and scared to death, Brenda had the presence of mind to know that if the bastard was to be caught, it was then or never. Her body trembling with adrenaline from her shock, and blood dripping from her forehead, she quickly told the female dispatcher all she could: "My name is Brenda Van Ark. I've just been beaten and robbed. I'm in the lobby of the Woolworth Building. He did it just outside. You can catch him if you send police now."

The voice on the other end said, "Describe him."

"He's black and tall and muscular. He's incredibly strong. He grumbles that kind of jive-talk the young street gangsters talk, but in a distinctive voice, like low and gravelly, yet kind of melodic like the low tones of a tuba."

"Tell me more—like the color of clothing." The dispatcher was not much interested in the tonal qualities of the crook's voice.

"I couldn't tell. You see, I'm . . . I'm blind," said Brenda. "Hurry, send a car."

The dispatcher sighed in disappointment. "I'm sorry, miss, but your description narrows the possible field of culprits to about three or four hundred thousand. We can't just stop every black young man on this description."

"Here's more, then. The creep wore a mustache and small goatee, an earring on his right earlobe, a hat, maybe a beret, a wool jacket, Levi's type pants, and a big clunky bracelet on his right wrist. He smokes too, I could smell it on him."

"That's something to go on. I'll roll our mobile units to your area to look for the guy," said the voice to Brenda. "And I'm sending another officer to you now. Stay where you are and I'll stay on the phone with you till they get there. Oh, by the way, are you all right?"

HELP ON THE WAY

In five minutes two black police officers cruising the area heard the dispatcher's bulletin and spotted Lyle Diderot, well-known East Side gang leader of the Whiz Kids, as he ambled down a nearby street like he owned the place. Diderot was big, black, and wore a beret, an earring, a clunky bracelet, a wool jacket, and Levi's. A lighted unfiltered Camel dangled from his sneering lips.

The cop riding shotgun pointed to Diderot and said to his buddy, "Let's stop that one." The driver pulled to the curb ahead of Diderot and both officers got out of the car and set up a two-man sidewalk blockade as the Field Marshal approached.

"Hold up, bro," said the driver to Diderot.

The Field Marshal stopped his ambling ten feet short of the two cops. "Whatchu want, pigs? Don't fuck with me. I ain't done nothin'. Leave me be."

The two cops inspected Lyle Diderot. He fit the radio dispatch perfectly. The driver, ignorant of Brenda's visual limitation, instructed his buddy to call in and have the victim brought to the scene for a show-up identification. He unbuttoned the flap on his hip holster and said to Diderot, "Somebody wants to see you. She'll be here in a few minutes, and until she is, you are not going anywhere. Don't move."

Field Marshal Diderot did not move anything but his lips. "Man, this is bullshit. I ain't stayin' around here with two pigs waitin' on some bitch."

The driver put his hand on the butt end of his gun as Diderot showered the two cops with more obscenities than Larry Flynt could print in a standard-sized dirty magazine. The two were unaffected by the verbal indignities. Actually, they were happy to be where they were; this wasn't gang turf. The Field Marshal was in the DMZ of gang-war land. A supportive crowd would not form to make the confrontation more dangerous than it already was. New Yorkers just walked by the three men like they didn't exist.

ON LOCATION

When Brenda arrived on location, she asked to be allowed to run her hands over Diderot to aid in her identification. Lyle was not cooperative and had to be held by the cops while she made her examination. She first felt for the clunky bracelet on his right wrist which had been squashed into her face during the assault. She felt the beret, the wool jacket, the Levi's, and the earring on his right earlobe. She smelled his foul tobacco-stained breath. She heard him protest, "Get dat blind bitch offa me! What da fuck is goin' on, man?" The voice was familiar, distinctively low, and sounded like a tuba.

"Ma'am, can you identify this man?" asked one of the cops.

Brenda centered herself before Diderot by grabbing each of his elbows in her hands. Then she swiftly rocked her right leg backward and drove it forward with all her might so that her knee's upward thrust landed squarely on Diderot's groin. "You're damned right I can," she said. And she continued kneeing and kicking and screaming, "Give me my purse back!" until the cops pulled Diderot out of range.

Brenda's identification was enough to arrest the Field Marshal. She was taken to the hospital for the routine swabbings and scrapings so that the DNA boys could see if Diderot's body tissues or hairs or clothing fibers turned up where they didn't belong.

I know all these sordid details because Lyle Diderot became our client after a couple of young thugs delivered a bag of cash to our offices and said that the Field Marshal of the Whiz Kids requested the legal talents of one John Wilkes as soon as possible in the matter of his liberty. Or, as they put it in their own vernacular: "Get yo' fuggin' ass over to the court and get the Marshal some bail for us to tho' down."

RETAINED

After examining the contents of the brown shopping bag, Wilkes's first words to the two punks were: "Gentlemen, we shall do it!" To me he said, "To the Tombs!" This seemed to satisfy the two thugs that Wilkes had an appreciation of the immediacy of their demands.

One tough, a short guy wearing a tightly wrapped red bandanna over his head and missing his two front teeth, then said, "Marshal's got court tomorrow on dis bullshit beef. You get him out tomorrow."

I tensed as the toothless Bandanna said this. The punk's eyes had that sociopathic hardness which says, "I'd kill you in the morning for ten dollars or maybe just 'cause you look good for killin' and I won't give it another thought for the rest of my life." You know the type.

Demands for results by clients were very dangerous. Wilkes looked into the fellow's lizardlike eyes. "I make no guarantees over what happens in the courtroom except for my best performance. From your presence here, I assume you well know that what I give is usually enough to carry the day. But not always. I don't buy judges. They're only sold at private sales. Unless you're in a position to promote one of the bastards to the appellate bench, bribery will only get you five-to-ten at Attica."

Wilkes pushed the money bag across the table. It hissed as he slid it toward the two punks. "If you guys want someone to guarantee results, you'll have to get someone else."

Years of experience in the law business teaches you to never oversell yourself. Clients are there to see you because someone apparently thinks you're pretty good. Underplaying yourself has the remarkable reverse psychological effect of solidifying that impression.

Anyway, when you're dealing with clients who have a demonstrated capacity for armed robbery, assault, head bashing for fun and profit, or worse, you don't want to disappoint with puffed proclamations of greatness. You don't guarantee what you don't own. Courtroom acquittals are not part of the office inventory. They have to be earned on the battlefield.

THE TWO JAKES

As Wilkes spoke, I knew he was thinking of Jake Turnish, a lawyer who had recently promised some cocaine-connected Colombians way too much by way of performance. But that was Jake—an average lawyer with a fatal proclivity for self-overpromotion.

Jake's fee arrangement was based on two mistaken assumptions. The Colombians mistook his enormous fee as a guarantee that the fix was in and that a pass out of serious legal difficulty was given. But this wasn't the old country where money was the invariable get-out-of-jail-free card.

Jake mistook the Colombians too-easy willingness to part with a ton of cash as an example of their desire for his vast legal talents. Easy come, easy go. In reality, it was simply a wanton squandering of ill-gotten gains. The resulting cultural miscommunication cost the Colombians thirty years each.

It cost Jake Turnish his right to continue breathing. They did it as they did in the old country. Jake was kidnapped and taken to a remote area outside of town. The kidnappers chained his upper and lower torso with two chains. Each chain was then connected to a car. The Colombians then expressed their disappointment in Jake's representation by driving off in opposite directions.

When you're in the law business, you make sure the client understands the limitations of the practice. Fee arrangements can be the ultimate test of an attorney's skills at communication.

TOUGH LUCK

The two toughs before us didn't want to hear talk about Wilkes's limitations. The Bandanna looked to his buddy, a well-muscled black youngster wearing a black beret, torn purple T-shirt, black Levi's, and high-top Reeboks. His eyes advertised that here was a young man for whom life, liberty, and the pursuit of happiness were solely his to enjoy by freely taking it from others. Muscles spoke: "Marshal jus' told us to hire you, man. Dat's it. Don't need no speech. You do what needs to get done."

"Fine," said my friend, "just so's we understand each other."

Muscles and the Bandanna left without acknowledging any understanding. They were just two guided missiles launched to drop their payload and return to the silo. They were beyond understanding. After they were gone, I put the bag of money in the office safe. Wilkes and I then went directly to jail to see our new client.

THE MARSHAL

Field Marshal Lyle Diderot had been the longtime leader of the Whiz Kids; he led a gang which got its name because of the obscene acts the gangsters performed on a fallen enemy following a street rumble. Diderot stood six and one half feet of muscle, was black as a moonless night, and had a face that would terrify his own mother. His eyes were colder and more menacing than those of Muscles and the Bandanna.

He came into the interview room, sullen and quiet, and sat heavily into the battered, gray metal chair. The legs of the chair shrieked on the dirty cement floor as he skidded on it. He lit a Camel and blew smoke at us. He didn't say a word.

Wilkes usually greeted clients with an offering of his hand and an introduction, but he assessed that this situation called for another tack. "Your soldiers came to see me today and said you wanted to hire me." He said this flatly through the cloud of gray smoke.

"Yeah," said the Field Marshal as he crossed both of the arms across his chest. His big eyes glared at Wilkes. His cigarette dangled from the right side of his mouth. "You get me outta here. I never touched that blind bitch. Man, what kinda fuckin' case is this, me gettin' fingered by a blind bitch? Why she tryin' to hang this beef on me?" His voice was distinctive and crackled loud and low. I thought it would make a great singing voice, one that could carry for miles.

"I don't want to hear anything about the facts here," said Wilkes. "When I get you out, we can talk, but I don't want you talking to anyone in here. You know what I mean?"

The Field Marshal made a clucking sound with his mouth. He looked contemptuously at us, as if to say, "Shit man, I know better than you can imagine." Then he said, "Shit man, I know better than you can imagine. I been in here before. Ain't nobody alive gonna go snitchin' off the Field Marshal."

Wilkes and I knew what he meant. The Whiz Kids were a well-known gang, which is to say one so dreaded by its rivals it could terrorize a gang off a block of turf without having to even rumble for it. Their authority in the Tombs was stronger than on the streets—there were so many of them in there—and they were exceedingly ruthless in taking their vengeance on those who would turn against them. This thought caused Wilkes to think of something very close to home.

"I told your soldiers that I will do my usual best in your defense. I'll throw all I've got at the prosecution case. But I don't control results."

Diderot cracked what would pass for a smile on his puss. The corner of his mouth with the cigarette in it rose a fraction for an instant and then receded into its normal scowl. "You take care of the case and I'll take care of the jury."

I saw Wilkes wince. "I am sure that your very presence in the court will convince the jury of your innocence," I offered in an effort to turn the talk from jury tampering. Discussions in the Tombs between attorney and client were supposed to be confidential, but we knew that was bull. If the room wasn't bugged, the walls were not thick enough to mute our words from the nearby guards and snitches.

Diderot turned his big head and stared at me. "Yeah, me and about a hundred of my warriors in full battle gear," he said. "I know how to win. You just get me outta dis shithole."

Wilkes nodded. We left the Field Marshal to his keepers and walked back to the office at Wilkes's normal Olympic pace. I gasped to my friend that no bail for the Field Marshal would mean he would await trial among the freedom-loving, perjuring inmates who would jump at the chance to hop on the stand and frame the Field Marshal. "Even against a fearsome brute like Whiz Kid Field Marshal Lyle Diderot, some fool is gonna think the D.A. can protect him and is gonna sing for his supper. This is just the type of case for it."

STATE *V.* DIDEROT

State v. *Diderot* was a case for it because it had High Profile written all over it. The victim was pretty, blind, white, smart, defenseless, and innocent. And Lyle Diderot was, well, Lyle Diderot. An arrest of this powerful and well-known Field Marshal in itself might not attract local media attention, but with Wilkes defending, and with the Beauty and the Beast plot line, it was certain to attract media. Every snitch in the Tombs would be looking forward to reading enough of the story in the paper to make up a convincing confession of the Field Marshal's. But any snitch would have to weigh the D.A.'s promises for probation and protection against the odds of the Whiz Kids cutting his throat.

My comments brought Wilkes out of his reverie. "I really doubt the canaries in the Tombs are gonna dare come out to sing on the Field Marshal. Even if the paper boys provide all the lyrics. His gang's too strong, especially in the Tombs. But snitches can be stupid. One of 'em might go for it."

We reached the office and Wilkes began answering calls from the newspaper and TV reporters who had heard that the Field Marshal had hired him. I began preparing the bail papers.

Y. KNOTT

"That'll be denied, counsel," intoned Judge Yulburton Abraham Knott in response to my friend's hour-long pitch for bail the next morning. "You really can't be serious, Mr. Wilkes."

Drawing Y. Knott as our judge in Diderot's case was a tremendous shock brought on by our ill-timed and inauspicious challenge to the first judge to get the case, Arthur Rimbaud, known to members of the bar as the Count Draco of the criminal bench. Trials for the defense before Count Draco were like Chinese water torture. The judge's motto was, "I never saw a defense attorney I didn't dislike." Even so, we would never have cast that devil out if we'd known who was waiting in the wings.

Judge Yulburton Abraham Knott was supposed to be out of the criminal draw. He had been trying only complex civil cases for years after having been happily driven to this civil case exile by the concerted action of sane defense attorneys who challenged the son of a bitch off criminal cases. That left Hizoner with nothing to do but sit in chambers and write, under the pseudonym "Grotek," grotesque futurist visions of a twenty-first century justice system. These he peddled to small circulation criminal justice magazines.

Judge Knott prided himself on his good looks, keen intelligence, and perpetual regal bearing. He also gloried in the swiftness of his criminal trials, which he accomplished by doing everything possible to end the proceeding quickly in favor of the prosecution. This invariably meant a judicial castration of the defense case.

When the court clerk announced the surprise assignment of the Diderot case to "the courtroom of the Honorable Y. Knott," Wilkes reeled from the defense table in horror. He turned and looked at me with wide eyes and cried, "We could get more justice from the KGB."

Our client, Field Marshal Diderot, did not comprehend the unexpected disaster that had just beset his case. "Say hey," he said to me, "why not? What's dat mean? Why not this courtroom?"

I elected not to inform the Field Marshal about all of the details of Y. Knott. He would learn all he needed to know soon enough.

We were informed by the clerk who saw our shock that the new presiding administrative judge had just that morning assigned this case to Knott in a move to make sure all the judges took a fair share of the criminal cases.

Within ten minutes we were in Knott's court. Wilkes's army of chattering reporters and veteran groupie court watchers followed us there. Knott's longtime clerk, Alvin Scribner, called the case of *State v. Diderot* as the judge bounded on the bench. Knott's dark blue eyes peered over the top of our client's lengthy rap sheet. The papers partially hid a face both drawn and bloated. Upon the sharp, angular, pale face hung out-of-place floppy white cheeks. The white head atop his black-robed body looked like a white shell on a lava bed. Vesuvius spoke in response to Wilkes's bail pitch: "Look at his record. In 1963 he fired a gun four times into a bus full of people."

"That's ancient history, Judge. Read the reports," said Wilkes in defense of his client. "The bus backfired twice. Mr. Diderot believed someone was shooting at him from inside the vehicle. When a man's been shot at as much as this man, what do you expect? You can't deny him his survival instinct. Fortunately, no one was injured, er, seriously."

Judge Knott then lamented the poor marksmanship of the mystery man in the bus. Still reading and embellishing from our client's rap sheet, the judge said, "Top this one, Wilkes. In 1965 your boy shot a man in the back. On Orchard Street no less."

"Again, ancient history exaggerated by the corrosive passage of time. I am informed, Your Honor, that my client mistook a pedestrian's ill-timed flatulence for the sound of gunfire. Of course, he fired in self-defense, albeit imperfect self-defense."

Knott spoke to the packed courtroom: "Your client seems to have an insatiable appetite for violence." The judge smiled slightly as he said these words. The phrase pleased him. He thought it captured the essence of the defendant before him. An even more pleasant vision came to him. He saw a struggling Field Marshal Lyle Diderot being led to his final seating on Sparky, the electric chair in which Con Ed once upon a time had made cons dead. He knew it would never happen, but he could dream, couldn't he? Dreaming is what made him so creative in his futurist writings, in trying and settling all those huge business suits, and in computerizing his docket with an original software package so that things could flow with maximum efficiency. He returned his thoughts to the business before him. "Perhaps this will put you in a bit of a pickle, Wilkes, but put yourself in my position. Would you release this man? What bail would you fix?"

Judge Knott enjoyed torturing attorneys by putting them in impossible positions. At sentencings, he used to ask defense counsel, "Sir, what sentence would you give your child-molesting, murdering client?" Or, he might ask the attorney, "If I order his release from custody today, would you be willing to permit him to stay at your home under house arrest as a condition of his five years of probation?"

Many attorneys, taken by surprise, stuttered and stammered at these unpalatable suggestions, which was Knott's objective. If the defendant's own attorney would choke at the idea of his release into the free world, then surely the good Judge Knott, by preventing it, was a fine fellow and the public's great protector. Making defense counsel look foolish and unreasonable also made the judge look very good. Judge Knott got a lot of satisfaction getting defense attorneys in trouble with their clients this way. That was why we all challenged him and drove him to the civil bench.

JUDGE WILKES

The tactic would not work on John Wilkes. My friend knew Knott well enough to anticipate the question, and he answered without hesitation. "Judge Knott, as a lawyer I could not say this, but since you ask me to act as judge, I can. Lyle Diderot appears here clothed with the presumption of innocence. The things you point out may test the cloth somewhat, but it still shrouds him. And what makes the cloak so complete and impenetrable is my own personal knowledge that he is absolutely innocent of these heinous charges."

The paper boys in attendance scribbled down every word Wilkes said, as he knew they would. The groupie court watchers murmured at Wilkes's audacity. Wilkes's last words were joined with a sweeping motion of his right arm and a half pirouette so that he faced the jammed, jabbering gallery. "By rights, you should dismiss this case right now, Judge. At a minimum, the Field Marshal should be released on his own recognizance."

Wilkes knew Knott would sooner give Son of Sam instant parole to a nunnery than Diderot bail. But if my friend could not get reasonable bail for his client, at least he could get good press. Wilkes continued to the gallery, "And I ask my many friends from the media to report my comments so that, hopefully, the guilty culprit will be driven by conscience to turn himself in and not let an innocent man suffer any further."

Every day of the week in a city of eight million there are at least five hundred men yearning to confess to anything. Getting the news people to receive their calls, and best of all, to report "yet another confession in the Diderot case," could only help saturate the city in reasonable doubt as to the Field Marshal's guilt.

Wilkes moistened his eyes a bit and looked over the attentive audience, to the mahogany-lined back wall and up to the ceiling. He lifted his hands to a prayer position in front of his chest and half yelled, "Please sir! Save an innocent man! Come forward at once. We can help you. We will help you! We must help you!"

"Your man's a trigger-happy menace," said a disgusted Judge Knott.

"Without a single incident of violence toward a female in his rather well-developed record," replied Wilkes as he turned to face the presidium. "There could be no better proof of innocence."

"Yeah, that's right, motherfucker. I ain't done nuttin' bad to no bitches." Our client, seeing our bail position faltering somewhat, added his booming voice to the debate. His gigantic frame rose from behind counsel table and nearly tipped it over. Three bailiffs ran to his side to make sure he stayed put.

Judge Knott saw that it was time to end this hearing before it got out of hand. With great solemnity he said, "Taking all of the facts and circumstances into consideration, and giving very serious attention to the comments of the district attorney, who has recommended bail in the amount of $750,000, I will concur in that amount. Arraignment and trial setting tomorrow morning at nine. We are adjourned."

Knott then rose and turned toward his chambers door. He hopped down the three short steps that separated the altar from the ground upon which we earthly mortals walked and skipped toward his door, whistling "Dixie."

THE HORROR

The Field Marshal left the courtroom yelling, "I been fucked! I been fucked!" To which Wilkes added, "And without the benefit of intercourse!" Our client was not a happy man, but now he understood why we were filled with dread when the case landed in Knott's chamber of horrors.

The die was cast. The resources of the Whiz Kids would not reach the astronomical bail set by Knott. Diderot's not being released pretrial necessitated something Wilkes abhorred—a speedy trial. The Field Marshal would not put up with delay if it meant more time living in a fashion to which he was unaccustomed in the despicable Tombs. Also, a speedy trial was necessary because the less time the Field Marshal spent in custody, the less chance of a stool pigeon coming forward to testify to an overheard phony confession.

Wilkes and I race-walked back to the Woolworth. Wilkes was anxious about the novel idea of going to trial too quickly. This anxiety brought on an explosion of work and temper. By the time we were in the office, he was firing out orders like a general under siege.

"Calendar a motion for a four-month continuance of the trial date and schedule the hearing tomorrow morning. Write up the papers tonight."

A continuance! I thought Wilkes had lost his mind. "That's the last thing we need," I argued.

Wilkes cut me short. "Of course we don't want one! That's why we're asking for it!"

I hurriedly wrote the motion. Actually, it was a brilliant idea. Judges hate defense lawyers. There is a Newtonian principle of judicial reaction to defense motions. The defense wish is the judge's command—to do the opposite. So the best way to go to trial promptly was to ask the judge for delay. While I wrote, Wilkes decided it would be a good idea to visit the Field Marshal and explain something about courtroom etiquette and our novel strategy in dealing with Judge Knott.

At the hearing the next day, Judge Knott sat and listened with an amused look on his face as Wilkes eloquently explained his need for time to prepare this very difficult case. He asked for four months, hoped for nothing, and expected whatever Judge Knott deemed worst for the defense.

KNOTT'S ASCENSION

And why not? Knott had the worst possible professional background to be a judge. A long time ago—so much time ago that those who did not remember would not have believed it—Knott had been a white-collar criminal defense lawyer. He also had a wife, Alice, who was the daughter of a very prominent Democratic party official in the city. The white-collar work and his wife's family connections gave him plenty of contact with the high and mighty. In New York the high and mighty buy and sell judgeships like seats on the stock exchange. It was thus inevitable that the ambitious Mr. Knott would become Judge Knott unless he disdained status, security, and power.

On March 4, 1959, at exactly three in the afternoon, Yulburton Abraham Knott was asked if he wanted the job. Eight minutes later he was sworn in.

Why defense lawyers make lousy judges was something Wilkes found bewildering. Here were these lawyers struggling every day to keep a sometimes mindless, arbitrary people-crushing justice machine from devouring clients. From within this machine the lowly defense lawyer invariably sought mercy and sometimes even justice. In the process, a lot of folks got wiped out.

Yulburton Knott saw enough human wreckage in his time at the bar to understand human weakness. He saw enough unfairness to understand things should be different. He observed, but he did not see. Instead, when he took the bench, it was as if the bias, unfairness, and harshness he witnessed as a lawyer were just training material for his life on the bench. On the bench, his true self emerged. Putting on the robe does that. It brings out the real you.

Judge Y. Knott became a tormenter of the people. They assigned him to the criminal calendar figuring that he would flourish in the land of his expertise. And flourish he did. Within ten years Knott was renowned as the most efficient, knowledgeable, and vicious pro-prosecution judge in New York.

And soon out of business. His inability to be fair to the defense made him subject to blanket trial challenges from the defense bar. When his court went dark for weeks at a time during the long gaps between trials, Knott put plume to parchment and wrote his fictional futurist blueprint of the ideal criminal justice system. He published two books under the nom de plume Grotek. The first was titled *Mobile One at Large in the New Republic.** The second book, entitled *Orbital Techtronic Cranial Infiltrators: Satellites in Space-Age Criminal Justice,*† followed shortly thereafter.

To Wilkes, Judge Knott's fantasies were the epitome of the judge's love for the speedy resolution of cases without the dreary delay of trial. His dream of a perfect tribunal was that of a greased conveyer belt of prison-bound guilty pleading clients. His docket cleared of the sludge of trial by jury would permit time for his important philosophical writings.

While Knott wrote of his dreams of Perfect Justice, worried court administrators, concerned about the waste of a courtroom and judge's salary, began assigning him to courts where no challenge could be filed by defense lawyers, like the criminal arraignment calendar. Even this did not solve the problem. The arraignment calendar is a dreary place. It is the court where the defendant, just arrested, first meets the judicial part of the criminal justice system. The meeting is brief. The defendant is dragged from a holding cell, read the charges against him, advised of his constitutional rights,

---

* An excerpt of this book appears at the end of this chapter.
† An excerpt may be found in *Wilkes: His Life and Crimes* (Ballantine, 1990), pp. 253–54.

heard on the issue of bail, and then pushed back to his cell. All in all, it takes about a minute.

Knott reduced that time to less than thirty seconds. Once, a poor black defendant was before him and asked for an appointed lawyer. Knott took delight in appointing him a V-6—an attorney who would be identified by anyone who knew anything about lawyers as a walking violation of the Sixth Amendment. Shiftless dolts were Knott's appointment specialty.

One defendant interrupted the judge's gracious offer of the V-6 by insisting his arrest was a big mistake. "I am innocent," he said. Knott, angered at this brief interruption of his proceedings, stared at the man as if he had just been convicted of mass murder. He said, "Save that. Tell it to your lawyer and we'll take it into account at sentencing."

During the 1968 Olympics in Mexico City there was a furor when two black American sprint medalists made a silent, public protest of American racism. While on the victory stand and as the National Anthem played, they raised their black gloved fists. Knott was in arraignment court the next day when about twenty black men came in on a big dope bust. Half of them—unaware of what they'd get—asked for appointed counsel. Knott said they'd have to swear to their poverty in order to qualify for appointed counsel. He told them all to raise their right arms, make fists, and take the following oath: "I'm busted."

There followed many disgusting incidents like this in Knott's court. When news of them got out, the court administrators decided to put Knott out to pasture. Defense lawyers made the criminal courts out of bounds for him. His nasty sense of racist humor would keep him out of the administrative calendar courts. That left one place for him. Civil.

That is where he had been for these many years when all of a sudden, like a hound out of Hell, he rises to preside over our case, all because some new administrative jerk without a sense of history thought all the judges should pitch in on the criminal backlog. And this case was an especially bad case for Knott to handle. It was a criminal case. John Wilkes, archenemy of the world judiciary, was defending. The defendant, Field Marshal Diderot, was a big, mean-looking gang leader with a record that was long play. Worse yet, Lyle Diderot was black.

HEIGHT OF EPITOME

But this time at least our Machiavellian strategy was playing into Knott's obsession for speedy justice. We actually wanted to go to trial quickly. In order to get there, we had to make sure Judge Knott believed it was the last thing in the world we wanted.

Wilkes and I appeared with Diderot the next day for trial setting and the ruling on my motion to continue the matter for four months. The smiling court clerk, Alvin Scribner, was lounging in his chair beneath the judge's presidium. Alvin had been Knott's court clerk ever since Knott took the bench in civil. In stark contrast to Judge Knott, most of the lawyers liked Alvin. He was a lifer in civil service and never got overly involved in the work.

As soon as we arrived, Alvin buzzed Knott and we were under way. Wilkes reiterated our position. "Due to the seriousness of the charges, the newness of the case, and my own very full trial calendar, we will need a continuance," he lied.

"Well, counsel," said Judge Knott, "since trial will not take place today, I will obviously be continuing this case for a short period of time. Just how long a setoff do you want?"

"I need at least four months to interview all the witnesses," responded Wilkes. "Obviously, I haven't had a chance to interview anyone yet."

Miles Landish, the assistant district attorney handling the hearing, rose from his wooden chair. He had the physique of a sumo wrestler, the head of a block of wood, and the disposition of a rattlesnake. He was on this case because, like a masochistic prizefighter who refuses to stay on canvas after being decked for the eighth time in the round, Landish went out of his way to volunteer to prosecute cases Wilkes would be handling. His colleagues in the D.A.'s office gladly stepped aside.

He now offered, "Mr. Wilkes's comment is very interesting. As he well knows, other than his client and the victim, there were no witnesses."

Wilkes turned to the moon-faced prosecutor. "That you know of," he said. "Judge, you know how it is. The prosecutor doesn't even look for evidence once he thinks he's got his man. The assailant of Ms. Van Ark is still out there. He's a witness. His whole family could be witnesses. There may have been a hundred people who walked by and didn't report what they saw. Probably the same folks who years ago heard Kitty Genovese screaming for help and went back to sleep as she was being killed in the street. I need time to at least go look for them."

"That'll be denied, counsel. Trial will be in two weeks. Give them the date, Mr. Clerk."

Alvin lifted the computerized trial calendar and gave us a date in just fourteen days.

"Two weeks!" Wilkes screamed. "That's not enough time to iron out book and movie rights! I need more time!"

"Do the best you can." The judge smiled as he rose from the bench and, whistling again, disappeared into chambers. The race to trial was on.

Mobile One at Large in the New Republic by Grotek

The nation's urban force of police androids is now, happily I might say, quite widespread. The public, tired of so many senseless civilian deaths in the cities and revulsed by the tremendous losses of human officers killed battling the forces of anarchy in the streets, insisted on a solution far more drastic than the simple, cheap, and utterly worthless political solution of the 1990s—the repeal of the first eight amendments to the Constitution.

The National Institute of Justice, under the brilliant leadership of retired Supreme Court Justice Kevin Needingham Moriarity, resolutely worked with the brightest humanoid engineers, brain simulator software consultants, and federal police planners to develop the Mobile One androids. The goal was to take the human dying out of police work and make the androids the most feared crime-fighting force on earth. Moriarity was the modern Oppenheimer of this tireless work. His androids are on the streets today successfully fighting to bring about the annihilation of the worst of urban crime.

Androids are designed to be imposing sights. Each weighs 210 pounds and stands six feet four. Advances in the plasticity of high-tech materials gives them the agility to run the hundred-yard dash in world class time even while firing their light laser guns with deadly accuracy at fleeing criminals. To protect the expensive 2-986 Series B computer head components, they wear white-gleaming titanium helmets held on with blue leathersynette chin straps. What appear to be oversized mirror-lensed sunglasses add an ominous look, but they are really cameras taking in everything within a distance of one mile for complete computer analysis.

From the neck down they are decked out in fully zippered dark blue jackets. The material, leathersynette, has the tough, leathery look resembling that worn by the old-fashioned street cops. The extinction of leather-producing animals of course required the use of a synthetic body cover. The synthetic, leathersynette, is far better than leather. It stops bullets.

At the waist, suspended from a wide leathersynette belt, hang the usual array of headbusters, shiny cuffs, and the latest in laser hand weapons. Blackjack boots rise from the feet to surround blue leathersynette pants around the knees. Although the androids wear so much leathersynette that they creak like old wooden ships when they move, the sound is misleading. They can chase down any hoodlum who dares to test their foot speed.

Over the left breastplate of each android is pinned a large gold six-star badge on which is emblazoned, MOBILE ONE NPA: MAH. The initials stand for "National Police Android: Mobile, Agile, Hostile."

The NPA vehicles, the Mobile One units, contain sophisticated destructive armaments, most of which are still classified and cannot be described here. It is no secret, however, that the arsenal includes bazooka-launched missiles capable of small, clean microthermonuclear deliveries to appropriate targets such as fortified drug houses, massage parlors, or unlicensed abortion clinics. (An unexpected societal side benefit of the Mobile One NPA use of such force is the reduction in city budgets for adverse condemnation suits and blight clearance projects.)

Mobile One's programmers at the National Institute didn't need to make the androids so menacing. They just could not resist the temptation. The public fully supported the measures taken. After fifty years of uncontrolled lawlessness in the streets, the people wanted to fight back hard. The embittered majority of citizens, led by Justice Moriarity's slogan of protest—"Should the guilty be allowed to run about freely just because the police have no evidence against them?"—convinced Congress to fund the Department of Justice android program and mandate putting the androids into action within three years. And with Moriarity leading the way, the magnificent task was accomplished on time.

Hank and Frank

"Stop that one," says Hank to his partner Frank. Hank points out the window of his dark blue Mobile One unit toward a scruffy-looking youth making his way down Hill Street carrying a huge trispeaker ghetto blaster. Frank quickly wheels the police van to the curb and the startled kid freezes in his tracks.

Hank and Frank jump out of their vehicle exactly as they have done more than one hundred times that day. They approach the trembling youth. If they had been human, Hank and Frank would have sensed the boy's fright—a piss-in-your-pants terror triggered not by an imagined horror, but by the certainty of what was to come: detention, detection, discipline. A stop by the new Mobile One androids leaves nothing to the imagination.

The kid points to his silent trispeaker blaster and cries, "It's off! It's off!" Hank and Frank ignore the comment.

Hank approaches the motionless young man standing on the sidewalk holding his big radio. "We're Mobile One units," he says in his harsh, loud, metallic, computerized voice. "You've been selected to take the RABI's test." The youth looks up to the two cops and cringes. He sighs, "It's off, really it's off."

The Random Android Brief Inquiry (RABI) was also Moriarity's brainstorm. Once the androids were ready to hit the streets, if they were to be effective, they needed authorized programming to stop anyone and find out if they had committed or were about to commit an act prohibited, or about to be prohibited, by law. Early scientific testing on controlled populations revealed an accuracy rate of over 95 percent. And this was curiously increased to 99 percent when the androids were given olfactory senses.

Hank and Frank escort the kid to the rear of their Mobile One van and open the red doors for the test. The interior walls are covered floor-to-ceiling with sophisticated crime-stopping computers. Illuminated in the middle of this elec-

tronic horseshoe is a comfortable chair covered in blue leathersynette, stuffed with foam and perched on a shiny chrome pedestal.

The kid walks unaccompanied to the chair, sits down and swivels to turn his back to the open end of the van and the androids. "As you know, I must read you this warning," says Frank. "We ask only one question. You need not answer, although you have the right to if you want." Frank points to an orange-colored metal cone sticking out of the wall facing the suspect. "That sensing module will tell Mobile One all that needs to be known."

The young man moves not a hair follicle as the van doors are closed. The one question asked of all persons subjected to the RABI's exam is, "Have you done, or are you about to do, something illegal?" The kid hears the question and says nothing. The computer nevertheless clicks into a frenzy of activity: hundreds of tiny lights flash, little knobs, disks, and wheels turn, levers go up and down.

The kid is guilty as hell.

Guilt is easily determined by Mobil One's computers. They monitor every physiological and mental function and instantly feed the subject's thoughts into polygraphs, which, with amazing accuracy, isolate innocent stress from guilty knowledge. Once guilt is detected, the computer then determines the seriousness of the crime contemplated or completed. The crime level will determine the precise laser punishment to be inflicted instantly by the Mobile One's laser-firing mechanism. The entire process, from interrogation to confession to adjudication to sentence and punishment, takes less than five seconds.

Hank and Frank open the rear van doors. The kid has both hands covering his singed, smoking ears. He moans softly. The computer noiselessly spits out a punishment receipt which Hank gives the kid. It says,

SUSPECT RECEIVED A TWENTY-FIVE MILLISECOND LASER BURN AT THE NONLETHAL BUT AUGMENTED INFRACTION LEVEL FOR A VIOLATION OF MUNICIPAL ORDINANCE §16,653.41(A)(1)(V)(III)—ANTICIPATED PLAYING OF PORTABLE TRISPEAKER IN PUBLIC PLACE ABOVE ALLOWABLE DECIBEL LEVEL.

* Burn level augmented ten milliseconds because of prior similar offense within one year

NEW YORK POLICE DEPARTMENT, DIVISION OF PUNISHMENT

Hank tells the kid, "Obey the law." The kid jumps out of the van and goes his way.

Frank sniffs the air, turns to follow the smell and sees an elderly, disheveled-looking woman coming down the street pushing a battered market cart filled with junk. Frank points at her and says to Hank, "Stop that one."

2

The Reenactment

*"Innocent and guilty are harder to separate
than Siamese twins."*
CHARLIE CHAN

"This dog has a blunted affect."
DR. VLADIMIR KNUDSON

A lot of people thought Wilkes was crazy. Sunday, I was among them. At Wilkes's direction I was in the office scrambling to put together the pretrial motions in the Lyle Diderot case for filing on Monday, just ten days prior to the start of trial. Wilkes was home reviewing the police reports in order to work out the investigative assignments for our sleuth, Uriah Condo.

Working in the office on some of the weirdest, most hastily prepared motions ever to be filed in a New York court of law was definitely not my idea of a good time. The weather aggravated my irritation. November in New York is usually an arbitrary bitch—cool breezes one day abruptly turn to arctic blasts the next. This day was different. The sun dominated a cloudless blue sky, and the afternoon temperature climbed to a perfect seventy. It was a glorious day to be outdoors, and I wasn't.

.　.　.

GOING THROUGH THE MOTIONS

I was to pump out a motion to dismiss the whole case because our client's name was slightly misspelled in the indictment and because the document charged him with the crime of "aggravated a salt" rather than assault. When I argued with Wilkes that these were hopelessly frivolous technicalities, he shouted, "Write 'em, goddamn it! Make 'em clean up the charges like they should. An indictment isn't a goddamned college term paper! They're not getting away with sloppy pleadings or anything else with us. There's plenty of case authority to cite. Just look in my file cabinet drawer labeled Technical Objections. Then look for the file labeled Very Technical Objections."

I looked and found an old file bearing the name. It had nothing in it. I complained to Wilkes. He was still contemptuous. "Look in the same drawer under S," he said.

I asked just what it was I was looking for under S.

He answered, "Supertechnical Objections."

So I looked under S and I found the supertechnical objections file and it was thick with paper so old that the edges were crumbling. Scribbled on the pages in Wilkes's handwriting were abstracts of ancient cases, two of which seemed relevant enough to stretch to our case. The first was an 1880 California case entitled *People* v. *St. Clair*, 56 Cal. 406, in which the Supreme Court of the Golden State reviewed a theft conviction in which the word "larceny" had been misspelled in the indictment as "larcey." The very able jurists held that there was no such crime as "larcey" in the state of California. Appalled at the injustice of convicting a thief under a nonexistent (or misspelled) crime, they reversed the conviction. You can look it up.

Wilkes's note beside his abstract read, "Great state! California!"

The next case I found in the supertechnicality file was of even more ancient origin. Wilkes had handwritten a quote from Professor Radzinovicz's *History of the English Criminal Law* (vol. I, 1948). The professor reported an ancient case involving the trial for high treason of a man named as Christoporus Layer. The defense had objected to the indictment for misspelling the accused's name as "Christopherus, and also that one of two sentences in the indictment was expressed in "incorrect Latin."

Wilkes's margin note read, *Quen etiam laudet virtutem eorum, qui potentiorem facere linguam Latinam,* which he later explained to me meant, "praise for the patriotism of those who aim at strengthening the Latin language."

Citing these two ridiculous authorities, I wrote the motion to dismiss the indictment for failing to spell the charge and our client's name right. I wrote it a little more forcefully than that, calling it "the most fundamental denial of due process of law to hale into court the wrong man for the wrong crime."

REENACTMENT REPRIEVE

I moved on to the next motion. This one was for a courtroom reenactment of the alleged assault on Brenda Van Ark, a motion I found beyond comprehension in this case. Why would we repeat for the jury a live recreation of the crime? What could better bring home the horror of the act to the jury? This was another lousy idea and I developed a virulent case of writer's block dealing with it. For about five hours I just sat in my office blankly looking out the window and feeling the warmth of the sun as it splashed its rays on my face. I nodded out.

As I often do, I dreamed about floating freely through warm blue sky and looking down on rolling green fields for as far as the eye could see. No thoughts of the bustling, grimy city; no pressure to be here or there in impossible time limits; no outrageous work demands. I soared without a care, like a small windswept tuft of cloud, roaming freely and mindlessly wherever the wind would direct. I never felt so good.

RING! RING! RING! The ring of the phone was like an alarm going off in my head. My brief escape into sunny dreamland was over. Groggy and grumpy, I roughly picked up the receiver. It was Wilkes.

"It's a great day," he bubbled, "and you shouldn't slave away in the law mines all weekend," conveniently forgetting that he had virtually condemned me to that fate by demanding his ludicrous motions be written by Monday morning. "Climb out of the dusty books and come on over. We'll barbecue some juicy T-bones."

I needed no persuasion. When it comes to eating, I am a decided carnivore. "Damned right! I'll be right over. Anything you need me to pick up on the way?"

Wilkes paused for a second and said, "Hum, yeah, there is one thing. Bring the steaks."

He hung up. I should have been angry at this, but I was more moved by the thought of getting out of the office and away from those impossible motions. Anyway, we'd just been paid in Diderot's case, and I was bucks up. I didn't mind buying the meat.

WHIZ KIDS

When I received the phone call from the Whiz Kids telling me that Diderot had been arrested and wanted Wilkes to represent him, I was surprised. Wilkes was well known both for his brilliance in court as well as his huge fees. I thought the fee quote would scare them away. I said to the gangster voice, "Mr. Wilkes has long admired the Field Marshal and would be eager to represent him for thirty-five thousand up front in cash."

"Ya git it tomorrow," said the voice on the line, and hung up.

I'd heard that before many times and went on about my business, forgetting about the curious call. Until I read the Adell Loomis story in the morning *Times* the next day:

WHIZ KID GANG BANGS PIGGY BANK

Four masked and armed hoods entered the NYPD Savings and Loan yesterday morning and held customers and tellers at bay while looting the place. Bank vice-president Clinton Hooley, a retired police captain, said it was the largest heist of any NYPD bank ever. He said about $35,000 was taken.

Hooley blamed the job on the Whiz Kid gang. He said, "The little bastards made us lay down on the floor while they took every dime from the vault, the tills, and out of our pockets. Then they shot up the ceiling and pissed on all of us."

Investigating officer Joseph Tazaro states that the Whiz Kids are prime suspects and that police informants on the streets are now at work trying to confirm the gang's role in the robbery. He said, "A leak is inevitable."

Later that afternoon, when Wilkes and I looked into the large paper sack delivered to the office by the two thugs sent by Diderot, I felt sure this money was the booty from the recently unauthorized withdrawal from the NYPD bank. At the bottom of the bag were dozens of neatly stacked and wrapped bundles of bills with the pictures of Presidents Jackson and Grant staring up at me.

After the punks left, I mentioned to Wilkes the news article in the *Times* and my fears about the source of our fee. Wilkes just laughed. "You'll never take a fee if you've got to prove it's got a proper upbringing. Are you gonna tell everyone who comes in here that we won't represent 'em unless they prove their money is not dirty?"

"Well then, what do you tell them?"

"Not a frickin' thing. Ever heard of the presumption of innocence, Schoon? That's the way clients come to you, clothed in the warm fur of *the presumption*. I figure the presumption's big enough to cover their money too. As far as you know, those dear young boys have scraped together their paper route money so that they can send their Field Marshal a couple of Hallmark lawyers, Schoon. We should be flattered. They cared enough to send the very best."

BERTIE

We banked the money, I took an overdue draw, and had plenty of dough to pick up a couple a big steaks. I drove over to Wilkes's place and found him in his usual position, lying on his back on the sofa, his legs draped over its back. I said hello. He said, "Have you read the police reports, Schoon?" He knew that I hadn't had the chance, and before I got the door shut he was reading to me the victim's statement to the cops.

"I am blind. My German shepherd, Bertie, and I were walking down Broadway when a man grabbed me from behind and yanked me into a doorway or something like an alcove. His big hand covered my mouth and he said not to scream or he'd hurt me real bad, but I was fighting him right from the beginning. I bit his hand, which was gloved. He threw me on the ground and yanked at my purse but I hung on. Then he clobbered me with a fist and I guess I let go and he ran off. His name is Lyle Diderot and he lives in my apartment building. I know it is him because of his voice. It is big, booming, and gravelly like Louis Armstrong's."

Wilkes put the report down on his stomach. He was still laying on the sofa. His head turned to me and he grinned. "There's something, eh, Schoon? Something very wrong, eh? Got it?"

"I sure do," I guessed. "They got the wrong man. They should have arrested Louis Armstrong."

"Nope."

"Okay, how about her not saying it was Diderot when at the scene?"

Wilkes sat up. I noticed he was still in his bathrobe and pajamas. "A point to be urged, but not the one I'm thinking of. It's the dog."

"What about it? She hardly mentions it."

"Precisely. This crime should have been dog-bites-man news. Just like in the Sherlock Holmes story."

A dim fifteen-watt light went on in my mind. "Oh yes, the one about the dog that didn't bark when it should have. Are seeing-eye dogs trained to go to the rescue of their mistresses in distress?"

"Sure they are," said my friend as he rose and relieved me of the sack of steaks. "At least a little chewing, eh? That's why we're making the motion for the reenactment of the crime before the jury. If that dog so much as lifts a paw to defend Ms. Brenda Van Ark, we'll win this case. I got Condo workin' that end of the case right now."

POETRY IN MOTIONS

On Monday we filed the motions I wrote up on Sunday. The hearings on them were set for that Friday, Judge Knott's day set aside for motions and sentencings. We arrived in court at nine-thirty in the morning. Knott, as usual, punctually strode to the bench with the quickness and spring of a cat jumping into position to survey a line of mice. He scanned the multitude of murmuring lawyers and nervous defendants who sat before him. /

Then he spoke his first words of the morning: "I've got about two hundred years' worth of sentencings to hand out this morning, so let's get on with it." He said it matter-of-factly, as if he just announced the number of square feet in the courtroom, but his words sent a palpable shock wave through the crowded court. Family members gasped and moaned, anticipating the worst for their loved one. Defendants yelled at their attorneys for getting their cases before this terrible judge. The attorneys just looked at one another and thanked God they were there as mouthpieces for the soon to be imprisoned.

Judge Knott continued. "Before I get to that, I'm going to take out of order the motions in the Diderot case. Where's Mr. Wilkes?"

Wilkes, surprised that the judge wasn't going to make him sit though the entire morning's slaughter, stood and approached the front of the court. "John Wilkes for Lyle Diderot, present and ready." Assistant District Attorney Miles Landish also announced ready.

"Then bring in the defendant, Lyle Diderot, Mr. Bailiff, and we'll get this one out of the way in short order."

Lyle Diderot lumbered into the courtroom, scowled at everyone, and sat heavily at counsel table beside Wilkes. The people in the gallery quieted.

"I've called this case first because it can be disposed of very quickly. I have not read your forty pages of motions, Wilkes, because it violates my five-page limitation. Tell me why I should even hear the motions due to that procedural default?"

Since Knott had not been in criminal cases for about a decade, no one knew about his five-page limit on motions, a rule that was consistent with the judge's orientation for expedition at the price of substance.

Wilkes answered quickly, "Because my client's right to fair play should not be sacrificed due to my attempt to thoroughly present his position. I note that my adversary did not object on the ground Your Honor raises, perhaps because he too was unaware that you would be importing your rules from civil cases to criminal."

Lyle Diderot looked up to his attorney and said loudly to Wilkes, "What's dis bullshit about five pages, man? You screw up?"

The judge picked up my beautifully crafted motions and handed them to his clerk, Alvin Scribner, and said, "Give him back this gobbledygook and we'll ask Mr. Wilkes to pick out his best five pages for us."

Alvin passed them to Wilkes. The motions were soon in my hands and I had the job of ripping out five of the most relevant pages to give back to the judge. It was not an easy choice since all of the pages were pretty much equally unpersuasive. I did the best I could and sent the much abbreviated version back up to Knott, who didn't even look at them except to make sure there were only five pages.

"I would like to argue the motions now," said Wilkes.

"That'll be denied, counsel," said the judge in his familiar reflexive singsong which sounded a little like Buddy Holly's "That'll Be the Day." Well-el-el, that'll be denied, when you say object, well-el-el, that'll be denied . . .

"Your Honor, then I must request permission to make an offer of proof to the court of what I would say if I could argue my motions."

"That'll be denied, counsel."

"Then I must move for the opportunity to file the thirty-five pages of pleadings recently denuded from my motion papers as a proffer of what my offer of proof would have been had I been allowed to make it. Just so that the record is complete. *Your Honor.*"

Wilkes said "Your Honor" in a tone that easily could have been mistaken for "You piece of shit."

"Denied. Denied."

"Then I move for—"

"Denied!"

"I must move—"

"Wilkes. Every motion you make will be denied!"

·   ·   ·

OFF RECORD

"Then please inform my client and me which motion is denied and why," said Wilkes. "We are entitled as a matter of right and common sense to that much. *Your Honor.*"

Lyle Diderot stood up to face the judge and looked at him with an expression that said, "Go ahead, try and deny my motions, motherfucka."

"Oh, Mr. Wilkes," said Judge Knott. His voice turned to a most patronizing falsetto. "I always say that the elaborate argument does not need an elaborate answer. Just a correct one. In this case, the correct answer may be said eloquently in four little words: Your motions are denied." With that, Knott looked to his court reporter and said, "We'll go off the record for a moment now."

Early in his career on the bench, Knott learned that he could say whatever he wanted without fear of looking bad on the record if he did one important thing—eliminated the record. He told his court reporter to keep her hands off the stenograph machine. On the record, he tried to be civil. Off the record, he could excoriate any attorney unmercifully who ticked him off. Attorneys couldn't respond in kind since, after all, you were still speaking to a judge. More or less.

Satisfied that his reporter was twiddling her thumbs, Knott lit into my friend. "Wilkes, this motion hearing is a complete waste of my time. Your motions are the most frivolous I have read in the last ten years. Your reliance on precedent is virtually nonexistent. Your block-headed legal reasoning would not challenge the intelligence of a chimpanzee. I find that you have engaged in playing games, and for toying with the court, I shall now—"

"Motherfucka!" I saw the defense table tip forward, rise and become airborne. Lyle Diderot was on the rampage. He heaved the huge, heavy mahogany table and smashed it up against the presidium. BLAM! Instantly, four bailiffs jumped him and smothered him in cuffs and chains.

Knott, mouth open and in awe of what he had just seen, didn't finish his sentence. As the bailiffs were pouncing on Diderot, Wilkes said to the judge, "Since the court's ruled on my motions, we have no further business before you. You're out of session and clearly don't need me. Anyway, I see a lot of people anxiously waiting for the business of the court to begin."

Wilkes gathered his files from the table, turned his back to Knott, and started walking out. As he reached the door he turned to make one of his short parting speeches, this one a warning to the defendants about to be sentenced. "My friends, sentencing speeches in this court are dangerous business. They remind me of the old Russian proverb: 'In this country, we enjoy freedom of speech. Unfortunately, we do not enjoy freedom *after* speech.' Good luck to you all. You'll need it. *Do svidanya.*" With those words, he pushed upon the doors and disappeared.

Knott, hatred etched in his blue eyes, stared at the swinging doors. Then his eyes shifted and looked for targets of his wrath still within his reach. The bailiffs were still all over Diderot in the process of dragging him back to his cage in the Tombs. Knott announced, "We are back on the record." His court reporter's fingers jumped to her machine and started moving on the steno keys.

"In light of this outrageous outburst of unprovoked violence by the defendant Diderot, by which he attempted to assault this court's person with a deadly weapon by throwing a table at me, the defendant will be chained to his seat during all future court appearances. I find this is necessary in order to preserve the dignity of the courtroom and to ensure the right to fair trial for all concerned."

He looked at our client, who was unsuccessfully fighting off a platoon of bailiffs. "And if you yell out any more profanities, you will be gagged. Do you understand me, sir?"

Prostrate, being pummeled and raging against the attack, Lyle Diderot had the presence of mind to turn his head to the judge and say, "Yeah, motherfucka, I understand. I understand that this here's a railroad and you is the fuckin' engineer."

"That does it," said Knott excitedly. "Did you get all that down?" he asked his court reporter. She hadn't missed a syllable and nodded affirmatively. To Diderot: "Next appearance, you will be wearing leg and wrist bracelets. You will be chained to your chair. Your filthy mouth will be gagged tightly."

Knott stood up from behind his throne and uttered the words judges live for. "Now bailiffs . . ." He pointed to the door that led to the holding tank. "Take him away!"

Before he was hauled out, Diderot yelled to Knott, "You is one dead motherfucka!"

And so ended the pretrial motion phase in *People* v. *Diderot*. Another day in the Temple of Justice.

Or so I thought. As soon as I got back to the office, Wilkes, in between screaming profanities at Judge Knott, gave me a laundry list of assignments to be done within twenty-four hours.

"Renew the reenactment motion," said Wilkes, "except this time do it as a motion in lemonade." The more precise Latin phrase, motion *in limine,* means motions brought just before trial. Wilkes suggested I call our investigator, Uriah Condo, for an important lead on the motion. I did and then promptly filed the motion papers.

SURPRISE ME KNOTT

On the day of trial, we were prepared for the worst. We faced an unimpeachably innocent crime victim whose only vulnerability on the stand might be the accuracy of her ear-witness identification. She was blind, after all. On the other hand, we had to hope for a blind jury because Lyle Diderot was too scary to look at. On top of that, he had been ordered bound and gagged for the duration of the trial. Better evidence of guilt could not be manufactured.

"I have a surprise for you, Mr. Wilkes," said a lively Judge Knott just as he sat in his throne behind the dented presidium. Knott's voice was highly charged. It crackled as he spoke, and his gestures were jerky, as if he were plugged into an electric outlet.

Wilkes lifted his long, thin frame from his chair and stood in anticipation of an expected cruel hoax. He said, "You are going to recuse yourself from this case, perhaps?"

"No. I'm denying your five-page motion to have your client unchained during trial."

Wilkes grabbed his chest with both hands. "My heart! My heart!"

"Very funny, Mr. Wilkes. Your client's last appearance in court lost him the right to appear here as a civilized person. I have read your motion that I not gag him so that there might be attorney-client communications during the trial. I will not grant that motion either. But I will allow you to slide the gag off his mouth when you think he wishes to speak to you. If he abuses that privilege, he shall forfeit it too. If he takes the stand, the gag comes off entirely unless he utters more obscenities, at which point I shall expel him from the court."

To this, Lyle Diderot, gagged and chained to his chair, voiced his objection by loudly screaming a high-pitched sound which, but for the gag, would have come out as, "Fuck you, motherfucka!"

Judge Knott looked to Diderot and then to Wilkes. "You see why? This man is simply out of control. Now, back to your motions *in limine*. I am also denying the motion for the reenactment. But I am seriously considering your suggestion that the court appoint the eminent Dr. Vladimir Knudson, a renowned veterinarian and canine therapist, to examine the dog Bertie and make a report to the court on his findings. What say you to this, Mr. Landish?"

Landish just shrugged his shoulders. He did not know what we knew. Our investigator had discovered that Judge Knott and his wife Alice had a Pomeranian dog named Poo Poo, which was either the sickest dog in the world, a born hypochondriac, or pampered beyond comprehension. Poo Poo Knott apparently went to the vet for every sniffle, dry nose, cough, itch, rash, vomiting episode, hard bowel movement, soft bowel movement, pink eye, hot ear, excessive barking, hoarseness, loss of hair, or tartar buildup.

The vet, after scores of visits with an otherwise perfectly healthy dog, observed the onset of an emotional problem with the mutt. He referred the Knotts to a dog psychiatrist, none other than the esteemed Dr. Knudson. Knudson had been seeing Poo Poo twice a week now for a couple of years.

We figured that as a last gasp measure, we would suggest the examination of the dog Bertie by the judge's own vet, Dr. Knudson. If Bertie was a normal dog, as we felt confident, then the jury might wonder why he sat silent as his mistress was attacked. We could argue that if Bertie did in fact attack and maul the assailant, as any well-trained dog would do, that this was the clearest proof our client was innocent. He had not a mark on him upon arrest.

We knew the judge would never grant the motion for the dog examination unless we appealed to some ulterior motive. First, the judge had to think we really didn't want it granted, but were making a record to have an issue for appeal. Also, by adding that we wanted Knudson as the only qualified expert, we knew this would appeal to Knott's ego. He'd like throwing some business his own dog therapist's way. Even better to have the expert testify against the defense—and at our expense to boot!

Miles Landish finally responded to the judge's question: "What's the doc supposed to do with the dog? Take his temperature or his IQ? Hah! Hah! Hah!" The assistant district attorney laughed so hard that small tears appeared at the edges of his squinting eyes and trickled over rosy mounds of cheek flesh.

Wilkes stage-whispered to me, "Perhaps the doc can deprogram the dog from Landish's coaching."

"We know the defense is somehow going to try and exploit the dog's silence and inaction," said the judge, ignoring the whispers. "Perhaps the expert can determine what the dog Bertie's normal reaction would be to an assault such as the one this defendant committed on Ms. Van Ark."

"MODURFUGUH!" said the gagged Lyle Diderot. The words, though muffled, came out unmistakably. Wilkes quickly followed with, "My client objects to the assumption of facts in Your Honor's last statement."

The judge laughed off the objection. Looking to our chained and gagged client, he said, "Purely a hypothetical assumption for the moment, Mr. Diderot, at least until the jury hears the evidence and rules on the case. And so I will appoint Dr. Knudson to conduct this examination of the dog Bertie and order that the dog be made available tomorrow at the doctor's office. And this is to be at the defendant's expense. You are to pay the good doctor his full rate. Right, Mr. Wilkes?"

"I guess," said Wilkes. "My investigator will be there to observe and pay the bill on the spot."

"Then it is so ordered."

SWEATY PALMS

I shall skip most of the trial evidence, as you have heard what was to come. The prosecution case was highlighted by the contempt citations handed out by the judge to my friend Wilkes. The first occurred early on when Wilkes, loudly and in front of the jury, demanded that Knott take the chains and gag off so that "in the great American tradition, my client gets a fair trial." Wilkes knew these shiny and noisy clinky restraints were devastatingly prejudicial, worse even that Diderot's huge, fearsome appearance or the gang of thugs in the gallery giving him moral support—if not the hope for a daring courtroom escape.

Wilkes complained at a bench conference, "The jury will think that if a man can't control himself in a courtroom with all the guards around him and the chains, isn't he just the kind of wild man who would do what he wanted with a blind woman on the street?"

Judge Knott responded to this as follows: "I shall instruct the jury on this, Mr. Wilkes. I shall tell them: Ladies and gentlemen, the mere fact that the defendant is chained, manacled tightly to his chair, gagged, and being closely watched by several armed bailiffs during the course of this trial should be of absolutely no consideration to you in determining his guilt."

As an afterthought, the judge added, "Er, ah . . . or innocence. Nor for that matter should they be concerned with the jail clothing he is wearing, nor his rather disheveled odoriferous appearance. I will also tell them that they should not consider any of the petty quarrels you instigate with me, Mr. Wilkes, during the course of this trial."

And so he did. In the great American tradition. After that, he issued the first contempt citation against Wilkes for bringing the issue up in front of the jury.

BLIND JUSTICE

Pretty, bright, and blind Brenda Van Ark then testified very convincingly that Lyle Diderot was her assailant. She recounted the attack and described her attacker by his clothing, size, smell, and voice. She said she had made an identification of a man in police custody minutes after reporting the attack because she knew Diderot. He lived in the same building. She told how she felt his garments, smelled him, and heard his distinctive Louis Armstrong voice. It was the same man. She said she didn't know what action, if any, her dog took during the assault.

She was so sympathetic and credible, Wilkes couldn't touch her in cross. The only thing he got out of her was that she never saw her attacker. Not much of a revelation coming from a blind girl.

The cops then testified to arresting Diderot in the vicinity of the crime dressed exactly as Ms. Van Ark had said her assailant was dressed except that he didn't have gloves on or her purse. But he did have a couple of hundred bucks in cash, an amount that was just about what Brenda had in her purse. They found the gloves—with her tooth marks on one—and her emptied purse in a garbage can at a point between the scene of the crime and the place of Diderot's arrest.

Landish then called a jailbird to the stand to testify to a "confession" Diderot allegedly made to him in the Tombs. Landish didn't have a statement from the guy. It was now so common for these snitch creeps to give the prosecution what they wanted that an understanding, as is common between two professionals, existed. The creep would hint at what he could say, but wouldn't commit himself until he was certain he got his deal for time served.

Landish was too lazy to go over to the jail and seal the deal the cops had made with the snitch. New York's dungeons are smelly, ugly places unfit for human habitation. No slumlord could get away with putting people up in such pits. No place for a busy man like

Landish. Anyway, he figured he could get the confession for free and subpoenaed the guy thinking he'd get what he wanted.

Wrong. When the creep hit the witness stand and saw Lyle Diderot, bound and gagged and seething, and the gallery which was half packed with ferocious Whiz Kids, he denied ever hearing Lyle say anything.

This led the judge to call for a bench conference. Knott assumed the witness was holding out from previous statements given to the prosecution. And Knott wanted the jury to hear a confession, the closest thing to an evidentiary bombshell known to the law. Perhaps he could pry the confession out of the creep with a few threats of contempt.

"Mr. Landish, has there been witness intimidation here?" asked the judge.

"That's the only thing that can explain this," said Landish. He was embarrassed to admit he hadn't guaranteed a deal for the snitch's testimony.

Wilkes offered another explanation: "No, there's no evidence of that. I think the snitch doesn't want to be exposed for perjury."

Judge Knott said, "I see some evidence of intimidation. Just look at the gallery. Look at those vicious thugs out there."

All three of them looked to the gallery. The jury turned to look. Even our bound and gagged client turned, as best he could, and looked. There sat several dozen vicious thugs, loyal followers of the Field Marshal of the Whiz Kids, Lyle Diderot.

There sat guilt by association.

Landish took this as a cue. "Well, hey, why don't I just put on evidence that Diderot is the leader of the Whiz Kid gang and that the jury should consider that in figuring out why this witness refused to talk."

Wilkes interjected, "Why not just ask for a directed verdict of guilt? Anyway, your witness didn't refuse to talk. He just said he didn't know anything."

Knott leaned back to think a minute. The case was rolling along in the right direction. A confession would be a very nice addition, but not really required to bring in the proper verdict. Knott saw no reason to take the time necessary to threaten the creep or explore the intimidation matter. "No, you can't do that," he said to Landish, "although I have been considering an instruction to the jury that they should not take into consideration the presence in the court gallery of certain persons identified with the cause of the defendant."

"Sounds good to me," said Landish.

"Sounds like it's time I move for a mistrial if you do that," said Wilkes. "Judge, you have already transcended the bounds of neutrality and aligned yourself as a member of the prosecution team. How about throwing us a crumb and putting a lid on more instructions to the jury about not considering this or that when you know damn well you are indoctrinating them to consider it."

This outburst produced contempt citation number two, but the judge did not give the jury instruction about not considering the presence of the gang as evidence of guilt. Of course, the jury wasn't blind. They could see the gallery. They could see the Field Marshal's unruly supporters.

The trial was not all unrelenting bad news. There were a few good spots, like when we recessed, had lunch breaks, and when the day ended. A stipulation was entered that although there was physical evidence of the physical beating, no physical evidence was recovered to allow DNA identification typing. "Therefore," added Judge Knott, "we've heard a lot about the magic of DNA testing in the news, but I instruct the jury not to consider in its deliberations the absence of such evidence."

This agitated Wilkes more than anything yet. He got up from counsel table shaking with anger. He bellowed, "Preposterous! Of course the jury should consider the lack of evidence in their determinations. That's an absence of proof! That's reasonable doubt! You've told them to ignore the best evidence of innocence. Objection! Mistrial! Recusal!"

That outburst produced contempt citation number three. But Knott knew Wilkes was right and altered his instruction to the jury to say that he only meant that the lack of the DNA evidence wasn't "dispositive one way or another."

The worst of the quarrels between the judge and Wilkes occurred when Wilkes took off Diderot's gag to hear what his client had to say during Brenda Van Ark's damning testimony. Lyle's helpful suggestions to Wilkes were overheard by everyone in the court. He told Wilkes, "Man, that bitch is lyin'. No fuckin' way do I do dat kinda shit on her, man. Prove she's lyin'. Prove it, motherfucka!"

This outburst proved disastrous. First, Brenda said, "I hear him again! Yes, that's the voice of the man that attacked me!"

It also led to the permanent gagging of the defendant by Judge Knott, this time a roll of tape wrapped so many times around the circumference of Diderot's head, he looked like the Mummy. Wilkes objected by pointing out that he could not competently represent a defendant whose voice was removed by the court. The judge responded that he doubted the truth of that, and from what he had seen, the defendant could not have done worse without an attorney.

To which Wilkes replied, "Well, there is no doubt about one thing. He could have done a hell of a lot better in any other court."

It was the truth, of course. The Yugoslavs have a saying: "Tell the truth and run." But Wilkes couldn't run. He got contempt citation number four instead.

You might draw from these exchanges that Wilkes and the judge were not hitting it off very well. After the fourth contempt and the defense case going quickly into the toilet, Wilkes was so furious he whispered not so softly to me, "That black-robed butcher's dead meat."

After which our bound and gagged client rattled his chains at the judge and added in solidarity with his beleaguered mouthpiece: "DIE MODURFUGUH!"

I didn't ask the judge, but I'm sure the feeling was mutual.

JOYOUS JUNCTURE

At this joyous juncture in the proceedings, the prosecution called Dr. Vladimir Knudson to the stand to try and explain why Bertie the dog had been so ungallant as to sit by in silence while his mistress was brutally assaulted. Miles Landish asked the vet, "You examined the dog named Bertie, the dog owned by Ms. Van Ark, correct?"

"Yes," said the doctor. He wiggled his left foot nervously over his right knee so that the oversized tassels on his white loafers bounced up and down. The heavy, gray tweed sport coat worn too tightly over a thick green wool sweater and white shirt and tie caused him to sweat. The doctor was suffering from a common courtroom malady, stage fright.

"Describe the examination, Doctor," said Miles.

"Well, of course, it was a routine visit. Forty-five minutes. Bertie is a well-nurtured German shepherd Seeing Eye dog with a healthy, thick fur coat, as is typical of the breed."

Miles Landish, only having talked to the doctor briefly by phone the day before, was unaware of the doctor's terror of the court proceeding, just as he was unconscious of it as he questioned him in court. He asked, "And as a result of your analysis, Doctor, did you come to a conclusion as to the mental state of the dog Bertie at the time of the crime?"

"I did."

"Please tell us your expert opinion."

"This dog has a blunted affect." The doctor looked the jury up and down. His thick horn-rimmed glasses gave his eyes the look of saucers. He continued, "More important to the question, this poor creature suffered from a transitional disassociational fugue state at the time of the crime, brought on by the inexplicable violence he witnessed. Bertie was helpless to go to the aid of his mistress, poor woman."

"Poor dog," interjected a beaming Judge Knott to his nervous friend on the witness stand.

"Objection! Your Honor is now commenting on the evidence," yelled Wilkes. Diderot, rocking violently side to side in his chair, chains clinking, joined him with a few more muffled incoherent profanities.

"Oh," said Knott, "I'll let the jury be the judge of that. Overruled."

"In other words," said Landish, "this dog was oblivious to what was happening around him at the time of the assault?"

"Absolutely," said Dr. Knudson, wiping heavy perspiration from his clean-shaven face with his bare hand. "In lay terms, he was out of it. Totally incapable of goal-directed action."

Landish then asked, "What is the cause of this unfortunate dog's mental problem?"

Dr. Knudson brightened at the prospect of giving his diagnosis. "Well, of course I'm not a Freudian by training," he said, "but I would say that a combination of underlying causes were present. I think Bertie had a difficult upbringing, what with the separation from his parents early on and then the separation from his Seeing Eye dog trainer. These separations during the first years of his life gave him very low self-esteem, which was aggravated by the chaos of life in this city. I think the assault on his mistress was viewed by him as another separation, which the poor dog just could not fathom."

"So he froze?" asked Landish.

"Worse, he was catatonic."

Landish turned toward Wilkes and said loudly and smugly, "Thank you so very much, Doctor. Your witness, Mr. Wilkes." Landish sat down smiling. He had every reason to smile. He put on a damned strong case. When Brenda Van Ark testified, half the jury wept. When the jury looked at the defendant, they cried again, but in fear. And Diderot could not take the witness stand for two reasons: first, his violent prior felony convictions would then be introduced to impeach his credibility—assuming he had any to impeach; and second, he was an even more frightening person when he spoke than as a gagged courtroom ornament.

KNUDSON ON CROSS

Now it was Wilkes's turn to cross-examine the vet therapist.

"Vladimir?" he asked. Wilkes hoped to appeal to any xenophobic feelings among the jury. An irritated Judge Knott, recognizing the ploy, instantly jumped to his friend's assistance.

"You sir," referring to Wilkes by pointing a long, thin finger at him, "shall give this witness the respect he is due by referring to him as Dr. Knudson. Do you understand?"

"I understand, Judge," said Wilkes, "perfectly."

"Now, Dr. Vladimir Knudson, you are a doggie doctor, right?"

"So to speak, yes," said the shrinker of dog heads.

"How long have you been an animal alienist?"

"Well, we no longer are referred to as alienists. But I have been a veterinarian with a subspecialty in canine mental diseases, disorders, and defects for about twelve years." Knudson continued to sweat but now even more profusely as my friend began to grill him.

Wilkes walked up to the witness and graciously handed the vet his red handkerchief, which was eagerly accepted by the witness to soak up a face full of sweat. Wilkes then asked, "Well, Dr. Vladimir Knudson, please tell the ladies and gentlemen of the jury how it is you determined the dog Bertie was nuts at the time of the assault on Brenda Van Ark."

Normally, Wilkes would never have asked such an open-ended question to a hostile witness, it being contrary to the cardinal rule of cross-examination. However, there are exceptions, such as when whatever the witness responds is guaranteed to make him look stupid.

Knudson said, "Well, I interviewed him and carefully observed his behavioral responses to certain stimuli which I introduced into the session."

"You interviewed him? Just how did you communicate with the hound?"

"Nonverbally, of course." Knudson wiped more sweat off his forehead with the red hanky and caught the drops rolling quickly down his cheeks. "I looked into his eyes. The eyes are always very revealing as to the dog's mental health. I checked his overall demeanor and looked for keys to his personality, you know, like is he hyper or noninvolved with his surroundings, does he respond to petting and the like. More than that, of course. As I just stated, I observed his behavioral responses to certain stimuli which I carefully introduced into the session."

My friend approached the witness. "Would these be the equivalent of what we call the battery of psychological tests used on human subjects?" asked Wilkes. "You know, like Rorschach, Bender-Gestalt, MMPI, and the like?"

"Yes. Very much the same thing." Knudson wiped himself and then handed Wilkes his drenched handkerchief. Wilkes in turn handed the soaked hanky to our investigator, Uriah Condo, and whispered loudly, "get rid of this." Condo dutifully left the courtroom.

"Well, did you try to stimulate anger in Bertie?"

"Of course, given the purpose of the examination, I wanted to see if he would react in an angry manner. I thought this was the purpose of the session." He pointed his left hand palm up toward the jury as if he were about to blow them kisses. "To help the jury with the question of why Bertie didn't bark or attack your client during the assault."

Wilkes pressed the attack. "And just how did you do that, sir?"

"Well," said the doctor, "I knew Bertie loves to chew on Ms. Van Ark's slipper. One was provided me at my request and I let Bertie play with it, which he did a little, and then I took it from him. I then tried to taunt him with it by simulating my own play with the slipper."

Wilkes interrupted. "Did you chew on it yourself?"

"No, no. I merely pretended to."

"Doctor, please take one of your shoes and show us how you did that."

Dutifully, Dr. Knudson took one of his loafers and pulled it to his face. Much to the amusement of all who watched, he began simulating chewing on it while making the noises of a glutton mid-feast.

The doctor then said, "I did that on all fours right next to the dog for about a quarter hour. Then I put it before his nose and quickly withdrew it. Taunting him with it, you know. The dog didn't react. He didn't grab it or make any attempt to play with it. This complete lack of reaction, coupled with my other tests, convinced me that Bertie suffers from the lingering impact of a psychotic break with reality occasioned by the assault on his mistress. He is just devastated by that crime. He cares about nothing."

"Yes, Doctor. You say in your report here that you have recommended an immediate commitment to the sanitarium and psychotropic medication. You suggest that a program of electroconvulsive therapy would not be contraindicated."

"Yes. There just aren't many modest treatment modalities available for his ailment."

"So the dog's just a basket case, eh?"

"Yes, sir. In fact, were Bertie human and on trial, I would declare him legally insane at the time of the crime."

"Isn't it true, Dr. Vladimir Knudson, that all of your opinion assumes that the normal dog response to the crime would have been to attack the assailant of his mistress?"

"Yes. That's how this type of dog is trained," said the perspiring witness, now seeming more confident with his testimony.

"So," said Wilkes, "if he'd have attacked his taunter—you in this instance, in the experiment—then he's a normal dog who would have attacked the taunter of his mistress."

"Precisely," preened the vet.

"And you tried to get Bertie angry at you to stimulate such responses in your office."

Wilkes looked to me and stuck out his hand. "Hanky, please." I gave him one and he handed it to Knudson. The doc began wiping his face. He then said, "You have it correct, Mr. Wilkes."

Wilkes turned to the jury momentarily. "Let us just take a look at crazy old Bertie shall we?" Wilkes gave me the signal to go get the dog. I ran out and got Bertie, whom we had subpoenaed from the sanitarium to the trial. Bertie and I appeared at the door of the court. Judge Knott said, "I told you, Wilkes! I told you there'd be none of this!"

• • •

MONGREL MOTION

"This is for identification purposes only," replied Wilkes. I was having trouble containing the aroused Bertie, and before Wilkes could further explain himself, Bertie escaped my loose grasp of his leash, bounded over the rail in one leap, barking and howling all the way, and jumped on the vet. Teeth snapping, mouth frothing and snarling, the dog was all over Knudson.

The doc screamed, "HELP! GET THIS MONSTER OFF ME!" He tried to beat the dog off with the loafer he still held in his hand. Loud cheers and whistles of support for Bertie came from the Whiz Kids section of the gallery. Knott pounded his gavel. Bertie growled that horrible growl the big cats make when attacking and devouring prey. Landish hollered out his objections. Diderot yelled through his gag, "Get that motherfucka, doggie!" Ms. Van Ark, detecting something amiss, screamed, "Bertie! Bertie!" With all the commotion, Bertie did not hear her.

Gallantly, Wilkes leapt into the whirl of fur, chomping teeth, and tearing paws, to pull the hound's choke collar and drag him off his psychiatrist. Two bailiffs came quickly to take over and haul the hound away, but Bertie dug his paws into the floor and with his head turned toward Knudson snarled and snapped all the way outside the courtroom.

Knudson, whimpering, was sprawled across the witness stand as if he'd just fallen into it like a turd from heaven. The damage was considerable: his green sweater was ripped down the middle; his tweed jacket had one sleeve torn almost completely off; both of his shoes were on the floor; and his horn-rims were tilted diagonally over his moist face so that one fogged lens covered his mouth.

"No further questions," said Wilkes. He walked in front of defense counsel table, whirled to point to the witness, and said, "Some blunted affect!"

Judge Knott was, of course, enraged. His face was bright crimson as he stood pointing at Wilkes and opening and closing his mouth. Finally, a word came, a very familiar one. "Contempt!"

"I suggest a recess," said Wilkes, "to permit the expert witness to compose himself. He appears rather decomposed."

Knott slapped down his gavel and stomped off the bench and into chambers. Wilkes said to the baffled members of the jury, "Well, folks, court is apparently out of session. See ya tomorrow."

FINAL ARGUMENT

A lawyer facing overwhelming adverse evidence has a problem. The relevant evidence is available to him, but it is of absolutely no use. Faced with this dilemma, desperate lawyers seize upon marginal points and argue the hell out of them. Good lawyers make the insignificant seem relevant. Great lawyers make the trivial point the single most important element upon which the trial must turn. And they always pick a point of minutia on which they will win.

When it came time for Wilkes to argue the case, he had the pertinent part of Dr. Knudson's testimony blown up onto a huge cardboard display so as to leave the indelible visual imprint of his testimony with the jury: "If he'd attack his own taunter—me, in this instance—he's a normal dog who would have attacked the taunter of his mistress."

Wilkes told the jury, "Dr. Knudson has proved they got the wrong man. It is clear that Bertie is a normal dog. He's not crazy. He did attack his taunter right before your very eyes. And, if I might say, he did so with some enthusiasm. You saw the results. He left his mark on Dr. Vladimir Knudson, didn't he? So it is clear he attacked the assailant of his mistress and left his mark. Lyle Diderot, as he was innocently walking down the street without a criminal thought on his mind, didn't have a scratch on his body and his clothes were perfectly intact. And they have nothing else as evidence except the mistaken voice identification of the unfortunate blind woman. Lyle Diderot is here, wrongly accused, because of the sound of his voice. He's here because he sounds like Satchmo. That's no crime."

· · ·

INSTRUCTIONS

After the arguments, the jury was instructed by an ill-tempered Judge Knott. No sooner had the judge started instructing than Wilkes was forced to object to the judge's comments to the jury on the sufficiency of the evidence. Knott told the jury, "Under the law, I have the chance to comment on the evidence. I want to say that the jury should not consider in its deliberations the devious stunt played on the expert witness yesterday."

"Objection!" Wilkes rushed to the bench to make his objections outside the hearing of the jury. By this time Wilkes and Knott hated each other so much that every word between them was an acidic exchange of mortal enemies. My friend said, "The court is directing a verdict! It has again publicly joined forces with the prosecution and against my client and the Constitution! Unfairness personified! Mistrial!"

Knott leaned over and said to Wilkes, "You sir, as usual, have no respect for the law or for this court."

Wilkes slapped his hand hard against the presidium and retorted, "Oh no, Judge, I have the utmost respect for the law. The same goes double—no, triple—for the court. It is you I can't stand. This case has been two on one since the opening bell."

Judge Knott leaned back. A bitter smile formed on his face as he thought about what Wilkes had just said on the record. He had him. These were contemptuous words, and deserved as they might be, no court would reverse his contempt citations and jail sentence. Knott said, "You, sir, are in contempt again. Your motion is denied. Now get back out there and shut up. We'll deal with all the contempts—how many now, five or six?—after trial. I view them as serious criminal transgressions."

After the bench exchange, Knott told the jury that they were free to accept his comments or not, but that he still saw no relevance to the "dog-bites-man stunt of yesterday."

Wilkes did not bother to get up, and stated from counsel table, "Same objection I just made at the bench in all of its previously articulated subparts."

The judge replied, "Same ruling with all of its previously articulated subparts including an additional matter to add to those serious matters we shall consider after the verdict."

The rest of the instructions were noncontroversial, and Knott read them verbatim from the pattern jury instruction book as if he were demonstrating his skills at speed mumbling. The instructions, incomprehensible if read slowly three times to the average college-educated linguist, were so much gibberish to this jury. Knott put the jury to sleep. Then he awoke them with the order to go out and deliberate on the fate of the defendant Lyle Diderot.

While they were out, Wilkes and I spent the time with the Field Marshal of the Whiz Kids back in lockup. Diderot was actually in a good mood, all things considered. He laughed that victory was certain. He said, "That dog scene was great! That shrink got eaten alive! Judge hated it. How da fuck you do that?"

THE RED CAPE

I could have responded to our appreciative client, "It was pure magic. All Wilkes's idea. During cross-examination, after Wilkes got back his sweat-soaked hanky from Dr. Knudson, he passed it on to our investigator, Uriah Condo, who went out in the hallway where the subpoenaed Bertie was calmly sitting and waiting to be called. Condo proceeded to taunt the hell out of the dog with the wet, red hanky for as long as he could before he got pushed away by the dog's custodian. Then he brought back the hanky and gave it to me and I gave it to Wilkes, who quickly gave it back to the sweating Dr. Knudson just before calling into court the now enraged Bertie. The smelly red hanky was like a matador's cape to Bertie, and when he saw it, he charged it like a bull. The rest, as they say, is history."

I could have said this, but I wasn't about to share the secret of this great trial strategy with our client. Magician's rule: never give up the trick. We might use it again. So I said, "Blind luck, I guess."

Before the Field Marshal could respond, we were informed that the jury, out only one hour, was back with a verdict. Wilkes said to us in a whisper, "This is bad. Way too soon." We walked back into court.

The gallery, a true rogue's gallery, was packed to overflowing with thugs jabbering, elbowing, and snickering like a mob about to watch a lynching. Except these were all Whiz Kids, a mean crew of bulging muscles, gold front teeth or no front teeth, and colorful head rags. It looked like the mayor had just emptied the Tombs to come see the verdict. If this jury voted guilty, they were in big trouble.

MOMENT OF TRUTH

Despite the support in the courtroom, the bluster was out of Diderot. I had never seen him so fearful. This was his moment of truth, and he was trembling. Perhaps he feared that his jury would give him justice. He leaned over to me and whispered, "Even if we lose, we can appeal all the way to the Supreme Court, right? We gotta brother up there on that court, you know. Can't lose. No way."

"Oh, yeah," I said to him, "Justice Clarence Thomas," while thinking that there wasn't a chance this damned case would ever see the rarefied heights of a Supreme Court hearing in Washington, D.C. Even if a miracle propelled it there, he'd have a much better chance at freedom going over the wall.

Diderot, Field Marshal of the Whiz Kids, looked at me like I'm some kind of idiot. "What? Who's that? That ain't the dude. Ain't chew ever heard of Whizzer White?"

3

Verdict in the Vortex

*"Nothing, but the wind, can pass the sun
without casting shadow."*
CHARLIE CHAN

*"Contempting the defense attorney is the judge's way
of making sure that SOMEBODY goes to jail."*
JOHN WILKES

"I am informed the jury has a verdict," said Judge Yulburton
Abraham Knott to the foreperson of the jury. They did. That is why
they were back in court seated in the jury box looking anxiously at
the exit doors as if salvation lay in the hallway.

That is also why there was a sea of ferocious-looking Whiz Kid
thugs in the standing-room-only gallery looking ready for a rumble
at the first indication of bad news.

That is why Wilkes and I were seated at counsel table with our still
bound-and-gagged (and, yes, now trembling!) client, Lyle Diderot,
Field Marshal of all New York City's Whiz Kid punk terrorists.
Watching him fidget fearfully and listening to his mumbled obscenities while awaiting *el momento de verdad* reminded me that few people
feel true peace just before their head is about to be handed them.

Taking this verdict is also why Judge Y. Knott looked.fit to be tied
up and put in the rubber room. His lips formed a wide upside-down
U on his deeply lined face. Normally, he looked rather distinguished,
with his longish white hair and shining blue eyes. Not today. Today

he looked like he was about to suffer one of his worst courtroom defeats, for not only did Judge Knott know the jury had a unanimous verdict, he also knew which way it went. Or, at least, he looked like he knew.

"We do have a verdict, Your Honor," said the foreperson, a black woman named Gladys Urdrea, in answer to the judge's ritualistic request. She spoke firmly, in a manner that said she was unashamed of the work of her group and damned happy that the job was about over.

"Very well, pass it to the clerk," said the judge with an edge of disgust. Old Alvin Scribner, the clerk, dutifully marched to the forelady of the jury and took the forms from her and then passed them up to the judge for his imperial inspection. Knott said not a word as he looked at the forms. As his blue eyes darted over the papers, he looked like he was reading his own death notice. What little color he had in his pasty cheeks blanched. He passed the forms to Alvin with the disgusted command, "Read the verdict."

Alvin dropped his head to read through his large rimless glasses. The courtroom was so completely silent everyone could hear Diderot's moronic mumblings. This was it, the pressure cooker was about to explode. Would it be those two little words that would bring an orgasm of relief and liberty? Or, as we expected, would it be a Hiroshima blast, that single devastating word which, like a nuclear detonation, brings on instant annihilation and, worse, a loss of business.

TWO WORDS OR ONE?

What would it be: two words or one? Instant joy or despair? Incredible victory or defeat? Riches or bankruptcy? Such are the stakes every time a jury speaks. Wilkes, Diderot, and I had no idea what was about to sound from Alvin Scribner's mouth, but dread was in the air. If Lyle Diderot lost this trial, with his record, he'd be sent to Sing Sing for many years. Lyle was frightened out of his mind. The Whiz Kids were edgy and apprehensive and explosive. Wilkes and I were scared shitless. We looked to Alvin for a hint of what was to come, our hearts pounding hard and loud, like sledgehammers on a kettle drum.

For years, while reading the verdict, Alvin Scribner made it a habit to face the winning party. That way, he gave both sides an instant head start on the shock that was to come. Getting hit with a guilty verdict is like having someone deliver a hatchet blow to the middle of your chest, or having a two hundred pound wasp sting you in the head. Having a couple of seconds to prepare for the jolt was a nice gesture on Alvin's part. It was one of a number of small but decent things old Alvin did in Knott's court. Such gestures made him a popular figure around the courthouse and made appearing in Knott's court slightly less horrible.

We looked to Alvin's body for the pivot that would signal our salvation or termination. Alvin stood holding the verdict form chest high. He read, "We the jury . . ." His body slowly started to wheel—oh God, no!—a movement in the direction of the prosecutor—out of habit, please!—as he spoke the words, ". . . find the defendant, Lyle Diderot . . ."

But then—was it, could it be?—thank God!—a mid-course correction back to face the center of the court, then a halt, briefly, as he said, ". . . also known as the Field Marshal, also known as Marshal," and then toward—praise Jesus and Peter in Heaven!—a magnificent full frontal turn toward us! Alvin, your frail old bod never looked so beautiful! We're gonna be saved! We're gonna win! Say it, Al baby! Say the magic words! SAAAAAAAAAAAAAAY IT!

". . . not guilty. Signed, Gladys Urdrea on behalf of the jury."

SOUNDS OF SILENCE

For a second there was a stunned silence. Most everyone thought Alvin made a mistake and waited for the correction. But Alvin simply plopped down in his chair beneath the towering presidium and looked upward to the fuming Judge Knott.

"Motherfucka!" One of the muscular Whiz Kids who looked like a young Sonny Liston yelled the first words to break the quiet. Then the other thugs in the gallery erupted in gleeful hand-slapping, jumping-jack high-fives, crouching low-fives, shoulder slams, cat whistles, shrill screams, and howling laughter. A few took off their head rags and twirled them. A half dozen jumped the rail and ran up to their mummified leader to slap his back and scream out joyous profanities.

It was the kind of mini-riot celebration you'd expect at a jail break, or if the mayor granted a surprise general prison amnesty. Bedlam prevailed. Between fives, the back slaps, the gleeful whistling and insane war whoops, they yelled, "Yeah, baby! . . . Not fuckin' guilty! . . . Motherfuckin' great! . . . Free da Marshal!" There was no order in the court.

Lyle himself was stunned into a momentary frozen quiet by the verdict, but he soon caught on that a good thing had just happened. He began rocking in his chair such that the chains that bound him began clinking while his chair tap-danced on the floor. Through his tight gag he shouted to Wilkes a barely coherent, "Nomoderfuginsheeeeeeiiit! Awitemon!" It was his way of saying, "Wonderful news, don't you think?"

JUDICIAL THOUGHT

Wilkes did not react. He just looked straight ahead and up at the presidium where a lava-constipated black-robed volcano was about to blow.

Judge Knott was still in disbelief. He looked at the happy anarchists crazily running about the court beneath him as if each one had won the Lottery. The insane rabble were ecstatic because this verdict had been stolen from him. FROM HIM! This verdict, this lie, this OUTRAGE, this . . . NOT GUILTY! Purloined from Lady Truth and her gallant Knight of Speedy Justice, Judge Yulburton Abraham Knott. Stolen by the cunning John Wilkes. He had deprived the twelve slobs in the box of what little common sense they had. These witless jurors were no match for that devil. They were supposed to be a fair cross section of the community. What crap! The only community these clowns represented was the psycho ward at Bellevue.

The judge banged his gavel loudly on his desk. BLAT! BLAT! BLAT! The noise in the court was at airplane takeoff level. He yelled for order while hoping that the floor would open up and swallow into the burning fires of Hell every last one of the raging black barbarians running amok below him.

Banging the gavel had no impact on deterring the celebrating hooligans. Judge Knott stood and yelled and banged, and banged and banged the gavel even harder, but the merrymakers from the gallery continued their partying in total ignorance of the Gothic figure standing and yelling at them. Knott yelled to the bailiffs to clear the court, an order the bailiffs, vastly outnumbered and keen to avoid losing a hand-to-hand battle with the ferocious Whiz Kids, pretended not to hear. Instead, the bailiffs got the Whiz Kids to shut up by speaking to them in a language they could understand. They pulled their pistols.

THANKING THE JURY

Things quieted a bit. Judge Knott, still standing, turned to the jury and shouted at them, "At this time, I usually thank the jury for its hard work." He paused as the crowd quieted some more. "I cannot and I will not do it in this case." As he spoke, his thin face, already the color of rose chalk, began to turn a deeper shade of crimson. "I cannot comprehend your verdict. How you could find this . . . this . . . CRIMINAL! . . . DEFENDANT! . . . NOT . . . NOT . . . I CAN'T EVEN SAY THE WORDS . . . NOT GUILTY! MY GOD!"

Once he choked out the words, the next phrase tumbled out quickly. "Christ! The evidence was there. It was there, I tell you. Where did we get you people? School for the deaf, dumb, and blind? Bellevue? The Tombs? The evidence was . . . just overwhelming!"

Knott stopped talking for a moment to glare at the intimidated jurors and let the courtroom noise subside a bit more. He pointed at the Field Marshal. "He didn't even take the stand to deny it! Unbelievable! He didn't even say, 'I'm sorry.' Well, congratulations, ladies and gentlemen of the jury, you have just turned loose on the streets of this city another violent predator whose criminal record goes back to the nineteen—"

THE CANONS

"Just a damn minute!" The harsh sound of my friend's objection rose above the nasty insults coming from the judge as well as the dangerous murmurings of the Whiz Kids. Their festival mood had quickly turned nasty. Some were whispering ominous things about the "honky" judge.

Wilkes said to Y. Knott, "You have no right to sit in judgment of my client. You were excused from that duty. That's why we elected to have trial by jury. Now, to insult these selfless men and women for doing their duty is just despicable. It is the worst thing I've ever seen. It is a flagrant violation of the Canons of Judicial Ethics, and sir, I am duty bound to report your outrageous misconduct to the appropriate judicial performance authorities, and you can rest assured that I will do so at the earliest opportunity. I demand a transcript of these proceedings."

Knott turned his malevolent, now very dark, blue eyes from the jurors to Wilkes like a marksman moving his sight from one target to the next. Wilkes moved to a place in the well of the court between the judge and the jury. The judge again pounded his gavel hard on the desk like a petulant kid and then pointed it like a gun at Wilkes. "We're going to deal with you, mister! You and your cheap dog tricks! You and your insults to this court, to the prosecutor, and to me personally. We have ways of dealing with the likes of you, mister. We call it contempt! Contempt! Contempt! Contempt! Contempt! Contempt of court!"

With that outburst, a sickening grin appeared again on Knott's face. If they ever come out with pictionaries, Knott's face is what they would put next to the phrase "sinister smile." Knott looked at Wilkes and thought about his new futurist work in progress, an essay on death penalty technologies of the next century. How quick and painless and cheap and efficient they would be. Why, it would be as if the dearly departed were hardly ever among the living. He

thought—happily—of that devil Wilkes being one of the first condemned persons to receive an application of the new Body Expirator
he was writing about. He wished he could fire the magic laser
injector and watch the instantaneous expiration of the vile creature
who publicly trampled the law inside HIS Temple of Justice. Such
conduct would be a capital offense in the next century. He was sure
of it.

"Oh, the contempts! Ladies and gentlemen," said Wilkes, interrupting the happy thoughts of the demented judge. Wilkes turned to
the jury, walked to the rail, and addressed them as if he were giving
opening argument. "Contempt is one of the sacred judicial rites of
rage. When the defendant is acquitted, contempting the defense
attorney is the judge's way of making sure SOMEBODY goes to jail.
I mean, EVERYONE can't just walk out of here!"

"That's enough out of you, Wilkes!" shouted Knott. Oh, to watch
Wilkes cringe in fear at my power as I pull the injector switch, and
poof! He is no more! Oh! The beauty and power of the Law!

Wilkes ignored the judge. "Contempt is used by the weakest of
judges, by the bullies of the bench who cannot keep order or stand
challenges or cope with not having it their own way. It's the act of
the coward. I hope you will all be witnesses for me at my contempt
trial."

"Shut up and sit down, mister!" screamed a beet-faced Knott. Oh!
To walk to the lifeless body of that devil and look down on the
extinguished enemy. Lady Truth and Justice vindicated!

Wilkes looked up briefly at Knott and then turned and leaned his
butt on the rail, crossed his arms over his chest and said, "You can
say what the hell you want, sir, but these fine people courageously
ignored your many exhortations during the trial to convict my client.
I'm sure that your bias in this case boomeranged on you. It was
probably responsible for the acquittal as much as anything I said.
Therefore, my client and I thank you for such a biased trial. As for
the jurors, in trial, they had to listen to you, but now they are no
longer a captive audience. They can get up and leave. You can yell
at the walls. No scalps tonight, Judge Knott."

FUTURE SHOCK

Knott stood in insulted silence. To have that chance to participate in the termination of the Archenemy! To personally be able to do it! Yes! No question about it! Future executions must permit the judge to be both judge and executioner! Computer appeals will only take a second or so before they uphold the conviction and affirm the penalty. Then off to the Body Expirator without delay! How glorious it will be! Fire and expire!

Wilkes turned to the bewildered jurors while Knott dreamed of perfect justice. My friend was doing his best to butter them up for when he would need them as witnesses in his defense. "Really," he said to them, "it's all right. You don't have to listen to the bastard anymore. You've done your job, and on behalf of my client and myself, we thank you for your courage and diligence. Court's over now. He's got no hold on you. Let's go home."

Wilkes went over to our table and shoved his yellow notepad and papers into his battered briefcase and started toward the back door. The jurors rose as one and followed. This brought Knott out of his reverie. He was not done fulminating. He looked to his court reporter and said, "Did you get all that down?" She nodded. "Good. Now listen. This is off the record now."

The court reporter instantly took her hands from the keys of her machine as if she just discovered they were coated with worm guts. Seeing this, Knott looked to Wilkes and continued. "I want the transcript of this trial immediately. We are going to have a contempt hearing. Yes, we are going to put Mr. Defense Attorney, John Wilkes, on trial for CRIMINAL . . . CRIMINAL! . . . CONTEMPT! Yes, indeed!" To the wall, devil! Fire up the Body Expirator! Fire and expire!

The jurors were at the door and proceeding out. Wilkes, always on the alert for an opportunity to ingratiate himself with prospective defense witnesses, was holding the door open and smiling his thanks to each of the departing jurors. He looked back at the judge, who yelled, "Stop! Everyone! All right . . . now . . . yes . . . all those whose business in this court is complete may now leave."

The last juror, the foreperson, Mrs. Gladys Urdrea, gave Wilkes a faint smile and touched him lightly on the arm before looking back in fright at the erupting volcano. She escaped the courtroom. Wilkes moved to follow.

THE NEXT FAIR TRIAL

"Not so fast, Mr. Wilkes. Your business in not complete. I am not finished with you by any means." The judge leaned over the bench so far, I thought he was going to fall into the well of the court. He pointed the stick end of the gavel at my friend and continued fulminating.

"We'll schedule your trial date tomorrow morning at nine. Alvin, you make note of that and look for an early trial date for the defendant Wilkes. And you, sir, I suggest you get yourself a GOOD . . . a VERY GOOD . . . and, if you know one, an ETHICAL defense attorney. I won't tolerate your trying to turn the contempt hearing into another three-ring circus. There'll be no dog tricks to save you. And no delays. Yes, considering the gravity of the misconduct and the irrefutable evidence in the record against you, I suggest a very capable counsel. Yes, one accomplished in the art of courtroom persuasion within the limits of advocacy and professionalism, and yes, one with skills unknown to you and your assistant, Mr. Schoontower. Yes indeed, and one last thing, Mr. Wilkes, don't forget to bring your toothbrush." Any last wishes, devil? A short will? No? Cigarette perhaps? No? Blindfold? No? Well, then, prepare for the eternal fires, Satan! You go straight to hell! FIRE! FIRE! FIRE!

I now decided to get into the act and interrupt the judge's cackling. "Your Honor, with all *due* respect," I said. By now I could taunt with the best of them—years of training at the foot of the master. "We must ask you to allow another judge to take over the contempt hearings given your inevitable role as a witness and, of course, the demonstrated deep emotional investment you have in the matter."

The mad marksman's dark eyes turned toward me and I felt targeted for destruction. "Denied!" he said. "I can be fair to Mr. Wilkes. I will give him a fair trial." And then destroy him! Lucifer shall not escape my grasp! Never! I shall preside over his eternal damnation and say to him, "To the wall, Satan! Prepare the Expirator! Fire! Fire and expire! Fire and expire!"

Wilkes said nothing. I said, "We will file our motions tomorrow."

The judge, now less agitated, said with frightening sobriety, "You can take your best shot, Mr. Schoonblower. You just file when ready, as is your legal duty. We can take whatever it is you deliver. This court can take it. No matter how petty or frivolous and slanderous the charge against us, this court can be fair. This court can persevere under adversity and accusation and still be the neutral magistrate which the law demands." And then: Fire and expire! Fire and expire! Fire and expire! Headline: "Today, that devil Wilkes was put to death by lawful order of the right Honorable Judge Yulburton Abraham Knott!"

LOVELY DEATH THREATS

We left him ranting. Wilkes was exhausted after the ordeal he had just finished, and pissed and depressed at the thought of the one to come. Now he would be the defendant. We opened the swinging courtroom doors and saw that the mood in the corridor was still one of unrestrained celebration. The Whiz Kids were congratulating a few terrified jurors when they saw Wilkes and quickly surrounded him, patting him on the back and making delightful—to my ears— death threats against the "honky pig motherfuckin' judge." Others assured us that the next time they got busted, they'd be sure to call on Wilkes, the Whiz Kids' new consiglieri. Just what we needed.

Wilkes shrugged off the congratulatory pats as if they were locusts practicing touch and goes on his back. He moved through the crush of punks toward the exit as if escaping a huddle of lepers. As he slid through the crowd, avoiding the offered high- and low-fives, he explained his early departure: "Sorry I can't stay and chat, but there is work to be done in preparing for my own trial in front of that honky pig motherfucka."

A loud chorus of encouraging best wishes from the Whiz Kids followed us out the door: "Kill dat old wrinkled honky piece' a shit!

Stick dat gavel up his motherfuckin' cracker asshole. Make him eat the big one."

We didn't stop to ask what the "big one" was, but quick-stepped through the elevator doors and pressed the down button. The doors closed before any of the gangsters could join us in our six-story descent to street level.

Outside it was bitter cold and gray. The wind slapped us in the face every step of the way as we race-walked back to the Woolworth. All the way, Wilkes was livid. He ranted about representing young gangsters. They were so wild and unruly, so lacking in understanding, so unprofessional. Then he railed about being underpaid for the case. "No amount of money can compensate me for the torture of defending anyone, much less a goddamned Whiz Kid, in front of Y. Knott. Remember this moment, Schoon, and kick me in the ass if I ever even think of filing a challenge against any other judge so long as Knott lives."

He loathed the prospect of the contempt trial which Knott was already insisting upon hearing himself despite the obvious reasons for his not doing so. This would mean countless hours preparing a motion to disqualify the bastard off the case. It would mean at least one appeal. It would mean a lot of wasted time.

There are three big drawbacks in getting contempted. First, if you're lucky and beat the rap, the whole thing is a big worrisome waste of time; second, if you lose, you can go to jail and be disbarred; and if you represent yourself, as Wilkes always did—with me as cocounsel—there's a third drawback. The pay is lousy.

By the time we got back to the office, it was just after four in the afternoon. Wilkes was thoroughly depressed. The thrill of victory was not in the air. Wilkes had me get started working up the disqualification motion papers for tomorrow's hearing while he went into his office, ignored the incoming phone calls—which I fielded—and sulked.

.   .   .

THE CALL

I took a call that came into the office within twenty minutes of our arrival. A very angry Whiz Kid was on the line, the one who looked like Sonny Liston, and he informed me emphatically that "da Marshal is still in motherfuckin' Tombs and the pigs ain't lettin' him out without a motherfuckin' court paper dat say he be free. You get da paper to the pigs. If you don't, your whole family's dead."

So much for our popularity with the Whiz Kids. Fame is fleeting. I went into Wilkes's office. He was stretched out on a sofa staring up at the ceiling. An open bottle of whiskey was on the side table and an empty glass rested precariously on Wilkes's chest. He didn't move as I told him about the phone call.

I offered to go see Alvin Scribner, Knott's clerk, and handle it. Shouldn't take a minute. All they needed was the release form. Knott couldn't refuse to issue it without risking a healthy civil suit for false imprisonment—to say nothing of what the Whiz Kids might do to him. And Alvin, despite being Knott's longtime clerk, was a reasonable guy and not at all a vulture like his boss. He'd clear up any paper roadblock to the Field Marshal's liberty.

Wilkes perked up. "You mean that son of a bitch Knott is keeping my acquitted client in jail?" He sat up. The glass rolled off his chest and fell to the floor. "That bastard! That . . ."

He got up and put on his jacket. "I'll take care of this personally." This seemed a bad idea to me. A Wilkes-Knott confrontation at this time would not be good, so I insisted that I could see Scribner and make sure the paperwork on Diderot got to the Tombs and freed his client. All very low-key.

He said, "No. You stay and prepare the challenge to kick Knott's ass off my case. I'll attend to this. Anyway, I want the satisfaction of liberating the Field Marshal."

Wilkes was like that. He loved to bear physical witness to getting people out of jail. It didn't matter how. Clients didn't much care how. Wilkes might be getting them reasonable bail or winning a jury acquittal or using some obscure legal technicality to flash at the system like a make-'em-gasp-in-their-robes-get-out-of-jail-free trump card.

"The client never asks, 'How?' " Wilkes would often say. "He asks, 'How long?'—as in 'How looooonnnnnng am I going to have to stay imprisoned in this shithole?' Clients don't care about how you do it as long as you do it. Use an Uzi and a helicopter or a release card from the judge—it doesn't really matter. Get them out! The quicker the better."

For Wilkes, getting them out from behind bars was the purest exercise of legal power wielded by the impotent defense attorney; he loved it when he could exercise it. And because freedom for the ne'er-do-well prisoner pissed everyone off, he loved it all the more. The assistant D.A., the police investigators, the jailers and judges, all cringed when they had to process the papers that would make an inmate an outmate. They felt they were forced participants to a legalized jailbreak.

So in that sense it didn't surprise me that Wilkes would want to get Diderot out of jail himself. But the ill will between him and Knott was off the charts. Maybe he'd be able to do it all with Alvin the clerk and not even see Knott.

Off he went, Diderot's file in his left hand, rumpled overcoat draped over his right arm, and a black cloud—another trial before Judge Knott!—hovering like a brooding omnipresence over his head. He was in a foul mood, but the prospect of sweet liberty for Field Marshal Lyle Diderot beckoned. Just the tonic to end an unbelievable day.

4

NAGATA

"Swallow much but digest little."
CHARLIE CHAN

*"Never pick a juror whose mouth puckers smaller
than a chicken's asshole."*
MELVIN T. TEASDALE, III

After Wilkes left to perform a jailectomy and secure the release of his client from the Tombs, I puttered around the office to finish our motion to knock Judge Knott off Wilkes's trial for contempt of court. Little did I know that someone was making that evening's writing and research one colossal waste of nonbillable time.

The subject of Wilkes's jail surgery, His Malignancy, Field Marshal Lyle Diderot, got out of jail just before five that afternoon— thanks to Wilkes's timely intervention at the courthouse and the cooperation of Knott's clerk, Alvin Scribner, in quickly processing the release papers. The headless body of the Whiz Kids gang now had its muscular brain back.

At about the same time, I took a very unexpected call at the office from a fellow with a distinct southern drawl. It was Melvin T. Teasdale, III, president of the National Association of Greatest American Trial Advocates, asking for John Wilkes. The group, I learned, was holding its annual national convention at that very moment at the Waldorf-Astoria. Teasdale's voice sounded an alarm when I told him of Wilkes's whereabouts.

"Whad'ya mean Wilkes is at the courthouse? Six months ago you guarandamnteed me he'd be here. Shit, boy, he's already more overdue than my first wife's alimony check. Remember, he's supposed to be here for dinnah, and there's the Grand Round Table where he's the featured speaker. Get y'all's behinds up here."

NAGATA

I thought, Oh shit! What with the Diderot trial and then the contempt hearing scheduled for the next morning, Wilkes and I had totally forgotten Wilkes's engagement as guest speaker at the NAGATA gathering. Or, I should say, I forgot. Wilkes never paid much attention to calendaring. My responsibility was to remember the dates, remind him in time to prepare, and then, at the right moment, push him in the right direction.

NAGATA was a membership-by-invitation-only group of well-heeled, elitist, megalomaniacal, white-haired or no-haired, potbellied, Caucasoid, male lawyers from all over the country. It met annually at swank big-city hotels or expensive resorts for the sole purpose of convincing its members that they were, in all humility, the last true champions of the greatest, most skilled, and brilliant trial lawyers association in the world. And, of all time.

In other words, it was a mobile, postcollege fraternity for aging adolescents.

There are many such trial bar organizations in the country, but under NAGATA's strict standards for membership, its associates had to admit they were the very best. In reality, most were well past living up to their self-proclaimed designation as Greatest American Trial Advocates, having long since given up their courtroom warrior spirits for the security of large law firms devoted to representing rich corporations and defendants with white collars.

They represented clients most defense lawyers dream about: powerful companies overflowing with enough filthy lucre to pay for and sustain centuries of litigation. These were essentially mindless, amoral clients who insisted on being overlawyered, who never questioned monthly legal bills, most of which exceeded an ordinary person's lifetime income, and who demanded nothing except the right to continue doing business—above, below, or within the law. To these clients, paying tremendous lawyers' salaries, litigation costs, and court fines was simply the fee for the right to do business without danger of going to jail.

I don't know why Wilkes agreed to speak at their annual meeting except that like most trial lawyers, he loved to hear himself talk and rarely rejected the opportunity to have an audience. But we both had forgotten the damned engagement.

What to do now? I had a very concerned Melvin T.—for Texas—Teasdale speaking from a portable phone brought to his table from the bar. We were already late for the meeting where we were to mingle with the NAGATA associates. While I stammered in search of a good reason for forgetting the engagement, I heard him speak with his waiter and order his beef "Texas rare." When the waiter asked for clarification, Texas Teasdale said, "Son, just knock off the horns, wipe its ass, and drag it on over."

I knew if Wilkes showed up this night, he was going to be in no mood to speak to a cluster of pompous tuxedos after the day he just had. Yet, if he no-showed, he would piss off some pretty well-connected people. Right now we were in need of important people as potential character witnesses for Wilkes at the contempt hearing as well as at the bar discipline proceedings that would inevitably follow. And what about those future referrals?

I said to Texas Teasdale, "Of course, Melvin, he's going to be there. He's been talking about nothing else all day. This is just a temporary trial lawyer's emergency. You all know how that can happen when you're in the middle of a trial."

This was a good point for getting Teasdale to be patient. I had just given him the trial lawyer's best excuse for being late or missing in action. A trial lawyer's first duty is to his client, and in the heat of trial by combat, nothing else in life matters. Not even dinner with the NAGATAs.

I continued, "We've got a taxi ordered to go straight to the Waldorf as soon as he gets back from court. And you fellows can prepare yourselves for one fine lecture 'cause Wilkes has been prepping for days on . . . what was it . . . I'm in such a fugue state right now . . . er, opening statements?"

"Son, the man's supposed to lead the Round Table on jury selection techniques. Say, what's your name again, fella?" Teasdale's voice still betrayed his irritation, although he could hardly voice it given the excuse I just gave him.

"Winston Alfred Schoonover," I answered, "silent law partner to the inimitable John Wilkes. Jury selection. Of course. Jury selection's exactly what I meant. He's ready, don't you worry. And looking forward to it. So, yeah, sure we'll be there. Soon as he gets back, which shouldn't be too long unless the judge has locked him up. Hah!"

Teasdale laughed, not knowing that if Judge Knott saw Wilkes that evening, the odds of Wilkes's being locked up were higher than a Texas oil gusher. But I continued dissembling. "Yeah, no sweat. You can plan on it. Bye bye."

EVER-READY WILKES

I cleaned myself up as best you can without the benefit of a shower or a change of clothes, and waited for Wilkes to put in an appearance at the office. Since he had forgotten the meeting, of course he had no clue he was to speak, much less of the topic with which he was to spellbind the NAGATAs. This was a trifling worry. Like any great attorney, Wilkes could talk for an hour on anything, sound knowledgeable and interesting, and not say a goddamned thing of substance the whole time. That's what made him so good as a speaker, conversationalist, and deliverer of jury argument. This was the natural by-product of years of the best verbal conditioning known to man: being well paid by clients to speak by the hour.

The problem wasn't the speech. The problem was whether he was planning to come back to the office at all before he went God knew where. Wilkes, half stewed and despondent, had left the office to free Lyle Diderot just after four P.M. I feared that once he left the courthouse, he could end up in a gutter as easily as back at the office.

I called Alvin Scribner at the court. He said Wilkes had come, and left after the paperwork to free the Field Marshal had been completed. I called his home. No answer. I called his girlfriend, *New York Times* reporter Adell Loomis. No answer.

At 5:30 P.M., I ran down to wait it out at curbside, intent on giving it about thirty minutes and then forgetting the whole thing. Outside it was still windy, and much colder than when Wilkes and I had marched victoriously back from the court following Diderot's miraculous acquittal. Now, Broadway was jammed with slow-moving rush hour traffic, and Wilkes was not in sight. I stood there, freezing my ass, checking out the passing pedestrian traffic in search of the National Association of Greatest American Trial Advocates' great American guest speaker.

Finally, at 6:15 P.M., I saw him staggering down Broadway bumping off people like a pinball. In his left hand he held a wet, brown paper bag shaped tightly around a half-exposed bottle of Jack Daniel's. In the other hand he carried a styrofoam cup which, when I first saw it, was upside down, being emptied into a wide-opened mouth like morning gargle.

"We forgot!" I said as I ran up to him. "The NAGATA meeting at the Waldorf! You're speaking on picking a jury after dinner."

PTSD BLUES

Wilkes stopped, pointed his bottle-bearing hand at me and said, "I say—hiccup—I say to all the great American trial lawyers, never, ever, pick a jury after dinner." I looked into his bloodshot eyes, which were at half-mast and which looked lazily back into mine. The smell of whiskey breath was overpowering. Wilkes, the usual teetotaler, was drunk because of Trial Lawyer's Teetotaling Exception Number 179: precontempt trial stress drama blues. He slurred, "That's all I know on the subject, so tell 'em to go fuck themselves. Take me home."

"Bad idea." I said as I eyed the cab-clogged street for an empty one. Getting a cab at rush hour would be about as easy as getting a judge to suppress twelve kilos of cocaine on a bad search. I stuck my arm out and waved indiscriminately at the passing yellow fleet of taxis being piloted through the street by a cross section of the Third World. They all ignored me.

With one arm flagging cabs and the other bracing the stuporous Wilkes to make sure he didn't fall over, I said to him, "Very bad idea. You can't piss these guys off. We could use some friends in powerful places right now. They could be witnesses at the contempt hearing. Good character and all that. You just can't no-show."

"Tellemstogoanfugemselbs," said Wilkes as his eyelids fell shut and his mind entered that glorious state of black nirvana that often follows a lengthy brain-soak in alcohol. His upper torso leaned heavily forward into me and I caught him in my arms as his rubbery legs buckled and then collapsed. I laid him on the sidewalk. I knew exactly what I had to do.

I ran to the nearby Guadalajara Café, a tiny, X-rated eatery where grease hangs in the air like thick London fog and the smells are of burned eggs and stale cigarette butts. Lunko, the short, barrel-chested owner, manager, waiter, cashier, janitor, bouncer, and chef, quickly responded to my order and poured two large "to goes" of the house specialty, toasted black coffee. Styrofoams in hand, I ran back to the prostrate Wilkes.

A few (this was New York City, after all) pedestrians were huddled around him wondering aloud if he were dead. I put the coffees down, picked him up, and threw him in front of the first empty cab that inched by on the street. Mercifully, it stopped. I then opened the back door, tossed Wilkes onto the backseat, and hopped in beside him. The cabbie, an angry Jamaican, pointed his fist at me and yelled, "I got to go get fare, mon. You getta fuck out."

Wilkes slid slowly off the backseat facedown onto the floor.

I yelled angrily, "My friend has twenty minutes to get an injection of medicine which he left at his hotel or he dies. We must get to the Waldorf! It is a matter of life or death. Here's a hundred bucks."

The cabbie's eyes filled with the look of a lawyer's greed as his hand filled with this lawyer's greenery. He smiled and turned to his two-way radio to tell his dispatcher, "Mon, I'm here at da World Trade and don see no ambassador lookin' fella. I'm heading back uptown." A moment later he was back on the line to Dispatch:

"Hey, mon, just got two fares to Waldorf. Headin' up dare now, mon."

With me force-feeding Wilkes burned coffee, and our cabbie happily jabbering in reggae mumbo-jumbo, we inched uptown toward the hotel—just another twig floating in a honking, swerving, gaseous river of slow-rolling metal.

THE TEASDALES

It took well over forty minutes to drift upstream to the Waldorf— enough time to empty the cups of java down a semiconscious Wilkes's throat. By the time we got to the hotel, he would still have failed any field sobriety test known to man, but progress had been made—by now he could have failed it standing up. I rushed him into the lobby and, taking direction from the events sign—which read: NATIONAL ASSOCIATION OF THE GREATEST AMERICAN TRIAL LAWYERS: THE GRAND BALLROOM—headed for the grand ballroom.

We entered a large banquet area devoid of human life. It was filled with large circular tables, each topped with a mess of half-empty food platters and bottles of wine. A couple of busboys, the Third World sons of the taxi drivers outside, were busy removing the wreckage. I asked about the diners and one of them pointed to another room off the dining area from where I heard the distinct prattle of party conversation.

With Wilkes in tow we entered the room. It was filled with cigar smoke, scores of laughing middle-aged men standing in black tuxedos in one group and an equal number of gorgeous bare-shouldered slender young women in evening gowns and diamonds in another. Everyone had a glass of something in their hand. A tall, wide-nosed man puffing on a cigar spotted us standing in the threshold and quickly approached with a pretty lady on his arm. As he did, the cubes in his tumbler of bourbon clinked noisily while the gray-white ash from his cigar dropped on the lapel of his black tuxedo. He didn't notice.

I surmised who approached and told Wilkes to either act sober or pass out because in between just wasn't going to do. Surprisingly, he made an effort. He stiffened his back and stood without my assistance. Ignoring Wilkes, the man introduced himself to me as Melvin T. Teasdale, III, president of the National Association of Greatest American Trial Advocates.

Teasdale was a large man in his early fifties, balding, and drinking. He looked much like the dozens of other jabbering men in the room. On his arm was a young blond-haired beauty wearing a black low-cut dress which amply displayed most of her chest. Around her long, lovely neck lay a broad band of diamonds the size of a bulldog's choke collar. Black gloves extended past her elbows, and on one wrist, affixed to the fabric of the glove, was a diamond-studded bracelet even wider than her huge necklace.

"Y'all er late," said Teasdale. "I'm Teasdale and this here's my wife, Kismet."

"Y'all er late," repeated the lovely Mrs. Melvin T. Teasdale. She removed her thin arm from her husband's and used both hands to sip some champagne out of a fluted glass.

Wilkes, for all his intoxication, made his first coherent comment since I threw him in the cab. "Better late than sober, I always say." He said this with only a slight slur while extending his hand to Melvin Teasdale. Melvin's eyebrows rose as his eyes turned to look at Wilkes. He had misfigured from our faces—mine alert and Wilkes's drooping—that I must be the featured speaker.

"John Wilkes, at your servicio, Señor Presidente." Wilkes bowed deeply. I wondered if he'd be able to straighten up, but he did and said, "Sorry we were delayed, but I spent the last hour trying to convince a lunatic judge that when a jury acquits a defendant, this means he has to let him go. A lot of judges find that hard to fathom."

"You mean y'all had a client in . . . in jail?" asked an incredulous Mrs. Melvin Teasdale the Third as she stuck a gloved, diamond-banded hand palm down and limp at the wrist so that you didn't know if you were to shake it or bow and kiss it. She wondered what kind of lawyer would be trying a case with a client who lacked sufficient funds to instantly post bond. She said, "I'm Mrs. Melvin T. Teasdale, the Third, but y'all may call me Kissy."

Melvin put his stogie in his mouth, his arm around his wife, and hugged her a bit as he said, "But this little darlin's the second Mrs. Melvin Teasdale the Third."

THE NUMBED MEDULLA

Wilkes's eyes were unfocused, but he was performing magnificently for a man operating with a numbed medulla. He squeezed Kissy's hand and fell forward in the process, so that his face almost plunged down her neckline. Catching himself, he let his head fall to her extended hand and gave it such a slobbery kiss, it left a moisture pattern. "John Wilkes, fresh from the bloody juridical battlefield, my lady." He straightened up and said in a very loud voice, "Victorious, yet wounded; acquitted, but contempted; and now honored most greatly as the featured Round Table speaker on the vagaries of jury selection to this, the greatest assemblage of trial attorneys in the cosmos. And, uh . . . here is my esteemed partner, Winston Alfred Schoonover."

Kismet's small nose, now engulfed in the stinking, whiskey vapors expelled along with Wilkes's words, wrinkled abruptly. Instinctively, she took a big step backward in self-defense and then drawled, "And just what kind of a case was it you tried, Mr. Wilkes? We hear so much about the Wall Street problems down in Texas. One of those insider tradin' cases, no doubt."

He was swaying so much as he stood there, I grabbed his belt near the small of his back to make sure he didn't tumble into Kissy's half-exposed front. "Not quite," he said. "My client, a punk gangster from the Lower East Side, was charged with assaulting and robbing a poor little blind schoolgirl."

The faces of Mr. and Mrs. Melvin T. Teasdale reflected their shock. They stiffened in a fixed expression of curled-lipped revulsion, appalled at the type of case we handled. Mrs. Teasdale particularly reacted as if we had informed her we worked in the city sewers and had just come up after a hard day of dung patrol. The two Texans looked at each other.

"A crime of brute violence?" asked Kissy Teasdale. "You represent . . . real criminals? Surely this case must have been, uhm, forced upon you. I guess that mean old judge just made you do it. *Pro bono publico,* ain't that what y'all call it? Is that—"

"Nope," interrupted Wilkes. He swayed forward again as I tugged back on his belt to keep him upright.

"Well then, what on earth could bring you to represent a monster accused of beating a blind girl?"

"Simple, ma'am. Thirty-five thousand bucks."

Kismet reflexively put her sparkly gloved hand to her ruby mouth, quickly turned her head toward her husband and then back to Wilkes. She could utter no audible reply to the vulgarians who stood before her. It was obvious now. It was too clear. These were the dregs of the great profession—low-down, filthy criminal street lawyers.

"Sorry about the attire," I said, to change the subject. Amidst the tuxedos and knockout gowns, we were wearing the daily uniform of the criminal defense attorney: rumpled two-piece brown suit, pastel-colored shirt, food-stained striped tie, and scuffed shoes. "We had no time to take the acquittal, convince the judge to free our client, and, late as it was, go home and change."

"Well, pardners, this is a bit out of the ordinary," said Texas Teasdale as Kissy spent a minute examining the both of us with the contemptuous look of the doorman at Gucci's or the maître d' at Le Cirque. "Let's go on in," said Melvin Teasdale. "We're about to start the damned business meeting. I'll introduce y'all at the Round Table."

GIRL'S BEST FRIEND

Before we could maneuver through the crowd—the place was pure gridlock, worse than the rush hour congestion out on the street—up glided a gorgeous redhead, all cleavage and sparkling jewelry, to see our hostess. She squeezed between Wilkes and me as if we did not exist and addressed the lovely Kismet. "Why Kissy Teasdale, that's the most sublime bracelet I've ever seen," cooed the redhead.

Kissy bussed the woman so lightly on the cheek her ruby lips never made contact. Kissy said, "Yes, Melvin picked it out for me just before we got married. It's an early Bulgari piece, much better than anything they're making today. But you know Melvin and I have to be so careful these days about our purchases because the bitch, Melvin's Ex, is still on the warpath making noises that he held out on her when they divided up their property. As if she didn't get enough! Do you know that little bloodsucka is threatenin' to take us back into court based on what she calls our curious post-property-settlement conspicuous consumption. Can you imagine? But never mind that. Let me look at you. Why, darlin' Sarah, I see you've still got that pretty lil' old birdy pin. That's black onyx, ain't it?"

Sarah was the redheaded trophy bride of an aging thrice-divorced NAGATA luminary whom, we later found out, was the fifth vice-president and climbing steadily up the vice-presidents' seniority ladder to the top. She looked down at the gleaming bird precariously pinned to the itty-bitty shoulder strap holding up her black gown. The bird had yellow and white gold wings. Huge diamonds formed the eyes and beak. Small, granular stones were clustered on the rest of the glittery head and body.

"Yes, but I should never have worn it with this gown," sighed Sarah. "Nothing but flesh to pin it to! It looks like it's perched on my clavicle. Ha! Ha! Ha!"

Kissy smiled at Sarah. "Why you pretty thing, you simply *had* to wear that gorgeous lil' ol' pin. You know, the best time to wear your diamonds is when you're very young. Big stones make a woman look old, don't you think?"

President Teasdale ignored the bird chatter and pulled on Wilkes. Somehow my friend had grabbed a tumbler of bourbon from a passing waiter and was imbibing again. As he finished the drink with a single swallow, Wilkes stuck his head between the small space where the two chatting women stood and said, "Ladies. Ladies. Why bother with jewelry and gowns? Why not just paste thousand-dollar bills, stocks and bonds, and certificates of deposit all over your skinny little naked bods?"

.   .   .

ROUND TABLE

The women's heads snap-turned to see the source of this outrage just as President Teasdale and I jerked Wilkes out of harm's way. We pulled him through the thick crowd to a round mahogany table big enough to seat about a score of tuxedos. The center of the table was dimly illuminated by a low-hanging light which displayed just about every conceivable variety of liquor bottle beneath it. This is where the Round Table events would take place.

Wilkes and I were seated just as Wilkes finished yet another drink. Somebody poured him another. Teasdale loudly called out, "Round Table! Round Table! Gather 'round."

Because of the size of the table, the eighty or so members had to group their chairs in multiple concentric circles around it. As they did, the women, having heard the male primal call to arms, moved to the bar side of the room to continue chatting about jewelry and gowns, the Broadway shows, their spouse, his Ex (and the trouble she was causing), or ancient history—their former lives as legal secretaries.

At the round table, Wilkes and I were surrounded by the chairs holding up the tuxedos. The lighting was so dim and the mist from low-hanging cigar fumes so thick, you could not make a face out past the first row. Teasdale opened the meeting. "Gentlemen. First thing, I want to introduce our guests, John Wilkes and his partner Winston Schooner, both distinguished members of the trial bar of the great state of New York . . ."

"But not for long . . ." mumbled Wilkes.

His words were smothered by a swallow of bourbon and Teasdale's next comment. "And in the NAGATA tradition, Mr. Wilkes will lead tonight's Round Table after-dinner discussion on the topic of the fine art of jury selection."

Polite applause and the tinkling of clinking ice cubes in tumblers broke out from the seated tuxedos hidden in the darkness. Wilkes downed his drink. Someone poured him another. As the applause quieted, he stood abruptly and said loudly, "I know I am to speak on jury selection after dinner, but I can tell you this, you fine bastards, never pick a damned jury after dinner!"

I pulled Wilkes down and hot-breathed a "Not yet!" into his ear, but being numb from the neck up, nothing registered. He was operating on drunken reptile-brain instinct, the higher levels of cerebral functioning having vanished once again.

President Teasdale continued, "But before we get to the fascinatin' education component of our meetin', let's first deal with the issue of elections for next year's officers. As is the custom, the six vice-presidents of the executive committee have nominated the new officers, who will be the following: First Vice-President Ronnie Lipton of Tallahassee will vainly attempt to replace me, your President for Life. But I shall resist unless I lose my loyal support of y'all."

Loud, good-natured booing erupted. "Resign now!" some tuxedo yelled. A burst of applause greeted the suggestion.

"Well, shucks," said a beaming Teasdale, "looks like I been run outta town. This here's a coup d'etat. Ronnie will be next year's president. As such, your most important duty next year is to get me an expensive wall plaque to commemorate my outstanding years of service to this great organization. Now, the other vice-presidents have shown great and discriminating leadership qualities by renominating themselves to another year in office. In keeping with our traditions, all those willing to rubber stamp these nominations, as is mandatory under the NAGATA bylaws, will now signify by shaking the ice in their tumblers."

A few tumblers were clinked, but only—as far as I could tell—by members who were in the process of raising their glasses to take a drink. Wilkes's tumbler was clinking the loudest as he drained yet another glass. Everyone else booed and hissed as Teasdale said, "Well then, once again we have a unanimous selection of our slate of next year's officers. Congratulations, men."

The crowd booed the announcement. No one really gave a damn who ran this outfit except those who, in the democratic tradition of club service, were nominating themselves for uncontested office.

First Vice-President Ronnie Lipton then rose to his feet at our right. He cleared his throat, waited for the unappreciative group to get quiet, and said, "Thank you, thank you. I shall strive to match the excellent example of President Teasdale, who did such a fine job this year. And, Mel, we're gonna surprise you tonight because as a token of our appreciation, the organization now presents Melvin Teasdale the first NAGATA President's Cup with his name inscribed on it. We will make this an annual tradition, Mel, and you are the first to be honored. Congratulations."

Lipton lifted an ugly gold trophy the size and shape of a small bathtub, put it on the table and slid it toward Wilkes and me, expecting us to pass it to Teasdale. "CONGRATULATIONS!" he said again to the crowd, hoping to inspire applause for the presentation, but the circled congregation did not oblige.

When the trophy got to us, Wilkes grabbed it, held it high over his head like a Wimbledon winner, and bellowed—what else?—drunkenly, "Thank you members of NAGATA for this award. Though I am not a member, I shall not forget your generosity. But! I am humbly reminded of the old saying, 'Awards are like hemorrhoids. Sooner or later every asshole gets one.' "

This brought on thunderous stomping of feet and loud supportive expletives from the crowd. "Then, give it to the asshole!" said one of the tuxedos. Others shouted approval of the idea. Teasdale, not waiting for Wilkes to hand him the gold, stood, leaned over, and grabbed his prize from Wilkes's head. "I earned this," he said, laughing, "and I want the membership to know: your president is no asshole."

Teasdale raised his trophy in one hand and his drink in the other and guzzled amidst more loud, affectionate booing. Then he wiped his mouth with his sleeve and announced, "Now, my friends, we have the matter of new nominations. Our colleague from the great state of California, Guy Olson of San Francisco, wishes us to vote on his invitee, Gene Phillips, of . . . er . . . what city, Guy?"

A short, serious-looking, balding man stood from the second row directly across from Wilkes and me. "Emeryville, just across the bay from the city."

. . .

THE BLACK BALL

"Emeryville?" a voice from the darkened back row shouted out. "Never heard of it." I heard murmurs in the rows behind me. Someone whispered, "Olson? Say, isn't he still at Advocate level?"

"Hell, no!" Another whisper from behind. "He's a measly Associate."

Someone in a louder voice from behind where Olson stood said, "Never heard of this guy, Gene Phillips, but I read his résumé in the program package. The guy's so unremarkable, I already forgot what I read."

A loud clinking of bourbon tumblers applauded the anonymous detractor who continued, "We're a big enough group without adding more no-names. I vote the black ball."

The black ball obviously was a negative vote, and I could tell from Olson's face that this single black ball would mean the defeat of the nomination. Olson turned toward the voice from the darkness and said, "More no-names? More? Look, I *know* this man. He's an excellent trial attorney and has been for twenty years. He's tried all sorts of jury—"

"Your best bet in jury selection is the deaf juror," interjected the very drunken Mr. Wilkes as he again tried to stand and begin his speech. "They never hear enough evidence—"

I pulled him down hard in his chair before he could get upright. He continued his drinking and shut up.

Another voice from the darkness shouted, "What cases has he tried, Guy? The usual P.I., divorce, bankruptcy, and traffic crap? What's this guy got to offer NAGATA? Looks like a black ball to me too, I'm afraid." More ice-clinking applause greeted detractor number two.

Guy Olson was taking this seriously. He was openly angry. The nomination seemed to be going into the toilet, and if it was to be salvaged, he had to put all of his personal prestige on the line. "No, hold on. I said I *know* this man. He is of excellent character, and as one of the few black defense lawyers in his community, he has served his neighbors well by taking on all kinds of cases other lawyers refused to take, from the most common to the most complicated. He is a trial lawyer's trial lawyer, and a damned good one. And besides that, I think it's time we broke NAGATA's color barrier."

Once Olson said the words "black" and "color" a terrible silence seized the group. It was as if a thug had announced, "Your next word is your last." Olson sensed the futility of his situation and let loose with a last desperate salvo: "There isn't a black face in this group. Gentlemen, this isn't the Klan!"

The group remained silent. Not even an ice cube tinkled. After a few moments of embarrassing quiet, Teasdale broke the hush with the code words for defeat. "Of course, Guy, this nomination cannot, must not, and will not be black-balled based upon the color of a man's skin as opposed to the content of his character."

Wilkes then blurted out, "Always blackball from your juries an accountant who picks his nose when answering questions." Wilkes didn't bother to stand for this precious jury selection tip. He pushed the tumbler of bourbon up to his face and drank deeply.

President Teasdale called for additional comment on the nomination, but before anyone could respond, he called for the vote. All in favor of the nomination were to stand. No one joined Olson on his feet except Wilkes. Olson, quickly seeing his isolation, sank miserably into his chair.

TIPS FROM OBLIVION

Wilkes, oblivious to his surroundings, stayed on his feet—a remarkable achievement in itself—with drink in one hand, and the other with a bottle of bourbon splashing a refill. Reloaded, he broke the silence by continuing his premature lecture on jury selection. "You know," he said as his body teetered, "I've always wanted to rack up the first twelve in the box and say, 'Judge, no need to question these fine folks. We'll take 'em as they sit.' Now, this ain't a bad move if it shames the D.A. into doing the same thing, 'cause the odds are, given the mental health of this country, there'll be at least one psychotic among 'em. Guaranteed hung jury."

The tuxedos grinned and chuckled at Wilkes's advice. It was a far better thing to concentrate on comic trivia than the nomination they had just slaughtered.

"Well, it appears our friend is eager to regale us with jury selection stories for the Round Table," said a delighted President Teasdale. He was eager to move on to another topic, and smiled at Wilkes, who was busy into his next bourbon. Teasdale put his arm on Wilkes's shoulder and said, "Mr. Wilkes, let me add my contribution to your astute observations on jury selection. In Texas, our rule is to never pick a juror whose mouth puckers smaller than a chicken's asshole."

A loud chorus of chuckles and cube tinkling applauded the president's advice. I stood and whispered to Wilkes that it was now time for him to perform. He began, "Always warm up the prospective jurors. . . ." As he spoke these words, he gesticulated wildly with his right hand so that his refilled bourbon and cubes flew out and drenched the first two rows of tuxedos.

Taking notice of the stained shirts on the well-dressed fellows in the first row, Wilkes told them, "Bourbon fits you fellas very well."

With his tumbler dripping in his hands and his mind too sotted to be the least embarrassed by his faux pas, he continued. "As I was saying, or spraying—hah!—always warm up the prospective jurors for what's to come. I start with something low-key, like, 'Ladies and gents, in this trial you will hear prosecution witnesses and witless perjurers. But then, I repeat myself.' "

The tuxedos were all smiles and chuckles and tinkling glasses of bourbon. A voice in the darkness added, "Never pick a juror who wears a beard and mustache, weighs over three hundred pounds, and wears a see-through T-shirt." This comment momentarily sucked the merriment out of the smoke-clogged air until the voice added, "Unless she's blood-related to your client."

"Good point," said Wilkes in the middle of the tuxedo laughter. He put his empty glass on the table and took a big gulp of air. I noticed he was sweating, his face was ashen, and his eyes seemed about to roll back into his forehead. He leaned forward on the table, face staring downward, and propped himself up by locking his elbows and resting on his clenched fists. He could not be long for the conscious world.

GOD SAVE THE JURORS!

Then he did the damndest thing. He pounded the table hard several times with his fist. "Knock on wood!" He pounded the table again. "Jurors! God love 'em! Thank God we're still able to select juries." He said this with surprising force, as if he were reborn to sobriety. The recuperative powers of the man never ceased to amaze me.

Wilkes continued, "Imagine this nightmare—having to try all your cases to the drooling, black-robed vampires. They'd love to get rid of juries just so's they can suck the life and liberty out of our clients without that time-wasting jury trial baloney."

Upright now, he lifted his newly refilled tumbler of bourbon, took a swig, and continued. "Today, I just finished a trial before one no-good-lying-cheatin' sonovabitch, a judge named Yulburton A.—for Asshole—Knott. Hates me. Tried to railroad my client with every cheap trick in the book. By the time the trial ended, the shithead contempted me six times. I felt like taking a machine gun and drilling the bastard right on the bench and then skipping out of the courtroom. I am fed up with judicial crooks who violate the law and then not only get away with it, but are rewarded for it!"

The tuxedos clinked their ice cubes, blew smoke, and loudly stomped their feet in applause. Several yelled, "Here! Here!" and other bravos. Wilkes happily guzzled his drink empty and nearly fell over in the process. He would have fallen over had it not been for a young busboy standing close behind him. The boy was carrying a portable phone and had approached the table without our notice during Wilkes's soliloquy. Until my drunken friend fell into him.

"Phone call for one John Wilkes," the boy said meekly. He stuck the phone under Wilkes's long, red nose.

Wilkes looked at the youngster strangely for a second—the kind of weird look man will give the first creature he meets from outer space. "I'm one John Wilkes," he said, "but I see more than one of you."

The busboy held out the phone until Wilkes grabbed it and stuck the business end in his ear. He told whomever was calling to speak louder as he could not hear for all the noise in the room. "Say what?" Wilkes yelled. "Speak up! Who wants me over there? Now? Chambers? Tonight? What? At this hour? I can't hear you. Say . . . What? Who? Shit!"

With that, he slammed the receiver down and announced to his audience that the call was from the chambers of Judge Y. Knott and that his presence was urgently required for reasons he could not comprehend. Wilkes grabbed his refilled glass of bourbon and lifted it as high as he could reach, spilling half all over himself as he did. "The blood-sucking vampire judge gets me at nine tomorrow morning and not a goddamned minute earlier!"

Then he collapsed backward into the busboy as the tuxedos rose as one and gave him a standing ovation.

— 5 —

Detective Mulraney

"Maybe some people on sea of matrimony wish
they had missed the boat."
CHARLIE CHAN

"Man, when we got married they musta made a mistake.
We took different vows: me to be faithful
and her to be celibate."
DETECTIVE JAIME PEREZ

NYPD Homicide Inspector Michael Fitzpatrick Mulraney, known
in Homicide as Mike "the Hanky," was looking forward to taking Jill
out to a delicious Chinese dinner at eight that evening. He had
broken the date with his wife two Fridays in a row due to two
untimely murders. (New Yorkers are not very considerate about the
time they choose to slaughter one another.)

Tonight, Mike felt good. Things had been slow this day. It had
been the standard fare: a slashing of a bum in the Bowery and a fatal
shooting between two dope dealers in Harlem. Mulraney was not
counting last night's murder of the woman walking her dog on
Riverside Drive. Wasn't his shift.

Fortunately, his buddies Perez and Fortunata got those crummy
assignments. He had called Fortunata that morning and assigned
him the slashed bum case. Frank was not pleased and yelled into the
phone the first question invariably asked by a New York homicide
dick in need of direction to the evidence: "Where's the beef?"

Mulraney pushed paper all day in the Dorm, the large, walless room filled with desks, which a score of homicide detectives called home. Like good cops everywhere, he loathed the paperwork aspect of the job, but being in the Dorm for a day was a rare event in the life of a homicide investigator in such a murderous city as New York. To be in the Dorm and not pounding the pavement, following leads given by witnesses, or at the scene of the corpse, was a temporary escape from the real world. Mulraney could not remember the last time he spent a full day there, and now it was late afternoon and his thoughts were on the sumptuous meal that was waiting to be cooked for him. Let's see, would he order his favorite, the extra-hot Hunan twice-cooked pork? Yes!

The garlic aromas. The heat generated by the sharp spices. The sensational tastes! His mouth watered so freely just thinking about it that a trickle of drool ran out the corner, to be quickly sopped by the ever-present hanky. And say hey! Maybe tonight he should be more adventurous and try something new. He was already hungry and it was not even five-fifteen in the afternoon.

MULRANEY

Michael Mulraney was forty-four years old, loved Chinese food, baseball, solving crimes, Willie Mays making the catch in the old Polo Grounds at 155th and Eighth Avenue (he was there), sex, his wife, his work, his partners, good jokes, clean jokes, New York City, garlic, loyalty, rock and roll, the Mets, chocolate shakes, chocolate ice cream, Hershey bars without nuts, steak and potatoes, Notre Dame and everything Irish, whiskey, the football Giants, boyhood memories of the baseball Giants, boxing, the Knicks, witty bathroom graffiti, his allergy and asthma medication, and Jimmy Breslin—in just about that order.

He disliked hypocrites, politicians, being stumped on a case, no sex, lawyers, liars, liver, the late Horace Stoneham, the Yankees, subways, salesmen, taxicab drivers, cold-blooded murderers, Dwight Francis Lorton, the Jets, rap music played loudly, rap music played softly, scotch, credit cards, credit card bills, air travel, New York air, doctors, stupid bathroom graffiti, hot-blooded murderers, dust and mold, taking allergy and asthma medication, needles, and being idle—in just about that order.

Mulraney's thoughts of dinner continued even as the short, plump Detective Jaime Perez laughed his way into the Dorm with a sullen-looking Frank Fortunata close behind. Perez was holding an official NYPD envelope over his head like a trophy. He gleefully yelled to Mulraney, "Hey, Hanky! I got my upgrade!" Perez looked back toward Fortunata. "And he didn't!"

THE SHITBALL!

The tall, strong-framed Fortunata fell into one of the ugly metal chairs near Mulraney and said dejectedly, "Once again, hard work, honesty, and intelligence get their just desserts. The shitball!"

Mulraney was still deep in thought of the restaurant date just two hours away, envisioning the omnipresent Chinese waiters hovering like food angels to whisk away empty plates and return with the next steaming ones, repeatedly filling the half-full water and wine glasses, and all done with such a quiet delicacy, you barely noticed them. They made you feel like an Oriental potentate.

Mulraney had barely enough interest in Fortunata's lament to look at him and grunt, "Huh?"

Fortunata looked as if he were about to reveal that Perez committed that day's homicides. "Look, Mike, you remember last week, me and Jaime, we both take the promotional exam. I get called in first. Sitting there is the three-headed panel with Chief Lorton, some old retired chief named McArdle, and the public member, Father Charles J. Laughlin. Get this, the guy with the O-ring around his neck is a former beat cop who got born again in Vice and turned in his blues for a penguin outfit. Sweet Jesus, can ya beat that?

"Anyhows, I answers all their questions perfect till the tight-ass preacher starts in like he's gonna squeeze a confession out of me. He asks me about my work habits. What it is, I says, is I bust my butt eight days a week by cramming the work into five or six thirty-hour days.

"And then the Holy Father throws a curve. He says, 'What about Sundays?' Well, I tell it straight. I says, 'When I'm not on shift, I sleep on Sunday.' So then he asks, 'Oh, so no church on Sunday?'

"Can you believe such a question! Gotta be unconstitutional. But what the hell am I supposed to say? So I treat it like it's a comment and not a question and don't say nothing. I look to the chief to help out with a question, but there's just a long silence. The chief and the other dummy look at me like Lucifer just sneaked into the muscular body of Officer Frank Fortunata to take the Homicide Detective Promotional Exam in his place.

"The chief then says 'That's it,' and my interview ends on that sour note and I slink out of the hearing room. Like the nice guy that I am, I tell my great buddy Jaime Perez here how it went. And what does this fat atheist go in and do! The first thing the chief asks him to do is introduce himself to the other two guys and outline his background in the department. But Friar Perez here says, 'Father, gentlemen, this is a time of trial for me, and I wonder if I might start this hearing as I do every single morning after I awake—with a prayer of thanks to the Lord.'

"And Brother Jaime Perez here, who ain't been inside a church since he got excommunicated at age twelve for crawling underneath the pews and peeking up the sisters' habits, he gets on his goddamned knees, crosses himself, and mumbles an Our Father. He mumbles it 'cause he don't even know the whole thing. And guess what? This motherfucking heathen gets the highest grade on the promotional!"

Perez, who is sitting on a desk, throws his head back and roars. Mulraney laughs too. This is vintage Perez, always the clever opportunist, convenience liar, and laughing conman. Qualities that made him a great dick.

Perez slaps Fortunata on the back and says with his slight Puerto Rican accent, "Amigo, maybe next time I'll be on your fucking promo panel and you'll remember to say your prayers, man!"

Mulraney smiled widely, which gave the appearance of being very much with his friends, but his thoughts had quickly refocused on the evening ahead. The great meal, the after-dinner drive home, his wife's sheer nightgown (a recent gift from him), and the love they would be making on full bellies in a heated bed within minutes of their arrival home. Jill, despite nineteen years of marriage to him, still loved a good romp in the hay.

Not like the other guys' wives who were the continual butt of jokes in the department. Like Perez and Fortunata. They talked as if their marriages were nothing but slow, tortured pleas for affection. Perez's continual joke was, "Man, when we got married they musta made a mistake. We took different vows: me to be faithful and her to be celibate."

GETTING BUZZED

The buzzing of the intercom on Mike the Hanky's desk brought him out of his daydream. Perez and Fortunata's jesting ceased. It was exactly five-twenty in the afternoon, and a buzz on the intercom, if answered, could ruin a weekend. The three of them looked at Mulraney's phone as if it were the Messenger of Doom.

Mulraney hit a button on the phone and a gruff voice on the intercom said that he should "get down here to my office at once!" A numbness in his gut quickly spread into his chest and then to his throat and head. He sneezed into his ever-present cheap white handkerchief. Dreams of a delicious dinner and a warm, sweaty screwing faded. Like a switched TV channel, the scene in his head was now much different. From the Chinese dinner station, he was now making a personal appearance on the reality channel and inventorying a death scene. Not a dead meat case! Not tonight!

The glee was off Perez's face. He knew, as did Fortunata, that the fellow with the all-too-familiar voice on the intercom was Chief Lorton, and he could only have murder on his mind—and work to be assigned. Perez and Fortunata looked at each other and hoped that the slaughter to be investigated was not so massive as to require more than one dick on the job.

As Mulraney got up from his chair, Perez looked to his watch and said, "Well, gotta go too. Movies and—Christ! I'm late to pick up Juanita! Damn it! No nooky for a week unless I materialize in midtown in ten minutes. Shit! I'm outta here. See you guys."

"Hold on," said Fortunata as he ran after Perez. "You're my ride."

His buddies gone before he took his first step, Mulraney began walking through the Dorm and the short distance down the empty hallway to see the chief, Dwight Francis Lorton, the longtime head of the Homicide Bureau. He prayed that the meeting was just another of the chief's frequent reminders that THEY were pressuring him to light the darkness, to find the unfindable and solve the unsolvable. Lorton's method of motivational leadership was to call you into his office and make you listen for hours as he verbally crucified himself with detailed descriptions of the threats and punishments from THEM.

Not that the chief convinced anybody. No one believed his whining complaints about menacing warnings from on high. He had been making them for years and nothing ever happened. But nothing ever happening was the best proof to the chief that he was being punished.

WORST-CASE SCENARIO

To the chief, the worst of all the unsolved crimes in Homicide is the unsolved murder of a cop, followed distantly by the unsolved murder of anyone else. But there was one type of homicide case that was worse than a cop-killing, or a buckets-of-blood family mass murder, or a grisly interracial torture-mayhem butchery in the park, worse even than a Harlem gang-bang execution of a busload of nuns from New Jersey—the unsolved high-profile murder that THEY figured any competent head of Homicide would have solved before rigor set in.

By the tone of Lorton's voice, Mulraney feared he was going to be presented a worst-case scenario from the top of the list. He ended his march down the drab hallway to Lorton's office hoping that he was only headed for a Crucifixion Speech. But please, not a cadaver detail! Not tonight!

Mulraney sneezed hard into his hanky as he entered Lorton's

office. Sometimes he sneezed so hard, deep, and loud, people feared his lungs were coming up. The worst were not only loud and lengthy, but featured moist phlegm noisily gurgling in his chest and rising to flood the awaiting cloth. The hanky, receptacle of these cacophonous blasts, was in his fingers most of the time, dealing with the various by-products of one of the world's worst cases of late-onset allergies. Mulraney was grateful it was only seasonal. As his specialist told him, "You are lucky. The worst seasons for you will be summer, fall, winter, and spring."

Mike the Hanky coped with the nuisance by living on prescribed air purifiers, dehumidifiers, oral inhalers, nasal inhalers, antihistamines, and an inexhaustible supply of plain, white hankies. Allergists had experimented on him with shots of cortisone, a new pill called "Big Bertha," and even sinus surgery. Nothing helped. Several times in his life he took desensitization shots two or three times a week, but once when the nurse forgot to put antigen in the needle and pumped a hundred cc's of air into his arm, he quit shot treatments. Allergies are rarely fatal. Embolisms easily can be.

"Bless you, Mulraney," said the chief automatically at the loud retort of Mulraney's sneeze. The chief was beyond suggesting that Mulraney see someone about his chronic malady. He saw Mulraney eat prescription antihistamine pills like popcorn, sniff nasal decongestants like a three-ounce-a-day coke addict, and suck his oral inhaler like it was a skin diver's oxygen tank. The chief was totally desensitized to Mulraney's allergies. "Look," he said, "we're in a jam."

Mulraney knew at that moment his worst fears were about to be realized. Lorton was not in a jam. He, Mulraney, was. The chief was about to spread him thin on another new case—and by the tone, it was going to be a worst-case scenario for sure.

It was time to change the subject. "You mean Fortunata's appealing his promo exam score?"

Lorton stood behind his desk as if standing would make his announcement more dramatic. His looks were not bad, although age had eroded a once-handsome face. The blue eyes were faded a bit and were supported by big, dark puffy bags. The face was worn with wrinkles and distorted by white doughy cheeks which gave him the look of a gerbil. Yet despite a body in decay, the chief was still a vain man, and it was said in the department that he never saw a mirror he didn't like.

He ignored Mulraney's trivial question. "We just got word of a murder in the goddamn courthouse. This one is absolutely top priority in the bureau, and I want you down there immediately. I don't have to tell you this is very bad news for us, what with all the goddamn unsolveds we got. THEY are already all over my case, and now this! Sheeeeiiiit!"

Mulraney blew his nose. His head was stuffier now than it had been all day. Numbness, headache, and a slight nausea, the concomitants of head blockage and sinus pressure, were making him woozy. There was no hope for tonight. But he had to try and get out of it. He owed it to Jill. "Christ Almighty, why me? I picked up the last two Friday night slaughters. I got family plans tonight. Why not Carter, or Viglioretti, or Melloy? Let them dance around the carcass tonight."

Mulraney was true to his two buddies, Perez and Fortunata, not to suggest their names. Not that it mattered. They had taken preemptive action and were long gone.

Lorton looked to his best detective and did something unusual. He told the truth. "Why? You have to ask? Because, Mike, you are the best I've got and this case has got to be done right. The other guys get their exercise jumping to conclusions, and most of them are wrong. Tonight, I need someone to get me facts, and pronto. Damn it, Mulraney, someone just murdered Justice Yulburton Abraham Knott!"

"Holy shit!" said Mulraney. Somehow, the murder of a judge on the Supreme Court lessened the feeling of extreme inconvenience, although it did nothing for his allergic reaction. Mulraney sneezed three times before he could get out a muted through-the-hanky "Where?"

"In his chambers. Stabbed in the back." Lorton saw Mulraney becoming attracted to the bait. They both knew this would be page-one material tomorrow, the biggest thing in the city, a great challenge to any dick. The *Daily News* alone would cover half the front page with one of its classic headlines, SUPREME COURT JUSTICE KNOTT GETS DEATH PENALTY! The other half would be a color picture of the bloody corpse being pushed into the meat wagon.

Lorton continued, "Mike, you can see why this one needs special attention. The mayor and the police commissioner are gonna want daily briefings from me on this. Tomorrow I'll give you two men, any two you want, but tonight I need you over there to take charge and preserve the scene. And you know the commissioner, Mike, he'll want a lead, and he'll want it quick."

Lorton began pacing behind his messy desk. He only called Mulraney "Mike" when he wanted something from him. Tonight he was taking a gourmet meal and some overdue hot love from him. Oozing phony sincerity, the typical introduction to the Crucifixion Speech, Lorton almost wept as he said, "So many cases, Mike. So many pressures on me. So many demands for quick solutions."

Blah, blah, blah.

Before Lorton could mount the cross and begin the speech in earnest, Mulraney said, "Okay, okay. I'm outta here. I'll call you from the court with the particulars."

HOMEWARD BOUND

Four merry, sotted NAGATA members helped me carry the long, rubbery frame of the drunken John Wilkes out of the Waldorf and to the curb on East Forty-ninth Street. Wilkes, lapsing in and out of consciousness, was a dead-weight carry most of the way. This troubled his polluted pallbearers not a bit, as they were pleased to lug the night's star and guest speaker on jury selection, holding him upright as he intermittently—during brief periods of coherence—regaled them with whatever old jokes entered his sotted brain. Meanwhile, I tried to perform a miracle on Forty-ninth Street by flagging down a taxi.

"Where was I? Oh, yeah . . . the motion to knock Judge Knott off my hearing tomorrow . . . and so I told old Schoon he could not file the motions he'd written, see. And Schoon, he looks up at me and he holds that little old fifty-page motion in his hand like it's his pet hound and I've just condemned it to death. He asks me, 'Why can't I file it? You haven't even read it.' And I look at the paltry pile of paper in his hand and says, 'Cause it don't weigh enough.' "

This was both untrue and not that amusing, but it drew loud howls of laughter from the plastered pallbearers. All but one let go of him while doubling up in giggles. Wilkes then turned his soused puss to his sole bearer and breathed a perfumed breath in his face. "My rule is that no motion is worth filing unless it weighs at least one pound."

Still laughing hard, their bodies mini-convulsing, the pallbearers sat or fell onto the sidewalk. As this included the last remaining pallbearer, Wilkes not only slipped back into unconsciousness, he also fell flat on his back into the gutter. Only my quickly placed hand cushioned his head from striking the curb. This activity was well-timed because Wilkes, lying prone in the street with his head in the gutter, was blocking traffic, and a cab was the first vehicle to screech to a stop about ten feet in front of Wilkes's body. Wasting no time, the pallbearers and I quickly picked up Wilkes and headed for the rear door of the taxi.

WEIRD SUKARNO

"No dead man! No dead man in cab!" said the cabbie, a short, stocky Indonesian-looking man whose face bore a striking resemblance to the late President Sukarno. We paid him no attention and stuffed Wilkes into the backseat.

"Not dead. Drunk," I said. "Dead drunk." To assure the man, I leaned Wilkes's head against the left rear-door window so that his mouth kissed the glass. Within moments Wilkes's breath was fogging it. "Look," I said, "he lives!"

Sukarno leaned over the backseat and put his broad, flat nose near Wilkes's mouth, and then recoiled at the first whiff of toxic fumes. "He plenty drunk." The reassured cabbie smiled. As he looked at me with that grin, I recoiled. He had no upper front teeth and his lower front teeth were on the longish side, giving him the menacing look of a werewolf.

Sukarno added, "Him puke in car, cost you fifty bucks extra. Okay?"

I nodded. "To the Village," I ordered. The cabbie hung a left on Fifth Avenue and began racing south toward Wilkes's place in the Village. By the time the taxi made the left turn, I became aware of the car radio.

". . . and coming up at news on the hour, we'll have more about the judge who was killed downtown at the courthouse today, but now, let's get back to rockin' and rollin' with an oldie, Little Anthony and the Imperials singing . . ."

Jesus! A judge dead! I grabbed Wilkes's limp upper arm and shook it. His head stayed stuck to the window, but his eyes opened a bit and he said in a slurred Gabby Hayes voice, "They got more than their money's worth tonight, eh, Schoon?"

"That's right," I said. "They got not just one speaker. They got one and a fifth."

"Just the tonic for a man on the eve of his execution," he said sleepily.

"Think you got problems. They just reported a judge was killed today. In the courthouse."

"Who?" said Wilkes. His eyes opened wider and his head turned a notch to focus on me.

"They didn't say. Wait a sec. Hey, Sukarno, how about putting it on the all-news station."

Our taxi driver dutifully pushed a button and the sounds switched from Little Anthony to a man's voice saying, ". . . the judge's body was discovered in his chambers just after five this afternoon. Homicide Detective Michael Mulraney has told this reporter that the cause of death was one or more stabs from a knife to the back. He says they have few leads at the moment, but that the investigation has just begun and more will undoubtedly develop."

Sukarno turned his head to annotate the news report with his insight into the event. "Very bad. Filthy stinking communists. Just like in my country. We kill them all. Plenty good. President should order same here, now."

The news reporter then played a recorded sound bite from the crime scene and Detective Mulraney's statement, ". . . Mrs. Knott and the judge's clerk found the body just after five . . ."

Mrs. Knott! MRS. KNOTT! GODFREY DANIELS! Somebody murdered Yulburton Abraham Knott! I looked to Wilkes. His eyes were open and clear and looking into mine. I said, "Wilkes! For God's sake! Judge Knott's been murdered!"

". . . we have no suspects," said the voice of Mike "the Hanky" Mulraney, "for the time being."

"Suspects?" said Wilkes to the radio. "They could fill Yankee Stadium with the people who would like to see Knott dead."

"Filthy drug-dealing commies," said Sukarno, twisting his neck to give us another view of his fangs. "Death too good. First torture many days. Then kill. But slow. Just like in my country."

I looked at Wilkes. He stared blankly ahead, eyelids again on the way down, listening to the news report of the death of his nemesis. A lousy fearful feeling came over me. Wilkes, amazingly for his condition, detected the look and said, "Don't worry, Schoon. Anyone who says they saw me with the judge this afternoon is psychotic and thus incompetent as a witness to testify against me."

"Because?" I asked.

"Because they'd be hallucinating if they say they saw me with Knott. I never came within sight of the bastard."

We both sat in silence the rest of the way to Wilkes's place: I, because I was deep in thought and worry about what the next few days would bring; Wilkes, because he fell back into unconsciousness.

Sukarno, however, filled the void with brilliant suggestions on finding and punishing the killer. "Communist do it. So kill all communists. All. Then you be sure to get right man. Just like in my country."

— 6 —

A Previous Homicide

"He sinks into thy depths with
bubbling groan,
Without a grave, unknell'd,
uncoffined, and unknown."
LORD BYRON

"God, man! The sardines!"
JOHN WILKES

It was a moonless night. For ten minutes Wilkes had been silently looking out the office window at the unusually thick fog below. A sea of dark cotton had washed over the smaller buildings and the city streets. Nothing could be seen except scattered glowing patches of fog illuminated by the city lights below.

I had just turned the television on in my office and was paying very little attention it. A weird cable game show called "To Catch a Crook" was on. When I noticed that the game's host was our old acquaintance, Jack Twink, from the game show "Take All You Can Get,"* I snapped to attention. Twink was said to be the perfect game-show host because he was pleasant, good-looking, and dumber than a fence post. Original thought never passed closer than twenty

---

* Faithful readers will recall that Twink hosted the game show "Take All You Can Get" when Wilkes appeared as a contestant and won a ton of money by answering all the questions asked of him on his category, Oscar Wilde. See *Wilkes: His Life and Crimes* (Ballantine, 1990), pp. 53–67.

feet from his brain. For some reason he was popular, and the network had him hosting several quiz shows.

DEAD OR ALIVE

The idea of this show was for Twink to describe to the television audience all the crooks listed on the current Most Wanted list. The crimes were reenacted by actors picked for the parts because of their resemblance to the actual perpetrators. Huge financial rewards were offered as prizes to whomever in TV Land could bring in to the TV show the scoundrels shown in the depictions. And they could bring them in dead or alive.

The rules were simple: the quicker the capture, the bigger the award; the more heinous the crime committed by the crook, the bigger the award; the more violence involved in the capture, the bigger the award. Any help from the police in the capture disqualified the viewer from the competition. The game was thus something of a cross between bounty hunting and contract murder.

Jack Twink was just announcing "a sensational development on our recent airing of the Boy Bank Robber Case." It seemed that citizen Earl Turning from Yonkers, a devoted follower of the show, had just captured the young crook featured in last week's episode. The Boy Robber was seventeen years of age and number ten on last week's Most Wanted list.

The severity of the boy's crime alone earned Earl Turning twenty thousand dollars from the show. Because he made the capture within a week of the first televised description of the wanted boy's crimes, he got a ten-thousand-buck bonus. And because Earl Turning had the presence of mind to make the capture with a maximum of violence—all totally unnecessary—and to have his sons with him to videotape the entire bloody event, he got a whopping fifteen-thousand-dollar bonus.

Shaky pictures of the beaming Earl with his two sneering sons in the booth of a pizza parlor flashed on the screen before me. Each wore the look of an arrogant matador having just slaughtered a defenseless, picadored-and-bled-to-death bull. It was like that moment of truth in the middle of the corrida when el matador stupidly waves his silly little hat at the crowd, importuning them to roar at the judge for the award of a dismembered ear or tail.

The mob always loves butchery, whether in a bull ring, at an athletic event or, best of all, on the tube. The crude videotape of the Turnings at the pizza parlor taking their prey was perfect for television—three armed men surprised and beat the shit out of a seventeen-year-old pimply pizza eater.

It sucked me in. I saw the business ends of the Turnings' handguns within an inch of the slumped, unconscious Boy Bank Robber. Shot in the stomach—thank God they didn't show that!—and obviously beaten about the head, the Boy Bank Robber was bloody and facedown in a half-eaten pizza.

Then the picture flashed from the crude video footage back to live action as Earl got his whopping check and Jack Twink said, "Hey ho! Yes indeed! Proof again, ladies and gentlemen, that John Q. Citizen can still do it! Proof that you too can catch a crook. And make big bucks while you're at it."

The thought crossed my mind that each week, this game show was inciting a million gun-toting vigilantes to bounty hunt all over North America for a few desperadoes. In the mindless stampede for TV fame and prize money, the lives of millions of innocents were made unsafe. But as stupid as the show was, I kept it on. I needed the company—something to drive out of my head the terrible thoughts that were whispering about John Wilkes having had something to do with last night's murder.

OPIATE OF THE MASSES

They were unthinkable thoughts, and I tried to blot them out with the mind-numbing opiate of junk TV. I didn't want to think, but I couldn't keep the voices quiet in my mind. After all, it was an angry Wilkes who had headed back to see Judge Knott in chambers after the verdict so he could get his client out of jail. No one else knew this or the cops would have been here already. Surely, they would never seriously think Wilkes did it.

Would they?

God! There had been so much hatred between them during the trial. So many vicious insults. So many contempts. So few objections sustained. The cops would love to take Wilkes in. Every prosecutor in town would say he was good for it and try to make the charge stick.

And last night at the Waldorf, Wilkes had publicly, although very drunkenly, called for the machine-gun death of the judge at the NAGATA convention. He had said Judge Knott and his kind were the biggest crooks of all time, hypocritical thieves of human rights who rigidly governed over courtrooms to ensure results they wanted.

As I sat and thought, I saw Wilkes walk by with a bottle of whiskey, something he usually avoided except in times of stress. About the only time defense lawyers don't feel stress is when they are unconscious, so Wilkes, in search of the stressless state, had been carrying the bottle steadily since the last day of the Diderot trial.

I went out of my office into his and sat across from him at his desk. He was leaning over the back of his swivel chair with his bottle-filled hand moving downward from just below his moistened chin. He had just taken a big swig, and a drop ran from the corner of his mouth down his wet chin, and skipped off onto his open shirt.

"Why the hangdog look?" I asked. "I wouldn't think you'd take Knott's demise so hard."

Wilkes said nothing. He sat down in his chair and took another gulp of Jack Daniel's. He turned his chair so that his back faced me and he looked out the office window. I worried. What if the cops came tonight and he was stone drunk? What if he then said something stupid and incriminating? Another NAGATA speech would prove disastrous.

I popped the big question: "Did you see Knott after court yesterday?"

"Nope," he said to his window. "Just Alvin, and then only for a second. Alvin said he had already processed the papers to get Diderot out of the Tombs before I even got there."

"That's damned good news under the circumstances," I offered.

·   ·   ·

MILLENIA CLUB

"No, not so good. I did go to the courthouse. I planned on seeing the asshole all right, but Alvin took care of everything so I didn't have the excuse. Alvin warned me not to even try to see the bastard. Said Knott was crazy mad at me 'cause Diderot got off. Said the judge had been looking forward to sentencing Diderot to forty to fifty years. Said if Knott had sentenced Diderot, he'd have made the Millenia Club."

"What the hell's the Millenia Club?" I asked.

Wilkes swiveled around in his chair and looked me in the eye. "It's for judges who have dished out over a hundred thousand years in sentences during their careers. Alvin said the judge had been out of the criminal draw so long that he hungered like a sports addict for the chance to put up some big sentencing numbers."

"But you never saw him? Right?"

"Why, Schoon, I'd say you're worried that old John Wilkes may have personally plunged the dagger into the back of the erstwhile Judge Y. Knott." He smiled and took another huge swig out of his bottle.

"Certainly not," I lied. "But as you know, mistaken identification plus motive and opportunity can easily lead to a wrongful prosecution. But I know, for Christ's sake, I know you couldn't do anything like that."

"You don't know shit," said Wilkes. "You know, if the police come right now, I should tell them about the man I really did kill. Tonight reminds me of that night so much, the night I killed Captain Muddock. The fog out there is just like . . ."

As his voice trailed off, I didn't react. Wilkes was prone to make outrageous comments, and by this time in my career with him, I had heard all of his stories, or so I thought. This one, although new, had to be another of his great leg pullers. His quiet mood suggested that he was not kidding, though, and I said to him through a forced smile, "I am not familiar with your previous homicide."

"Well then, sit back and listen. I was eighteen, just out of high school, and bumming around the country the summer before college." He took another slug from the bottle, wiped his mouth with his shirtsleeve, rose from his chair and walked a few feet to the window behind his desk. He was still tightly clutching the neck of the bottle. Staring down at the fog, he said softly, "That damn fog sure reminds me of that goddamned night."

Wilkes then did the strangest thing. He dropped the bottle and started jumping and scratching himself all over. His hands worked rigorously over his upper body while he alternated hopping on one foot and then the other. The free leg rubbed the calf of the other, which bore his weight. This continued for about fifteen seconds until he shrieked: "The sardines! God, man! The sardines!"

The tone of his voice was frightening because it was so unusually high pitched and aching with helplessness. I thought I was eyeballing a man mentally coming apart. I stood up to go over to him—to do I know not what—when he turned to me and with a pained expression on his sweating face said, "I'll tell you about it."

He picked up his bottle and sat down heavily in the swivel chair behind his desk. His face was ashen.

DARK TALE

"I've not told you this dark tale because I've tried to blot it out. Never saw any point talking about it. Not sure there's much in it now. It may freak you out, but you want to hear it. In 1938, I killed a man in Monterey, California. A man I'd barely known but a man I hated more than any man in my life. Even more than Yulburton Abraham Knott. Hated! Hated! Hated!" He pounded a fist on his desk and then took another swig of whiskey.

Coming from Wilkes, who I knew hated (and was hated by) enough judges, prosecutors, probation officers, cops, bailiffs, and civil and criminal attorneys to fill a large auditorium, this was quite an admission. The guy in Monterey must have been something. I was more struck with this thought than the revelation that he'd killed the man. That I didn't believe.

"I was eighteen and at the end of my summer adventure on the West Coast. I was looking for just enough work money in Monterey to get me back here for school. So each day I'd go down to the wharf hoping to catch on with one of the commercial fishing ships, go out for a week or two and then head home on the money I earned.

"Fisherman's Wharf was really something in those days. They still call it Fisherman's Wharf now, but more as an epitaph for what once was. Back then it was filled with hardworking, loud-talking, constantly cussing fish people. The noise of the place was something, but the smells, God, the smells could make you want to stop breathing. You could smell that wharf five miles away. Schoon, the B.O. of our clients is sweet cologne compared to that horrible smell!

"The sound of the place let you know right away Monterey was a hardworking town. Cannery whistles blew regularly to let the cutters know fish were in and ready to be cut. Women, mostly Chinese and Japanese, worked in the open wharf pounding abalone with wooden mallets. The loud pounding gave the place a kind of rapid, irregular heartbeat.

"Cats and rats and gulls fought and screeched at your feet over the fish scraps tossed on the wharf by the fish butchers. Orientals, Italians, Portuguese, Spaniards, and Okies all jabbered at each other in their native lingo. Ships and boats blew their horns to let you know they were going out, or coming in, or just there. It was all noise, but the combined cacophony was the town's music.

"Looking for work early each morning, I went into all the retail fish businesses to see where they got their catches and to try and make contact with a captain in need of another hand. After a few days, I fell into a job.

CAPTAIN MUDDOCK

"It was about two one afternoon when I first laid my eyes on him. He ran into the fish store so fast, I thought he was just a full-bladdered fellow in desperate search of the bathroom. He asked the owner if there were men looking to work sardines: 'One of my sonovabitches quits on me thirty minutes before we gonna ship out. Bastard scum! I need a hand.'

"I immediately stepped forward and volunteered my nonexistent fishing skills. He looked me over quickly and snorted, 'I got no time to pick and choose. You'll have to do, pencilneck.'

"I looked over my new boss. Captain Joe Muddock was a short, gruff, no-nonsense middle-aged man with a big potbelly and a hook nose. His eyes were big and black, his voice loud and gravelly, and his sun-weathered face puffy, bearded, and littered with small red boils. He was the ugliest man I ever saw.

"Muddock gave me my prelaunch training in the sixty seconds it took to walk the short distance from the market down the wooden wharf to his trawler. He said, 'Listen up, pencilneck. We go out two-thirty sharp every afternoon. Return five in the morn. We catch sardines at night an' we divide the shares from the catch equally. Exceptin' the boat, the trailer, and the net gets an extra share. I deduct equal for gas and oil. I charge you for your gear. Any questions?'

"He didn't give me a second to ask any. He just kept walking fast and rattling off rules. 'You get paid at one in the afternoon the day following a trip. No bastard gets a share who loses or breaks the equipment. No bastard gets a share who falls in the ocean. No bastard gets a share who don't work even if sick. And no bastards get a share if we don't catch fish. Those is the rules, pencilneck. If you don't like 'em, don't set foot aboard my ship. Any questions?'

"He looked at me as he popped the question. I saw something in those dark eyes I didn't like, something wild and mean, but I needed money and said, 'Nope, no questions,' saluted him and climbed aboard.

SS *MUDDOCK*

"We were at sea thirty minutes after I hired on. To me, a nautical novice, the sixty-foot boat named the *Muddock* looked like any ordinary tug I'd seen in New York harbor. The stern, however, was distinguished by its covering with a huge fishnet. The net was what this trip depended on. Spread out, it could cover half a city block. In water, it could encircle tons of fish at a time. Lead weights along the bottom made it sink fast, and cork baubles at the other end kept the top at the surface. There were rings fastened to the bottom with a rope running through them.

"Once the sardines moved within the net, the boat circled, enclosing them in it; by pulling the ring rope, the net would close. Then it was time to scoop out the fish with a smaller net attached to a boom on the boat and put the fish in the trailer. The trailer—actually just a large floating bathtub as big as a house—was pulled behind the ship and served as a hold for the catch. It could hold sixty tons of fish.

"I was outfitted for the trip with three items of gear worn by the working crew: cotton gloves, an oilcloth that covered my front like a big bib, and a pair of heavy, cumbersome, black rubber hip boots. Muddock gave me my boots and other gear with the following advice: 'Wear these and you won't be dancing in seawater and sardine shit all trip. Fall in and you'll sink like a rock. Hah! Your last drink'll be a sardine-shit cocktail! Hah! Rent on the boots and bib and gloves comes outta your share, boy. Any bastard that loses 'em don't get no share. Any questions?'

"The first afternoon and night at sea were beautiful. The ocean was calm as we left the harbor promptly at two-thirty. The sky was clear and powder-blue. Within an hour porpoises were following us. I was told this was a good sign.

"And it was. We hauled in tons of sardines that night. It was exhausting work dropping the net, scooping fish, dumping them in the trailer, and then hauling in the heavy net and stacking it. By our return, everyone was stinking and exhausted and swearing off another trip, but by one o'clock that afternoon everyone was back for their money and committing themselves for another trip.

"It was the middle of the Depression and you didn't turn your nose at a paying job staring you in the face. Even a job with Captain Ahab at the helm.

PENCILNECK

"As the week wore on, I grew to hate Muddock. I hated him 'cause he cheated me out of most of my share each payday by bullshit lies like, 'You got sick, pencilneck. You didn't work hard enough, pencil-neck.'

"Hell, everyone got seasick, and who in the hell wouldn't on the rolling sea in a tug moving within a suffocating, nauseating cloud of diesel fumes? But Captain Muddock looked for every excuse he could think of to deny me my fair share.

"He'd claim that I was 'a still-learning pencilneck' and wasn't entitled to a full share; or that I was a 'worthless pencilnecked bookworm who ought to be thrown overboard as bait.'

"As the week progressed, with us hauling in tons of sardines every night, Muddock went out of his way to nag, bully, and humiliate me at every opportunity in front of the crew. One trip, he dropped a bucket of sardines on the deck behind me while I was hauling in net. You need a clean surface even with boots on to get leverage to haul in a lead-weighted net that weighed at least a ton. I fell on my ass as soon as I stepped on a fish, and the captain's potbelly got a good shaking when he laughed about it. 'Look at the pencilneck, mates,' he said to those nearby. 'Fell on his arse! Where's your sea legs, boy? Y'er no help to us on y'er arse, boy!'

"Other times he'd come up to me and ask if I'd done a task he claimed he'd asked me to do, but never had. Then he'd berate me for neglecting my duty. 'Pencilneck, how can you do book learnin' if you can't remember what a man tells ya five minutes ago? Maybe he needs a good keel haulin' to improve his memory, eh, mates? Whadya say?'

"The crew, composed mostly of lifelong fisherman and a few itinerants catching on with any job around, was intimidated and unresponsive to Muddock's comments. He was mean and crazy, but these were hard times and they needed the work. No one said anything. Not even me."

LAST NIGHT

"By the seventh night, the tension between Muddock and me was electric. Muddock was spending all of his time on deck berating me from the time we left harbor until we returned. It made the crew so uneasy. I figured the reason why Muddock didn't just fire me was that the bastard enjoyed tormenting and cheating me too much. Why I took the abuse is another question. I needed the money and wanted to get home. But now, I was filled with rage. I think maybe I was hooked into staying for an opportunity to take my vengeance.

"The sea was the heaviest it had been all week as we chugged out of the harbor that last day. We chugged up small mountains of waves and slipped quickly down the other side. The sea was too rough for the porpoises that day and we didn't see any.

"As the sun set, I got sicker than usual, turned lime-green and puked. Muddock was on my ass like a bloodsucking insect, telling me, 'You weak, no good sissy pencilnecked geek. No peckerwood gets a share if he won't work. You're gonna be dead weight on this trip too, ain't ya?'

"Despite my nausea, I kept the watch for the fish. I should have been lying down on a bunk below deck, but if I did that, I would automatically lose my share, as I had discovered on a previous trip. Nothing much happened until we spotted our prey. Until we saw sardines, the only thing you could see was a small wedge of the moon, the bright stars above in the dark sky, and occasionally the faint, distant lights of another fishing boat.

"You couldn't hear anything out there in the darkness except the distinct 'chucka, chucka, chucka' of the diesel engine. When we stopped the engine to haul in fish, you might hear a distant, happier crew singing to a banjo player. It was eerie out there with no shoreline in sight and the barely audible singing voices coming out of nowhere.

"There were no singers on the SS *Muddock*. Except for Muddock, we were a quiet lot."

SPOTTING

"The way we spotted sardines was to look for their glow in the water. It was a spooky sight I'll never forget—seeing huge sections of faintly luminous seawater in the black of night. It's like the fog out there tonight, Schoon, illuminated from below with the streetlights. Reminds me of that sight.

"They told me the schools lit up the ocean because of the moonlight's reflecting off the fish. They traveled in such densely packed schools that they gave off an unbroken dim light the length and width of the school.

"That last night, we were slow to see any glowing water because of the roughness of the sea. The growing swells made me feel more nauseated than ever, but I kept at my job.

"I saw the first school near midnight. It was a big group, judging from the area of glowing water, and we lumbered over the swells to position our tug and begin dropping net. Net dropping was an arduous task under calm conditions, and much more difficult in winds and rolling sea. Everyone on board helped off-load the net as we circled the glowing water. Muddock barked out orders like an admiral in battle: 'Watch the rig; let it out faster; mind the ring rope! Don't tangle it! Oh, it's a big school, you lucky bastards! You'll be workin' your arses off tonight hauling this load in! Hah! Faster! Faster, you bloody bastards!'

"Once the net was out, we finished circling the sardine school and quickly began tightening the ring rope. This was the most demanding part of the job, even with winches screeching to pull in the rope. Captain Muddock continued yelling out orders with his normal nastiness, reserving his special wrath for me. 'Come on, pencilneck, get to pullin' the ring rope! Pull hard, damn you! Hah! I've seen more muscles on a squid's pecker!'

"We tightened the rope as tight as we could. To the port side of the S.S. *Muddock,* I now saw a caldron of millions of frantic doomed sardines, thrashing in frenzy, and bringing the surface water to a white boil."

SCOOP

" 'Start scooping!' yelled Muddock. While most of the crew pulled the huge trailer hull close by the edge of the net, I and two others manned the scoop net, a device suspended from a big overhead boom. We swung the boom so the net could be dipped into the foaming sardine mass, gulp five hundred pounds of fish and swing over to be off-loaded in the trailer hull.

"Maneuvering the scoop would be tricky. The swells of the sea had to be timed so when we scooped we got fish instead of air. Muddock, sensing the difficulty, appointed me as the designated scooper. I grabbed the long thin pole that moved the scoop net up and down. Muddock was on my back screaming vulgar instructions. 'Watch the boom, pencilneck! Scoop now! Bastard! Mind the swells! Now, pencilneck, now! Scoop!'

"I guided the scoop net over the sardines with the long pole while the others positioned the swinging boom as best they could. We were pitching so violently, I had to hold on to the low side rail so as not to fall overboard. The swells were huge rolling mountains of surging water, and the wind at my back made staying aboard all the more difficult.

"Muddock was on my shoulder yelling in my ear. 'Dig now, dig now, pencilneck!' But I timed the swells poorly and my first scoop just scraped the teeming surface to grab about ten pathetic sardines. I quickly dug again and this time missed entirely.

"Muddock was furious. He yelled, 'Arsehole!' and violently grabbed for my pole just as a swell rose to wash the deck with flipping sardines and sea. Muddock's legs slipped, the boat lurched in the swell, and he fell forward into me. His momentum forced me half over the rail, and I dropped the pole into the water. As I turned my neck, I saw his face within an inch of mine. I could smell his putrid breath. His black eyes were enlarged and enraged. I remembered seeing his yellow, worn-out teeth as he mouthed one word: 'ARSEHOLE!'

"As soon as he got his balance, he took a step back and pushed me hard—I swear to God!—over the rail and into the sea. Not wanting to travel alone, I hooked onto the bastard and took him with me."

• • •

AFTER THE FALL

"We splashed right into the middle of the entrapped sardines. Instantly, I felt millions of slimy, raspy-rattling fingers crawling over every inch of my body. What little water I first sensed in that horrible darkness was now gushing into my hip boots and weighting me down like thousand-pound cement shoes. I was already underwater before I understood what was happening. I was sinking into the dense, squiggly sardine muck!

"I remember the feeling of fear as well today as I did those many years ago. If you've never tried swimming in a giant can of sardines, you'll never know the horror of drowning in it. Sardines were in my clothes, face, eyes—everywhere. They were crushing me. I tried dog-paddling, but I could not move my arms and legs fast enough. I was about to drown in one big sardine-shit cocktail.

"In a few seconds I was already feeling out of air. I was thrashing about just like my condemned sardine neighbors when, by God, I felt a broom handle. It was the scoop net pole which I knew was still connected to the ship's boom. I moved my hands over the loose pole to the wrong end, which led to nothing. I reversed direction and slid my hands up to the scoop net at the other end. I pulled down hard on it to get rid of the slack. I got more slack. I pulled down again. Nothing. I was still descending and about to black out from panic and lack of air when the rope stiffened and I began to pull myself up and out of my nightmare.

"As things seemed about to turn for the better, conditions quickly worsened. Muddock, I now discovered, was just below me, grabbing my ankles, ending my northward travel and holding me down. I couldn't pull his weight with mine in that crush, and I wasn't about to spend a great deal of time trying.

"Muddock, I thought. Muddock's holding me down! Muddock! This ugly pirate sonovabitch had spent the week degrading and robbing me of my wages. He had just pushed me overboard. Tried to kill me. He was not going to take me down to the bottom as his deathmate.

"I was out of air. My chest was ready to explode, and there I was with Captain Muddock escorting me to Davy Jones' Locker. I bent into a pike position and ripped one of his hands off my leg as he simultaneously pulled himself up with his other hand. I stabbed out with my free hand and felt for his head. When I found it, I put my free foot on it and used the top of his head as a base to push off for the surface. As I launched, I felt his head give under my boot.

"I continued pulling myself up with the scoop net. My head broke water just as I let my mouth fly open to gasp for air. I got a mouthful of foam instead, but the boom started pulling me up, and soon I was back aboard the S.S. *Muddock*."

MALICE

"Captain Joe Muddock was listed as drowned in the official papers. And he sure as hell was that. When they found him in the net later that night, his lungs had plenty of seawater and sardines in them. But his neck was broken too. They thought he broke it in the fall.

"I was never even asked about what had happened while in amongst the sardines with the captain, and I sure as hell didn't volunteer. What happened down there with Muddock was known only to me, the sardines, and the deep." Wilkes paused a bit to see if I was still paying attention. Seeing that I was, he took another swig and continued.

"I've never regretted what I did. I hated the guy. I *hated* him! He was like Judge Knott—pure meanness—and like the departed Hizoner, he delighted in torturing the people forced to work with him."

Wilkes got up and went back to the window. It seemed to me that his instinctive act of survival under unbelievably freakish circumstances didn't come close to murder. So what if he hated the guy? It was a desperate act borne of necessity.

I shared my thoughts with my friend, who acknowledged their wisdom. "You're right," he said. "In the water, where we were unseen and buried alive, it was a reflexive act of self-preservation. But I also know I never tried to pull him up. I did the opposite not for lack of air or fear or cowardice, but because I had malice in my heart. I sent him to the bottom to drink that sardine-shit cocktail without the slightest regret. That's just what I feel about the late judge."

Wilkes took another big swig, got up and walked over to the window, and continued staring at the slow, rolling fog below. There was no point in arguing the matter. I said nothing, joined him at the window and looked down at the patchwork of glowing fog and darkness. I thought for a moment about the death of Captain Muddock.

And of Judge Yulburton Abraham Knott.

— 7 —

The Chase

"Woman's tongue like sword that never gets rusty."
CHARLIE CHAN

"I tink I been entwapped!"
BECKY BUTTERMILK

"Let's see, the last three judges who were murdered in the city—first there was Judge Crater, who disappeared long ago in the great Argentine style. Then there was that poor judge here in the city who got shot by the father of some gal 'cause she lost her wrongful termination suit in his court. And most recently, there was the mob hit on Judge Joseph Blugeot. Now Knott gets stabbed in the back. That's different. That's a lead already, isn't it, darling?"

Mulraney and Jill were warm under their covers and talking shop. Jill knew that solving the biggest murder case in the department would give a very big boost to her husband's career. To the extent merit had anything to do with elevation in the department—a debatable point—solving this case could pave the way for a giant leap upward.

Jill was bright—as bright as her husband, who was very bright himself. To Mike, she was his best sounding board on his tough cases. She worked as an editor and researcher at the Norton J. Pencroft Publishing Company, a prestigious publisher of educational books and high-tech training texts. She was also a voracious reader of mysteries. Her intelligence, her excellent grasp of police work, and her vast general fund of knowledge, made her an invaluable resource for brainstorming.

So there they lay. Naked under the covers, warmly entangled in each others' arms and legs, and chatting away about the recent murder of Judge Yulburton Abraham Knott. Mike the Hanky was reminded why he loved his wife so much. She could have been there bitching at him for breaking off their dinner date—the third in a row—but she was enthusiastically collaborating with him like Dr. Watson.

"It is a lead, sweets," he whispered in her ear just before kissing it. "A stabbing means closeness, obviously in the physical sense, but also maybe by relationship. The killer and the judge probably knew each other."

Jill rolled out from Mike's entangling appendages, onto her side, and propped her head on her arm. She was every bit as intrigued by this case as her husband. It was a mystery, a puzzle in need of a solution, and helping solve it was exciting. "I agree," she said. "And from the way you describe the crime scene, I'd say it was a payback. Since there really was no place to hide in chambers, and nothing was disturbed, the judge must have let the killer in. No sign of a struggle means the judge didn't mind the person being there."

DEATH CHAMBER

Mulraney thought about the crime scene. He had arrived in Knott's chambers just as the bloodied body was being lifted belly down onto a cart. Someone had planted what looked like a golden tent stake in the judge's back. Judge Knott looked a lot older than the last time Mike the Hanky had appeared in his court ten or more years ago. Although still relatively lean, the judge had grown soft. A small potbelly hung like a speed bump from his torso, and the face was wrinkled and the skin loose. His hair was almost pure white. There was something peculiar about the judge's face that caught Mike's eye. It was not just the look of decline that comes with age; it was not just the peculiar blood-drained look. This look the Hanky had seen before on the lifeless faces of many of the middle-aged corpses viewed at murder scenes all over the city. It was the look of corruption.

Jill continued, "I researched the murder weapon for you. Your tent stake was the judge's fancy letter opener, a beautiful Italian piece. Very expensive. The handle is twenty-two karats of intricately sculpted gold with carvings of a lion's head at the top and three scenes of the Labors of Hercules depicted underneath. Marvelous workmanship. The blade is thick ivory. Cost someone well over a grand. Easy.

"The murder weapon was there on the judge's desk when the killer arrived. So maybe the killing was unplanned. Maybe the judge really pisses this person off and like, zap, it's payback time."

Mike rolled into his wife's body and kissed her neck. She wrapped her arms around his back, pulled him tightly to her body and said, "Mike, tell me again about the poem."

When Mulraney arrived, the judge's chambers was being printed by the lab boys, who were making their usual dusty mess. The judge's huge polished mahogany desk dominated the chambers and was situated so that he could have seen anyone come into the room. There was no sign of a struggle, and no one strange was reported in the area just before the killing.

Mike made mental notes of the room's debris: hundreds of law books neatly arranged in their wall shelves; stacks of briefs and motions on tables and chairs; and on the judge's neatly arranged desk, galleys of Knott's lunatic futurist writings which he authored under the pseudonym Grotek. Mulraney read the title to the galley on top of the pile: "Back to the Future: A Socioeconomic Argument in Favor of a Laser Beam Rack and Screw in Modern Criminal Justice."

The color monitor of the judge's computer terminal was still on, but the screen was blank. Mulraney went over to it and hit the page down key, curious to see if anything was there. To his surprise, a document jumped up on the screen. Resting in yellow courier script on a royal-blue background were the following glowing words:

•   •   •

LOST AT SEA

Inscrutable waif,
tide of silence ebbing in my arms,

your gentle black cries of sorrow
smash furiously
upon the shore of a mind's peace,

crumbling it
under the surging pushing wash,

a swelling dark desolation
pulling me out—

out with the unrelenting current
to the unknown depths of a brooding sea.

"That's it," said Mike after reciting the poem from memory. "He wrote it, I guess." Mulraney had asked Jill to try to find an author of the poem, but she found nothing. Both Mulraneys lay quietly for a minute thinking of suspects.

Then Jill, still hugging Mike's body to hers, spoke. "The poem is important. Who is it about? A lover? Maybe his wife? The wife, bailiff, and court clerk found the body. That makes them suspects, with wifey at the top of the list."

"Yeah, I gotta see her first. And then there's John Wilkes," said Mulraney. "He just finished a trial in Knott's court. Knott held him in contempt and planned a hearing on it the next day. Wilkes and Knott hated each other. The judge would have put him away, that's for sure. Have to check him out. His client too. Field Marshal Lyle Diderot, chief punk of the Whiz Kids. Coulda been any of the Whiz Kid slimeballs too."

"Was urine found on the judge's clothing? That's the Whiz Kid signature, isn't it, Mike?"

"It's their signature. His clothing was soaked with so much blood, you couldn't tell. But the lab boys will check it out for sure."

Jill said, "It could have been a disgruntled litigant, witness, or friend or relative of a litigant or witness. Or maybe a soured business associate or angry golf partner. Or maybe a pissed-off court watcher." She grabbed Mike's cheeks, put her face close to his so that their noses touched, and said, "In other words . . ."

It was the usual suggestion made as a case investigation was beginning. Mike completed her sentence: ". . . there are eight million stories in the Naked City, and every goddamn one of 'em's a suspect."

They laughed, grabbed each other and made love like two sex maniacs just released from years of solitary confinement.

MEANWHILE, WINSTON SCHOONOVER

Seeing as how Judge Knott had been knocked off, I tore up the motion I had begun writing to knock Knott off Wilkes's contempt hearing. Now that the hearing would never take place due to the lack of the complaining witness, the motion was (as they say in the business) moot. In place of a contempt trial would be an interview by the cops about Knott's murder. Wilkes had been to the courthouse too close in time to the murder to be safe from suspicion, but he seemed unconcerned about it now. His melancholic sardine story of the previous evening was history, and he was busy doing that which he loved best—happily interviewing a potential client in the office.

As she reclined across from Wilkes, Becky Buttermilk, Miss Potential Client, looked as cheap as a skid-row hooker. Yet beneath the cheapness, the gaudy makeup, above the ill-fitting skimpy clothes, was as plain a face as ever looked in a mirror. As plain as homemade sin. She had long, straight, obviously dyed canary-yellow hair. Her face was painted thick with violet lipstick, ruby cheek rouge—over a white powder base thick enough to ski on—black mascara, and purple eyeliner strung out to the temples.

Her face could have been a Crayola Rorschach Test.

But really, you wouldn't be looking too closely at her face because Becky Buttermilk had the most sensational body ever to grace the law offices of John Wilkes. And she was not bashful about showing it off. She wore a tight, short black leather miniskirt which was not long enough to cover her bright red undies when she sat. Her low-cut, flimsy, discolored silk blouse rose briefly out of the skirt to barely cover the biggest, most beautiful bosom I'd ever seen. Although almost totally exposed by their owner, Miss Buttermilk delighted in frequently bending over in her chair to give her interviewers a more in-depth view of her manifest frontal charms.

For me, it was carnal love at first sight. I made it a point to assist Wilkes in conducting this interview of our luscious prospective client and sat next to my friend as he quizzed Miss Buttermilk on the nature of her legal problem.

"What brings you here, Ms. Buttermilk?" asked Wilkes as he looked at her chest, half expecting her breasts to talk back to him.

"I'm in so much twubble, Mr. Wilkes," said Becky. Her voice was high pitched and she spoke with a lispy speech impediment which made her sound like Elmer Fudd. "I was workin' as usual at my pwace of empwoyment—dat's da Love Tub Tumble—and dis customer comes in and wants da Love Tub Special, which means he just gets in the Jacuzzi and I get in with him and we get naked and pway awound. Fifty bucks is all it costs. It's willy a bargain."

"And when you say play around, does this include copulation?" Wilkes asked. This was a rhetorical question. Anyone who got naked and played in a love tub with Becky Buttermilk was bound for sexual contact.

AWOUND DA WORLD

"You mean do we do it in the tub? No way, Mr. Wilkes," said Miss Buttermilk. "I just pway awound naked in the tub wid 'um. Maybe I wub up against 'em and maybe let 'em play kissy-face wid me, but if they weally wants to get sexual, dey gotta rent a room and pay me wots more money. The amount depends on what dey wants. Like, you know, if dey wants to go for just a stwaight scwew, dat's a certain amount, and for a bwow job, it's a widdle more, and for evewything—I call dat Awound da World—well, dat costs more. I never even went to da room wid dis guy. We just got naked in da tub and pwayed around like, ya know, spwashing and wubbing and kissy-facing."

Ms. Buttermilk briefly gestured as if she were in the hot tub splashing water, then dabbed her black silk hanky close to her eyes as if soaking up tears, and purposely dropped it in front on the floor. She slowly bent over to pick it up and exposed her wonderful assets to us. We were all eyes. I dreamed of being the lucky guy in the tub on the receiving end of Miss Buttermilk's playful attention.

FWEEBIE RULE

"But what brings you here, Miss Buttermilk? It's no crime to take a hot tub with someone. At least, not yet. What's the legal problem?" asked Wilkes.

"Well, see, I bwoke a rule of mine. No fweebies. See, I liked dis guy right off. I was wery attwacted to him. He was fun and came on to me weal nice. So when we pwayed I got carried away and, you know, one thing wed to another and I ended up giving him a fwee bwow job wight in the tub. I was being weal nice to da guy. No extwa charge, see?

"And in da middle of da bwow job and wid me far, far under da water and settin' some kinda wecord for bweath holding, he sup- posedwy starts shouting dat I'm under awwest. Later, he says he yelled it out many times, but I don't bewieve it. Never heard noth- ing. I keeps going at it under da water holding my bweath weal good, and he supposedwy keeps yelling dat I am under awwest. But dat's bawoney! He's a wiar! He never pulled me off, Mr. Wilkes! Only when he ejacuwates and I come up for air does he announce dat he's an undercover cop. And now I'm charged with some weird sex cwime, er, what you wawyers call it? Dirt you eat. Dey calls it something funny like oral sod on me."

"Oral sodomy," I offered.

"Yeah! Dat's it! Dat's what they called it, Mr. Schoonblower. And dey also adds a charge of pwostitution, but I ain't no pwostitute. I opewate a very wespectable business estabwishment. I tink I been entwapped, Mr. Wilkes!" said the excited Miss Buttermilk as she seductively squirmed in the chair. "I can't go down on no cwiminal beef, Mr. Wilkes, 'cause I could lose my business license. See, I have been the pwoud owner of the vewy pwofitible Love Tub Tumble for over five years."

"Well, well," said Wilkes, "a very interesting case. But I'm interested in how you got referred to me."

Becky opened her tiny purse and pulled a recent article from the *Post* which referred to Wilkes's miracle acquittal of Field Marshal Lyle Diderot. "This says you pulled off a gweat victowy. I knew then dat you'd be just the man for me 'cause dis could be a hard case to win, Mr. Wilkes. I need a fighter like the wawyer who won for Mr. Wyle Diderot. Dat's you, Mr. Wilkes. I want you to win this case for me."

FEE TALK

"I'd be honored to represent you, Ms. Buttermilk, but first, of course, there is the matter of my fee." Wilkes was about to converse in fee talk, that uniquely expensive language known by all those who would try to engage his services. Its alphabet was simple: an Arabic number followed by many zeroes. Faithful readers of these sagas know too well of my friend's unyielding and uncompromising tenacity in convincing clients to part with their worldly wealth in order to employ him to their cause. I wondered how he would fee talk with the titillating Ms. Buttermilk.

Becky Buttermilk dropped her hanky again, leaned over to pick it off the floor and again gave us a wonderful view of the twins. She said softly, "Why, Mr. Wilkes, of course I expect to weimburse you for your work. I was thinking that perhaps I could offer the services at my store to you and Mr. Schoonblower on an unwimited basis— for several months at weast."

Wilkes looked at me and laughed. He pulled a slip of paper off the desk and scribbled a note. "As tempting as your generous offer is, Ms. Buttermilk, I must decline. I never mix pleasure with business. It's like the ladies in your business say, 'If you got the money, honey,

I got the time.' Our fee is always paid in coin of the realm."

He leaned across the desk and handed the note to her. "I was thinking of something in this range."

Becky took the note and looked at it. Her eyes bulged and her beautiful chest heaved as she read the figure written on the paper. Then tears, real tears, formed and immediately took on a dark color as they began coursing down through her black mascara and purple eyeliner. When they reached her ruby-rouge and white-powdered cheeks, they took on a new purplish-orange hue before disappearing into her black hanky. The resulting tear trails and hanky wipes left an ungodly crisscross of vibrant color on her face.

"Oh pwease, Mr. Wilkes, pwease! Take me! Take my case! Your fee is too much. I can pay, but less. Can't we cxpwore some alternative form of payment?" She stood up with a bounce and turned her stunning body slowly around in front of us to make very clear the alternative she had in mind.

Wilkes quietly and carefully scrutinized the proffered fee gyrating so magnificently before him. "You are very persuasive, Ms. Buttermilk," he said. "But we're a cash-only business here. And as for the amount I request, I like to recall to my prospective clients the old saying of the unknown nineteenth-century British essayist and critic of life, John Ruskin. He said, and I quote, 'It is unwise to pay too much, but it is worse to pay too little. When you pay too much, you lose a little money—that is all. When you pay too little, you sometimes lose everything because the thing you bought was incapable of doing the thing it was bought to do.'

"These are very wise words, Ms. Buttermilk. Pay too little and you may get nothing in return. There's never any danger of paying too little in this office."

The standing Miss Buttermilk appeared uncomprehending. Tears were now coming fast and slipping quickly down her many-colored cheeks to fall freely into that great crevasse formed by the convergence of the two immense fleshy mountains. She stepped to the edge of Wilkes's desk and leaned heavily over it. Wilkes's eyes plunged into her neckline.

"I pwomise I'll be your very favowite client, Mr. Wilkes. You can be my favowite client. Pwease, just knock off a few zeroes from dis paper and we gotta deal."

In the entire time I was with Wilkes he never, ever reduced his fee for anybody. Of course, this wasn't just any body. This was the kind of body that horny sculptors would immortalize in marble if they could quarry enough of it.

But Wilkes had never taken an alternative to cash as a form of payment. There were always offers. Clients offered vacation homes, fast boats, exotic cars, expensive jewelry, you name it. We never took any of it for one simple reason: the great danger of accidently accepting stolen merchandise, which, when repatriated to its rightful owner, leaves you with nothing except a potential criminal charge for receiving.

Miss Becky Buttermilk's offer was a little different. Until this day, no one had ever offered their body to pay Wilkes's fee. You wouldn't catch a receiving case for taking it, but you might catch a case of something worse.

BREAST REDUCTION

Wilkes continued staring at the Buttermilk breasts. If they could talk, they would have been eloquent spokespersons for the cause of Becky Buttermilk's retainer. I know this because Wilkes then said words I'd never heard up to that time. "Your offer is very attractive. I will subtract one digit from the proposed fee in return for three months of transferable passes to the Love Tub Tumble."

Becky Buttermilk straightened up at this enormous ten thousand dollar markdown. A toothy smile appeared on her multicolored smeared and moist face. She stuck her hand out toward Wilkes. "It will be a weal pweasure, I'm sure. It's a deal."

Wilkes stood and stuck his hand out. Ms. Buttermilk grabbed it and, with surprising strength, pulled him into her and then warmly hugged and kissed him. Wilkes hugged and kissed back.

While I watched the two satisfied customers sealing their business deal, the phone rang and I left the room to answer it in my office. I said hello and was chilled. The voice on the other end said, "This is Detective Mike Mulraney of NYPD Homicide. I'd like to come over and see you and Mr. Wilkes. It's about the Knott homicide."

8

Alice

"Roots of tree lead in many directions."
CHARLIE CHAN

"Ay, que chalupas!"
ADMIRER OF BECKY BUTTERMILK

A little after five in the afternoon, Alice Poplar-Bennett Knott, better known in the legal community as Mrs. Judge Yulburton Abraham Knott, heard the doorbell. She was expecting her visitor. Calmly, she rose from her chair and walked to the door.

Alice Knott was born to the Poplar-Bennett family, which meant she was born to wealth and status. She was an only child, gifted in endeavors athletic and quite intelligent, although isolated in her youth behind her parents' wall of contempt for all other people of lesser station. The offspring of lessers were off-limits.

From the time she left the womb, little Alice was treated like an adult Poplar-Bennett and was expected to act like one. Educated at the best schools the East had to offer, it was while she was at Smith that she met Y.A. He was a senior in law school and she was in her last year at Smith. The marriage to Yulburton was not encouraged by her parents, as Y.A. did not come from wealth or status. He was a mere commoner seeking the hand of the Poplar-Bennett princess.

Had her parents known that Y.A. was to become a lawyer specializing in criminal defense, albeit white-collar cases, they would never have approved the marriage. Alice might not have either. But they all felt a lot better about Y.A. when he became a judge, thanks to a few of the family's adroitly placed political contributions.

THE KNOTT HOUSE

As she walked to the door, her maid approached and Alice waved her off without a word. She answered the door of her lovely home. Standing in the doorway was Mike Mulraney, busy putting away his hanky after a big blow.

Mulraney studied Mrs. Knott as she stood at the door. She looked far more imperious than on that dreadful night last week when her husband died. Now, although early fiftyish, she looked fifteen years younger. In fact, as they looked at each other, Mulraney pictured her sitting comfortably on a well-cushioned sedan chair held aloft by four Nubians and looking down on him like he was the most insignificant particle in the universe.

Alice was tall, on the thickish side, although not to the point of unattractiveness, and impeccably dressed in the best brown dress suit that Bergdorf Goodman had to offer. Her tightly drawn face, the product of a recent laser lift, bore the mark of early beauty even though the fresh-skin tones of youth had long ago faded.

"Detective Mulraney, please come in," she said rather haughtily. "We've been expecting you. You're late." Her tone was a surprise to Mulraney. He had the lasting memory of her that deadly night at the courthouse. There, she was totally out of control, a condition Mulraney now assessed as rare for her. She had alternated for hours between blubbering mush and wild fury. It was the anger that was predominant, but there were tears aplenty too, and all of Mike's hankies got soaked once she ran through all the Kleenex in the building.

Mulraney entered the Knott house thinking of that night and the purpose of this visit. He was there to take a follow-up statement. That horrible night, understandably, Alice Knott, for all her anger, her weeping and general incoherence, did manage to give a brief statement to Mike the Hanky. She said she had arrived at her usual time at the courthouse to pick up her husband and take him home.

The chauffeur was waiting down at street level with the limousine motor running while Alice took the judges' elevator to avoid rubbing shoulders with the rabble in the public elevators.

That this was her daily ritual, Mulraney confirmed with court-house attendants, played out for years with a you-can-set-your-stopwatch-by-it reliability. Except for Wednesday afternoons. That was when the judge would leave the court early and take a cab uptown to the New York Athletic Club for a workout.

MURDER NIGHT

On murder night, Alice said she gave her usual knock on the chambers door, expecting the perfunctory "Come in, my dear" as she was already letting herself in the door. But there was no answer this time and the door was locked. She sought out the judge's clerk, Alvin Scribner, whose tiny office was just next door to Knott's chambers.

Alvin said he thought the judge was in chambers, expressed surprise at the door being locked, and joined her at the judge's door. He knocked and tried the door. He then went for his key, returned and opened it. Through her tears and wailing on murder night, Alice told Mulraney of the dreadful sight she saw: "He was there, lying facedown on the carpet, his white shirt saturated in blood from shoulder to waist with *that thing* sticking out of his back."

That thing, Mulraney discovered, was a beautiful gold-handled letter opener, a wedding anniversary gift to the judge by Mrs. Knott. When Mulraney saw it the first time, it was embedded in the middle of the judge's starched and once-white monogrammed shirt. The bloodied golden handle, topped with a sculpted lion's head roaring like the MGM cat, was driven in past the hilt.

Between her wails and screams that night, Alice told him, "Alvin and I rushed to my dear Y.A.'s side. My poor, poor Y.A. We . . . we, Alvin, he screamed for the bailiff, for anybody, and then he and I . . . tried to . . . turn him on his side. We tried, but the blood . . . the blood was running all over my hands . . . Oh! The awful . . . the horror! . . . and Alvin tried for a second to . . . gently

. . . pull the knife out, but he couldn't. I thought it was a nightmare. But it was real!''

Mulraney would long remember that night for what came out of Mrs. Knott's mouth next. She looked at Mulraney. Their faces were close. Their eyes locked for an instant and Mulraney saw the unspeakable animal terror. She then let out a scream loud enough to shatter glass, the type of scream that curdles blood, something out of a horror film, a scream to pierce the most calloused soul. That was all he got from her for the rest of murder night.

Now he was with her again. He had waited until after the judge was buried before calling on her again for the follow-up. The interval gave Mulraney a chance to get his bearings on the case and follow up the few apparent leads he had. One thing was certain, from her statement and the nature of the mortal wound, the killer had just done his deed when she and Alvin Scribner found the judge. The running blood told him that. Dead men don't bleed that much. The judge was just about dead when they arrived, but not quite. Damn! Why couldn't he have just whispered out the name of his killer? It would have made the investigation so much easier.

In search of clues, Mulraney supervised the search of the judge's office. After fifteen years on the bench, the judge had quite a mass of paperwork around, to say nothing of the hundreds of case folders and many files in the hard disk of his computer. Of great interest to Mulraney was the safe. He asked Alvin Scribner for the combination, and noted that Alvin was hesitant to give it up, claiming respect for the dead, judicial secrecy, and other bullshit reasons. The little old bastard even excused himself to go call an attorney for advice! For being so sensitive to the judge's privacy, Alvin became an immediate suspect in his death.

One among many. Of course, it could be anyone, but the way police work went, you first checked out the closest targets on the scope. That was usually good enough.

.   .   .

SAFE EVIDENCE

After Mulraney threatened to get a court order to open the safe, Alvin relented. Inside the safe Mulraney found a bunch of court papers, opinions, and floppy disks, but no money or other items of value. One of the items he found was a year-old receipt for a small stock investment owned by someone or something named "S. Trubluy." The stockbroker's name was Albert Rhinestrum and the listed brokerage was Baynard, Pith, and Willikins. Mulraney assigned newly promoted Detective Jaime Perez the job of checking that lead out.

The crime scene spoke to Mulraney, and it said the judge knew his killer. It said there was little likelihood of a sneak attack. The judge's desk was positioned such that he could see anyone in the room. There was no sign of a struggle, no one heard raised voices or screaming, and no one strange was reported in the area before the killing.

THE NEXT STATEMENT

Mulraney, guided by Mrs. Judge Knott through the elegantly appointed foyer and hallway, landed in the spacious living room which looked like it was out of Buckingham Palace. Alice sat down with her pet dog, a yappy Pomeranian, and began petting it. Her manner was deadly serious and negative enough to attract magnets.

"We've discovered some interesting things in the last week," said Mulraney. He pulled his hanky out and sneezed into it. From his coat pocket he pulled a piece of paper out. "Must be allergic to your dog. Say, we found this in your husband's safe at the courthouse. It's a stock receipt in the name of a Mr. S. Trubluy. Very curious name, don't you think? The S stands for Snivlakno. A stockbroker named Albert Rhinestrum over at Baynard, Pith, and Willikins handled the deal, according to the receipt. Ever heard of these guys or the stocks?" He handed her a Xerox of the original receipt.

"Absolutely not," said Mrs. Knott before she even looked at the paper. "Never heard the names. As for stocks, not a dime of our money went into stocks. *My* inheritance, however, was partially invested in the stock market, but that was *my* money, and Y.A. did not touch it. Daddy insisted that Y.A. agree that what came to me from my family was to be my separate property. One of those prenuptial arrangements, you know."

Mulraney sneezed. "Must be allergic to your sofa. Not to worry, I'm only sensitive to things organic and inorganic." He then asked her, between wheezes, the usual questions about unusual activity, curious people visiting, phone calls, letters, and the like. She said she was unaware of anything suspicious.

"Enemies?" he asked before he wiped his nose.

"Well," she said snottily, "there is the human refuse he dealt with every day at the courthouse. He always complained about them. Constantly complaining about the filthy beasts."

"I understand," sniffed Mulraney through his hanky. "Any defendant stick out in your mind?"

"What? Say that . . . Defendants? Oh, no! I was talking about the defense attorneys. They gave Y.A. such a bad time. But now that you mention it, the criminals too, yes, he invariably complained about the low class of criminal who came into his court. No honor among thieves these days, he'd say. Bad as the attorneys. Yes, I suppose any of those horrible men could have done this."

"What about Alvin?" asked Mulraney.

"Who?" Alice didn't have the faintest idea who Mulraney was talking about, even though she probably saw her husband's clerk four times a week for the last fifteen years.

"Scribner. The judge's court clerk. The man who opened the door to the chambers that night?"

"Oh, that little shriveled old man. The man's a complete nonentity to me. He hardly spoke when I saw him. Rarely spoke with him. Y.A. never discussed him at home. What can I say?"

Mulraney blew his nose into his handkerchief. He thought Alice was a cold fish. She wouldn't stoop to talk to her husband's hired help. "I don't believe whoever did this went there to kill him, ma'am. Wouldn't have used the letter opener."

THE BLADE

Her eyes watered. "That was my gift to him," she said. Then tears began falling. Mulraney handed her his handkerchief, which she waved off with a look that said, Are you trying to pass me live cancer cells?

"It was a beautiful Italian piece. Very expensive. The handle, as you've seen, is twenty-two-karat sculpted gold. Did you see the detailed carving on the handle, the wonderful lion's head at the top, and three scenes of the Labors of Hercules depicted underneath? There were twelve altogether, you know. Marvelous workmanship. Simply marvelous. The blade is so gorgeous too—the finest ivory."

Mulraney wiped his nose and thought that the Mrs. was showing more emotion today about the letter opener than the death of her poor hubby. He knew that the letter opener cost her well over a grand, but that wasn't big bucks for her budget. Only rich people can get caught up in things like ornate gold-handled ivory-blade letter openers.

Mulraney envisioned the Knott marriage. He saw two stone-cold planets in fixed orbit around each other, bound together not by love, but by the law of gravity. No matter. It was over now, and unless he planned on going into an asthmatic coma, it was time to bid Mrs. Yulburton Abraham Knott adieu.

Mulraney's breathing was labored. His head was pounding and felt like it was stuffed with one hundred pounds of mercury. His lungs were fast filling with fluid, and with each breath made noises like a homemade accordion. He was getting close to that point of panic where he felt like he was about to drown in his own goo.

THE BIG QUESTION

But before he left, he had to pop the big question, the disarming one he had saved for last, the one he wanted most to see her react to at her most unguarded moment. He handed her another piece of paper with the "Lost at Sea" poem on it. "We found this on his computer that night. I assume he wrote it. Are you familiar with it?"

Mulraney watched her eyes dart across each line. Her face was blank and stayed that way right down to the bottom line. No reaction. Mulraney was disappointed.

She finished it and looked to him. "No. I have no idea if he wrote this. Y.A. was very creative, you know, so he could have. He was always writing something unique, something very different from the wearisome mumbo-jumbo he had to work with every day at the courthouse, you know. He wrote so well. He should have been placed on the Court of Appeal years ago."

Mulraney coughed and wheezed. "Sounds like the poem's about someone in despair and it's bumming out the speaker. You know, like the one person is very attached to the other, and what bothers one, bothers the other. Like two lovers, maybe. What do you think?"

Alice's finger tightly gripped the paper with the poem on it. "I think I haven't the foggiest notion of what or whom the poem's about. It could have been about anything. And, it could be about absolutely nothing. I might add, he never wrote me a poem." This was said by Alice so icily, Mulraney thought he saw her cold breath fog as she spoke. More to change the subject than to express concern, she asked, "My good man, are you entirely all right?"

Mulraney was covering his face with his hanky like it was an oxygen mask. He lied and said, "Oh, fine. Just fine. Little allergic reaction. Just filtering the air." But he was eager to leave before he stopped breathing altogether. He left the copy of the poem with her and bid Mrs. Judge Yulburton Abraham Knott adieu.

Five minutes after leaving her house and taking two Seldanes, two Actifeds, four Tylenols, three plungerfuls of his oral inhaler, and a couple of whiffs of Afrin up each nostril, he was breathing again. No question about it. Better living through chemistry!

Of course, there were side effects. The Actifeds made him drowsy; the albuterol in the inhaler made his heart beat twice as fast as normal; the Afrin brought on nonstop sneezing and explosive nasal discharges for about five minutes.

Mulraney, driving a car in this condition, endangered everyone on the streets of Manhattan. But he drove back into town, drug-drenched and thinking of the deceased. Mulraney had not known

Knott, but he had heard of him. The judge was a tough, law-and-order, no-nonsense kind of guy who wrote quirky essays in his spare time on futurist criminal justice. Now, Mulraney was getting to know him a lot. He was a technologically up-to-date jurist, a friend of the police, and when he got a little cranky, loved to dole out time and the contempt citations. He was feared by the criminal element and their mouthpieces. And he was smart. He married money.

Late that afternoon, Mulraney called the law offices of John Wilkes to set up an interview.

BUTTERMILK ARRAIGNMENT

I got Mulraney's call that evening at the conclusion of our interview with our voluptuous new client, Becky Buttermilk, accused oral sodomist. Because Wilkes and I were to be in felony arraignment on her case the next morning, we agreed to meet Mulraney there, as he said he only had a few questions and that he didn't need to inconvenience us at the office.

A master calendar court such as felony arraignment is always a noisy, crowded place. Lawyers, courtroom attachés, and newly accused clients are moving in and out all the time as their cases are called and disposed of within a few minutes by the court. The spectacle is something of a mix between taking church communion and cow-branding. Attorneys and restless clients sit on the hard cathedral benches waiting their turn for a visit with the high-branding priest. In time, the case is called, and in a few seconds a stinging scratch of paper—a multicount felony complaint—is given the accused, while God's appointed servant mindlessly intones a meaningless liturgy before moving on to the next case.

Wilkes, Becky, and I sat in the back row of the crowded courtroom. Becky came dressed for the occasion. Her powder-caked plain face was richly painted with bright purple eye shadow, orange rouge, and fluorescent-red lipstick. She wore yellow patent-leather high heels, a tight red-leather micro-mini which barely covered her bottom, and a flimsy, see-through, lavender-colored tank top which gave maximum exposure to her imposing protuberances.

That was all she wore. No coat or sweater. No bra. Not even undies. She did tie her long, canary-yellow hair back into a ponytail. This kept her shoulders bare and added to her near-naked look.

She almost started a riot.

As we sat and waited for Becky's case to be called, every male attorney who knew Wilkes—and a lot who didn't—came up to him to talk about nothing at all. Wilkes had the seat next to the aisle, Becky was next to him, and I was to Becky's right. The visitors were there to get an up-close view of Ms. Buttermilk's magnificent anatomical features. The clients of the lawyers who followed were not so indirect. They came up and pointed at her and uttered such charming phrases as, "Man, check this out!" or *"Ay, que chalupas!"* or "Whadyasay baby, you and me, let's get it on outside." The more polite just drooled in silence.

Within a few minutes there were twenty guys standing next to us making way too much noise for anyone to hear the cases being called by the court clerk. I saw the bailiff come out of the well of the court and run toward us. Surely, he would soon be breaking up this group of gawkers, droolers, and would-be molesters. But when he arrived, he just stood among them and rubbernecked himself!

JUST WOOK!

Sweet Becky was amused by the attention. She said, "Just wook at all da cwiminals, Mr. Wilkes. And da wawyers. And da sheriff. Hi! Fewwahs! Hi!" She raised her right arm and waved vigorously at the swelling group of admirers. This motion set off ripples of jiggling bosom which not only titillated the growing group of oglers, but caused several of the more excited ones to try to enter our row and make a move on Becky.

Wilkes, sensing danger to his client, acted immediately. He got up so as to block the aisle and yelled, "Up! Our case has been called by the judge!" He guided Becky to her feet and we started leaving our row on the side opposite the oglers. The bailiff, seeing that he could get a better look at Ms. Buttermilk in the front of the court, shouted to the crowd, "Sit down and shut up or you'll be thrown out." Then he sprinted to the front of the court to check out the accused oral sodomist as she bounced her way there.

The commotion in the back of the court had already stopped the proceedings by the time we got to the front of the court. Wilkes said to an irritated judge, "Your Honor, John Wilkes and Winston Schoonover appearing as retained counsel for Ms. Rebecca Buttermilk. She's number forty-seven on this morning's calendar. A thousand pardons for interrupting these proceedings, but I must ask for your indulgence and seek priority in the arraignment of Ms. Buttermilk. Ms. Buttermilk, please step forward."

Just as the judge was about to pound his lifted gavel and angrily reproach Wilkes for his presumptuous interruption of the morning cattle call, he got his first close look at our half-naked client. His jaw went slack. He dropped his gavel. He said, "Mr. Clerk! Call number forty-seven!"

STATE V. BUTTERMILK

Before a hushed audience the clerk bellowed out, "Case forty-seven, the state of New York versus Rebecca Buttermilk, also known as Becky Buttermilk, also known as Nancy Gdanzig Wyzkowski." His voice had that distinctive resonance of a peanut vendor at the ballpark yelling, "Get yer red hots!"

Wilkes and I looked at each other. Becky sensed our bewilderment at her additional moniker and whispered, "Dat was my weal name until I changed it. Weally. Wegally changed it in court. Weally."

Wilkes allowed me to do the verbal honors. I said to the court, "We state that the true name of the defendant is Rebecca Buttermilk. She is present in court on a notice to appear this morning."

At this moment the eyes of the duty-day assistant district attorney seated at a table covered with high stacks of case files were madly racing over Becky's paperwork for the first time; in a second he stuck out his arm without even looking in our direction. At the end of the arm was his hand, and the hand clutched the complaint. He was the only one in the courtroom who had not yet noticed Becky.

I took the complaint as the prosecutor looked down to the open file on his table to read the charges to the court. He read, "The defendant is charged with one count of attempted oral sodomy on an undercover officer and one count of running a house of prostitution at an establishment called the Love Tub Tumble. Defendant has a record during the last ten years. Let's see, under the name of Nancy G. Wyzkowski, she has, uhm, let's see now—two, four, six, eight, ten—yes, twelve arrests for prostitution and one conviction, which was later dismissed for some reason not reflected in the file."

Another surprise. Becky had neglected last evening to tell us about Nancy's record. Becky whispered loudly in my ear, "Da conviction was for twespass, Mr. Schoonshower. And hey! What do dey mean attempted owal sodomy? No! No! No! Dat's wong too! I weally gave da guy a bwow job. Weally! It was no attempt! It was entwapment!"

As the words "bwow job" floated over to the prosecutor, he lifted his head from the file for the first time and swung it in our direction. "All things considered," he said, "we recommend bail in the amount of ten . . . ten . . ."

At that instant Becky dropped a Kleenex on the floor between herself and the prosecutor. She squatted a bit, then leaned over like a ballerina to pick it up and give the assistant a smile and the grand view. Everyone in the gallery stood to watch. Even the judge leaned over his throne to get a better view.

" . . . ten . . . ten . . . ten . . . ten . . . ten . . . ten . . ."

"Yes, that'll be acceptable, Your Honor. Ten dollars," said Wilkes while the struck-dumb prosecutor tried to reel in his tongue.

Bang! went the gavel. "So be it," said the judge. "Ten dollars bail. Give them a trial date in thirty days, Mr. Clerk."

THE CALL OF JUSTICE

And so he did. We escorted our client out of the court's swinging doors—to the leers of all—and into the hallway. The hallways in the Criminal Courts Building are like the streets of a Third World country in revolution. On any given day, as the attorneys, cops, clients, jurors, witnesses, clerks, groupie court watchers, and security people walk to their assigned courtrooms, they pass the humanity hailed there by the call of justice. Weeping mothers suckle infants on wooden benches while their man is dragged off to Attica. Family meals are served out of brown paper bags and eaten on the floor while Daddy testifies for his liberty, and poor preteens—the sons and daughters of men in trial—run up and down playing football or soccer, or just yell their heads off, oblivious to how Daddy's doing on cross-examination. Teenage addicts nod off or shoot up, drunks puke on themselves, a transvestite kisses his lover, mothers pull sonny's hair, sonny punches out Mom's lights, thieves steal, gangs make war, and weapons flash. It's the city turned outside in—the streets of the courthouse are the mean streets of the city.

Lenny Bruce once said that the only justice you get in the halls of justice is in the halls. No more. The halls of justice are far too dangerous a place to see anything resembling justice.

MEET MULRANEY

But the hallway is where we met Detective Mike Mulraney. He was on the floor pulling two brawling punks apart in front of the door to felony arraignment. "Hey! Assholes!" he said to them. "You don't want to miss your arraignment. Then you'll get busted for bail jumping and they'll put your virgin asses in the joint, where they wouldn't be virgin very long. Now, get the hell in there." He lifted the two young men up by their T-shirts and shoved them through the swinging doors and into felony arraignment.

"John Wilkes, at your service," said my friend as the two brawlers disappeared into the court. Wilkes seemed almost happy to meet Mulraney. Curious, I thought, since Mulraney was there to ask questions about the murder of Judge Knott.

Mulraney ignored Wilkes's greeting. He wasn't being rude. He just couldn't take his eyes off of the smiling Becky Buttermilk, who was at Wilkes's side as we approached. "Yes, yes," he said after a few moments of gaping. He spoke to Becky. "And who have we here? Wilkes, this must be your assistant, Wilma Stoopover? The lady with the deep voice I spoke to over the phone last night?"

"You spoke with me, Winston Schoonover," I said. Nobody ever gets my name right. I made the introduction. "Mike Mulraney, meet Becky Buttermilk, at the moment a damsel in distress."

"She doesn't look like she's in distress," said Mulraney.

This was true. When you looked at Becky, you didn't picture distress. Undress, yes. Distress, no.

Becky stuck out her hand. Mulraney eagerly grabbed it, gave it a firm shake, and watched the resultant waves of undulating chest flesh. "Pweased to meet you, Mr. Muwaney," said Becky. She performed a small curtsy while still connected by hand to Mulraney. "Are you wepwesenting dose two fewwahs you just pushed into da awwaignment court?"

"No, ma'am. I'm a homicide detective. Nice to meet you. I don't want to bother you and Mr. Schoonopper. I promised Mr. Wilkes I'd just take a few seconds and ask him a few questions about a case I'm working." Mulraney let go of Becky's hand and started walking away. Wilkes said he'd be right back and followed.

"Pweasure meeting you, Detective Muwaney. Weally," cooed Becky. She all but jumped him as he retreated with Wilkes, but I managed to grab her elbow to restrain her. "He's weally attwactive," she said.

BUTTERMILK BUST

They disappeared from view just as a recess in the arraignment court began. With Becky in tow, I went back into the courtroom to talk to the assistant district attorney. I wanted discovery. I asked him if Becky's file contained the police arrest report on her case.

The assistant looked up at me and Becky. He said, "Ah, yes, the celebrated Buttermilk bust. Let me see." He looked in the piles of files for Becky's. "Eureka!" he said with a laugh at finding it, and then a second later, "A miracle! A police report actually in the file! This is unique, almost unprecedented! Here." He handed me a copy saying, "Our feeble description of the Buttermilk bust."

Becky and I took a seat to read the report. In pertinent part, undercover vice officer Charles X. Tuttlebell wrote:

On the date in question, I went into the Love Tub Tumble wired with a transmitting device in my jacket. I met suspect Buttermilk in a small lobby in the front of the store. She was alone, scantily clothed, and represented herself as the owner of the place. I said I wanted a Jacuzzi.

She asked, "Will that be the hot, the sweltering, the scalding, or the blistering Love Tub Tumble?" I know from informant information that the hotter the tub category, the more sex the customer gets and the greater the expense.

I said just a regular hot tub would do. She said, "Fifty bucks for thirty minutes." I paid in premarked money, was taken to a small room with a Jacuzzi and told to undress and get in, which I did. At this point, I was without the transmitter which was left in my clothing.

I sat down in the Jacuzzi. Ms. Buttermilk, who had led me into the room, took off her clothing and got into the tub with me. When I was seated in the water, she grabbed my penis and made it erect. Then, just as my penis broke the surface of the water, she attempted to put her mouth on it. I was able to stop her just prior to any copulation. I announced I was a vice officer and arrested her for attempted oral sodomy and running a house of prostitution.

I couldn't help laughing after finishing the report. Many of the police reports I've read have been fictional inventions of the police officer's imagination. For years I read about how our clients "freely consented" to allow cops without a warrant to search their cars filled with dope, or "abandoned" contraband right under the officer's nose, or "freely waived" their right not to speak to the constable.

But this report was a Gold Medal whopper. No man could get into a hot tub with a naked Becky Buttermilk and resist her attentions. Especially a vice cop.

Becky's reaction to the report was less cheery. She looked at it resting on my lap and slapped it. "Dat's bull! I weally did bwow da bastard, and he never stopped me. He ejacuwated too, right in the tub when I was under da water. After he got his jowwies, den he busted me."

Becky's version of events, while perhaps more embarrassing to

Officer Tuttlebell than his version, only proved her guilt. So truth in this case was no defense. If we stuck with Tuttlebell's version, at least we could argue that the officer was mistaken about Becky's intentions. Or something.

WILKES RETURNS

"I wondered where you went."

I looked up and it was Wilkes, recently returned from the Mulraney interrogation. Judging from the time he was gone and his happy demeanor, it was a brief and not unpleasant inquisition.

"Here's Becky's arrest report," I said as I handed him the report. "Read these four paragraphs."

"It's widdled with untwuths, Mr. Wilkes," said Becky as Wilkes read. "Weally."

Wilkes finished reading the report. "Becky," he said, "in this case, the untruth will set you free."

—— 9 ——

Taking Stock

"Cannot see contents of nut until shell is cracked."
CHARLIE CHAN

"It is possible for Officer Tuttlebell to be a truth-teller. If so, he is undoubtedly the proud owner of something belonging in the Guinness Book of Records (which amazingly has no record listed for the world's longest penis)."
FROM WILKES'S MOTION PAPERS IN
STATE V. BUTTERMILK

Alvin Scribner was, until someone planted a letter opener into the back of Yulburton Abraham Knott, the late judge's court clerk. Compared to the judge, Alvin was the most affable of men. Compared to anyone else, he was shy to the point of retiring. In fact, Alvin lived for the soon-to-come day when he would be retiring. In the meantime he continued his mundane clerking duties in his usual mousy way.

Short, thin of body and hair, plagued by poor eyesight, and with a posture comparable to the Hunchback of Notre Dame, he was about the oldest, unhealthiest-looking fifty-four-year-old man alive. He was also, in Detective Mike Mulraney's opinion, one of the unlikeliest murder suspects he had ever investigated.

But then, life is full of surprises.

Alvin Scribner had loose, jaundiced skin fissured with deep wrinkles which gave him a baggy, malarial appearance. Both of his eyelids twitched occasionally from a nervous tick. His faint hazel eyes squinted behind thick, rimless glasses which allowed him to see most of what was before him. When he walked, his head faced the floor as if life had just dealt him a painful defeat, and he shuffled so slowly you would have thought he was walking to the electric chair.

Mulraney thought the man physically incapable of plunging a knife deep into anyone's back. The man was so frail, he could have been the poster boy for the ninety-eight-pound weakling.

Despite appearing two steps from death, Alvin had no serious medical problem. He was instead a typical modern employee of the modern bureaucracy whose only malady was the omnipresent contagion of the public workplace, the disease Mike "the Hanky" Mulraney had repeatedly seen all over the civil service world.

TERMINAL CSA

Alvin Scribner had a bad case of what Detective Jaime Perez called "the Civil Service Alzheimers"—the spirit-killing, mind-numbing, initiative-despoiling, clock-watching affliction that is the ruination of all bureaucrats, whether petty or notable, whether in service to the public or private business, whether in the big city or small village. Delusional thinking is typical of CSA-infected workers. They believe their guaranteed-for-life employment is "personal improvement time," which, unhappily, is occasionally interrupted by short, nauseating periods of exertion in the name of forced labor to the public.

CSA-infected workers have no other thoughts than for more and more AND MORE of their Big Five Manias—SECURITY! MONEY! BREAKS! VACATION! PAID HOLIDAYS!—and for less and less of their Five Great Phobias: responsibility, accountability, initiative, supervision, and, least of all, work. The Five Great Phobias fuel the energy CSAs expend organizing CSA unions which lobby to augment worker guarantees of more of the Big Five Manias and less of the Five Great Phobias.

Alvin has a bad case of CSA. He has dawdled through thirty years of clerking as if he were a compensated court watcher. About fifteen years ago luck landed him the assignment as clerk for Judge Yulburton Abraham Knott. This was good fortune because Judge Knott was challenged so frequently by criminal defense attorneys he rarely tried a criminal case. This meant a lot of on-the-job leisure time for Alvin between the occasional civil trials.

Mike Mulraney arrived at the courthouse and took the elevator up to the floor where Alvin was working in the clerk's office. Mike was not in a good mood. His boss, Chief Inspector Dwight Lorton, had climbed up on the cross that morning and given his Crucifixion Speech again. He had said, "The new police commissioner told me this morning that he had heard a rumor that the Homicide Bureau was best in the department at successfully closing a case. Now he tells me he's beginning to think it was just a rumor."

Lorton's parting words to Mike were: "It's been over a week since the Knott murder, and no leads. We need a break on the case or the commissioner's gonna do something. Mike, I don't want to think about what that might be. But whatever it is, remember this, Mulraney—shit rolls downhill."

Mulraney, desirous of avoiding the fecal avalanche, went straight to see his leading suspect.

FIRST DEGREE

Alvin was expecting the visit, thanks to Detective Mulraney's call that morning. Alvin did not think much of it—just a routine search for leads, he guessed. When Mulraney arrived at about quarter to noon, Alvin led him into a small, unkempt closet converted into a storage room in the back of the clerk's office.

Mulraney noted Alvin's apparel—brown slacks worn so thin on the butt as to shine, an open collar topping a white stained shirt that could pass as a used baby bib, and a gray wool button-down sweater. The shoes were penny loafers in bad need of polish.

A rat scurried underneath a cardboard box when Alvin turned the light on; it was followed to safety by a platoon of scampering cockroaches. Mulraney sniffed the air. It had the musty smell of damp cardboard. That meant mold. That meant an allergic reaction. He was sneezing before he even sat down on one of the two beat-up gray metal chairs Alvin dragged in from the outer office.

Despite the bad air, Mulraney thought it was the perfect interrogation room. The light was poor, the room tiny, and the feeling claustrophobic.

His eyes watered immediately and he sneezed a second time as he sat down. Then he blew his nose into the ever-present white hanky. From his coat pocket he pulled out his antihistamine pills and quickly popped two down the hatch without benefit of water. A saliva cocktail. Neat. Just like always.

Mulraney's severe allergic reactions were misleading to the witnesses who looked on in awe at this sick man who appeared on the verge of blowing out his insides. His awful symptoms relieved the initial tension of the interview. Witnesses felt the physically defective man before them would surely be conducting a brief and superficial interrogation so that he could go directly to the hospital and get under an oxygen tent. But Mulraney's first question quickly changed that.

"I want to follow up on our talk on the night of the murder, Alvin," sniffled Mike. His nose was now totally plugged, which made his voice nasal and deadened. "What about a guy named Trubluy? Every heard of him?"

"Who?" asked Alvin. He looked to his watch. Lunchtime was only twelve minutes away. Should he say something about it?

"First name's Snivlakno. Eastern European maybe, I dunno. We found his name on a Baynard, Pith, and Willikins stock receipt in the judge's safe. You remember the safe, Alvin, the safe you would not open for me that night until you called your lawyer. By the way, who'd you call for advice that night?"

"Our civil service union has attorneys for us," said Alvin meekly without answering the question. His initial unconcern turned to embarrassment and alarm. Mulraney wasn't sugar-coating his interrogation. There was nothing superficial about these questions. He was going for it. "Say," said Alvin, checking his wristwatch. "Lunch is in about twelve minutes and I gotta take it then."

"Don't worry about it, Alvin, you'll make lunch. Now, in the safe we found a floppy disk, and our boys can't get into it. It's got a password entry. None of the other floppies have passwords. Got any idea what is in the disk or what the password is?"

Alvin's frail body shivered a bit as he said, "No. I was under orders never to touch the judge's computer. Wouldn't know how anyway." He fidgeted in the chair and continued looking at the floor as he thought about the lies he was telling and the need to escape this room and this interrogation.

"What about the stock investments? You know anything about the judge making them? Ever heard of Albert Rhinestrum, the stockbroker at Baynard, Pith, and Willikins? His name was on the receipt too."

Alvin, now extremely hunched over and looking to the floor, said: "I don't know about any of this. I don't even know if the judge made investments or had a broker or was acquainted with this man Rhinestrum. I was only the court clerk. I mean, the judge and I got along fine on the job, but I wasn't his buddy or personal adviser. Judges don't fraternize with the help as a rule. We lived in different worlds and went our own way."

"Okay, Alvin," said Mulraney. He sensed the mendacity. All cops sense mendacity. This is because they assume everyone lies. Usually, they're right. Cops believe only that which is irrefutably corroborated, and even then they're dubious. But what the hell would a court clerk like Alvin want to kill the judge for? Maybe he was driven crazy by one too many paper cuts, or a shortage of paper clips, or maybe the last pot of office coffee was too weak. He had the CSA after all.

Two days ago Mulraney had assigned Frank Fortunata to check out Alvin's financial background, and the early returns showed that he had been living within his civil service means. Yet, something was troubling Alvin. Mulraney thought it time to unsettle the witness a bit more. "The lab found a partial print of yours on the handle of the murder weapon."

Alvin instantly straightened his crooked back and a pink color filled his yellow cheeks. His eyes widened and he looked Mulraney in the face for the first time. "So what! God! I told you that night! She was screaming in my face! She—Mrs. Knott—was screaming for me to pull it out! God! She screamed it so loud. She was so hysterical. I tried once but it was stuck, uh, it wouldn't come easy and there was the blood and I—"

"Just the same, yours are the only prints on the murder weapon, Alvin. Doesn't look good."

"For Christ's sake! I didn't kill the judge!" protested Alvin. He was close to tears now. "Why would I do such a thing?" He crossed both arms over his lower chest and bent over slightly, as if he had a stomachache.

Mulraney noticed a ballpoint pen in Alvin's left shirt pocket held in a plastic holder, a fashion felony with the trendy set, but normal wear for the likes of Alvin Scribner. He asked to use it and said, "The autopsy report is no surprise, Alvin. Knott was killed by a single stab in the back which punctured his heart, causing him to bleed to death. An expert blow or a lucky shot. Anyway, the angle of the back wound is downward and to the left, strongly pointing . . ."

As he was saying this, Alvin's shaking right hand reached into the pocket and handed over the cheap, government-issued ballpoint pen.

". . . to a right-handed murderer." Mulraney grabbed Alvin's right hand. It was moist with sweat. "Got anything you wanna say, Alvin?"

Alvin instantly withdrew his clammy hand from the arm of the law as if he were pulling it out of a pot of molten lava. "Do I need a lawyer?" he asked pleadingly. His eyes were tearing, but no tears fell.

Mulraney stared him in the eyes. "I dunno, Alvin. Do you?"

Alvin did not reply for a moment. He looked to the floor. The first tears fell like tiny bombs and smashed silently on the filthy linoleum floor. Finally, he choked out, "I did not kill Judge Knott. It's time for lunch. I wanna go."

Mulraney got up and gave the familiar order cops give to all prime suspects: "Don't leave town. Call me if you wanna talk. You know how to get in touch."

Alvin followed Detective Mulraney like a beaten dog out of the closet. When he saw Mulraney leave, he went to the phone and made a call to his lawyer.

ITALIAN STALLION

Back at Homicide, Detective Frank Fortunata was sitting at his desk writing a report on the Knott case. As Mulraney asked, he had checked on Scribner's finances and living conditions and then attended the Knott funeral—a large affair held in a big uptown church—to browse and listen. He heard nothing suggesting a lead. There had been a lot of emotionless speech-making about the tragic loss of a fine public servant, but they could have been speaking about the retirement of the city rat catcher.

So matter-of-fact was the event, it seemed more like a business meeting than a church funeral for a murdered Supreme Court justice. Fortunata was not surprised. He thought most lawyers had no heart, especially the politically ambitious, and that accounted for most. Now, if they'd gathered to mourn their losses from the recent stock crash, there would have been enough tears to float an ark.

"Hey, Stallion! I hope our corpse cutters did a good 'topsy on da judge 'cause I hear Mrs. Judge turned him into a crispy critter." It was Detective Jaime Perez bouncing into the room to happily announce news of the cremation of Yulburton Abraham Knott. Perez had a nickname for everyone. The pathologists at the morgue were the corpse cutters. Frank Fortunata was the Italian Stallion.

"Old news, amigo," said Fortunata to his short, plump, and bubbly partner. "When they didn't drop him in the dirt at the funeral, I asked. Said he was just out of the oven."

"Well, man, the Hanky wants me to go interview Mr. Piss over at Payhard, Piss, and Whatchamacallit. You know, the brokers. Broker? What the hell does a broker do, Stallion? I know I'm broker than you, but shit, Puerto Ricans don't know nothin' about stocks and bonds. My portfolio, it's got a lot of bills, man, but no T-bills. No way I'm the guy for this job, Stallion."

"Amigo," Fortunata smiled, "your expertise is limited, but you can't expect to investigate cockfights and stabbings the rest of your life. Think of this as a stretch."

Perez knew the Italian Stallion would not be budged from his desk for this job, but there was no harm in trying. "You should do it,

Stallion. Really, man, you could pick up a free investment opportunity for all your loose change."

"Bullshit," said Fortunata. "I got my paperwork to finish here, and then I gotta go get some snot-nosed computer whiz out of jail to crack the code on the disk they found in the judge's safe. It's got a password and our guys can't crack it. The Hanky wants the kid who busted into the bank's codes and stole a ton of money. Thinks he can open the file for us. This one's all yours, amigo."

MR. LEWIS PITH

"The name Trubluy is a very familiar one," said Lewis Pith to Jaime Perez at the prosperous-looking headquarters of Baynard, Pith, and Willikins. Pith seemed young to be a partner. He had a thick head of brown hair which he brushed up and back, a clean-shaven handsome face, and could have passed as a contestant for yuppiest-dressed man of the financial district. He wore a blue shirt, a red-orange tie, a tan linen suit, and brown suede wing-tipped shoes—the complete designer ensemble. Now he was seated in a leather throne with his shoes resting on his beautiful and neatly arranged rosewood desk.

"I suppose you are here to pursue Albert Rhinestrum for the theft of the Trubluy account. We've been waiting for someone in law enforcement to look into it. Still, it's a mystery to us what happened to that account or the client or, for that matter, our employee."

Jaime Perez was startled by the flood of unexpected information flowing from Pith's mouth just seconds after introductions were completed. He had just arrived and shown Pith the stock receipt from the Knott safe, and now all of a sudden here comes an outpouring. It was like touching the kitchen faucet handle and having the pipes burst.

"Man, you ever seen either of these dudes before?" Perez flashed Pith a photo of Judge Knott and his clerk, Alvin Scribner.

"Nope," said Pith. "You could show me Trubluy's picture and I wouldn't know it. Never saw the man. But I can show you the record of Trubluy's stock transactions with his broker, our former employee, Albert Rhinestrum. Trubluy dealt exclusively with him."

Pith pulled a file out of his desk. "I've been saving this for the day someone would come in and check on the account. I thought maybe the client or a relative might come in before you guys. I remember I got two calls about it shortly after the theft. Two different men called, but they wouldn't identify themselves. I made notes of the calls on the cover of the folder. By the way, you can have this copy, Detective Perez."

He handed Perez an inch-thick file folder which Jaime opened and then scanned. It was a long computer list of stock and bond buys and sales dating back ten years. Feigning understanding of the transactions on the documents before him, Perez said, "In other words . . ."

"Well, it's very embarrassing to our firm, but it appears that our former agent, Albert Rhinestrum, after an amazingly successful investment history, dramatically increased Mr. Trubluy's portfolio; then, the fellow apparently liquidated it all in a very short time span six months ago. I'd say he stole well over three million dollars and just disappeared."

THE CRACKER

Jethro Wilmore, also known as the Hacker-Cracker, was in jail awaiting trial in Manhattan for moving enormous amounts of other people's money into his accounts through the use of a personal computer, a modem, telephone lines, and his genius at breaking the password barriers to the big bank computers. Bank codes are probably the most sophisticated in the world, as good as the military's, but Jethro was not to be denied. Many hackers saw such passwords as intellectual challenges, but not Jethro. He broke them for the money.

It was not difficult for Frank Fortunata to talk the skinny, pimply Hacker-Cracker into joining forces with the police. Jethro lived to play with his Apple computer each waking hour, a convenience not available to those waiting trial in jail in the Big Apple. Jethro was about to die of boredom.

Jethro got caught on his bank crimes more for his reckless driving than his illegal forays into the bank computer vaults. He had more drunk driving and speeding tickets in one month than an untreated alcoholic gets in three lifetimes. This terrible driving record necessitated multiple crackings of the Department of Motor Vehicle computer to erase his awesome record of driving citations and thus save his license.

One day, Irma Etius, a DMV programmer afflicted with CSA, was putting five more of his speeding tickets into the department's data base. She started the work at 4:15 P.M., and by 4:55 P.M. she had only input three. Irma took her last five minutes on the job to check off the three tickets she typed in, straighten her work area, and watch the second hand on the wall clock as it swept through the final ticks from 4:59 P.M. to 5:00 P.M. At precisely five she joined the thundering herd and bolted out of the office.

The next morning when Irma returned, she thought it strange that the three tickets she had input into the computer were no longer in the file for Jethro Wilmore. She noted this only because it irritated her that she would have to repeat the typing of the three tickets, a task a normal typist could perform in one minute. So she typed all five tickets into the computer.

The next day, by chance, she received another Jethro Wilmore ticket to enter, but when she pulled up Jethro's file in the computer, she discovered all five of the tickets were erased again. This angered her. She lashed out at a fellow female employee whom she had long suspected of attempting to drive her crazy. This led to a physical fight which led to an investigation of the incident which eventually— one year later—led to Jethro's arrest for fiddling with the DMV computer.

This led to disaster for Jethro. During the search of his apartment for the DMV offenses, the investigators hit pay dirt. They uncovered Jethro's computer printouts of his vast and newly acquired bank resources.

Frank Fortunata told him the offer. "Jethro, if you help us, we'll help you. We want you to crack a code on a computer file."

Jethro quickly agreed to try to break the password on Judge Knott's floppy disk. "In return, I have a few modest requests. Actually, I'll make you a deal. If I can't crack this file, then just tell the judge I tried to help. If I crack the code, I want this criminal case dismissed. In any event, I want a big room in a nice hotel to live in while I work for you, and computer games to play with during my down time."

Fortunata said he'd look into it, but could not promise him anything at the moment. In an hour Jethro was sprung from jail.

At the station, Mulraney was with his boss, Dwight Lorton, and the computer technicians. They were looking over the computer paper generated by all but one of Knott's files when Fortunata and Jethro entered the room.

Without so much as a greeting, Jethro eagerly sat down at the judge's IBM computer, booted up the software, and purred with satisfaction to be back in the saddle. The floppy disk in question was in the open A drive. Jethro called it up. At the bottom of the screen, it read: ENTER PASSWORD. Jethro typed in the name Knott, and the screen responded, "File is locked."

Mulraney said, "The Hacker-Cracker, I presume." He introduced everyone around the machine and said, "This won't be easy, Jethro. We've tried calling the software company to get around the password, but they say it can't be done. It's not a mainline software. Knott got some customized stuff for his computer. The password could be seventy-five characters in length, and they tell us you'll destroy the file information if you just blunder into the guts of the software and try to pull up the text. Gotta have the password."

Jethro looked to the men standing around him. He was pleased to have the undivided attention of the police and yet not be under interrogation for one of his computer crimes. "Yeah," he said. "Okay. Seventy-five characters, eh? That means it could be any combination of numbers and letters and spaces and punctuation— all of it invisible. That means you take all the letters, twenty-six, and all the numbers, ten, and all of the others, punctuation and symbols—thirty-two in number, and that adds up to sixty-eight combinations possible for each of the seventy-five possible marks in the password."

Jethro looked at Mulraney through his old fashioned horn-rim glasses. He was in ecstasy. This was a job for a genius. Perfect for him. He ran his hands through his greasy hair and then rubbed them together. Jethro started typing on the computer screen while saying to it, "That's sixty-eight different combinations for each possible space in the password. So for the first space, there are only sixty-eight possibilities, but for the first and second spaces together, there are sixty-eight times sixty-eight, and for the third space, sixty-eight times sixty-eight times sixty-eight, and so on up to the max possible of seventy-five spaces. That's a huge number of possibilities, enormous, impossible . . . let's see, let me get you a number on that, uh, okay, the log of sixty-eight equals one point eight, and seventy-five times that equals about ten-to-the-one-hundred-thirty-seventh power; in other words, ten times itself one hundred thirty-seven times, or a ten followed by one hundred thirty-seven zeros. And that, my fine, fine, finest friends of the New York Police Department, is how many combinations it will take a computer to figure out the password by the brute force method."

Dwight Lorton brightened at the thought of a solution. He said, "Brute force! A computer can figure it out then? Great boy! Go to it!"

A MATTER OF TIME

"Sure," said the Cracker, "if it had the time, sure."

"Great," said Lorton. "Son, you take all the time you need and we'll give you all the support you want. Just crack that code. We need to know what's in that damned file."

"Sounds good to me, sir, but let me give you a little idea of how much time we are talking about. Do you know how many combinations ten followed by one hundred thirty-seven zeros is? Obviously not. So let me paint a picture for you. There are about ten-to-the-seventieth power electrons and neutrons in the entire expanse of the universe. You all know about electrons and neutrons, the basic components of the atom. Well, there are countless billions of atoms in the universe, my friends, and more electrons and neutrons in almost every atom.

"Therefore, my fine friends of the New York Homicide Bureau, the total number of possible password combinations we are facing is far larger in number than all of the electrons and neutrons in the universe. Need I go on?"

Seeing the jaws of his audience slacken, Jethro continued. "Okay, now men, let's just talk the mechanics of a possible brute force solution. Know what a gigaflop is?" Without waiting for an answer, he gave it. "It's a process capable of performing ten-to-the-ninth floating point operations—that's ten-times-ten nine times, or the number ten with nine zeroes behind it, or one billion operations. The Cray computer is capable of processing at gigaflop-per-second speed, which is one billion operations per second. There's faster stuff around, maybe three or four gigaflops per second that I . . . but, uh, er, that's another story."

"Can we get access to a Cray? Would it help you?" asked Lorton. "We need this thing broken. We need a lead."

Jethro stuck up his palm. "Hold on there, comandante. Let me finish. Now to give you some idea of what we have as a problem here, the age of the universe is about ten-to-the-tenth years old. That is, maybe ten billion years, twenty billion at the outside, give or take a coupla billion.

"Now, to solve this little code problem we would need a Cray operating for longer than the universe has existed to try all the possible letter, number, and other symbols for each of the seventy-five space possibilities. And this assumes you have the hardware—a computer—capable of accepting the possible solutions fed at the rate the Cray gave them out, and there's no such animal in existence, see. So forget it."

Fortunata was frustrated at the brat's attitude. "Well, Jethro, looks like you just calculated your way out of one nice hotel and one cushy job. Back to the slammer for you, bud."

"Not so fast, Detective Fortunata," said the Cracker. "I am, after all, in custody for allegedly busting into the most sophisticated bank computers in the world. That means I allegedly got past some pretty tough codes. I have another approach besides just plugging in all possible combinations, which is a hopeless approach.

"First, let me go into the guts of the program and look around. I might try to end-run the password if it's possible. With this particular customized software, that is highly unlikely. I gotta be careful 'cause the writer might have booby-trapped the file with a self-destruct virus. If I trigger that, it's so-long file—just like on 'Mission: Impossible.'

"Second, I'm gonna ask you to get me one of the software exchange programs and I might try to wash out the password by trying to convert it to generic or exchanging the data from one software program to another. These options don't hold a lot of promise, but you never know.

"Third, we'll try the Dumbo-assault method, which is the simplest and most obvious means of cracking the code. People are unbelievably lazy and stupid about passwords. They use their birthdays or names of kids or pets. No more than eight to ten letters usually. It's unlikely your judge Knott did any different."

Lorton asked, "If you assumed only ten characters, couldn't you solve it by the brute force technique?"

Jethro said, "No way, even with only ten letters and the sixty-eight combinations, it would still take, uhm, er, let's see, about thirty years for the Cray to do it, assuming you had the hardware to process it at that rate. No way, man.

"So the best way to do this is the logical way. The Dumbo method. I just try to guess the password through inductive reasoning. In other words, I guess a lot. I'll want all the information you have on the judge. Absolutely everything. Biography. Family tree. Friends. Pets both living and deceased. Education. Hobbies. Medical history. Military record. Law career. His big cases and favorite clients. Everything. I'll draft all the combinations in assault programs and we'll let the attack computer methodically introduce all of them. That's our best shot."

"Done," said a disappointed Dwight Lorton. "Give him whatever he needs, starting with the printout of the judge's cases, his writings, and whatever in the hell else we got."

.   .   .

BECKY BUTTERMILK MOTIONS

"Great! Fantastic! Just great, Schoon!" Wilkes was in his office reclining his long, lean body on the top of his desk. From his desk sofa he was busy reading and yelling out his approval of my just completed draft of the motion to be filed in defense of our lovely client, the recently busted Mistress of the Love Tub Tumble and alleged oral sodomist, Ms. Becky Buttermilk. Wilkes thought the motion was "great" because it was exactly what he directed me to write. Here is what he was enjoying so much:

POINTS AND AUTHORITIES IN SUPPORT OF JURY VIEW

1. FACTS. Detective Charles X. Tuttlebell has sworn in an affidavit that at the time of the alleged attempted act of oral copulation, he was sitting in a large, heart-shaped Jacuzzi in a commercial establishment known as the Love Tub Tumble, a health emporium owned by the defendant, Becky Buttermilk. Tuttlebell swears he was in three feet of hot bubbly water with his buttocks resting comfortably on the bottom of the tub when the defendant—without her head going under water—allegedly attempted to perform an act of oral copulation on the officer's exposed penis.

2. PROFFER. The defense intends to prove that Officer Tuttlebell's concocted evidence is both incredible and a physiological impossibility. Although not stated in his affidavit, the defense assumes that at the time of the alleged act, his penis was fully erect, at attention and partially out of the water. For this to be true, Officer Tuttlebell's penile appendage would have to measure well in excess of three feet so as to allow him to be immersed in the water and for the alleged act to occur without the alleged oral copulator getting her head wet.

3. DISCUSSION. This is a remarkable allegation, unique in the annals of crime or anatomy. Officer Tuttlebell has either gone to great lengths to falsely portray himself in a most flattering manner, or has the world's largest human penis. For it is written in Morris's classic text, *Human Anatomy* (N.Y. The Blakiston Co. 11th Ed., 1953) at p. 1535, "The flaccid penis varies from 8 to

12 cm. in length and 3 to 4.5 in diameter, being subject to wide variations both in individuals and races. . . . During erection it increases in both length (12 to 18 cm. [5 to 7 inches]) and breadth (4 to 5 cm.)." Dr. Jacobus reports in *Simons' Book of World Sexual Records,* pp. 54–55 (N.Y. Bell Pub., 1975) of his survey of several hundred men and the discovery of a 12-inch penis on a Sudanese man. The penis was described as "more likely the penis of a donkey than a man." In the same book, Dr. Robert Chartham reports of an Englishman's phallus which measured 10.5 inches.

While the defense is aware of unconfirmed sightings of penile members of greater size, we are aware of none the great span inherent in Officer Tuttlebell's story. This is not to dismiss the claim. Given the advances in science, the court must always allow for such possibilities as phalloplasty, prosthetic extension, or donor transplant.

Nor can one rule out enlargement through disease. *Simons' Book of World Sexual Records,* p. 56, reports, "There can be little doubt that the largest of all human penises result through the various effects of penile and scrotal elephantisasis [sic]. . . ." The author reports the horrible effects of the disease: "this condition is sometimes depicted as a vast sphere, as much as two feet across. . . . In one picture before me a vastly inflated penis is shown reaching as low as the knees."

Thus, it is possible for Tuttlebell to be a truth-teller. If so, he is undoubtedly the proud owner of something belonging in the *Guinness Book of Records* (which amazingly has no record listed for the world's longest penis).* Officer Tuttlebell, as well as his penile member, are now the most important witnesses against the defendant, and because the defendant has a constitutional right to confront and examine the witnesses against her, she must be allowed to test the officer's statements concerning the expanse of his alleged extremity.

It is inevitable that Officer Tuttlebell, as the only eyewitness, will take the stand in the prosecution of this case. In a recent telephonic interview with counsel for the defendant (see at-

---

* The book mentions just about every other dimension of the world's tallest man, Robert Wadlow. He reached a remarkable height of eight feet and eleven inches, but there is no mention of penis size. Even extrapolating from his vast height, his ring size of 25 and shoe size of 37, his erect penis could not have been over 13 to 15 inches.

tached affidavit of John Wilkes, Esq.), Officer Tuttlebell refused to confess to the actual length of his penis. Whether from false modesty or false testimony, it is clear that the prosecution witness is now excluding from the defense potentially exculpatory information. Fortunately, there is neither a modesty exception to the constitutional right to evidence, nor such an exception in the aptly titled Penal Code. The jury must be allowed to weigh the evidence first hand.

The question before the court is the manner in which the defense will be allowed to test the prosecution evidence. Several alternatives come to mind. First, of course, are the normal mechanisms of cross-examination to test the officer's credibility. But the issue to be litigated is more than just a matter of credibility; it is a matter of highly questionable physical evidence.

The defense asserts, upon information and belief, that the officer has self-servingly enlarged upon the truth in his sworn evidence and that his penis is at least two and one-half feet short of its claimed extension.

4. PRAYER FOR RELIEF. The defense moves for a jury view of the penis in question under the "Best Evidence Rule." This would require that Officer Tuttlebell be ordered to expose and introduce his private member to the ladies and gentlemen of the jury during trial. If it is in a state of flaccidity (or not at least three and one-half feet in length at the time of exposure), then the officer must be compelled by immediate court order to cause his penis to become erect so that it may be measured in such an altered state.

While such a jury view during trial may stretch the limits of courtroom decorum, it is absolutely required to fulfill the defendant's right to a fair trial and demonstrate that the officer has, in flamboyant fashion, extended the truth beyond the limits of human experience. Further, the view must take place in open court to comply with the defendant's Sixth Amendment right to a public trial and the public's "right to know" what takes place in the conduct of the People's courtroom business.

For these reasons, the defense would strenuously oppose any prosecution suggestion that the officer be allowed to submit to a privately conducted physical examination by a physician or land surveyor who would then testify to the jury as to his or her findings.

When he finished reading the motion papers, he looked up and laughed. "You know, if I had a dick that big, I'd sure as hell show it off. Hell, I'd do it at Yankee Stadium and sell tickets!"

"Wonder what they'll do when they get this?" I said. "I mean, after they stop laughing." What was funny to me was not so much Officer Tuttlebell's "lie" as to the length of his dick, but his mendacity in claiming that Becky never performed the act of oral copulation on him. Such an admission by him would cost him his job. Undercover cops aren't supposed to get laid or blown by prostitutes, at least not while on the job. According to history, as reflected in police reports, they never do.

Before Wilkes could answer me, the phone rang. I picked it up. The voice on the other end was subdued. "Hello, is Mr. Wilkes in? I need to talk to him. In fact, I think I need to retain him."

Wilkes was looking at me, reading my facial response. His expression asked, "What?" I put my hand over the speaking end of the phone and whispered, "Prospective client." The voice was strangely familiar to me. I asked the voice who he might be, and he surprised the hell out of me when he answered, "It's Alvin Scribner, Mr. Schoondozer. With big troubles. Let me speak with Mr. Wilkes."

— 10 —

The Hacker Hacks

*"Young man suffer from overdeveloped impulses and
underdeveloped control."*
CHARLIE CHAN

*"It was a just a shitty little case to the People of New York,
but to Becky Buttermilk, her right to run her house of prostitution was on the line."*
W.S.

Becky Buttermilk's oral sodomy case was about as petty as they come. Cases like hers usually deal out at the first court appearance with a plea to reduced charges of disturbing the peace, public nuisance, or trespass. The prosecutor propositioned Becky with such offers, but she would not cop a plea. As she said in her inimitable way, she would accept only a "dismissal and a pubwic apowogy."

It was just a shitty little case to the People of New York, but to Becky Buttermilk, her right to run her house of prostitution was on the line. She knew a plea to any charge would jeopardize her business license and her right to keep open the Love Tub Tumble, an establishment which, until recently, specialized in expensive Jacuzzi baths and watery ejaculations.

Wilkes delighted in having a client so resolute in demanding her sacred right to trial by jury. But it meant a busy week at the office preparing for trial, a process made difficult by the distracting calls from worried suspects in Judge Knott's wrongful termination case.

Alvin Scribner, for example, the late judge's doddering old clerk, called Wilkes frequently after Mike "the Hanky" Mulraney scared the bejeezus out of him with accusations of bumping off his boss.

Wilkes also got a call from Lyle Diderot, Field Marshal of the Whiz Kid gang, who also was interrogated by the Hanky about his whereabouts after his release from the Tombs on the evening of the murder. The interview was cut short when, midstream in the conversation, the Field Marshal succeeded—in customary Whiz Kid fashion—in urinating on him. The Field Marshal's phone call to Wilkes came from the Tombs following his arrest for pissing off the officer.

I thought it unseemly that the Knott murder suspects were calling Wilkes for advice. Christ! He was a suspect too!

DOUBTFUL PENIS

The day before trial, my motion filed on Becky's behalf for a jury view of Officer Tuttlebell's questionable three-foot penis was denied after the prosecutor explained to the judge that Officer Tuttlebell had simply made a mistake in writing his report.

"The officer states he does not now have, and never has had, a three-foot penis," said the prosecutor.

Nevertheless, the court, at Wilkes's insistence, ordered an examination by a doctor for measurements of the dubious penis. Wilkes also asked for a blood sample of the officer to be taken for purposes of making sure the offending instrument was free from communicable diseases. He told the judge, "I ask this as a safety precaution for the health of my client."

"And all my cwients, past, present, and future!" said Becky in my ear, but in a voice loud enough for everyone who wasn't asleep to hear. Fortunately, as it is with all but the most disorderly defendants in the courtroom, her words were ignored by the judge.

"Objection to Mr. Wilkes's motion," said the prosecutor, who also ignored Becky's comment. "There was no sexual contact in this case. Only an attempt by Ms. Buttermilk."

"Another MISTAKE in Officer Tuttlebell's report!" countered

Wilkes, spitting out each word as if it were poison.

The judge sat back in his throne and took a long look at our client. He studied her manifest charms; he looked again at the provocative charges and Officer Tuttlebell's suspicious report. Then he looked at the lean and cocky vice cop, Charles Tuttlebell, sitting next to the prosecutor at counsel table.

VICE

The judge scrutinized Tuttlebell. Judges hear the rumors about bent vice cops, the crooked ones—about their enjoyment of drugs during (and before and after) narcotic stings; about their flagrant looting of the cash boxes in gambling cases; about their outrageous sexploits with the hookers in the aptly named undercover investigations. These fellows were worse than the petty crooks they chased. Charles Tuttlebell had Vice written all over him.

Wilkes sized up the judge's thoughts and said helpfully, "Judge, the officer SAYS he got naked with THIS woman in a Jacuzzi, and that as soon as she grabbed his thing, he supposedly arrested her. We deny the limited nature of the accusation. My motion for blood is based upon his very questionable report, and human nature."

And rumor and innuendo, I thought, the two staples that motivate much judicial action.

The judge turned his head from Tuttlebell, looked again—longingly, it seemed to me—at Becky, and bellowed, "So ordered!"

I prepared the order for the doctor to take measurements of the Tuttlebell dick, withdraw blood and turn it over to us.

The blood, that is.

BUTTERMILK ON TRIAL

Wilkes faced the jury the next day. Becky Buttermilk sat calmly between Wilkes and me at counsel table. Her bright, wild yellow hair was pulled by a small black ribbon into a tame ponytail. Her dress, cottony and virginal white, fully covered her voluptuous body, filling in the lovely curves and hiding the splendid mounds in loose fabric—a tragic, but fortunately temporary, loss to the ogling world of one of earth's beauteous shapes.

Her makeup was shaded down to the vivid pastel tones of a Renoir, a great improvement over the fluorescent reds and purples that usually accented her face. Instead of a hardened microdressed hooker in neon paint, the transformed Becky Buttermilk now resembled a cute, moderately overly made-up ingenue-hooker. This was the makeup and costuming demanded by the case.

Officer Tuttlebell took the stand as the prosecutor's first and only witness. He stated right off that he had made a mistake in writing his report of the incident. He was not sitting on the bottom of the Jacuzzi when our client attempted to orally copulate him. He was floating on the top of the water so that his penis was entirely exposed to the air. And no, he did not have a three-foot penis. Only a "normal penis."

In this, the officer was not far short of the truth. Tuttlebell's physical examination revealed, according to the physician's report, "a normal, healthy male penis which, in its flaccid state, was just a hair under three and one-half inches in length."

What Tuttlebell was lying about was in saying that Becky never actually copulated him. Since our three-foot-penis defense was now going to be short of the mark, Tuttlebell's biggest lie would now become our defense. It was to be the defense of truth—an unusual event in my friend's career, and rather dangerous under the circumstances.

CROSS-EXAMINATION

Everyone knew the case would be decided, one way or the other, by Wilkes's cross-examination of Officer Tuttlebell. I produce below the reporter's transcript of the examination, which I have briefly interrupted with two explanatory comments.

Wilkes began cross by, as they say, coming out swinging:

WILKES: So you are telling us you don't have a three-foot penis?

TUTTLEBELL: Yes.

Q: So that was a big lie . . .

A: No.

Q: . . . about a small truth?

A: Hey, I don't got to take this.

Q: So, when you wrote your report of the incident, you made a mistake? Is that it?

A: It appears so, counselor.

Q: And instead of being seated at the bottom of the pool with your penis extending up three feet through the water's surface, as you wrote, you were floating on your back, right?

A: Yes.

Q: So you admit to this jury you do not have a three-foot penis?

A: Not on me, counselor. [Laughs]

Q: Well, are you aware of the measurement taken by the physician yesterday?

D.A.: Objection. Irrelevant.

TUTTLEBELL: Hey, the doc said when flaccid.

COURT: What is the relevance?

WILKES: A measurement of three and one-half inches, under the circumstances, is entirely relevant.

COURT: How's that?

WILKES: He says his report is a mistake. If it weren't for this trial, we'd never know that. We'd be left with an inflated impression of the officer's endowment. I think it goes to his mental state and propensity for exaggeration.

COURT: The fact that he has a three-inch penis?

TUTTLEBELL: And one-half! When flaccid!

BECKY: When stiff! It's a wegular pygmy pecker! Make him dwop his twousers!

COURT: Quiet, Ms. Buttermilk.

BECKY: Sowwy, Yowona.

WILKES: Well, it goes to the weight, Your Honor.

COURT: Yes. To the weight of the evidence. Objection overruled.

Q: Three and one-half inches, right?

A: Like the doc said, counselor, when flaccid.

Q: And when erect?

A: Double that, minimum.

BECKY: Bull!

COURT: Quiet, Ms. Buttermilk!

BECKY: Sowwy, Yowona.

WILKES: So you say.

TUTTLEBELL: So I know.

Q: Now, you are a professionally trained report writer, correct?

A: We are trained to write reports, yes.

Q: And to write them with great care?

A: To write down what happened, counselor.

Q: Accurately?

A: Accurately, counselor.

[I should insert at this point, for those unfamiliar with courtroom practice, that many cops on the witness stand use the word "counselor" not as a sign of respect, but only as an epithet for the defense lawyer. It's like an in-house joke, except it's no joke. Crooked cops would rather tell the truth under oath than use the respectful form "sir," or the horribly servile "Mr. Wilkes." Being respectful to the enemy is too demeaning, so the word "counselor" has evolved in bent cop jargon as a means of avoiding the contempt citation, which would come if the officer ever uttered in a court of law his synonym for "counselor"—"ASSHOLE OF THE UNIVERSE!" But let us continue.]

VERY CROSS EXAMINATION

WILKES: So, as a professionally trained police officer, you inaccurately stated in this report that you were seated when actually you were floating on your back with your penis standing tall and at attention?

D.A.: Objection. Argumentative and compound.

WILKES: I withdraw the part about "standing tall."

COURT: Answer if you understand the rephrased question, officer.

A: I was inaccurate in saying I was seated in the Jacuzzi.

Q: Did Becky tell you to float around with your penis erect and out of the water?

A: No. I just did that to make it more convenient for her.

Q: For her to grab your penis?

A: Correct.

Q: Now, she's in the water too. Floating or seated?

A: She's seated. Seated kind of next to me.

Q: You're sure she was seated? Remember, in your report you said you were seated, and now you say you were floating on your back with your penis flying high and dry.

A: She was seated, counselor.

Q: So her head was out of the water?

A: Yes.

Q: And then you float by with your penis, shortened by some three feet or so, standing—

D.A.: Objection, argumentative. There's no evidence of that.

COURT: Right. Sustained.

WILKES: I stand corrected. Officer, were you flaccid at that moment or did you show her your tallest mast?

A: I was erect, if that's what you mean, counselor.

Q: So on your own and without a word from my client, you brought yourself to the point of an erection and then exposed your upright penis to her and floated it right under her chin, right?

A: That was the idea, counselor.

Q: And you say my client then attempted to orally copulate you by doing what?

A: Well, when I floated under her chin, she grabbed my penis with her right hand in preparation for oral copulation, but I arrested her before she made oral contact.

Q: Might I suggest she was merely pushing away the tiny object with which you were attempting to jab her?

A: Suggest anything you want. But that's not the truth.

BECKY: IT WAS SELF-DEFENSE!

COURT: Quiet, Ms. Buttermilk.

BECKY: Sowwy, Yowona.

WILKES: But she's seated all the time in the Jacuzzi, right?

TUTTLEBELL: Right.

Q: When she grabbed it, as you say, how close was it to her chin?

A: Couple of inches.

Q: As I understand your testimony, when you got into the Jacuzzi, no one talked about sex?

A: Didn't need to. She's a pro. She knew what was supposed to happen. This was a house of prostitution, counselor.

WILKES: [To the court] He knows better than that, Judge! This man's a professionally trained witness. He's testified many times. I move to strike his gratuitously self-serving, conclusionary comment about this legitimate Jacuzzi establishment being a whorehouse. [Points finger at witness] IT'S A LIE AND HE KNOWS IT!

[This was a masterful example of Wilkes's speaking objection strategy. He yelled it loud and angrily to let the jury know the officer was not playing by the rules. The crucial point was to insert in the long-winded speaking objection at least one word (here, the word, "conclusionary") which properly stated a basis for the judge to strike the answer, and surround it with as much self-serving commentary as possible.]

COURT: Strike the words "house of prostitution." The jury will ignore it. Don't do that again, officer.

Q: Now, when you got into the tub, no one said anything?

A: Nope.

Q: And just what did you think was supposed to happen?

A: She's gonna give me sex.

Q: So that was what was on YOUR mind?

A: No, that's what she thought.

Q: That's a convenient, after-the-fact justification, officer. Are you a mind-reader as well as a poor report writer?

A: No. I'm neither, counselor.

Q: The jury will decide that. I'm asking just what were you thinking as you floated naked as a peeled banana in the warm, swirling waters of that little pool with your perpendicular penis aimed at my client's chin?

A: I wasn't thinking, counselor. I was getting my job done.

Q: A blow job?

A: No, counselor. My job was to see if she was running a house of prostitution.

Q: And it is your testimony that you had no sex with her?

A: That is correct, counselor. When she grabbed my penis, I arrested her immediately.

Q: So you did not force her into an act of oral copulation and ejaculate?

A: No, counselor.

Q: You are not mistaken in that too?

A: No, counselor.

Q: Recognize this?

A: A wadded-up Kleenex. Never seen it.

Q: Do you know that the forensic people have examined the tissue paper used by my client that night to swab out her mouth just after you arrested her? It was still in the wastebasket in the Jacuzzi room of the Love Tub Tumble.

A: I don't know nothin' about it.

Q: Well, do you know that with DNA testing we can find out who the donor of sperm is by just examining a tiny drop of it and matching it with a suspect's blood?

A: You don't say. Congratulations.

Q: I do say. Remember that blood you gave upon order of the court?

A: Taken in violation of my rights, counselor.

Q: Well, think very carefully before you answer this next question. Officer, I ask you once again under the penalty of perjury, did you, or did you not, have oral sex with my client in that Jacuzzi?

D.A.: Objection. Asked and answered.

BECKY: Yeah, except he wied the first time he answered.

COURT: He can answer again. Quiet, Ms. Buttermilk.

BECKY: Sowwy, Yowona.

TUTTLEBELL: I am not on trial here.

WILKES: Not yet. But I put it to you once again, Officer Charles Tuttlebell of the vice squad. Reminding you, as is my holy duty as an officer of the court, of the heavy—some would say draconian—penalties in the state of New York for the crime of perjury, and your absolute constitutional right to remain silent without fear of recrimination, did you, or did you not, require my client to have oral sex with you on the date of the arrest?

TUTTLEBELL: Judge, do I have to dignify that with an answer?

COURT: Yes, you do.

TUTTLEBELL: Well, I ain't.

D.A.: The question is compound and argumentative.

BECKY: TELL DA TWUTH!

WILKES: Perhaps I can enlist the assistance of the court at this point.

COURT: Answer the question.

TUTTLEBELL: This is ridiculous! I am not on trial. I refuse to answer. Judge, I refuse to answer any more of this asshole's questions.

WILKES: Officer, I will be perfectly happy to oblige you and not ask you any more questions, but only upon hearing from the judge the two most beautiful words ever heard in any court of law.

COURT: [Pause] Case dismissed!

At that, Becky jumped into Wilkes's arms and gave him a warm hug and big kiss. "Gweat work, Wilkie! I'm back in business! Tewwific!"

With that, she released my friend and bounced gaily down the aisle to the door. There, she turned and yelled to us—before a packed, admiring courtroom—"Don't forget to use the fwee passes I gave you and Schoon to the Love Tub Tumble!"

Leaving those lovely words floating in the air like laughing gas, she disappeared out the swinging doors. It was not the last we would see of Becky Buttermilk.

THE FIRST CRACK

"Geez, this is going to be easy," said the Hacker. He was in his room at a nice hotel going through the investigative reports the NYPD gave him to help come up with the password to the mystery file on Judge Knott's floppy disk. The stock receipt found in the judge's safe with the odd name of "Snivlakno Trubluy" was the first item to strike him as peculiar. He typed the letters on the computer the police had provided him:

SNIVLAKNO TRUBLUY

The idea was for the Hacker to figure out possible passwords and then program all possible variants of the password into an attack program. Each attack program would be fed by his computer into another computer which contained the mystery file. Hopefully, one of the attacks would be successful and penetrate the password barrier.

He typed the letters backward.

YULBURTONKALVINS

He laughed sarcastically. He separated the letters with a couple of spaces and laughed again at the screen. Only one type of police investigator could have missed this, he thought.

"An idiot!" He said it aloud to the screen.

As he looked at the reassembled name of Snivlakno Trubluy, he wondered how it was possible that the idiot police had ever caught him for his own crimes.

YULBURTON K   ALVIN S

— 11 —

The Bath

*"Long road sometimes shortest way
to end of journey."*
CHARLIE CHAN

*"But he was not watching television.
He was dead."*
W.S.

New York. Nighttime.

Detective Mike "the Hanky" Mulraney lay in a bathtub filled with water so hot it turned his freckled skin bright red. The faucet trickled scalding water to keep what was in the tub near boiling. A wet washcloth covered his face, giving him the look of a pharaoh in the first stage of mummification. Despite the difficulty in sucking air, the wet rag actually made it easier for him to breathe—the filtered hot, moist air was just the ticket for his clogged sinus passages and lungs.

The tub was his sanctuary when allergies attacked. If he did nothing to stave the allergic reactions, the suffocating effects of asthma followed. As hot steam fogged the room and smothered reactions, Mulraney soaked in the hot tub, sucked in the steam, and breathed.

Often as not, Jill would join him there, and often as not, a love-making romp in the water ensued. On this night, the Mulraneys romped in the tub like humpbacks in heat and made a watery mess of the floor.

After, a clear-lunged Mike said, "God! Sex is great for fighting allergies. That was good." He laughed as he noticed the flooded floor. "Did the earth move, or what?"

Jill giggled. "No, just the water. Call out the towel squad. This place is a mess!"

CUI BONO

After laying down some towels to soak up the water, Jill sat naked on the edge of the tub with her feet in the water. The mystery of who killed Judge Yulburton Abraham Knott was on her mind. "The last stock report from the file indicates the broker, Albert Rhinestrum, liquidated everything six months ago, got a ton of money and split. No trace of him since. So we must ask, like the ancient Romans, cui bono? For whom is it good? Who would gain by the death of Judge Knott? Who'd take money? Answer? Obvious. The broker."

"Yes, the obvious answer," said Mulraney. He thought of his suspects again as he had each day since the demise of Judge Knott. He had looked into Albert Rhinestrum's background—thirty-four, a broker for the last eleven years straight out of Harvard MBA, he had worked for the same firm since he started in the business. He was described by his coworkers at the brokerage as clean-cut, quite smart, a very competent workaholic, likable but standoffish, a loner with no known family, girlfriend, hobbies, religious or political interests. In fact, he didn't have any close friends as far as anyone knew. He had clients, lots of them, and that was about it.

Jill had it figured out—now that the Hacker-Cracker had told everyone that Snivlakno Trubluy was really a backward rendering of the names of Yulburton K. (as in Knott) and Alvin S. (as in Scribner). "There's no mystery," she told her husband. "The records reveal the stock investments began with an initial investment of $25,000 ten years ago, just after Knott went almost exclusively to the civil bench. A great place to get insider business information on the fate of a business in litigation."

"Yeah," said Mike, "when you're the judge deciding the fate of the business in litigation."

"Through very shrewd trading in stock options, he parlayed this sum over the years into three million and some loose change. Too shrewd, I'd say. No one's that good. Not without help, as in insider information. That information came from the judge and probably his clerk, Alvin Scribner. They both were in on it. Why else the stupid name on the stock document with their names spelled backward?"

Mulraney lay quietly in the tub thinking about ten years of brilliant stock investments. Rhinestrum had played the market like a wizard. From the time of the initial investment, he rarely lost a cent, and those losses he incurred were small, perhaps even purposefully done to throw off the government regulators. Overall, Rhinestrum made a killing in dealings with stock options. Mulraney learned that trading in options—the right to buy stocks in the future—was the truest gamble on the stock market. Guess the future and you may take big profits. *Know* the future and you can be as rich as you want.

Mulraney had ordered a printout of all the civil cases Knott handled in the last ten years. When he got it, he discovered an amazing coincidence of cases involving business litigants and near-simultaneous investments by Snivlakno Trubluy. Every time a business listed on the exchange was in Knott's court, an investment was made by Rhinestrum on the "Snivlakno Trubluy" account shortly before the deciding jury verdict or important judicial ruling.

TAKE EXCELLULITE

Take the investment Rhinestrum made in Excellulite, a company that marketed weight reduction products. In June it was selling for fifty dollars a share. Rhinestrum bought ten call options for a mere two thousand dollars. This gave him the right to buy one thousand shares of the stock at fifty dollars per share within sixty days.

Within that sixty-day period, something happened to the company, something remarkably good. Its stock shot past eighty bucks per share. Rhinestrum now controlled the right to buy a thousand shares of eighty-dollar-per-share stock for only fifty dollars a share. Now he could either sell his options or exercise the call and buy the stock himself at fifty bucks. Either way, he stood to make a tidy profit of $28,000 in less than two months.

Mulraney had checked the judge's docket at the time of the investment in Excellulite. A major class-action employees' suit was pending against the company before none other than Judge Yulburton Abraham Knott. It must have been one helluva serious suit, casting a cloud over the future of the company, because after Judge Knott issued an order granting the company's motion for summary judgment, the dramatic rise in the worth of the company stock followed.

Judge Knott's order in the Excellulite matter came ten days after Rhinestrum bought the options for his client, Snivlakno Trubluy; it was obvious Rhinestrum had the best insider knowledge upon which to make his move.

Jill broke into Mike's thoughts. "So the judge and his clerk were crooked, but the broker's crookeder; he sold off all the stock and split with everything."

"Yep, a real Wall Street stock split," said Mulraney weakly through the washcloth. "No honor among thieves these days."

"But why does Rhinestrum split with all the money? Why so greedy? He would have been making big bucks off these insider tips himself. They were sure things. He killed the goose which was laying his golden eggs. Can a coke addict run so much money up his nose?"

"Easy," whispered Mulraney through the cloth. "In New York, there's no amount of money to satisfy a high-living, Wall Street coke head. He could have been deep in debt to his supplier. Three million's a drop in the bucket to a Wall Street coke head."

"Financially, darling, you and I could drown in that one little drop," said Jill. "But we don't know why he took the money. All we know is that one day he drains the account without the judge or the clerk knowing it and splits. Then one day the judge goes to visit his money and finds to his horror that the keeper of the treasury has taken off. What can the judge do but grin and bear it?"

· · ·

RRRIIINNNGGGGG!

The family bathtub brainstorming session was interrupted by the clanging of the telephone. Mulraney spent so much of his time at home in the tub, he always had a phone within arm's reach. His wet hand grabbed the receiver and he answered. It was Detective Jaime Perez.

"Hey, Hanky. Man, you won't believe it, but I got a lead on that stockbroker dude. He's in a hospital in San Francisco. S.F. General."

Still lying in the tub with the warm washcloth over his face, Mulraney said, "How the hell did you find that out?"

"Say man, you don't sound too good. Hey, Hanky. You sick?"

Mulraney pulled the cloth off his face. "No, the wife and I are in the tub and I got a cloth over my head."

"Very kinky, man. Go for it. Don't mind me. Man, I'll call you back later, dude. But like I was saying. The Hacker, man. That kid's good, even if he is a little prick. The Italian Stallion hates babysitting the little shit. Kid says he gets bored working on cracking the code to the judge's computer file, so as a diversion he works on other possible leads. He wouldn't say how he got this little nugget, and I'll bet we don't want to know, man. He just said check it out, and I called the hospital and, guess what, that mother's there, man. Under his own name. No shit."

"No shit," said the Hanky as he pulled the drain plug from the tub.

HACKER-CRACKER

In his hotel room, Jethro Wilmore busily poured over reams of paper given him by the Homicide Bureau. Jethro's brilliance was only outshone by his amorality and lack of judgment. He was like a beautiful new ship, fitted with all the latest in technological machinery, but lacking in one basic component—a rudder. Prison psychologists opined that this condition may have been produced by his childhood, when his parents used the television as his constant babysitter, pacifier, and entertainment. Jethro learned his value system from the nighttime soaps.

In search of the password to unlock the floppy disk file, the Hacker had asked to read everything available about Judge Knott: "The password is somewhere in the judge's history, so give me everything you can get on him. Also, I want one hour a day out of this room to stretch my legs and breathe free air."

Upon hearing the request, Bureau Chief Dwight Francis Lorton said, "Give the little bastard what he wants. The commish wants a lead. The mayor wants a suspect in custody. The press wants a story. And I want that goddamned computer file opened now! The answer to this case is in that lousy floppy disk. I can smell it."

So NYPD obliged Jethro and gave the little bastard some free time and all their investigative reports of the murder, which the Hacker eagerly read like a page-turner novel. He had everything: the judge's home and office records, his mail and correspondence and phone records, the contents of his desk (you can learn a lot looking in a man's desk), his address books, calendars, magazine subscriptions, even the contents of his medicine chest in his chambers' bathroom.

In reading the boxes of material, Jethro learned more about Judge Yulburton Abraham Knott than anyone would ever want to know. He devoured the transcripts of the judge's last trial, *State* v. *Lyle Diderot*, with Wilkes defending; he also read the judge's docket of cases for the last ten years. More interesting reading came by way of the biographical material on the judge the cops got from Mrs. Judge Yulburton Abraham Knott. Here, the Hacker learned about the judge's deceased parents (Homer Knott, a bricklayer who rose in union ranks to become head of his local, and Agatha, homemaker mother of five), his siblings (brothers Noel and Howell, and sisters Lucretia and Mildred), his schooling (public all the way), health (remarkably good until the knifing), military (the highlight—he went to Korea in 1953 as an intelligence officer), and financial portfolio (his was modest; his wife's substantial—and separate).

The unexpected fun came with the reading of the lunatic futuristic essays on Perfect Justice written by Knott under the pseudonym Grotek. Jethro read about Hank and Frank, the leather-covered robotic policemen of the future who were merciless enforcers of the Computer Law; he read about the TCIs, orbital Techtronic Cranial Infiltrators, which could read minds from space and zap out the sociopathic thought-holder by activating a deadly, although somewhat inaccurate, laser device called the Cerebral Mushmaker.

To Jethro, a technofascist himself, these were delightful tracts, and his low opinion of the dead judge rose with each piece of futurist nonsense he read. Jethro and the judge had something in common: neither ever allowed the law to interfere with whatever in the hell they wanted to do.

From this information, the Hacker programmed thousands of possible password combinations to attack the mysterious locked floppy disk. Every one failed, but it was while reading the material that Jethro quickly figured that Snivlakno Trubluy was, very simply, "Yulburton K Alvin S" spelled backward. For this insight Jethro expected more than a pat on the back; he expected big concessions on his hotel accommodations. He told Detective Frank Fortunata that he wanted a TV, stereo, lots of CD albums, more room service, and some spending money. Most important, he wanted a promise in writing that he was not going to get any more time on his own beef. In fact, he wanted a dismissal.

Fortunata, the Hacker's liaison-guard to NYPD, detested the smartass kid but promised to take Jethro's demands to the chief. Fortunata called Chief Lorton from his hotel room adjacent to the Hacker's. He exaggerated the Hacker's demands only a little when he said, "Chief, the boy-genius is demanding a fifty-inch color TV with high resolution, a quadraphonic Sony sound system with all the heavy metal albums out in CD, a maid-cook on twenty-four-hour service to attend to his every need, and a raise in his allowance beyond the per diem he's getting."

Fortunata knew the chief hated heavy metal and giving raises. The chief responded, "That little sonova—"

"That ain't all, Chief. He says his one non-negotiable demand is a written promise that his case will be dismissed."

"Why that little shit. I'll tell you what—"

"Says we're a bunch of bumpkins for blowing the obvious, like missing that Snivlakno Trubluy bass-ackwards crap."

The chief said, "So, he comes up with a little minutia and thinks he's Sherlock Holmes, eh? Well, has our little Einstein figured out the goddamned password to the disk yet? Anything?"

"No," said Fortunata, "and ya know, Chief, I think the little worm knows that his worth will be spent once that piece of the puzzle is solved. I think he's stalling to keep from going back to jail."

As Fortunata knew, this last observation unpopped the champagne cork on the chief's anger. Lorton's words to Frank were loud and acidic as he moved into a short version of his patented Crucifixion Speech: "Listen to me, Frank. You scare the piss out of that little turd! Threaten him with MORE TIME IN CUSTODY! I need a lead! Now! Christ, I've got so many people pressuring me to make this case. The mayor's people, the commish, the press vipers, the public, and all my great admirers within the department who want this job. They're like dragons. And I feel the heat. So now you make that kid feel the heat, Frank. SIZZLE THE LITTLE BASTARD!"

FIZZLED SIZZLE

"Chief, you can count on me." Fortunata hung up. "It will be a pleasure." He smiled as he lay down on his bed thinking of how he would terrorize the Hacker in the morning.

Simultaneously, in the next room, the Hacker also hung up. As an information specialist, he knew the value of keeping on top of things, especially where his fate was concerned. In his spare time he had secretly hooked his phone line into Fortunata's to keep abreast of late-breaking developments.

The Hacker thought. SIZZLE ME! SIZZLE ME! THE KEY-STONE KOPS? NO WAY! IDIOTS! How on earth did these fools ever catch me? It's a disgrace to my intelligence! I almost deserve this fate for being so stupid. So now they want another lead. Hell, I could have solved the case already. It's obvious who did it. Okay. Here's an idea . . .

The next morning, before Fortunata could even utter his first hot threat, the Hacker provided him with the lead on the location of the stockbroker in San Francisco General Hospital. He hadn't figured how to get into the floppy disk file, but this was the best lead in the case so far, and Fortunata knew it.

BAGHDAD BY THE BAY

Within three hours of his bath, Mulraney was on a red-eye to San Francisco to see Albert Rhinestrum, his witness-suspect in the case of the murder of Judge Y. Knott. As soon as he was seated on the plane, he doped himself with an assortment of antihistamines, aspirin, coffee, nasal decongestants, and inhalers to prepare for the eventual descent from 35,000 feet to sea level. Unmedicated, Mulraney would certainly be in excruciating head pain from the effects of the changes in atmospheric pressure in his ears and sinus cavities. For normal people, the worst that happens is their ears plug up. For Mulraney, the pressure changes brought on explosive internal sinus pressures and unbearable head-splitting agony.

Just before the plane took off, Mulraney blew his nose to try and clear his inner-ear canals. The loud honking timbre of a goose filled the cabin. Several passengers turned around to look at the source of the loud sound. A small Latin-looking man seated to Mulraney's right gazed at him as if he were bubonic. Mulraney paid no mind. He was used to the attention his condition brought.

"Dude, you are a very sick man to drink that much plane java," said the man as they lifted off. The passenger noted Mulraney was washing down a handful of pills with his second cup.

"Yeah," said Mulraney as he downed the last drop. "I'm addicted to dark-colored hot water. It's consumer fraud to call this crap coffee. It's terrible."

"Like man, jet java's been stepped on a hundred times. Gimme that espresso. Man, now that's good shit. Really."

With that last comment, Mulraney closely looked at the Latino-appearing man next to him. He was small and skinny and his brown, oily face was flat, almost featureless. Yet, his body, even at rest in a plane seat, pulsated like it had been injected with a thousand cc's of pure energy.

Mulraney noticed the expensive, tasteless clothes, the dark tinted glasses, the diamond earring, gold rings, the gold Rolex on one wrist and the gold identification bracelet on the other. Mulraney knew this guy. He had seen him hundreds of times in the city. This was Mr. Coke Dealer.

"I could use some espresso," said Mulraney.

"Well, you ain't gonna get no expresso on this jet plane. Least not in coach. Man, I can't believe first class is full. I never fly back here, but tonight I couldn't even buy my way up front. I'll bet most of the jerks in first are airline employees flying free, and here I am ready to pay top dollar to go coast to coast. Can you believe it? Really!"

Mulraney grunted a response. He wasn't much interested in striking up a conversation with a dope dealer, but the dealer couldn't keep his mouth shut.

"Say man, you don't look so good. All them pills and stuff are probably worse than your disease. I can give you something for some lift, man. Good shit. Really."

Mulraney winced at the thought of what was to come. Busting this asshole in the middle of the night while airborne on a jet plane bound for the coast was not at all what he wanted to do. He was tired and wanted to sleep.

Mulraney tried to give the dealer an out. "Say hey, we're already at thirty thousand feet. That's pretty high. High enough for me."

"Dude, you ain't even left the ground yet till you tried some of this shit I got. It's really got legs. Better'n legs, it's got wings."

Mulraney's head ached. He didn't want to do it, but he was given no choice and duty called. "Okay," he whispered to the dealer, "I'll show you mine if you show me yours."

The dealer looked puzzled for a second, but then figured Mulraney was talking about flashing his buy money. Displaying a tight-lipped grin, he reached into his pocket and pulled out a clenched fist. Mulraney reached into his jacket pocket and also pulled out a clenched fist.

"Okay, man, on the count of three we open our hands and switch. But very discreetlike, you know," said the dealer softly. "Uno. Dos. Tres."

The dealer opened his palm just above Mulraney's lap. Resting there was a tiny glassine envelope of a white powdery substance. The dealer's grin widened as he looked at Mulraney's hand as it slowly opened.

"SHEEEIIIIIIIIIITTT!" The dealer's saucer-sized eyes bulged. In Mulraney's hand was a shiny badge which flashed the initials of the NYPD.

"That's right, asshole, a stinking badge. Really. We're over New York and you're under arrest." Mulraney quickly grabbed the dealer's wrist and cuffed him to the arm of the seat. He then informed the stewardess to call ahead and have the San Francisco police available when they landed.

Mulraney gave the dealer his rights. "Asshole, I'm gonna try to sleep and you are gonna keep your mouth shut so as not to disturb me, 'cause if you do, I'm gonna have to ask you to step outside. Got it?"

But silence was not in the cards. For the rest of the flight the dealer whispered sweet supplications into the plugged right ear of the half-awake Mulraney, imploring him to: "Gimme a break, man. I can make it worth your while. Really.

"Man, you don't want to waste your time on a little beef like this. Think of all that court time, the continuances, the paperwork. My lawyer will subpoena you to court on your vacation. It ain't worth it. I'm gonna get probation anyway. Really.

"I'll get into a rehab program, man. Really. Narcanon, I think they call it. Or is it Cocanon? Hey, I promise I won't do it again. Really."

As the plane descended for a landing, Mulraney's head started splitting, and Mr. Coke Dealer, convinced that he was about to go into custody, finally ceased his importunings for a break and concluded with a sincere expression of his feelings: "Pig, you are one cold motherfuckin' douche bag. You planted that shit. You got no witnesses. My word against yours. I'm gonna love watchin' my mouthpiece carve you two new assholes in court."

Mulraney said nothing in return. As soon as they landed and the passengers disembarked, he asked for the pilot, copilot, and a stewardess to come to his area of the plane. He told them of the arrest and said he wanted witnesses as he searched the man's clothes and carryons.

Before Mulraney even started searching, Mr. Dealer was screaming, "Plant! He planted all that shit on me! I've been framed!" Mulraney pulled ten glassine envelopes out of his pockets. From his carryon bag Mulraney found fifty more as well as two baggage-check stubs.

DEAD END

Inside the airport, Mulraney delivered the dealer and the evidence to the awaiting cops and wrote out an affidavit they could use in getting a warrant to open his suitcases when they came out of the cargo bay. Then, tired, head aching, and cranky, he taxied into the city and to the hospital.

At the registration desk he identified himself and was told that Albert Rhinestrum was on floor Five A. Room 513, to be exact. The lady at the desk looked at him funny as he asked if he could go right up. She seemed flustered for a second and then said to him, "Yes," but it came out like, "If you're crazy enough."

On the fifth floor, Mulraney made the walk down a hallway. Each room was occupied by a bug-eyed, emaciated man with a white sheet. Some had the sheets over their heads, some twisted around them like togas, others balled them up like pillows. Some of those that appeared conscious and awake were moaning. It didn't take long to figure that this was the floor for patients with AIDS. Home for human suffering. Bodies wasting. The fatality floor.

Toward the end of the hall was the TV room. Several patients in their bed sheets were slouched in chairs with faces pointed in the direction of the TV. Vacant eyes bulged out of thin, twisted, gaunt faces which bared the alienation and agony to which the terrible disease sentences all who carry it. The TV was not on. No one spoke.

Mulraney walked through the TV room toward Room 513. When he got there, he saw a man lying flat on his back, with his eyes half open and unseeing, apparently staring at the TV which was high in a corner where the ceiling and walls met. Albert Rhinestrum, emaciated and breathless, looked like a baguette of bones.

His TV was on. The surprise new hit of daytime TV was on— Jack Twink's quiz show called "Battle of the Network Savants." This show pitted an idiot savant against an almanac. The objective was for volunteers from the audience to stump the savant with questions they picked from the almanac.

"Now James, for ten thousand dollars, according to the almanac, page 145, what is the name of the man executed in the New York's electric chair whose last words were, 'I am about to prove that wood conducts electricity?' "

"Frederick Wood," stated the savant correctly, much to the amazement of game-show host Jack Twink and the questioner from the audience.

Mulraney turned to look at the face of Albert Rhinestrum. Albert was not watching television. He was dead.

Mulraney called out to a nurse. "Yeah," said the nurse, "he died about an hour ago. I haven't had time to move him downstairs yet. Better get it done now, though." She called for an orderly to move the dead man downstairs.

Mulraney introduced himself to the black orderly who came to push the gurney down to the morgue. He spoke without prompting. "Sorry, brother. He your friend? Another holocaust victim. Look at him. Sorry, but he looks like what they found at Auschwitz. That is what's happening. Must be the same in New York. Right?"

"Right," said Mulraney.

"This is the new holocaust, brother. Just like with the last one, nobody gives a shit 'cept those affected. These poor guys can't even get the latest drugs available. All given the death penalty. So many bright young men dying every day now. It gets to you. It's awful, man. I'm gonna quit."

Mulraney asked, "How many have you lost this month?"

"Shit, I must have taken ten guys down here myself. I dunno the total. It's bigger than anyone on the outside thinks, and getting bigger every day. This guy was special. Rich, smart, nice. Spent tons of money looking for the miracle cure. He told me he lived several months in Paris at the special hospital there looking for a miracle remedy. Looks like he found the only cure there is."

"What else do you know about this guy?"

"Not much. Don't pay to get to know these guys good 'cause then it takes something big outta you when they go. Takes enough as it is. They all go, sooner or later, and if you get too involved, it'll break you in half like a matchstick. So you keep some distance. Most of them understand. But this guy, toward the end, he was real nice. Gave all his money away."

After pumping the orderly dry of information, and there wasn't much more, Mulraney went back to Room 513 to look for anything that might connect Rhinestrum to the late Judge Yulburton Abraham Knott.

THE HACKER THINKS

So those sonsabitches want a solution, eh? Ain't good enough that I give them the only leads they got in this lousy case so far. Ungrateful bastards! But I ain't doing no more time on my beef, no matter what! No way! I ain't going back to jail. This password. I can crack it. I know Knott now. I know how he thought. I know the dude better than anybody. Even his old lady. He'd code this file with something from his crazy essays. Let's see . . .

The Hacker typed in: HANK AND FRANK.

Nothing. The computer read back: FILE LOCKED.

GROTEK.

FILE LOCKED.

ORBITAL TECHTRONIC CRANIAL INFILTRATORS.

FILE LOCKED.

CEREBRAL MUSHMAKER.

FILE LOCKED.

He had a feeling he was close. The password came from the futurist essays. He knew it. He kept pulling words and phrases from the essays to use as possible passwords, but after each entry, the computer responded in the usual fashion—"File locked."

Then he typed in, PERFECT JUSTICE.

The computer clicked. The blank screen filled with words. Jethro's heart began beating fast. I cracked the damned code! I am unbelievably brilliant! This was an act of pure intuitive genius! I can hear freedom ring! Perfect justice! For me!

But after reading the first words, Jethro gasped, "Oh, shit!"

— 12 —

The Plant

*"One cloud does not make a storm,
nor one falsehood make a criminal."*
CHARLIE CHAN

*"We're gonna arrest him. Let God and the D.A.
sort out the details."*
CHIEF DWIGHT FRANCIS LORTON

The Hacker read his computer screen:

For the government to launch the massive android-as-police-man-soldier in the War on Crime, and the equally essential Random Android Brief Inquiry (RABI) Test, would require the rubber stamp of approval of a final obstacle. The Law.

The test court case in the Supreme Court Computer was filed with the singular purpose of establishing the lawfulness of the android program and particularly the right to RABI detentions. And who better to design the legal strategy and argue the case for the government than retired Justice Moriarity?

His stunning victory for the two programs came in the case, *ICBM Police Software Products and Associated Government Subcontractors* v. *American Civil Liberties Conglomerate*. Ironically, it was one of the first cases ever decided with the participation of the newly appointed supercomputer, Justice Dray Giga Flop I, sitting as a justice on the court. (Today, of course, all of the justices on the Supreme Computer—as it is now called—are humanoid computers).

The Supreme Court Computer, speaking through Justice Flop in his first opinion, said that what was required to decide the case was a reasonable balancing of the interests involved. On the one hand, there was tremendous lawlessness in the streets. The rights of the lawless would have no weight.

Considering the brevity of the androidal detentions of citizens on the street, the high degree of accuracy in detecting criminals by such random stops and inquiries, and the overriding need for public order in a free and submissive society, the balance was easily struck in favor of the constitutionality of implementing the RABI program—at least as long as the error ratio for erroneous stops and punishments did not exceed 5 percent.

Justice Flop's opinion stated, "Statisticians tell us that true statistical significance begins at about 5 percent; thus, an insignificant number (i.e., less than 5 percent) of unfortunate false positive RABI test stops and punishments of criminal suspects will not cause the constitutional derailing of this splendid technological program benignly designed for the common good and desired by the overwhelming majority of our citizens and humanoid resident-aliens."

The Hacker could not believe his eyes. Is that all there is? Another Judge Knott weirdo essay about perfect justice? This is it? THIS? After all that work? Jethro thought of the ramifications of his discovery. If he turned over this worthless crap to the NYPD, he would be finished. No deals. No dismissed case. No liberty. No nothing. This would not do. Not at all.

Quickly, he went to work. He entered a block command and erased the entire file. Then, relying on the evidence provided him by the NYPD, he began typing in passages which would prove far more useful to the judge's murder investigation and—surprise, surprise—to the liberty of Jethro Wilmore, the Hacker-Cracker.

MULRANEY & LORTON

"I want Scribner arrested, Mike," said Homicide Bureau Chief Dwight Lorton.

Mulraney, jet-lagged, smelling like last week's garbage, head aching and sneezy, had just arrived from JFK with the news of Albert Rhinestrum's death in San Francisco. He wiped his face with his bare hands and felt the accumulated bear grease. He was in no mood to make any arrest.

"For what? We haven't got a murder beef on the clerk. Not yet." He wiped his nose with his shirtsleeve. He was tired and irritated. His journey was a round-trip to a dead end. Now the chief wanted to solve the bureau's biggest murder case with an arrest based on little more than suspicion of the heinous crime of insider trading.

"Yes, we do. Look at this." The chief threw on his desk a computer printout with the gusto of a hearts player slamming the queen of spades. "This proves the sonovabitch has been lying to us all along. Scribner told you he didn't know anything about the judge's finances. Look at that. He and the judge have been coinvesting in the stock market for ten years using insider information they got at the courthouse. Look at this! Look at it!"

The chief excitedly pointed to the document as Mulraney turned his tired eyes to the papers on the desk. There, in neat columns, were the dates and amounts of investments along with the names of the stocks and their current worth. The final two columns were titled "Knott" and "Scribner," and contained the amounts their respective shares were worth.

"That," said Lorton triumphantly, "cinches it. You will note that the figures exactly match those we found at the brokerage under the client name of Snivlakno Trubluy, which happens to be the names of Alvin S and Yulburton K spelled backward. The only addition on this document, and a very nice one at that, is the division of money between the judge and his clerk."

OPEN AND SHUT

Mulraney's eyes were too bleary to focus on the numbers before him. He took the chief's word for it and said, "So what do we arrest him for? Lying to a cop? A 10(b) (5) rap? Where's the murder beef in this?" He sneezed suddenly. There was no time to catch it with his hanky. The explosive sneeze-breeze lifted several of the computer papers and coated them in a fine phlegm film.

The chief's doughy white cheeks reddened. "Bless you! Damn you! God, man! Look! The beef is buried six feet under! How much more do you want?" Lorton was electrified. He got that way every time he was about to close a big case. For him, closure meant escape from his perceived crucifixion at the hands of the mayor, the commissioner, and the press for having failed to crack the city's biggest unsolved homicide case.

"You want evidence, man? Listen up, Hanky. The old bag of bones clerk and the judge made millions over the years. Then one day, just as Scribner's gonna be put out to pasture in a blissfully rich retirement, the judge tells him the money's all gone. Stolen by their broker, who's just been notified he's got six months to live and decides to go in search of the miracle cure for AIDS.

"Now, Scribner's been waiting for ten years to put his hands on the money. He doesn't believe the judge. He thinks the judge has either blown it all or is just greedy and is going to keep it all for himself. His whole dream of a luxury retirement is gone. You know what that leaves Scribner with, Hanky?"

"Yeah, his measly civil service retirement." Mulraney knew full well what Lorton thought, but he was too fatigued to play twenty questions. He sneezed again.

"No, damn you, it gives him one helluva motive. M-O-T-I-V-E. And you know what else he's got? He's got opportunity. That's O-P-P-O-R-T-U-N-I-T-Y. He's got access. He's the only person near the judge at the time of the crime. He's the last person to see the victim alive. Most killers are."

"AAAACCCHOOOOOO!"

"And we've got evidence, Mike. We've got his fingerprint on the murder weapon. The angle of the stab wound is consistent with a right-hand thrust, and he's right-handed. He's found with the judge's blood all over him. And we know he tried to call an attorney that very night while waiting to be interrogated. It's a solid case. He lied through his ass to you about his relationship with the judge and their crooked investments. Why? Because it was his motive to kill."

"AAAACCCHOOOOOO!" Mulraney sneezed again, without commenting on the chief's analysis. He was not impressed, but he knew the chief had his mind made up and that it was useless to oppose him other than to say, "All that doesn't mean we've got a provable case."

"Hanky, what the hell do you want? You think the guy's gonna come here on his knees to give us a confession? You think he's gonna beg us to arrest him? No, we got the bastard on the basics: motive, opportunity, evidence, especially the lies. We're gonna arrest him. Let God and the D.A. sort out the details."

"Well, I haven't slept in two days, Chief. So if you want him busted, get Jaime and Frank to grab him."

"Not to worry, Hanky. I've already sent them to the courthouse to take him in. I tipped the press too. They oughta be here any time now. But I want you to talk to him, Mike. He knows you. See if you can shake out a confession. That'll make it open and shut."

TV ARREST

Alvin Scribner was arrested in the middle of the workday at the clerk's office with cameras rolling and the whole world watching. Because of Lorton's convenient tip, the television stations were there to telecast the blessed event live to the city.

Detective Jaime Perez cuffed Alvin's trembling hands behind his back while Detective Frank Fortunata read him his rights. Alvin's coworkers surrounded them and watched.

"Gotta read this to you, Scribner. You've heard these a million times in court, but you know I gotta read 'em to you. You have the right to remain silent."

"For as long as you can," whispered Perez. Then he laughed.

"Shut up, Jaime. You have the right to an attorney—"

"If you are loaded with bucks."

"Shut the fuck up, Jaime . . . and if you cannot afford one—"

"The Legal Aids will surely be anointed. They might actually come see you too."

"Pay no attention to this guy, Scribner. Look, you know your rights. You're up on a murder charge. You wanna say anything or not?"

Alvin Scribner had not heard a thing the two cops had said. The shock of the arrest was like having his brains vacuumed out. Alvin was deaf and dumb and senseless. If the psychiatrists diagnosed him then, they would say he was in a transitional disassociational fugue state.

Which means he was scared shitless out of his mind.

Getting no response from their collar, Fortunata and Perez each grabbed an arm and half carried the paralyzed Alvin out of the office and down the gauntlet of horrified coworkers, indifferent cops, and a curious group of gawkers made up of judges, lawyers, witnesses, court-watcher groupies, and homeless people who live in the courthouse.

PANIC

Frenetic reporters pushed each other and pulled their cameramen to get into position to ask the accused a penetrating question to enlighten their audiences of thousands. Fear and panic were in the air, but it was not over Alvin's fate. No, what was in the air was the reporters' dread of being beaten out of THE BIGGEST STORY OF THE YEAR. It was a much bigger fear than the usual "my God I might lose the Pulitzer if I don't get the story" fright.

This was THE BIG FEAR: if someone else got a closer camera angle or fired off a better question, it might garner negative attention back at the station. Negative attention on this, THE BIGGEST STORY OF THE YEAR, could mean the loss of the good story assignments, or no raise, or a lecture on the need to be aggressive in getting THE NEXT BIGGEST STORY OF THE YEAR. And it could mean—God forbid!—a demotion, or even termination.

And then what? No job. No money. No bills paid.

And then what? Humiliation. Eviction. Starvation. Eventually, the whole family . . . dead!

So there was good cause for these high-strung, obnoxious reporters and camera people to elbow, shove, swear, grunt, shout, spit, bite, and kick their way to get THE BIGGEST STORY OF THE YEAR—they had to be the best on the scene to get THE BIG STORY. It was a matter of life and death—theirs and that of their families!

At least, that's the way they saw it.

As Alvin passed his position in the reportorial gauntlet of yelling, gesticulating humans waving mikes and cameras, Morty Qualls of Channel 79 TV shoved a microphone into his face so hard it nearly floored him. He then fast-talk-shouted a question all of his colleagues were drooling for Alvin to answer: "Alvin Scribner, you're old, you're bald, you're frail, you're on the verge of retirement at full pay, and now you're under arrest for ruthlessly murdering your former boss, Judge Yulburton Abraham Knott. Right now, tell our viewing audience, if you'd just look this way, Alvin. Alvin, turn in this direction. Alvin, turn around! ALVIN SCRIBNER, TELL US, DID YOU MURDER KNOTT OR NOT?"

Alvin's mind was numb. Electrical activity, if it hadn't ceased, was in a temporary brownout. Regaining his balance, he continued silently in the four arms of the law to the door and then out.

It was a typical arrest in a high profile case, effecting maximum mortification and terror on the citizen-accused. Hauling a chained defendant like a mad dog out of his workplace with flashbulbs and klieg lights popping was the perfect opportunity to start saturating the public with the stain of guilt. And, what the hell, if the accused ultimately got lucky and got off, at least the cops got in a few good licks.

AT THE BUREAU

Mulraney sneezed and blew his nose as Perez and Fortunata escorted Scribner into the Dorm. They sat him down in front of the Hanky. Perez said, "We read him his rights, but he ain't said a word, Hanky. I mean nothin' at all."

Alvin's nearly bald head was trembling and sweaty. His eyes squinted and twitched rapidly. He looked at Mulraney and weakly mouthed his first words: "I'm innocent."

"Hey, the suspect speaks," said Fortunata.

"Hey, Alvin, the last innocent died on the cross," said Perez. "Give it up."

"You lied to me, Alvin. Look at this." Mulraney shoved the computer readout of the investments under Alvin's nose. It was the Hacker's forged file, which, while counterfeit, also happened to be true. It was forged because the judge's locked file had no such information on it; but it was true because it more or less represented the judge's and Scribner's investments under the name Snivlakno Trubluy.

Alvin looked at the file for a moment. His eyes enlarged when he saw the column listing the money split. "These figures are wrong," he said indignantly. "I never was to get a fifty percent share. The judge insisted on getting seventy percent."

"You lied to me, Alvin," Mulraney repeated.

"Why don't you tell us about it," said Fortunata.

"Yeah, Alvin," said Perez. "C'mon, you'll feel better talkin' about it. Maybe we can help you, man. Like maybe you were angry 'cause the judge, he took all your hard stolen money, and like maybe you stabbed him a little bit in the back by accident."

Alvin looked at his three interrogators. Tears rolled down his yellowed and wrinkled cheeks. He sat up in his chair. "I've said enough." He pulled out of his shirt pocket one of Wilkes's business cards and read from the preprinted announcement on the back. Under the title READ THIS TO THE COPS IF ARRESTED, Alvin read: "Upon the advice of counsel, I assert my total innocence and also my right to counsel and to remain silent."

With that, his almost hairless head fell to the beaten gray metal table where his arms cushioned the fall. He began bawling like a baby.

FEE TALK

If monsters like Adolf Hitler, Joseph Stalin, Benito Mussolini, or Pol Pot, to name just a few recent mass murderers, had been arrested in New York for the first-degree murder of ten or twenty million souls, they would most certainly have called upon John Wilkes to defend them. Whether they could have afforded him is another matter entirely.

(Someone once said: "Kill one, and you're a murderer; kill millions, and you're a statesman.")

It was no surprise that Alvin Scribner had called on Wilkes for advice long before he was arrested. Formal arrangements, the fee, had not been negotiated. When we heard of Scribner's arrest on the radio, Wilkes and I dashed to the bureau to see our man in distress.

We found Scribner in a small room, waiting to be taken to court for arraignment and then to the Tombs. Wilkes sat down in front of him and came right to the point. "Alvin, we've already talked about this possibility. Now, we've got to deal with the matter of the fee before I can go down to court with you and enter a formal appearance."

Scribner was relieved to see us. "Thank God, you're here. You warned me about all this, Mr. Wilkes, but you just cannot prepare yourself for it. It was horrible. They arrested me in front of everyone. Cameras too. Don't get mad. I . . . I . . . I said a few words to the officers."

"Alvin," said Wilkes, "first things first. About the fee."

I always admired the direct manner of Wilkes's fee talks with clients. He got right to it. No use wasting time if you can't hook up. I could never do it as well. Nor could I ever even quote the extraordinary amounts Wilkes not only quoted, but almost always collected.

Alvin's relief quickly turned to visible distress at the outbreak of fee talk. His voice weakened to little more than a whisper. "Mr. Wilkes, my only asset was the money in the stock account. That's gone. I don't have any money in the bank. My house is mortgaged to the hilt. Maybe I could assign you my civil service pension?"

I laughed to myself. Wilkes was strictly a cash-on-delivery kind of guy. If Alvin had no assets, he would not have the indomitable John Wilkes defending. I waited for Wilkes to end the interview.

"No," said Wilkes. "I've thought about this a lot, Alvin. I'm prepared to defend you for an assignment of all of your literary and movie rights, such as they may be, in the story to this case."

WHAAAAAAAAAAAAAAAT? I was shocked! This was impossible! My ears were surely deceiving me. Wilkes never defended anybody for anything except cash on the barrel head. Legal tender. Coin of the realm. Real moolah. Mr. Green appearing in person. Nothing less. Taking an assigned interest in the life story of a shriveled clerk suffering from Civil Service Alzheimers, even one accused of murdering a judge, was about as profitable as retailing chocolate-covered chicken lips.

PRO BONO

"So this is to be a *pro bono* murder defense," I said sarcastically. I was confused. This was not Wilkes. Where was the slip of paper with the enormous retainer figure on it, the figure that always sucked the breath out of so many prospective clients, causing many of them to part forever with their earthly lucre?

"I know he's innocent," said Wilkes.

"Bless you, Mr. Wilkes," chimed Alvin.

Innocent? Innocent! Innocence never had the slightest thing to do with Wilkes's quest for the king's ransom as a retainer. It was never considered by Wilkes during fee talk. Much more relevant was the difficulty of defending because of the enormous amount of proof against the client. Now *that* was pertinent to the amount of the fee. But for Wilkes, considering innocence in fee talk was as out of place as a federal judge mentioning probation at sentencing.

I said, "The Indians made a better deal selling Manhattan."

Wilkes looked at me without replying. There was something he wasn't telling. Alvin damn well *knew* there was something Wilkes was not saying—he was not quoting his normal outrageous fee. Scribner readily agreed to terms: "Where do I sign?"

"Mr. Schoonover will draft the proper contract which will warn you of the potential conflict of interest in me taking literary and movie rights to your case. You see, some people might say that I would pump up the publicity in this case to make more valuable the book and movie rights. That might not be in your best interest, but it might be in mine. That sort of thing."

I still could not believe the words I heard. This was totally out of character. He would never do a case, much less a murder case, for nothing, unless . . . unless . . . unless Scribner had something on him. Like what? Wilkes had been contempted by Judge Knott half a dozen times the day of the murder. That's motive. Like how about Wilkes going to the courthouse just before the murder to pick a fight with Judge Knott? That's opportunity. Maybe Wilkes saw Alvin do the dirty deed, or worse, maybe Alvin saw Wilkes . . . Jesus! Wilkes, the killer of Captain Muddock, the tormentor of his youth. Now, the killer of his current tormentor, Y. Knott? Why not? Christ! Talk about conflicts of interest! Is the real murderer representing the accused murderer, or is the attorney the only eyewitness to his client's crime? How do I write *that* into the contract?

While I thought of death and conflicts, Wilkes said to his new client, "It's just as we talked about earlier, Alvin. Now, you and I must plan for bail. Did you contact your relatives?"

DESPERATE STRATEGY

That afternoon, Scribner was arraigned for the murder of Judge Knott and Wilkes made an impassioned plea for the setting of bail. Any bail. Our client was old and infirm. He had no record. He had worked in the courthouse for thirty years without killing any other judges; and last, even though everyone thought he was guiltier than hell, he was presumed innocent.

It is said in law schools that the presumption of innocence is the mighty bulwark against wrongful convictions. In the courtrooms we put it a little differently. The presumption of innocence when added to a cup of warm spit leaves you with a cup of warm spit. Asking a judge for bail by arguing the presumption of innocence is like asking Hizoner to drink a glass of liquid Drano to cure his hiccups.

In answer to the motion for reasonable bail, the arraigning magistrate hiccuped with the expected firmness, "That'll be denied, counsel."

Back at the office, Wilkes paced the floor like a trapped cat. He was agitated. Over what? Bail for Alvin? He knew Alvin would never be able to come up with freedom's rent. To get it, we needed something extraordinary to show a court.

While he paced, I heckled him about the fee. "This contract is worthless and will be worthless at trial's end. It's going to cost us a fortune to defend! What gives?"

Wilkes continued pacing. "You're wrong, Schoon. Already got a call from an independent film producer who wants to talk about options for movie rights after the trial ends and if—"

"If what?"

"If the case proves to be more than that of a stupid little greedy clerk stabbing his boss in the back over money."

"You mean you've got to get Alvin acquitted *and* at the same time make the case sensational enough to be movie material?"

"Something like that. Actually, the producer would like it if we could also find the real killer."

"Ridiculous," I said, and went to my office while Wilkes continued his constitutional.

After about three miles of pacing, he yelled to me, "Schoon, prepare an *ex parte* order to permit Garfield Bonzo to enter the jail tonight and conduct a confidential lie detector test on Scribner. If he passes, it may be his pass out of jail."

It was a desperate strategy, but I jumped at the chance of doing something to get my mind off of figuring out who killed Y. Knott. Maybe the lie-box test would answer the question. I quickly prepared the order and got it before a master calendar judge for signing. This was a routine matter, and the judge signed it that afternoon. I relayed it to Bonzo before five.

GARFIELD BONZO

Bonzo was a typical polygrapher. Uneducated. Untrained. Uncouth. He was from South Carolina originally, about fifty, and so overweight that if he walked twenty feet, he had to pause to catch his breath. Not to appear out of shape, he used this opportunity either to light up a big cigar or take a puff—which he inhaled.

He always wore mismatched plaid sport coats and pants, and the patterns clashed like warring armies. Burnt-orange suspenders held his pants so high aloft that the belt line was several inches above his belly button. I never trusted a man who wore his pants that high.

Bonzo had a huge Lyndon Johnson–shaped head with floppy Dumbo ears, a long, fat foghorn of a nose, and beady eyes. His hair was thin, receding, and slicked back. One look at Garfield and you thanked God that lie detector evidence was inadmissible at trial. Any credence in him or his results would have evaporated the moment he set foot in the courtroom.

Nevertheless, long ago Garfield Bonzo was the head polygrapher with the NYPD, where he was reputed never to have passed any suspect on a test. This gave him a measure of credibility with prosecutors, police, and judges. Wilkes characterized his popularity with the department as follows: "Bonzo's NYPD tests had the reliability of a broken thermometer which always reads seventy degrees. Sometimes, by chance of that day's weather, it was correct; most times not. But if you liked your air temperature reading at seventy, it was a very acceptable result. NYPD liked Bonzo's results."

Surprisingly, after leaving the NYPD and entering private practice, Garfield started passing a few suspects on his damned test. A lie-box pass for Alvin Scribner on his murder beef might prove persuasive when mentioned at a future bail hearing.

Late into the night, Wilkes and I waited for Bonzo at the Woolworth. To fill time, I drafted the ridiculous retainer contract, all the while thinking it would be less complicated and just as profitable to do the case for nothing.

THE LIE-BOX ANSWERS

At about eleven Bonzo appeared, polygraph machine in hand; he waddled into the office with the results of his examination of Alvin Scribner. Slowly and carefully he spread several three-foot sheets of polygraph chart paper out on Wilkes's desk. Wilkes, impatient, said, "Well?"

Bonzo gasped for air from the thirty-foot walk from the elevator to our office. Then he said, "Y'all be quiet. Let me examine. Let me examine my paper."

He looked reverently down at his polygraph paper like it was the Shroud of Turin. Then he leaned over and peered within an inch of the wild squiggles on the chart paper and followed the up and down lines as they moved laterally to his right. All the while he was mumbling: "Very interestin'. Humm. Countermeasure? No, just the cell door slammin'. Humm. Vagus effect here? Nope, he burped. Humm. Staircase breathin'. Humm. No control reaction here. Humm. Systolic rise is steep and reactive on a relevant here and here. And WOW! LOOK AT THAT GSR! HUMM. HUMM."

"Will you shut the hell up and just tell me whether he passed your goddamned voodoo test!" yelled Wilkes. My friend was in no mood to endure more of the witch doctor's chanting.

HE'S GOOD FOR IT

"Well, sir," drawled Bonzo, "I don't think you want me to mathematically score these here charts. I could, you know. Very precisely. But I'd say, Wilkes, your guy is good for this charge. Unless we got a false positive, or a guilt-complex responder, or a bothersome outside issue, or a bad set of questions, or a mistake, or machine error, none of which is likely."

"Maybe what we got here is all of the above, to which I would add the obvious defects in the examiner!" howled Wilkes. "Alvin Scribner did not murder the judge, and I thought even a boob like you could figure that out. You flunk the Wilkes polygraph, Bonzo. I know ground truth and you don't."

Wilkes grabbed his jacket and headed out of the office. "Pay him his money, Schoon. Pay him for giving us his expert opinion that our client is a lying murderer."

"The lie box don't lie," said Bonzo as Wilkes headed for the door.

"Except when turned on," said Wilkes as he disappeared out the door.

I handed Bonzo his check in payment for telling us that our client was a lying murderer.

"Oh, I would never say that your guy is guilty," said Bonzo to me as his meaty, hairy hand grabbed his pay. "I am just sayin' that Mr. Scribner's reactions to the question of whether he murdered the judge are consistent with deception-indicated criteria."

HACKER

After the arraignment Detective Frank Fortunata went back to the hotel to continue overseeing NYPD's prisoner, Jethro Wilmore. Jethro was anxiously awaiting the good news. Hadn't he given the NYPD just the break they needed? Hadn't he opened the locked computer file and found the proof of Judge Knott and Alvin Scribner's secret stock fund? Hadn't that proved Scribner to be a liar? Wasn't it the motive for the killing? Hadn't he just watched them arrest their man on TV based on his leads? Now it was time for just desserts. It was time for the coppers to let him go free and forget about those felonies, the money he stole, and that prison sentence.

When Fortunata got back to the hotel, he didn't speak to the Hacker. He went to his adjoining room and called his girlfriend, a call the Hacker overheard through the tap he had put on the detective's phone. Jethro only listened long enough to hear one fragment of a sentence, but it was enough: "The snot-nosed brat's not gonna like going back to the joint—"

Instantly, the snot-nosed brat put down his phone, defeated the special door lock meant to keep him in his room, and escaped. It was an escape he could have accomplished at any time during his comfortable detainment at the hotel, but Jethro waited patiently for the cops and the district attorney to reward him with his freedom in return for his magnificent contributions in nailing Alvin Scribner, killer of Judge Y. Knott.

The Hacker breathed the free, polluted air of the city. He was looking forward to once again challenging the city's many alleged hacker-proof computer defense systems.

Meanwhile, Frank Fortunata finished his sentence: "—even if it's only for the night. Then the deal goes down and he's a *free* snot-nosed little brat."

— 13 —

Junior

"Our own interest is another wonderful instrument for blinding us agreeably. The fairest man in the world is not allowed to be judge in his own cause."
PASCAL

"Impossible to prepare defense until direction of attack is known."
CHARLIE CHAN

"Lasciate ogni speranza, voi ch'entrate!"
JOHN WILKES (& DANTE)

Sitting in the office just before our court appearance, I heard Wilkes laughing on the phone. There was nothing peculiar in this except that he had the receiver cradled between his ear and shoulder and was making jerky motions with his free hands near his mouth. It looked as if he were pantomiming playing harmonica.

"What the hell are you doing?" I asked as he hung up.

"I was talking to our erstwhile client, the buxom Ms. Becky Buttermilk, proprietor of the Love Tub Tumble. She wants to know when we're gonna make use of the free passes she gave us. Business must be slow."

I glanced at the moist threads of dental floss twisted around his fingers. Wilkes noticed my look. "Oh that. I was checking out something. Schoon, prepare a motion to continue Alvin's case based upon a medical emergency. It's obvious to me that I am in need of an urgent dental procedure tantamount to oral surgery, and I need it performed immediately."

"Like what?" I asked.

"I need my teeth cleaned. Think I can get a couple of weeks' delay of the trial for that, Schoon?"

He laughed, and was kidding, of course. Not that he wouldn't have tried it in another case; it was just that our client, Alvin Scribner, was old, infirm, and most important, in custody. He would not survive in jail long enough to appear for trial if Wilkes applied the Old Wine Defense and continued the case for the usual couple of years.

This was the most unusual of Wilkes's cases. No big fee, no likely suspects to blame, and no attempts at delay. The chemistry was all wrong. "Let's go." I said. "We'll be late for court."

COURT WALK

It was a cold November morning, and we walked quickly across the street from the Woolworth Building, through City Hall Park and up toward Foley Square. Despite the wind and cold, Wilkes was positively upbeat. "You know, Schoon, they really haven't got much of a case against Alvin. So he lied to the cops about his lucky investments with the late judge. Big deal. So all the money's gone and Alvin got none of it. Big deal. So he has his fingerprints on the knife. Big deal. So he's got blood all over him? Big deal. Where's the evidence?"

"*That* sounds like evidence to me," I commented.

"Easily explainable. Alvin found the body. He tried to remove the knife. Of course he has blood all over him and his print is on the blade. The thing is, he didn't have blood on him when the Mrs. first saw him just before they entered the chambers. And so he lied about the investments with the judge out of misplaced loyalty to his crooked boss or his own survival instinct. Big deal. Things aren't so bad, Schoon. The D.A.'s case is razor thin. With the right judge, it might never even get to the jury and Alvin will walk with a close shave."

Wilkes's euphoria was making him delusional. I said, "Yeah, ninety percent of the judges would direct the jury to return a verdict, all right. OF GUILTY! And if the case does get to the jury, then what? Shoot for manslaughter?"

"Sure, but we'll also take a stab at a full-tilt boogie acquittal."

TONGUE-TIED

The Criminal Courts Building in Foley Square is only a few blocks north of the Woolworth Building. It is a big, dirty black-green building of neo-Stalinist architecture that feels as alienating and dangerous as a day at a war front, or sunbathing at Chernobyl or, worse, a night in the Manhattan YMCA. It looks like what we call it—the Temple of Doom.

The front doors open like a big mouth out of which sticks a seemingly permanent tongue of entrants lined up for magnetometer inspection. The line is filled with a rainbow coalition of black and brown and white and yellow people, some dressed in street clothes, others in three-piece suits, some holding briefcases and others ghetto blasters. On this day, like every day, the Temple would spit out most of the entrants it had swallowed. Others would be digested.

The line usually elongates during morning rush hours and moves slowly into the building. The magnetometer is so sensitive, just about any metal larger than a gold nose ring sets it off. When that happens, the would-be entrant receives the up-close and personal treatment from the cop with the handheld metal detector. He carefully sweeps the detector over every nook and cranny of the suspect while five guards approach and watch as if violence is imminent.

As one waits in line watching this ritual, the air is tense with expectancy—someone, someday, maybe soon, maybe today, maybe right now—is going to pull out an Uzi and start spraying the place.

Such is the joyful mood upon entry to the Manhattan Criminal Courts Building. While Wilkes and I waited in line, Wilkes looked

around and said matter-of-factly, *"Lasciate ogni speranza, voi ch'entrate!"*
It was from Dante, and it captured the mood: "Abandon hope, all
ye who enter here!"

APPOINTMENT WITH DESTINY

In time, we passed sentry inspection, received official entry into the
Temple of Doom, and went up the filthy elevator to the master
calendar court. We went there for three reasons: first, to learn of the
appointment of a trial judge; second, to get a trial date; and third,
because if we didn't show up as ordered, we would be arrested and
dragged there in chains.

The most important issue was the selection of the trial judge. Of
course, we could not hope for a judge who would have the slightest
defense bias; such jurists, contrary to the popular mythology, do not
exist. The best we could hope for was a judge who cared more about
appearing to be impartial than in overtly joining the prosecution to
form a tag team bent on convicting our client. Such is the difference
today between a neutral magistrate and a hanging judge.

The matter of assigning a trial judge in this case would not be
easy. On the one hand, the victim was a judge, a fellow member of
the black-cape society who, if not loved by all of his brothers and
sisters, was at least one of them. And the thought of a court clerk
killing his own judge was as menacing a threat as a judge could
imagine.

On the other hand, not many judges really much cared for Judge
Yulburton Abraham Knott.

But on the other hand, this would be a high profile case with
plenty of photo opportunities and a chance to shine in the light of
the megamedia coverage. Advancement to the appellate court could
quickly follow a grand performance securing a conviction.

On the other hand, there was the huge bottom-line-nervous-
breakdown-early-retirement-inducing, "I wouldn't take that case if
you paid me" factor: John Wilkes was defending. That alone would
scare off most of the bench.

So as we waited in the packed courtroom for the master calendar judge, Judge Julius Dungus, to grace us with his earthly presence, whispered rumors of the names of judges we might draw and to which pain parlor (courtroom) we would be assigned pervaded the gallery. The names of Holmes, Cardozo, Brandeis, Marshall, Harlan, Frankfurter, Black, Douglas, Warren, or Learned Hand were not among them.

JULIUS THE JAWFUL

Julius Dungus was the master calendar judge. He was the oldest judge in the courthouse, and over the many years of his career on the bench acquired a number of nicknames: the "Two Thousand Year Old Judge"; "Julius the Just" (Julius's favorite, but only used until he ruled in his first case); "Julius the Just-*Awful*" (during his first twenty years on the bench); "Julius the *Jawful*" (during the last twenty years).

No one really knew how old he was, but it was remarked from time to time in the attorney's lounge that he had eaten dinner with Judge Joseph Force Crater on August 6, 1930, at Billy Haas's Restaurant on West Forty-fifth Street and was one of the last persons to see the judge alive.

He was short and stooped. His head was completely hairless, and so undulated with large wrinklelike folds of skin that he looked like he had traded hides with a Shar Pei. Other than that, his small head was unremarkable.

His full set of false teeth were too big for his mouth. They were often so loose that they made loud sucking noises when he spoke. Attorneys have debated over the last twenty years whether the nickname the "Jawful" came from the outrageously oversized choppers or from the contraction of the nickname "Just Awful."

The Jawful could read on a par with a second grader, although his comprehension was not that high. Despite being nearly blind, he refused to wear glasses. He used a magnifying glass instead to read pleadings and the court docket. When he looked up and into the well of the court or at the gallery behind, it was blind justice at work.

The interior of his brain had to resemble a postnuclear battlefield:

millions of dead brain cells littering an area occasionally illuminated by the spark of a few mutant neural synapses. What killed them was a mystery. Age had something to do with it. Overuse didn't. Julius was not senile. He was just stupid. //

Over the decades, lawyers coming out of his court would offer exasperated descriptions of their moments before Julius. There was the familiar: he's off his rocker; he's not playing with a full deck; he's a gallon short of a full tank; he's a few bricks shy of a full load; his elevator doesn't go to the top floor; he's not rowing with both oars; he's half a bubble off level; no one's in the cockpit; the stairs don't go all the way to the attic; the lights are on, but nobody's home.

Or, the interconnected: there's a screw loose (he's not wrapped too tight); he's got a hole in his head (he's lost his marbles); his chairs aren't all pulled to the table (he hasn't got a grip); his car lacks an ignition (he's not firing on all pistons); he hasn't seen the ball since kickoff (he should have worn his football helmet).

Or, the innovative: he's one sandwich short of a picnic; his smoke won't go up the chimney; the butter's sliding off his toast.

To the ultimate: If brains were gas, he wouldn't have enough to fuel an ant's go-cart once around the inside of a Cheerio.

Julius's courtroom demeanor had two distinct phases: REM sleep and conscious inattention. To accommodate this, the clerks put up signs on each party's table which read: SPEAK VERY, VERY LOUDLY TO THE COURT! So you yelled everything in his court. This either woke him during phase one or caught his attention during phase two.

You looked at Julius the Jawful and you thought: Good Lord! This man is defending the Constitution of the United States! And you prayed for your country and your clients.

THE VOLUNTEER

"People versus Alvin Scribner," called Julius's clerk after the old man crawled babylike up the three steps to the platform that held his throne.

"Miles Landish, assistant district attorney appearing for the People of New York," yelled Miles Landish, who was appearing for *some* of the people of New York. Alvin Scribner could be excluded from that group.

"John Wilkes for Mr. Alvin Scribner, who is present in court and in custody," hollered Wilkes to the judge. Alvin was seated at the counsel table, hunched over and trembling in fear.

Julius looked through his magnifying glass at the sheets of paper in front of him. With his head no more than an inch from the paper, and the glass between his head and the desk, he looked like a scientist in search of a lost molecule. He began reading slowly from the paper on the desk.

"People versus Alvin Scribner. As you all know, this is no ordinary case in which to select a trial judge. Ordinarily, it would be a random selection, but not today. Most of the judges on the bench have declined the case because of their very close relationship with our dearly departed and deeply missed brother, Judge Y. Knott."

UH-OH

Right away we knew there was trouble. It was bad enough that we had to hear all the popping sounds of Julius's false teeth sloshing around his gums, but the fact that he had a prepared speech meant that what was coming was a product of premeditated and premedicated thought. From this deduction and the language used, we knew Julius didn't write a word of the words he spoke; they lacked his characteristic stamp of see-Spot-run twaddle. This meant a darker, more intelligent force was at work.

The Jawful continued his slow script reading: "After the voluntary recusals, only a few judges were left to choose from, and of these, one fine, brave, and fair-minded jurist has, at my request, accepted the assignment. He has assured me that his relationship with the deceased was limited to a few casual lunches, dinners at each other's homes, weekend seminar trips, family weddings, golf outings, fishing trips, occasional socializings, gift exchanges at Christmas, as well as judges' meetings."

As Julius read these words, I felt Wilkes tense at the table. A familiar premonition came over him. I sensed it too. It was the old feeling that a public screwing was about to take place and that we, as usual, were to play the roles of screwees.

"And so, having prevailed upon this fine judge to abandon his heavy civil calendar for the time being and accept the trial of this case which is so important to the city, I now formally assign this case for all purposes to the Honorable Lester J. Throckton, Junior. Trial in three weeks. We are adjour—"

At the name of Lester J. Throckton, Jr., Wilkes went ballistic. He exploded off his chair to his feet. "THROCKTON? JUNIOR? THIS CASE? NOT THROCKTON! YOU'VE GOT TO BE KIDDING!"

He was livid, in shock, partially crazed. The Honorable Lester J. Throckton, Jr., faithful readers will recall, was the Sal Minchinzi, mob-sponsored judge who Wilkes defeated in a race to sit on the Supreme Court. During the campaign, Wilkes called Junior corrupt scum and a mafia stooge in his famous Scumbag Campaign Speeches.*

THE FAIREST OF THEM ALL

"He has assured me he can be fair to all parties," said Julius the Jawful. "We should be grateful he will take this case."

"Yes," yelled Miles Landish, "Judge Throckton would be an appropriate selection for this case. The People accept the appointment." The prosecutor turned his neckless, chubby head to Wilkes and beamed a broad smile.

Wilkes ignored Landish and protested to the judge. "BUT I PUNCHED OUT JUNIOR'S LIGHTS! I LITERALLY KICKED THE SHIT OUT OF HIM IN A FIST FIGHT DURING THE CAMPAIGN! THIS IS RIDICULOUS! I MOVE TO RECUSE HIM FOR BIAS!"

* All documented for history in *Wilkes: His Life and Crimes* (Ballantine, 1990), pp. 138–79. Wilkes actually won the election but was disqualified for technical reasons having to do with the wishes of a certain mafia don and city officials desirous of a normal life span.

Julius was now baby-crawling down from the podium when Wilkes hit him with this verbal fusillade. While on all fours, he tried to spit out the words "Recusal denied," but what came out instead were his teeth. They shot to the floor and chattered—"clickety clack, clickety clack"—some ten feet to the wall.

Julius the Jawful, jaws now empty, mumbled a barely decipherable "Adjourned," and crawled to where his teeth rested, picked them up, and disappeared out the door as the enraged Wilkes continued yelling sarcasms: "OH, WELL, THAT SURE AS HELL SOLVES THAT PROBLEM! HE WILL BE FAIR! THAT'S THE RULING! THAT SETTLES IT! WELL, THAT DOES NOT SETTLE IT!"

Even after the judge left the court, Wilkes continued yelling to the crowd of reporters, court groupies, and lookie-loos. This was a good tactic. Whatever Wilkes said would help us with the motion to kick Throckton off the case, and the more outrageous the comments, the better the odds of a retaliatory response from the judge and more grounds for kicking his butt off the case.

"I CANNOT BELIEVE HE WOULD TAKE THE CASE IN-VOLVING THE MURDER OF HIS BELOVED FRIEND, JUDGE KNOTT. AND I CANNOT BELIEVE HE WOULD TAKE A CASE I'M DEFENDING. LADIES AND GENTLE-MEN! DO YOU THINK IT FAIR THAT I HAVE TO TRY THIS CASE IN FRONT OF A POLITICAL SCUMBAG WHOM I HAD THE PLEASURE OF SO LABELING JUST BEFORE I PUNCHED HIS LIGHTS OUT? LET'S CALL THIS WHAT IT IS: THE BEGINNING OF A JUDICIALLY SPON-SORED LYNCHING!"

As the bailiff came to grab Alvin Scribner and take him back to his cell, he looked up from the table at his fulminating attorney and began to weep uncontrollably. Loud mournful sobs filled the court. I put my hand on Alvin's trembling back, and Wilkes came over to give support as well. Alvin continued wailing.

The prosecutor also came over, but not to give aid and comfort. He had a packet of papers in his hands. He said, "I'd cry too if I was caught red-handed killing a judge. Especially after having confessed to it . . ."

"Oh, bull," said Wilkes.

". . . to a clergyman in the jail."

Alvin's sobbing stopped for a moment and his head turned to Landish. The bailiff guided him to his feet. He looked to Wilkes and cried, "I never said a thing, Mr. Wilkes. Honest! It's a lie."

Landish threw a sheaf of papers on the table. "Here's the discovery on it, Wilkes." He looked at Alvin. "Read it and weep."

At this, Alvin recommenced his loud crying and sobbed all the way to the back door of the court, where he disappeared with the bailiff. Wilkes and I stared at the papers on the table as if they were our death warrants.

Wilkes fell heavily into the seat. The balloon of morning optimism had long since popped. He continued gaping at the papers and began a chantlike mutter: *"Lasciate ogni speranza, voi ch'entrate; lasciate ogni speranza, voi ch'entrate; lasciate ogni speranza, voi ch'entrate; lasciate ogni speranza, voi ch'entrate."*

RESCREWSAL MOTION

After getting screwed in the courtroom, which was often, Wilkes took part of his fury out on me in the form of assignments. This screwing was no exception. I was to prepare the motion to dump Junior off of the case for bias toward Wilkes, and I was to do it that night. I didn't mind. Most times when I'd write motions for Wilkes I dreaded it because they were either frivolous, boilerplate, hopeless, or so technical as to be incomprehensible to the most learned legal scholar. I knew they were never in danger of being read by the judge, much less granted. The law clerks, programmed to write "That'll be denied" in as many ways as can be written in the English language, would be the only humans to gaze at them.

So I usually didn't care much for staying up all night to grind out Wilkes's motions on demand. But this was different. This WAS an outrage. Anger, and a computer full of stock recusal motions to work from, propelled me. So did the morning *New York Times* which—thanks to Wilkes's girlfriend, reporter Adell Loomis—editorialized about the inappropriateness of the appointment of a judge "whose ugly political feud with Mr. Wilkes, which included an embarrassing physical confrontation, makes his selection exceedingly inappropriate."

Wilkes insisted on drafting his own affidavit to support the "re-screwsal" motion, as he called it. He wouldn't let me change a word of it. Since it is probably an unprecedented document in the history of law, I reproduce it in its entirety.

JOHN WILKES
LAW OFFICES OF JOHN WILKES
233 Broadway
New York, N.Y
Telephone: (212) 232-2222

Attorneys for Alvin Scribner

IN THE SUPREME COURT OF NEW YORK
BOROUGH OF MANHATTAN

PEOPLE OF STATE OF NEW YORK	) CASE NO. 89666
Plaintiff,	)
	)
v.	) DECLARATION OF JOHN WILKES
	) TO RECUSE JUDGE THROCKTON
ALVIN SCRIBNER,	)
	)
Defendant.	)

BEING DULY SWORN, JOHN WILKES DECLARES THAT:

1. I hate Lester J. Throckton, Jr. I hated his father too.
2. He hates me as much as I hate him. So did his father.
3. During our political campaign against each other for a judgeship, he called me many foul names and his supporters actually threatened my life.
4. During the same campaign, I called him, among other things: "a corrupt sonovabitch," "a two-bit scumbag mafia stooge," "a brainless nincompoop," "a lube job," "a tax cheat," "a sadist," and "a black-robed pimp." See Exhibit A, articles from the New York Times which ran all of my speeches, collectively entitled, "The Scumbag Speeches."
5. I was the only candidate who spoke the truth. (See paragraph 4)
6. Prior to a debate with Throckton, I was perhaps overstimulated by the accusations and death threats against me and was required to nail Throckton with one punch which rendered him unconscious. At the time, he was wearing makeup.
7. Only a kangaroo could feel comfortable in the court of Judge Throckton.
8. Judge Throckton APPEARS biased against me. He IS biased against me. He ALWAYS WILL BE BIASED against me and anyone I defend. It is an affront that he was assigned this case; it is an outrage that he accepted it.
6. My client, Alvin Scribner, is on trial for the murder of a judge friend of Throckton's by the name of Yulburton Abraham Knott. Mr. Scribner is entitled to a fair trial somewhere other than a courtroom fit only for Australian marsupials.

I declare under penalty of perjury the above is true.

John Wilkes

PLEAD TO THE SHEET

After he finished the declaration, he turned his attention to the confession papers Miles Landish had given us. On top of the stack was a letter from Mr. Landish telling us of the discovery he was providing and ending with the generous offer of a "plea to the sheet," which, in plea bargainese, means plead guilty to everything charged. It said, "In light of the overwhelming evidence against your client and this confession to a volunteer clergyman at the jail, I am empowered to make an offer which will be open for acceptance for only one day. Your client may plead guilty to the sheet, and the district attorney will not argue for more than the maximum allowable sentence. Also, the district attorney will not add any additional charges such as could be alleged for the misconduct surrounding the joint investments with Judge Knott."

As he read this to me, Wilkes paced the office. He continued walking around the office as he read the jailhouse confession of our client to one known as Father Harold Leech. Alvin's alleged admission to Father Harry was short and, one might say, to the point. Alvin reportedly said, "When I found out he took all my money, I stuck the no-good swindler in the back."

I groaned. Now the case was hopeless. They had motive; they had opportunity; they had evidence; and now they had Alvin's confession.

Wilkes, however, began to chuckle. I thought it might be the laughter of a man gone insane. I mean, there was only so much bad news a fella could take in one day. Then it got worse. His laughter turned to loud howling and he began laughing so wildly and convulsively, he fell to the floor.

"Father Harry Leech!" he roared while on his duff. "It's the Father Confessor! By God, this isn't such bad news, Schoon! This could be a break!" In a moment, he jumped to his feet, ran to the Xerox machine, and duplicated a sheet of paper. Then he dashed back to my desk with the single sheet in his right hand.

"Schoon," he said as he stood triumphant before me, "you deliver this to Miles Landish first thing tomorrow morning."

He released the paper and it floated like a feather down from Wilkes's hand to my desk. Laying before me was a very unique piece of legal correspondence created by Wilkes. I asked, "What the hell is this?"

"That," he said, "is our response to the Landish ultimatum."

Here is what he gave me:

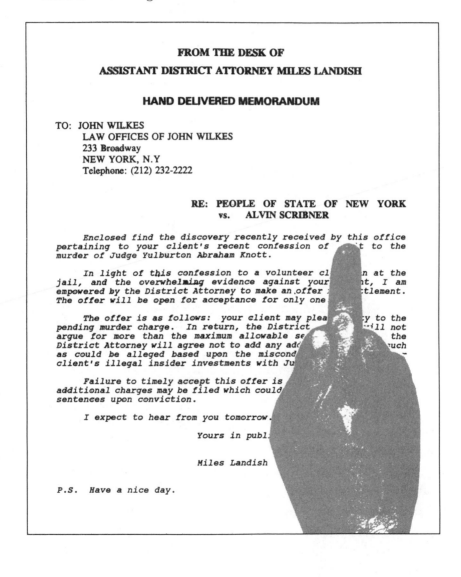

FROM THE DESK OF

ASSISTANT DISTRICT ATTORNEY MILES LANDISH

HAND DELIVERED MEMORANDUM

TO: JOHN WILKES
 LAW OFFICES OF JOHN WILKES
 233 Broadway
 NEW YORK, N.Y
 Telephone: (212) 232-2222

RE: PEOPLE OF STATE OF NEW YORK
vs.   ALVIN SCRIBNER

Enclosed find the discovery recently received by this office pertaining to your client's recent confession of ▢▢▢t to the murder of Judge Yulburton Abraham Knott.

In light of this confession to a volunteer cl▢▢▢▢n at the jail, and the overwhelming evidence against your ▢▢t, I am empowered by the District Attorney to make an offer ▢ ▢tlement. The offer will be open for acceptance for only one ▢

The offer is as follows: your client may plea ▢▢▢y to the pending murder charge. In return, the District ▢▢▢ll not argue for more than the maximum allowable se ▢▢ the District Attorney will agree not to add any add ▢▢ ▢uch as could be alleged based upon the miscond ▢ ▢ client's illegal insider investments with Ju ▢

Failure to timely accept this offer is ▢ additional charges may be filed which could ▢ sentences upon conviction.

I expect to hear from you tomorrow.

Yours in publ▢

Miles Landish

P.S. Have a nice day.

—14—

Ruby and the Voir Dire

"It takes very rainy day to drown duck."
CHARLIE CHAN

"Don't worry none. Da twelve we rack up ull never agree on nuttin'."
RUBY FULGIONI

Murder is an ugly crime to defend. Defending any case in the Temple of Doom is tough, but toiling in murder's gory muck compounds the difficulty. And when the victim is as innocent as a bystander, it's especially hard. But if the victim is a piece of work like Y. Knott, well, that's another thing entirely.

THEORY OF THE CASE

In all cases you need a theory of the defense. Maybe there is no doubt that the defendant did hack the victim to death with a hatchet. But maybe there is an explanation. Self-defense. Insanity. Alibi. Maybe all three. You might argue: "Did my client strike the fatal blows, ladies and gentlemen? Or, as we have shown, was he crazy someplace else thinking he was about to be assaulted by a group of cockroach-looking assassins from outer space?"

Immediately, images are conjured in juror minds of a wildly

free-swinging defendant far from the scene of the crime. He is chopping the air madly to fend off imagined oncoming hordes of giant acid-spewing insect aliens. He is defending himself. He is crazy. He is somewhere else.

It's a theory. It beats pleading guilty.

Or maybe the victim needed a little killing. Here, the theory of defense embraces the slaughter as a kind of public service—an act of waste disposal management. Jurors can relate to that. So maybe your client did shoot her husband in the back of the head while he was asleep on the couch. So what? He was a battering bastard, a drunken shiftless bum, and a faithless husband. He got what he deserved.

Of course, you can never verbalize such a moral justification for murder. Better to say, "Ladies and gentleman, this tragedy occurred to stop the ceaseless cycle of senseless violence that had driven this poor, maimed woman to the limit of human endurance. The gun was fired. Yes. But only as an act of anticipatory self-defense, an act that said to the sleeping, battering monster, 'You will beat me no more.' "

It's a theory. It beats pleading guilty.

In the case of *People* v. *Alvin Scribner,* we were finding difficulty coming up with a theory of the case. We had to merge Alvin's theory of defense ("I did not do it") with the prosecution evidence (which screamed, "YES, HE DID!"). Some of the prosecution evidence was irrefutable, and when you face irrefutable evidence, it is of utmost importance to harmonize it with the defense theory. In Alvin's case we lacked the harmonic voices to blend with all the prosecution evidence: the missing investment money, his admissions that he partook in insider trading with Judge Knott, the blood all over Alvin's shirt, his fingerprint on the blade, and now, the murder confession to Father Harry Leech.

The big problem for us was, Alvin's skinny little theory of defense was all we had for the moment, and it needed lots of bulking up. But it was a theory, at least, and it beat pleading guilty.

. . .

PTSD

Judge Throckton did not get around to responding to our motion to kick his butt off the case prior to trial. This was intentional. By not giving us his answer ("That'll be denied, counsel") until trial, he ensured there would be no way to take the issue to the appellate court for review. Judges like having rulings unreviewable. It gives them a sense of invincibility. In Junior's case, it guaranteed that he would preside over Alvin Scribner's trial.

When we made our usual race-walk toward the court that first morning of trial, it was with more than a sense of dread. Wilkes was positively suffering from an acute case of pretrial stress disorder. He was angry and jittery and stressed out as much as I've ever seen. I doubt he slept the night before. He had downed a full pot of espresso that morning, and the caffeine jolted him with a billion volts of internal electricity.

Wilkes had good reason to be concerned. We came to the court with a weak theory of the defense and little else. We faced a prosecutor armed with a ton of evidence and a black-robed butcher—put on the bench by the mob—of whom it was said (most often by John Wilkes), "He is the best judge money could buy."

THE BEGINNING

Before we even got close to the courthouse, the media maggots were swarming all over us. Cameras, lights, microphones of all sizes were crammed into Wilkes's face, while the paper-boys and girls, with pencils and pens pointed at us, joined in shouting out the usual penetrating questions.

"Gonna plead Alvin out today, Wilkes?"

"Just how many of Alvin's confessions does the D.A. have?"

"Is life the maximum sentence or is this a death case?"

Wilkes said only, "My purpose here today, ladies and gentlemen, is to ensure that innocence not suffer one more day." But the media would not take that for an answer and kept pestering him with stupid questions. So Wilkes said, "Get the hell out of my way so I can go do my job," and he began roughly pushing his way through the mob toward the Temple of Doom.

As a class, media people generally know no insult or embarrassment or good manners. They would not get out of our way. Instead, a slowly retreating army of loud question-yelling reporters surrounded us as we, like safari hunters in the jungle, slowly pushed and hacked our way from the street up the concrete stairs into the courthouse, through magnetometer inspection, into the elevator, up the elevator and off, and down the hallway into the courtroom known to us as Judge Throckton's pain parlor.

THE PAIN PARLOR OF THE TEMPLE OF DOOM

With our noisy entourage in tow, we invaded the crowded courtroom. The din in the pain parlor was even louder than that of our moving press party. More reporters were there, and on seeing Wilkes, they gave us the bum's rush. The surging force of a wall of human flesh body-slammed us back into the first media mob and then out of the courtroom into the hallway. We had to fight our way back in to the safety of the well of the court where, fortunately, reporters, courtroom groupies, and lookie-loos may not enter.

Wilkes got to the battered wooden defense table first and found a piece of paper resting there. "What the hell!" he yelled. He sat down heavily and read out an order from Judge Throckton. "Recusal denied," he read. "Both parties are requested to file briefs within one week on the issue of whether the affidavit filed by the defendant's counsel contains anything more than conclusionary defamations. If the pleading contains no more than such calumny, please answer the following question: Does defense counsel's pleading warrant referral to the bar association for disciplinary review and/or to the prosecutor's office for a possible perjury prosecution?"

Wilkes crumpled the order and threw it down right in front of the judge's throne. Such was the start to our day as we took our seats for the commencement of the trial of Alvin Scribner for the murder of Judge Yulburton Abraham Knott. Selection of the jury would come next.

RUBY

Wilkes didn't believe using professional psychological jury-picking consultants improved upon his own instinctive approach to selection of jurors. Generally, if Wilkes thought he could get along with jurors, if they were the type he might enjoy a lunch with, he kept them. If he disliked them, they were gone. That approach had served him well. He found that when he occasionally paid for one of the experts in jury selection, the costs were high, the process of jury selection too slow and complicated, and the results were not noticeably any better.

He thought that way until he ran into Ruby Fulgioni, a part-time Brooklyn tarot card dealer and jury selection expert. For him, Ruby was love at first sight.* She was about sixty, of plain and wrinkled face, frumpy, broad-nosed, slightly mustachioed, and just shy of five feet tall. Each day, she wore the same brown wool suit in declining stages of physical disintegration and increasing degrees of odor. Purple-framed glasses laden with sparkling rhinestones held up two Coke-bottle bottom lenses capable of stopping a cruise missile. This season, Ruby was dyeing her hair a flaming red and wore it in a page-boy style. She looked like Mr. McGoo in drag.

Wilkes loved her toughness as well as her smarts. She sounded like a retired prizefighter—pure Brooklynese—and she gave no quarter when it came to speaking her mind. We hired her because she could read people like a New York *Post* headline. One look from Ruby and she could spend an hour telling you the most intimate details about the person's life. Sometimes she was even right.

Most important, Ruby was cheap.

We heard her before we saw her that first morning of Alvin's trial. "Get your ugly meathooks off me buster or I'll brain ya. Now, lemme in." A burly bailiff was trying to keep her from entering the well of the court. I quickly went over and told the fellow she was part

---

* Ruby also helped Wilkes select the jury in his gallant, but ill-fated defense of Hank "the Lizard" Gidone. Ironically, that trial was held before the late Judge Yulburton Abraham Knott. See *Wilkes: His Life and Crimes* (Ballantine, 1990), pp. 94–96.

of the defense team. He looked at me like I was nuts, but he let her in. As she entered, she gave the fellow a hard look and spat out, "GESTAPO!"

As soon as Ruby got to our table, the bailiff hauled our client out of the holding pen. The first words Ruby said to us upon seeing poor Alvin Scribner being escorted to counsel table were, "Wilkie, are ya representin' anudder of the uptrodden today?"

"Down, down, downtrodden," said Wilkes. He put his arm around the now-seated Alvin Scribner. Our shriveled client was already showing his colors. His head was down on the table buried in his folded arms. He was quietly weeping.

"Dis here guy's yer defendant? Ya gotta be kidden!" said Ruby. She sat next to me on my right side. Alvin was to my left and Wilkes to his left.

"Well, yes he is," said Wilkes. "Perhaps not appearing as I would have choreographed, that is, standing in proud defiance and outrage before the scurrilously false charges laid against him, but a citizen in need nonetheless."

"Skip da bull, Wilkie." Ruby leaned over my lap to whisper to poor Alvin. "Don't worry none. Da twelve we rack up ull never agree on nuttin'."

Alvin lifted his head a moment to check out the source of these strange words. As soon as he focused on Ruby, his head fell heavily into his arms and he began groaning and squealing, "OH! OH! I'm gonna die in prison! OH! OH!"

Wilkes then noted our opponent, Assistant District Attorney Miles Landish, entering the war zone accompanied by Detective Mike Mulraney and a psychologist who would assist them with the selection of the jury. Wilkes looked at Ruby and said, "That's the opposition."

"Yeah, well, we'll kick der butts. You know da rules, Wilkie." [*See Ruby's Rules*] Ruby noticed the chambers door open and a figure appear. "Say hey! Wilkie, dat guy, didn't I see dat bum in da movies? *Retoin of da Livin' Dead*, wadn't it? Gees, it's da judge!"

• • •

THE MADE-UP JUDGE

Yes, it was Judge Throckton entering the courtroom. Wilkes and I didn't focus on his appearance as he mounted his throne. We were expecting immediate verbal fireworks from Junior in retaliation for the outrageous motion we had filed to kick his butt off the case. But Junior ignored us and greeted the crowd of potential jurors, members of the press, lawyers, witnesses, court personnel, groupies, lookie-loos, and the rest of the rabble present by informing us all that he was about to guide the jury through the process of jury selection.

Junior's opening act was a bit of a surprise. He was acting as if my partner hadn't just filed papers calling him "a corrupt sonovabitch," "a two-bit scumbag mafia stooge," "a brainless nincompoop," "a lube job," "a tax cheat," "a sadist," and "a black-robed pimp."

He was silent on the subject, content to let his court order deal with the issue for the time being. He appeared all business. He appeared in control. He appeared nonplussed. The reason: Junior came to this case utterly devoted to using the trial for one overriding purpose—to get even.

Junior looked cold and imperious up on the bench. This was nothing new. He was cold and imperious. He acted as if lording it over everybody were his manifest destiny. Though small, skinny, and runtlike in stature, Throckton looked tall on his throne, an appearance he enhanced mightily with a Whoopie cushion on his chair and a foot stool on the floor. When he stood, he was a foot taller.

Junior always wore makeup on the bench, a habit that began years ago when he ran against Wilkes for his judicial seat. The cheek powder made his face bleach-white. Junior's light powder-blue eyes were also disarming, if not shocking, because the whites blended into the very light blue irises so closely that it looked as if there were no color in the eyes at all. When combined with his powdered white cheeks, he had the bloodless appearance of an albino zombie. Overall, it was a spooky look, one you might expect to find when answering your door on Halloween.

Junior continued addressing the multitudes. "I need to ask you jurors this. Would the fact that this is a murder case, or the fact that the victim is the late, beloved Judge Yulburton Abraham Knott, or the fact that the defendant is the late judge's clerk, Alvin Scribner, or that the prosecutor is Mr. Miles Landish, or that the defense counsel is one John Wilkes, would any of this information cause any of you to believe you should not sit on this case?"

No hands raised.

"Good. Now, the fact that this case is destined to last in trial several weeks at least, would that cause any of you to have a problem sitting on this case?"

Every hand available for the raising went up, even those of the lookie-loos and courtroom groupies, even Alvin's (which I promptly pushed back down). Throckton looked over the forest of arms waving at him. "Please realize," he said, "that it is not only an honor to sit on a jury, but a civic duty."

No hands went down.

"This city's justice system cannot function without the volunteerism of ordinary citizens like you who give up a small piece of their lives in service to the great cause of justice."

No hands went down.

THE HARDSHIPS

Throckton was unperturbed. He had more in his arsenal than mere hopeful calls for charitable assistance. "Well, ladies and gentlemen, I trust those of you who are seeking hardship excusals have the required notarized letters from your physician or employer, or whomever, because I will not hear any pleas for excuse from service without notarized evidence. This is the law. Notice was given to you in section twelve found at the bottom of page three of your notice-to-appear instructions."

Most hands went down. A huge collective groan went up.

"Fine. I'll see any of the hardships up here. Mr. Landish and Wilkes may join me and we will hear from you."

Only about ten people were brave enough to approach the bench. Ruby and I stayed at the defense table while Wilkes and Landish went up to the throne to hear the jurors try and beg their way out of duty. Ruby elbowed me as the line formed. "Schoonie, dat guy, da cowboy. Gotta cute butt, ain't he? Take a look."

She was pointing to a tall white male, about thirty years old, who was last in the hardship line. He wore a three-day beard, long brown hair, a Levi's jacket buttoned to the naval, no undershirt, tight Levi's pants, dirty, scuffed brown cowboy boots, and a red neckerchief. Ruby looked at his butt intently. "Hummmm," she said, "poifect."

As Ruby contemplated the cowboy's derriere, and while Alvin wept, I listened to Junior talking to the first hardship. ". . . no notarized excuse? Well, then what are you doing up here? I cannot even consider your excuse from service."

The juror, Wanda Farouk, a middle-aged lady who ran her own bookkeeping business, was trying to explain that as a self-employed individual, she could not find a person to verify in writing her excuse from prolonged service. She had written her own note explaining and requesting it, but it was not notarized.

Wanda asked, "Do you mean if I have my own note notarized, I can have my hardship heard? How about if I just swear to it right now?"

"To move this along, Judge, it's fine by the defense if she's excused," said Wilkes loudly. This was a "win-win" remark. If she were excused, she would be grateful to Wilkes, as might the others in line. In fact, the whole prospective pack of jurors might take a liking to Wilkes just for this one courtesy. On the other hand, if the judge overruled her excuse, it would be the judge she'd hate.

Grasping this, Miles Landish tried to chime in. "Well, the district attorney's position is—"

Too slow. "You two will be quiet," interrupted Junior. To Wanda Farouk he said testily, "Madam, I am not in the business of giving legal advice. I do not make the rules. It is my solemn duty to execute them. Your hardship excuse is denied. Next."

With that, the cowboy and six other hardships gave up. Wanda's ruling doomed their chances. Within a few minutes the remaining hardships were dealt with in like fashion and returned to their seats. Then regular jury questioning began.

Junior started it with a request for his clerk to call the roll and the seating of would-be jurors. Fourteen were put in the box so that the lawyers could then question them with two purposes in mind: first, to throw off "for cause" those with admitted or obvious biases like being related to the victim, married to the defendant, or working for the New York Homicide Bureau; second, the lawyers for each side got ten shots, that is, ten "peremptory challenges" to be freely used to knock off any would-be juror. The only cause you need to use a peremptory challenge was best explained by Ruby Fulgioni to our client: "Because I don't want dat butthead widin ten miles of decidin' dis case."

VOIR DIRE: ONE, TWO, THREE

The first day of jury selection set the tone for the rest. The most important and time-consuming issue to be covered was the pretrial publicity. The media maggots had done a terrific job in publicizing our client's guilt with daily headlines and radio and TV spots. The only concession to fairness was that the word "murderer" almost always was prefaced with the word "alleged." So "News at Eleven" would trumpet, "Alleged murderer Alvin Scribner confesses to priest in jail!" Or the *Post* headline would scream, "I DID IT!" SAYS ALVIN, followed by a subheadline which read, ALLEGED MURDERER TELLS ALL.

After the ceaseless media barrage, as far as the public was concerned, Alvin's being an "alleged murderer" was synonymous with being the actual murderer.

Now there was jury work to be done to undo the media propaganda, and Ruby would prove invaluable in sizing up which of the would-be jurors we would ax. Her advice always gave a rough and colorful but intelligent rationale to Wilkes's impulsive, instinctive manner of jury selection.

Actually, we weren't selecting jurors. We were deselecting them. You toss out as many as you can, and what's left is your jury. As Ruby eloquently explained to our client when Wilkes was chattering away with the jurors, "Alvin. Al baby, can you hear me? Dis ain't gonna be no jury of yer choice, see. Yer jury's what's left over after we get rid of da woist."

Ruby's explanations of what we were doing seemed to soothe Alvin. He was no longer crying. His head was now coming up from the table to look around. That was progress. Maybe he'd actually watch what was going when his trial began.

THREE DAYS

It took three full days to voir dire the jurors on media coverage. Scores were deselected for cause because for them the media had destroyed the presumption of innocence and proved Alvin's guilt beyond a reasonable doubt. As one juror told Wilkes, "Sure I believe in the presumption of innocence. I also believe he's guilty. I must have read his confession a dozen times in the papers and I'll always have that rattling around in my head no matter how much law the judge reads to me."

After this juror was successfully challenged by Wilkes for cause, his statement caught on like an infectious disease. Over the next three days, juror after newspaper-reading juror repeated the refrain of that first juror—"I'll always have that confession rattling around in my head no matter how much law the judge reads to me."

After the first dozen said it, Alvin, who had been watching the proceedings upright and dry-eyed, had a turn for the worse. As another juror said, "I'll always have that confession . . ." Alvin's whole upper body starting shaking. Then he slumped forward hard so that his head hit the table with a loud thump just as the juror said, ". . . around in my head." This was followed by Alvin's loud mournful cries which echoed off the courtroom walls.

Junior looked at Wilkes and said, "Have your assistants either control the defendant's emotions or I'll have him removed from these proceedings."

To which Miles Landish added, "Yeah, it's a trick. A Wilkes ploy for sympathy."

This brought on Wilkes's charge to the bench for a sidebar conference and his first three motions for mistrial. "Your Honor, I move most respectfully for a mistrial based upon your comments threatening to deprive my client of his right to attend his own trial. Second, Your Honor, I respectfully move for a mistrial based upon Miles Landish's outrageously false accusation that my client's spontaneous and soulful cry of victimization is a defense trick. Last, Your Honor, I move for a mistrial based upon Your Honor's tardy denial of my motion to recuse you for bias."

Landish started to respond, but Junior put up his hand. "Let me expedite this. That'll be denied. Thrice. Now, get on with it, gentlemen."

Wilkes was beside himself. Alvin was perfectly playing the role of the guilty defendant. Ruby, too, was upset. She whispered to Alvin, "Quit yer blubberin', man. Yer gonna get my good suit all wet while you float yerself up da river."

By the time we ended the publicity portion of voir dire, we had eliminated just about every juror who could read. We also discovered that no one listened to radio news much, so there was no basis for axing jurors there. Most surprisingly, despite the tremendous TV exposure about the case, the nonreader TV-watching jurors claimed no recall about the case.

At the end of the three days of publicity questioning, scores of would-be jurors were thrown off the case because of their unshakable belief in Alvin's guilt. Our client, his head still in his arms on the table, wept throughout the process. By the end of the third day of hearing jurors proclaim him guilty, he lifted his puss long enough to sob to Ruby, "Stop . . . stop . . . this. It's . . . just killing me. Tell Mr. Wilkes to get on with it. I want my trial to start now."

To which Ruby replied, "Al baby, if we starts yer trial right now wid deze bums, you will be killed."

That shut up Alvin for a while.

FOUR, FIVE, SIX

The next phase of jury deselection was general voir dire. This meant getting the jurors to talk openly about their families, neighborhood, jobs, education, relatives, friends, and experiences with the law.

After they share this biographical information, you can start asking about how they feel about the criminal justice system, constitutional rights, and lawyers. A lot of lying is done at this point.

Prospective juror John Jasper Witherby said he was thirty-six, lived on Riverdale Drive, and worked as an executive for a Manhattan bank. He said he favored the death penalty for murder, long sentences for drug dealers, and community service and restitution for white-collar criminals. Ruby advised Wilkes, "Watch out for dat yuppy. Dem bums got no heart. Dey only care about gettin' to da theater by eight. Looks like a Rule Three, Wilkie."

He was axed.

Mildred Lytton was in her mid-fifties, plump and loud, and lived near the garment district. She invoked the name of God a lot when she talked. Ruby advised, "Church lady, eh? Kick her ass off, Wilkie. She's a Rule Five. No turn the other cheek in this one. She's an Old Testament hanger."

She was axed.

Wyatt Wonderlick, the cowboy of the hardship line with the tight ass, said he was an unemployed auto mechanic and actor, lived in a lot of places in mid-Manhattan, mostly with girlfriends, and had a father and uncle in Queens who were cops. He said he was going to ask for a hardship excuse because his dad was trying to line up a job for him fixing cars for the police department.

Wilkes's instinct said ax him immediately, but Ruby said he was a keeper. "He's a Rule Six, Wilkie, and I like his butt." Wilkes obeyed.

THE SPREADER

Wanda Farouk, the first of the rejected hardship cases, stated she lived in the upper Seventies and owned her own bookkeeping business. Ruby knew that D.A. Miles Landish would ax Wanda because Wilkes had ingratiated himself with her earlier. Ruby suggested to Wilkes, "She's a goner already, Wilkie, so make da most of it. Use da spreada."

My friend knew exactly what Ruby meant. The spreader was

Ruby's term for using a friendly juror who was certain to be kicked off the jury by the D.A. as a spreader of the gospel. You know this juror's going to give good answers, so although she's doomed, she can serve as the broadcaster of the good word to the others in the box.

Within a few questions it was apparent Ruby was right. Wanda took a shine to Wilkes. This was probably because she thought since Wilkes had stuck his neck out for her in front of Junior by suggesting it was okay for her to have a hardship excuse, that with an expression of warmth toward Wilkes now, he might follow up and, as a true humanitarian and all-around nice guy, bump her off the case so that she could get to her business.

Wilkes began by asking questions about such controversial topics as believing in goodness, morality, and the law. She was very agreeable and said yes to everything, but she spoke so softly answering Wilkes's questions that he approached close to the rail to hear her. "And, Mrs. Farouk, would you promise to give my client a fair trial? Speak up now so that we can all hear."

She said loudly, "Yes, of course I would, Mr. Wilkes."

Wilkes, now standing directly in front of her, then asked, "And why do you think that a fair trial is important. Speak up."

"Well," she said. Wanda was somewhat baffled by a question which called for more than a syllable of answer. She smiled, "Uh, it's—it's—well, it's the American way. It's just doing what's fair and right, isn't it, Mr. Wilkes?"

As she said these words, Wilkes smiled and reached over the rail with his right hand. He said, "Well, it sure is, ma'am, and may God bless your heart." Then he patted her on the shoulder, turned his head toward the throne and said triumphantly to Junior, "This juror is acceptable to the defense."

Miles Landish rose to object, but his holographic image, the judge, beat him to the punch. "There'll be no touching of the jurors, Mr. Wilkes. None at all."

Landish then asked her a few perfunctory questions and promptly kicked Wanda out of the box. We scored a few points with this maneuver. It was the last we would score for the rest of the trial.

In fact, when it came time to use the rest of peremptory challenges, Wilkes came to Ruby and asked for suggestions. Ruby said, "A bigger bunch of bums I never seen, Wilkie. Don't make much diff who gets kicked now. Da only ting you can do now is fire at random."

And so as the sun set on the sixth day, Wilkes randomly fired off the rest of his challenges as his client, head down and buried, wept like a plucked ostrich bound for the native stew pot.

We had a jury. Now the worst part was to come, the presentation of evidence. After the jury was sworn in and excused for the day, Ruby took a final, disgusted look at them as they merrily filed out of the jury box. When they left, she told Wilkes, "Dat jury, Wilkie, dey wanna party—a lynching party."

RUBY'S TEN DOS & DON'TS OF JURY SELECTION IN NEW YORK CITY

1. DON'T pick jurors who gasp when the charges are read.
2. DO pick jurors who have trouble understanding English.
3. DON'T select a juror who drools when he talks about capital punishment.
4. DO pick descendants of the Boss Tweed family.
5. DON'T pick religious jurors except for followers of the Satanic Masonics, Disciples of Alphonse the Apostate, the Moribund Tabernacle Divine Light Holy Mission, the Charles Crud Celestial Crusade, the Beelzebub Worshipers, the New-Age Satanic Revenge Society, the Post-Thermonuclear Anti-Christ Pre-Survivors Club, or the Unitarian Church.
6. DO pick disbarred attorneys, impeached judges and politicians, proctologists, and unemployed performance artists.
7. DON'T pick an accountant who resorts to her calculator to answer the question, "What do you feel about reasonable doubt?"
8. DO seek to seat jurors who raise their hands in response to the question: "Anyone been convicted of a felony?"
9. DON'T pick jurors who are evasive in answering the question: "Could you treat the defendant the same as if it were your only begotten son on trial here today?"
10. DO pick jurors whose last names being with letters beginning after S. As children, they grew up waiting long periods of time for their names to be called, and in the process developed a personality disorder known as "alphabet neurosis." The longer the trial goes, the more likely a nervous breakdown and a mistrial.

— 15 —

The Trial from Hell

"Never hunt rabbit with dead dog."
CHARLIE CHAN

*"One corpse on display in the courtroom
is quite sufficient."*
JOHN WILKES

Miles Landish was completing his opening statement to the Roy
Bean Family, otherwise known as our jury. Although the courtroom
was packed, it was quiet. A tenseness was in the air, as is common
when a kill is about to be made. Landish moved his large frame to
the rail and spoke loudly to the jurors. He was prone to spray his
words in wide spittle zones so that nearby jurors often needed um-
brellas and raincoats when listening to his perorations.

"In sum, ladies and gentlemen, guilt will be shown here, make no
mistake. We will prove beyond any shadow of a doubt that the
defendant is a liar, a thief, and a murderer. Pay attention to the facts
as they pour like the mighty Niagara from the witness stand. You'll
find that Scribner's fingerprint was on the murder weapon. He had
blood all over him when the police came. The murderer used his
right hand in plunging the dagger into the back of Judge Knott, and
this defendant is right-handed. The defendant illegally made millions with Judge Knott by using information they gleaned from court
cases to invest in stocks. The defendant lied to the police about the
investments because the missing money was his motive to kill. Fi-

nally, he confessed to a clergyman-prisoner at the jail following his arrest.

"Now, those are the facts! They will gush down from the witness stand, engulf this defendant, wash away any reasonable doubt, and drown him in his guilt. After hearing it, despite whatever pathetic smoke screen the defense attempts, you will not let guilt escape this courtroom. You will find it, RIGHT HERE!"

At this point Landish wheeled on one foot, aimed his arm in our direction and pointed his index finger straight at Alvin. "You will find guilt at that table sitting between these two CRIMINAL defense attorneys!"

Alvin, as usual, had his head buried in his arms on the table and was moaning. The moans—"OOOOAAAUUUUHHH! OOOAAAUUUUHHH!"—became louder and louder, such that by the time Landish reached the climax of his oration, they were as loud as the prosecutor's bellowing.

Landish made the most of it. "The defendant, ladies and gentlemen, even now as I speak of his crime, has his head hidden from you. So great is his shame for his foul deed, he cannot face you. But you can hear the dishonor in his cries, and I know they will not go unheard. You will respond. You will find Alvin Scribner guilty of the cowardly back-stabbing of Judge Yulburton Abraham Knott. Thank you."

Landish cocked his head high and lumbered over to his table and sat down. Detective Mike Mulraney, his case agent, gave him a thumbs up look that said, "Devastating."

SOMETHING FROM NOTHING

I looked to Wilkes. He had a look on his face that said, "Devastating." It was now his turn to address the jury, but he sat there as if in a trance. The only sounds in the court were Alvin's moans. Actually, Wilkes *was* in a trance. He was doing his best to disassociate from the predicament of telling this jury something about what our evidence would show when we had absolutely nothing to show them.

Judge Throckton cocked his head in puzzlement. "Are you ready, Mr. Wilkes?"

That snapped Wilkes out of it. "Ready if you are," he said, and then rose and stood behind Alvin's quivering back. He leaned over and put a hand on Alvin's shoulder. "Ladies and gentlemen, I shall be brief and to the point. I have known Alvin Scribner for many years as a clerk in this courthouse. I have known him as a trusted servant to the late Judge Y. Knott. I am presently honored to know him as a client. I have known his gentle nature, his loyalty, and now . . ."

Wilkes paused. He saw that Landish was getting up to object to his speech. He quickly went over to the rail, put both hands on it, and looked the jurors in the eyes. "I know all his secrets. You know I do. And I'll tell you this, as God is my judge, I know that Alvin Scribner is absolutely innocent of this charge. Thank you."

"OBJECTION!" screamed Miles Landish. "He can't say that!"

"WHY THE HELL NOT?" said Wilkes in mock defensiveness. "JUST WHY THE HELL NOT?" Wilkes knew very well why the hell not. The Marquis of Queensberry Rules of courtroom etiquette forbade an attorney from telling a jury what he actually knew about a case. But what the hell? What else could he say? He lacked the essential ingredient to talk about in opening statement: favorable evidence.

"YES! YES! SUSTAINED!" cried Judge Throckton. "MR. WILKES, YOU KNOW THAT WAS IMPROPER!" Junior turned to the jury. "Ladies and gentlemen, I am instructing you on something very important. What the defendant's criminal defense attorney just said was inappropriate; it is to be disregarded by you except as to how it may reflect the unseemly lengths to which some lawyers will go to win; it is to play no role in your consideration of this case in determining the guilt of this defendant; it is to be forever stricken from your memories. Mr. Landish, call your first witness."

"OOOAAAUUUUHHH! OOOAAAUUUUHHH!" moaned Alvin.

"I must beg the court to allow a motion at sidebar," said Wilkes. He wanted to make a motion for mistrial based upon the judge's comment to the jury about his performance.

Junior was ready for him. "No, Mr. Wilkes, that will not be necessary. We can't have constant sidebars and going back and forth or we'll never get through this trial. I believe I know the nature of the motion. An M motion if I'm not mistaken. That'll be denied, counsel. Now, sit down and make no more improper comments."

"Well," said Wilkes, "based upon what you just said, in addition to the first M motion, I have M motion number two to make."

Junior smiled. "With the same result."

"OOOAAAUUUUHHH! OOOAAAUUUUHHH!" moaned   you know who.

So began the trial from Hell.

EVIDENCE

With this auspicious start, Miles Landish bellowed, "The People of the State of New York call as their first witness, Mrs. Judge Yulburton Abraham Knott."

Up stood the tall, handsome, and fur-shrouded Alice Knott. She danced down the aisle like a painted Russian circus bear. When she sat down, she looked directly at our table and studied us like an entomologist might look at a collection of malarial mosquitoes. Wilkes leaned over to me and whispered, "Alice Knott, *videris de odio et atia*," which means, "Alice Knott, you look of hate and spite."

Landish launched into his direct examination. Mrs. Knott warmed to Landish's questions and became positively chatty as she told the jury about her regularly picking the judge up each evening at five, the door to chambers always being open except on the murder evening, when it was locked, her going to get Alvin to open the door, and then entering to find . . .

"There on the floor, my beloved husband, his life's blood gushing out of him." She pulled a hanky out of her purse and soaked up the tears. "It was horrible, absolutely awful."

Landish then asked the key question, the precisely formulated inquiry which he was taught, like thousands of others at prosecution gladiator school, was the query guaranteed to quickly unravel oodles of incriminating testimony: "And then what happened?"

"Then my world started spinning, literally . . . I, well, I almost fainted, but I remember running to Y.A.'s side. He was down on the floor on his stomach with that thing sticking out. Then, I remember the strangest thing happened. The defendant Scribner quickly reached out and grabbed the murder weapon and roughly pulled on it."

"And then what happened?"

"I screamed out, and then I noted what appeared to be a spot of blood on his right sleeve."

"OOOAAAUUUUHHH! OOOAAAUUUUHHH!"

Alvin's moanings were like exclamation points to the most harmful evidence. Wilkes had tried to convince Alvin during jury selection to either shut up, let us tape his mouth shut, or that he waive his appearance for trial and stay in jail all day. But Alvin insisted on being there.

Miles Landish didn't need Alvin's contribution to understand that what was just said by Mrs. Knott was important. This meant it was time to drill it into the jury consciousness. "You say you saw this blood spot on his right sleeve even before he touched the blade?"

Wilkes tried to deflect the damage. He objected. "Leading and suggestive. Assumes facts not in evidence. Compound. Asked and answered."

"Yes," said Alice quickly, without waiting for Junior to rule. "I'm quite sure of it."

Junior then gave Landish another opportunity to make his point. "Mr. Landish, what say you to these various objections by the criminal defense attorney?"

"I say it is very important for the jury to know that she saw the blood on his right sleeve even before he came close to the body, thus demonstrating—"

Wilkes interjected, "I object to this self-serving explanation of his improper question before this jury, and trust the jury will be admonished by the court in the same fashion it has previously been admonished concerning me."

Junior held up both of his hands. "Now gentlemen, let's quiet down. The answer may stand. I take it the prosecution is trying to show that the defendant killed the judge earlier, got blood on his sleeve, and was now trying to get blood all over him to hide the evidence. Thus, both the question and the form of the question are proper. Ask your next question, Mr. Landish."

"OOOAAAUUUUHHH! OOOAAAUUUUHHH!" moaned the defense's barometer of battle damage.

"I have two more M motions for Your Honor," said Wilkes as he slipped into his chair beside his moaning client. "May I approach the bench to articulate the precise bases for each?"

"That'll be denied as unnecessary. For the same reasons I stated in denying the first M motion, these two will be denied also," said Junior. "I know what they are, and they are meritless. To be totally fair to you, however, and in an abundance of caution so as to preserve every conceivable right of your client, you may submit your M motions in writing for reconsideration tomorrow morning."

After this exchange, it was apparent that objecting to anything was not only futile, but dangerous. Junior would, like an echo chamber, repeat the prosecutor's rationale and emphasize the most damning points to the jury. Alvin would then accentuate the harm by wailing loudly, as if each new point was an arrow shot into his body. Then Wilkes would make his M motions in front of the jury and get humiliated by Junior.

"Mrs. Knott, did the defendant say why he tried to pull out the blade?" asked Landish.

"No, no. He just grabbed it and pulled. I screamed at him not to. I knew it could aggravate the wound. But he just did it. Then he seemed to go out of his way to get Y.A.'s blood all over him."

"OOOAAAUUUUHHH! OOOAAAUUUUHHH!" These two wails of agony filled the courtroom and stopped the testimony. Landish used it as a poignant point of departure. "No further questions," he said.

TELLING POINT

Surprise testimony is the courtroom equivalent of the venerable bushwhacking. Witnesses who have been interviewed a dozen times can say the darndest, most unexpected things when they hit the stand. Mrs. Knott had not told anyone that she saw this alleged spot of blood on Alvin's sleeve before he tried to pull out the knife. Now she remembers. How convenient. Wilkes rose to question her.

"Mrs. Knott, didn't you yell for Alvin to pull out the knife from your husband's body? Isn't that why he tried to pull it out?"

Alice Knott stiffened when Wilkes asked this question. Her stare of hate returned. "Absolutely not." She reached for the glass of water on the witness stand and sipped.

"A little water clears us of this deed? Out damned spot?" said Wilkes quoting Macbeth.

"That's no question," wailed Landish.

"I'll sustain my own objection to that on the grounds of incomprehensibility," said Junior.

Wilkes continued as if oblivious. "You were interviewed several times by Detective Mulraney, the gentleman with the hanky to his nose seated over here next to Mr. Landish?"

"Twice."

"You never told him about this spot of blood on Alvin's sleeve before, did you?" Wilkes was holding Mulraney's interview reports, which reflected no such statement.

"I did so tell him," she said. "I told him either the first time, which was the night your client murdered my husband, or the second time, at my home following the funeral."

"His notes don't reflect it," said Wilkes. "I wonder why?"

"Objection," yelled Landish. "Assumes facts not in evidence. Mr. Wilkes is making gratuitous comments again, Judge."

"Sustained as to the question and the gratuitous comments," said Junior. "The jury will ignore them as previously instructed."

"Madam," said Wilkes, "didn't you tell Detective Mulraney that Alvin first yelled for help, he yelled for the bailiff, and then the both of you tried to roll your husband on his side so that Alvin could more easily and gently pull out the knife?"

"No. He may have called for help. I was screaming for help. He may have rolled the body. But I didn't tell him to pull on the knife and I DID SEE THE BLOOD ON HIS SHIRTSLEEVE

BEFORE HE TOUCHED THE KNIFE OR THE BODY!"

"OOOAAAUUUUHHH! OOOAAAUUUUHHH!"

"Well, since you rolled the body first, the blood very well could have got on his sleeve as he came in proximity to the body and before he reached for it, couldn't it?"

"No. I know that the first time I saw his sleeve it had blood on it. I first saw his sleeve when he first reached out to the body."

"Well, wasn't the body hemorrhaging like a park fountain when you first got there?"

"Absolutely not. The blood was . . . my God, Your Honor, do I have to respond to this?" Alice dabbed her hanky at her eyes and then looked to Junior for relief.

Landish followed her lead. "Objection. Invasion of privacy." It was a ludicrous objection to the trained legal mind, but then Landish wasn't a trained legal mind.

Junior gave Alice his warmest look of support and then said to Wilkes, "I'm sure Mr. Wilkes will be *extremely* brief on this point in light of *who* is on the witness stand and the *gruesome* subject matter."

Now, it has never been in Wilkes's nature to be brief on anything in the courtroom, particularly in the hopeless case. For one thing, the longer the trial, the longer it takes to convict. Also, as time marches on, witnesses die and evidence gets lost. So, as long as you're in trial, there's still hope. Wilkes wasn't about to quicken his pace, and he knew that for the moment he could put off the judge by uttering the following lie which is routinely stated to judges by attorneys everywhere in the world: "Just a few more questions, Judge."

Wilkes continued. "Okay, Mrs. Knott, let's try and paint the jury a picture. Was it spurting like water from a high pressure garden hose when you got there or more like a kid's squirt gun?"

"Sir, I don't wish to paint pictures. I'll tell you this. There was profuse bleeding in the area of the wound, but none was flying from the surface of the body." Mrs. Knott said this tear-free and with the coolness of a coroner.

"None that you saw, you mean?" said Wilkes. Then he reverted to Macbeth: " 'Yet who would have thought the old man to have had so much blood in him?' "

"Sustained," said Junior. He pointed his gavel at Wilkes stick end first. "One more of those and you are out of here, mister."

Alice responded. "None that I saw was flying about. No blood got on me until I actually touched the body to turn it, oh God!"

With that, like a faucet, out came the tears. Wilkes was getting nowhere. Lady Knott was harder to pin down than a beebee on greased glass. We'd have to call Detective Mulraney to the stand to try and impeach Alice by showing she did not tell him about the blood spot on the sleeve during their interviews.

"How big was the spot on his sleeve?" he asked.

"Bigger than your heart," cried Alice into her hanky. "About the size of a quarter."

"OOOAAAUUUUHHH! OOOAAAUUUUHHH!"

On this accented downbeat, the joust with Alice Knott ended and the prosecution took a big lead out of the gate.

DR. DEATH

Landish next called Dr. Lane Springwood, the pathologist who had conducted the autopsy on Judge Knott. Springwood had for years tremendously enjoyed "working the beef" at the medical examiner's office and then testifying in court about his findings. He loved the investigation, the physical act of cutting and sawing into cadavers, and even grew to like the smell of his work. For obvious reasons, he had gained the nickname of Dr. Death around the courthouse.

Landish pinned on an easel huge pictures of the bloody, naked body of Judge Knott. Dr. Death's people had cut away the clothing so that the knife blade was still sticking out of it. Once the pictures were up, there didn't need to be any testimony, but the pathologist testified that in his expert opinion the cause of death was—surprise, surprise—the blade of a sharp instrument penetrating through the back and nipping the aorta. The victim bled to death. The angle of the blade in the body indicated insertion by a right-handed person.

After Dr. Death identified the bloody photos, Landish said, "I move to have the pictures of the body admitted into evidence."

Wilkes rose. The judge expected an objection to exclude the introduction of the gory autopsy photos as evidence, which he was prepared to instantly overrule. But Wilkes had a different motion in mind. "Your Honor, although it pains me to say this, court decorum and the Penal Code demand that I move for Mr. Landish to zip up his pants zipper."

"WHAT?" yelled Junior. He looked at Landish, who was standing by the easel near the front of the jury box.

"Penal Code, Your Honor, abridged edition," answered Wilkes.

"OUTRAGEOUS!" yelled Landish as he looked down and over his belly to see that his zipper was indeed flying at low mast. He quickly zipped it. His face was red and a slight, embarrassed smile appeared for a second.

"Yes," said Wilkes, "I make this motion to avoid cumulative evidence. One corpse on display in the courtroom is quite sufficient."

"SIT DOWN!" said Junior. "I shall not dignify that remark with a response. We'll have no more of that. I warn you, sir. I have given you tremendous leeway. That ends now. The jury will ignore the comment of the criminal defense attorney. Call your next witness, Mr. Prosecutor."

There was good news and bad news to report about the jury reaction to Wilkes's motion. The bad news: Not one of the jurors even smiled at Wilkes's remark. The good news: Juror Wyatt Wonderlick, the urban cowboy who Ruby had liked, not only wasn't smiling, he wasn't even awake. Perhaps he would sleep through the entire prosecution case and then hold out during jury deliberations on the ground that he hadn't heard one word of damning evidence.

Wilkes had nothing at all to ask the pathologist, so he only spent about two hours questioning him. We learned that Knott's heart weighed 490 grams, that multiple sections of the coronary arteries were examined by the doctor and showed no evidence of occlusions, that sections of the myocardium revealed no evidence of an infarct, that there was no abnormality of the tricuspid, pulmonic mitral or aortic valves, and that but for the one slice out of the aorta, there was nothing at all wrong with the body that a good knife pulling wouldn't have cured.

The closest thing to a relevant question was, "Sir, did you find any recently consumed pizza in the judge's stomach?" to which the expert answered, "No pizza at all."

With the entrail-reading finished, so ended the first day of evidence. The prosecutor had a no-hitter going.

TAKING STOCK

The next day, Landish put on elaborate evidence of the stocks the judge and Alvin bought through their insider trading with stockbroker Albert Rhinestrum. This was to show Alvin's motive for murdering the judge—that he thought the judge blew all three million bucks just as Alvin was planning a comfortable retirement. First, officer Jaime Perez hopped on the stand and testified that shortly after his arrest, Alvin admitted to everyone at the police station that he and the judge had made the investments. He also testified that Alvin signed his name on the booking sheet with his right hand.

A police technician then put up a bunch of charts he had created to show that the stock purchases all came just before a judicial decision related to the business was about to be made in the courthouse. The technician told the jury how a computer file was found in the judge's safe which, after the password was cracked, revealed the complete record of investments Alvin made with the judge. This record dovetailed almost perfectly with that found at a local stock brokerage under the strange name of Snivlakno Trubluy.

Wilkes couldn't do anything with this witness on cross. We had no defense to the insider stock-trading evidence. Our client admitted it. But we hadn't heard anything about having to get by a password to enter the judge's file.

"What was the password that opened the file?" asked Wilkes.

"Perfect Justice," said the technician.

"How did you figure that out?" asked Wilkes.

"I didn't."

"Someone else, then. And just whom might that person be?"

"A young man by the name of Jethro Wilmore."

Wilkes didn't recognize the name, but being recently learned in the ways of computers and word processing, I took an interest in computer crime news. Jethro Wilmore was the infamous Hacker-Cracker, a computer criminal of recent fame who was supposed to be in prison. I sent Wilkes a note.

"Sir," said Wilkes, reading from my note, "is this the same Jethro Wilmore who is known as the Hacker-Cracker, the fellow convicted of stealing enormous amounts of other people's money through the use of his personal computer and the telephone lines of Ma Bell?"

"It is," said the technician.

"Let me ask you this, then. Was anyone present when the Hacker purportedly cracked the password?"

"Not that I know of."

"What was he getting paid for this work?"

"I have no idea."

Wilkes turned to Junior. "Well, I want to know, Judge. There is no proper foundation for the introduction of this exhibit since the witness who allegedly cracked the password is not here. We were never provided any information that a felon serving time would be working for the police in this investigation. We need to know what he was paid for this work. I suspect he was given his liberty for it. This is a stunning development. I must make another M motion based upon it."

This was a break for us in the sense that any departure from the unrelenting avalanche of incriminating testimony was good.

"Wait a minute," said Landish. "This is ridiculous! The defendant has confessed to having the secret insider-trading deal with the deceased Judge Knott. This is trivial at most and irrelevant in reality."

"This raises major constitutional questions of equal protection and due process," replied Wilkes. "When did the Hacker become an employee of the New York Police Department? What did he get for this? How do we know this file is authentic?"

Junior looked at Wilkes. It was the look a train engineer might have on his face as he saw terrorists about to blow track just ahead of his speeding engine. "I believe the computer file is self-authenticating, Mr. Wilkes. Further, given your own client's admissions on this issue, this fellow Jethro Wilmore's role in the matter is extraneous to the core issues before us. I won't waste the jury's time with further inquiry into it. You have your own investigative resources to explore it on your own if you like. All motions about this which you have made or are thinking of making are hereby denied."

And so, the train rolled over the terrorists.

"OOOAAAUUUUHHH! OOOAAAUUUUHHH!"

BOMBSHELL

"Thank you, Your Honor," said Landish. "I next call to the stand, Lewis Pith."

Pith was a partner at Baynard, Pith, and Willikins, the stock brokerage firm that employed Albert Rhinestrum. He testified Rhinestrum handled the account for Snivlakno Trubluy until the day of his disappearance with all the money in the account.

Landish asked, "And then what happened?"

"Well, I remember after he disappeared I got two calls about the account. Two different men called, neither of whom would identify himself. I made notes of the calls and the dates on the cover of the account folder."

"Yes," said Landish, "and do you think you could recognize the voice of either person if you heard it again?"

"Well, I dunno. I could try certainly."

"Your Honor, at this time the People of the State of New York seek a court-ordered voice exemplar from the defendant Scribner. We would like him to read this statement taken from the notes Mr. Pith wrote on the folder."

Before Wilkes could utter an objection, Junior said, "So ordered. The defendant will read the notes now."

Alvin, who was listening between moans, lifted his head from his arms long enough to see Landish stick the Pith folder under his nose and say, "Take it."

"Let the record reflect that the defendant has taken the file WITH HIS RIGHT HAND," said Landish. He pointed to a few neatly printed sentences and said, "Read this."

Alvin's eyes, swollen and bloodshot from weeping, looked to where Landish's finger pointed. As commanded, he began reading, "May I speak to Albert Rhinestrum, please? May I speak to someone, then, who can give me information on the Snivlakno Trubluy account? The money's gone? You're sure? Gone?"

"Yes, that's the voice from the second call," said Pith.

"You say that's the voice of the man who made the second call?" repeated Landish, as if hard of hearing.

"Yes," said Pith, pointing to Alvin. "It was a distinctive voice, scratchy and worn like the one that this man has. I don't think I'll ever forget it."

Alvin looked at him oddly. Before either Wilkes or I could get his hand over his mouth, Alvin said, "Mr. Pith, I didn't ask 'The money's gone?' as you have written here. I asked you, 'The stocks are all gone?' "

"Sorry old boy, I thought I got it down right," replied Pith.

So ended day two of the trial from Hell. The prosecution was so far ahead, it was out of sight.

— 16 —

Father Harry Leech

"If befriend donkey, expect to be kicked."
CHARLIE CHAN

*". . . but the mouth of them that speak lies
shall be stopped."*
PSALMS 63:11

We were having morning java at the Guadalajara Café near the office, a needed fix of caffeine before we hiked up to the Criminal Courts Building for another day of getting our brains beaten out. Maybe we should have loaded up on an anesthetic instead. Anyway, Lunko, the short, barrel-chested owner, poured us each another cup of his fresh brew. Wilkes told him to put it on our tab. Lunko belched in response, which meant okay.

Wilkes was blue and not saying much. He was slouched over his coffee like he had scoliosis. His face was ashen, his clothes needed pressing, and his shoes were scuffed and dusty. He looked like he felt.

I was reading the *Times* coverage of the story of the trial by Adell Loomis. "Hey," I said, "Adell's giving us good coverage, considering what's happening. She mentioned your name three times above the fold on the front page."

"Yeah, I read it," said my depressed friend into his coffee. "She said, 'John Wilkes's defense sustained a number of major blows yesterday as witness after witness took the stand and tied strands of incriminating evidence to Wilkes's client, accused murderer Alvin

Scribner. With the evidence raveling around the defendant, and continually chastised by Judge Lester J. Throckton, Junior, Wilkes struggled vainly to keep the taint of evidence from his client.' "

Wilkes's recall of the passage was exact. His memory was amazing. I glanced his way as he turned in my direction with a contemptuous look of, Don't you get it?

"For Christ's sake, Schoonover! Adell's my girl! She's my goddamned girlfriend and even she can't sugar coat disaster! Man, I don't even wanna see the *Post*."

It was true. Adell's story wasn't so good. That's because reality wasn't so good. This was one of the few times when the news about an event of which I had personal experience fairly matched what actually happened. Usually, the media take a news event and use it as a fictional story idea for "News at Eleven."

"At least she caught the bit about the deal the cops made with the Hacker-Cracker. What an outrage! That ought to embarrass the hell out of NYPD. Shall I get Condo out looking for the kid?" I asked. "And maybe have him check the kid's criminal files. Find out if anyone represented him and if the deal was put on paper."

"Sure. Why not?" said Wilkes with disinterest. "Hey, Lunko, gimme one of your best dunkin' doughnuts. I wanna create an oil slick."

While Wilkes played drown the doughnut, I called Condo and gave him his new investigative assignments. He clued me in on what he had been doing, and then Wilkes and I began the Bataan Death March toward the Temple of Doom. On the way, I informed Wilkes of what Condo had come up with on the prosecution's next witness.

BACK IN THE TEMPLE

With the trial moving rapidly and easily toward its inevitable result, both Landish and Junior appeared relaxed for the third day. Their juggernaut was speeding right on target to its destination—Alvin Scribner's oblivion—and they felt good about it.

Landish called his next witness to the stand. "The People of the State of New York now call to the stand Father Harry Leech."

Out of the door that connected the court to the holding tank appeared a convict so rotund, he made even the stout Miles Landish look like a ninety-eight-pound weakling. A giant ball of blubber with mouth and eyes waddled to the witness stand carrying a bible.

Harry Leech looked like a movie star. In stature he resembled the Blob, while facially he looked like Jabba the Hutt. Harry was a con who spent his time in custody trying to roll close to high profile defendants to "take confession" and snitch them off to the D.A. in return for time off his sentence. He became known as "Father" Leech because of the miracle of his presence; it seemed that every inmate who got within speaking range of the bastard gave confession.

Over the years, after getting caught for his burglaries and robberies, going to jail, taking confession, and then making deals with the D.A., Leech decided to make good on the moniker and joined a prison cult known as the Church of the Sing-a-Song. The church was an in-(big)house joke created by cons to con the prison administration into giving its members special religious favors—like nightly meetings for worship, where the sacred church rite of seven-card stud could be played; for Sunday services, where the blessed sacrament of watching and betting on Sunday football could take place; and most important, adherence to the church's special dietetic requirement—filet mignon.

CONFESSION CONVERSION

Miles Landish was happy to have Leech as his witness. He couldn't have cared less if Leech was lying about the purported confession he took from Scribner, just as long as he didn't admit it to him or on the witness stand. He just wanted Leech to sing his a cappella tune for the jurors, to convert the reasonable doubters into believers in guilt. And a confession usually did just that.

After having Leech identify himself, Landish asked him about his contact with inmate Alvin Scribner in the lockup. Leech sat with his open bible resting on his huge belly. Like a professional witness, he looked to the jurors when he answered.

"As soon as Alvin entered the cell, sir, he confided in me. He sought the Lord's regeneration, and I tried, with all my humble abilities, to give him solace. The sinner unburdened himself."

Leech then lifted the bible and read, "And I said unto Mr. Scribner, and I am quoting Zechariah 3:4, 'I have caused thine iniquity to pass from thee, and will clothe thee with change of raiment.'"

"Tell us what he told you, Father," asked a respectful Miles Landish.

"Mr. Scribner said that after finishing a snack of pizza in chambers with the late Judge Knott on the afternoon of the murder, the two sinners got to talking about the millions they had made in their secret stock deals. Judge Knott then made the most unfortunate statement. He told Mr. Scribner he had blown all of their secret stock money, the money Mr. Scribner had long been planning for his retirement. The judge said he was sorry. Scribner said he was too. He grabbed a letter opener on the desk and stabbed the judge to death."

"OOOAAAUUUUHHH!" Our client, with his head down and his moaning up to megadecibels, accentuated the incriminating testimony for the jury.

"And that's what this defendant, Alvin Scribner, told you, right?" Without waiting for an answer, Landish sat down. "Thank you, Father."

Leech looked at Landish with surprise. He had forgotten to get the best of the confession in. "Actually, Mr. Landish, the exact words he said to me were, 'When I found out he took all my money, I stuck the no-good swindler in the back.'"

On that note, the five-minute direct examination of Father Harry Leech was completed.

Wilkes's cross-examination took a bit longer—two days.

BIBLICAL JUSTICE

If it were not so horribly perverse, it would be amusing to watch a liar take refuge in the bible and the law and use them to peddle perjury for freedom. Imagine the moral makeup of a man who would do such a thing without so much as a thought of the consequences to his victim. But such perversions are inevitable. As long as lies can be bartered for favor, perjurers will swarm to the witness stand like flies to the dung pile.

Wilkes rose to cross-examine. He was furious, of course, and eager to take on this maggot. There is no finer satisfaction for the lawyer than verbally dicing up a snitch on cross. But Father Harry Leech was as close as one could come to being a professional perjurer, and with a judge and prosecutor serving as the Blob's bodyguards, it wasn't going to be easy. It never is.

WILKES: And so, Father Harry Leech, you're saying my client, who had not mentioned any involvement in the judge's death at the scene, or to the cops in various interrogations, or to his friends, or to his coworkers, or to other inmates in jail, or even to his attorneys—

LANDISH: OBJECTION as to what his client told him!

COURT: Sustained.

WILKES: Well, so how is it out of all the people in the world, he picked you to confess to?

LEECH: God works in mysterious ways. Hallelujah!

J.W.: A person he'd never seen before, he'd just spill his guts to? To the likes of you?

LEECH: The wonders of the Lord. I never question them, sir. I am HIS humble earthly servant and rejoice in HIS salvation.

J.W.: You smile when you say that. Do you always smile when you commit perjury?

LANDISH: OBJECTION! ARGUMENTATIVE!

COURT: Sustained. The jury will again disregard the comments of the criminal defense attorney, Mr. Wilkes.

LEECH: It is truth.

J.W.: Leech, you wouldn't recognize the truth if it smacked you in the face.

LANDISH: Objection to that outrageous comment. Request the court to admonish the criminal defense lawyer.

WILKES: [To Landish] Why sir? Was I outlandish?

COURT: Sustained. Sustained. The jury will again disregard the comments of the criminal defense lawyer, who, I might add, had better control his mouth.

CRIMINAL HISTORY

J.W.: How many felonies have you been convicted of committing, O Great Father?

LEECH: I don't recall exactly, sir. That was all before my rebirth in the House of the Lord. But to answer your question, more than two and less than ten.

J.W.: Let me see if I can jog your selective memory, Father Leech. Let's start with the present. What are you doing time for now?

LEECH: Relieving others of material goods upon the presentation of weapon. An unfortunate mistake in identification by the victim, I assure you. I haven't been sentenced and I expect we will clear it all up then.

J.W.: In other words, a jury like this one has already found that you committed strong-arm robbery. And now you are trying to get out of a twenty-year sentence by singing a song for your supper, courtesy of Lord Landish.

LANDISH: OBJECTION!

COURT: Sustained. The jury will again disregard the comments of the criminal defense lawyer. Ask a question without the argumentative monologue, Mr. Wilkes.

J.W.: Father Leech, what's next in your criminal history?

LEECH: Oh, long ago, a couple of burglaries, assaults, things like that. Again, that was all in my previous life, admittedly a rascally one, but again, prior to rebirth.

J.W.: So what we see now is the afterbirth of Harry Leech?

LANDISH: OBJECTION!

COURT: Sustained. The jury will again disregard the comments of the criminal defense lawyer. Mr. Wilkes, you are dancing with contempt now. I warn you.

J.W.: Leech, your crimes include crawling into people's homes at night when they're asleep and stealing their property, and if they awaken, terrorizing them with your gun and pistol-whipping them, right?

LEECH: Regretfully, some of my past conduct has resembled your brutish description, sir. But so long ago. And I have mourned for those victims, really mourned and prayed for them, and I have repented. My sins are washed away now. I spend my time volunteering to bring the word of the Church of the Sing-a-Song to others in prison. Anyway, no one came to great harm.

J.W.: Mr. Slipper, come forward. Leech, do you recognize this man?

LEECH: No.

J.W.: During your last burglary, you entered his house and hit him over the head and fractured his skull.

LEECH: It was dark. I didn't see faces. It was a long time ago in the other life.

SLIPPER: Two years ago! Let me at that son of a bitch! [Man restrained from attacking witness]

LEECH: Forgive me Father for I know not what I did!

J.W.: How many burglary convictions do you have?

LEECH: I can't remember. I can't remember everything I did in that other life.

J.W.: Is it amnesia or are you having trouble remembering because there are just too many crimes to recall?

COURT: Mr. Wilkes, when are you going to refrain from these improper comments?

J.W.: When he stops lying to this jury to frame an innocent man! Then he'll be freed by Lord Landish to sack and pillage our community and crush the skulls of good folks like Mr. Slipper or like the ladies and gentlemen of the jury or—

COURT: ENOUGH! That's contempt, which we'll deal with later. [To witness] Father Leech, can you just tell us all you know about your criminal record?

LEECH: That's it, Your Honor. Just ask me about one and I'll tell you what I know.

J.W.: Do you remember fracturing Mr. Slipper's skull?

LEECH: Not really.

J.W.: That's because you've assaulted so many people in your life, right?

LEECH: No. I just don't recall it, but my sin is ever before me, for "behold, I was shapen in iniquity and in sin did my mother conceive me." Psalms 51:5.

J.W.: I like it when you read from the Good Book, Leech. I've never seen the Devil quote scripture.

COURT: That's not a question.

J.W.: Okay, Judge. Leech, let me ask you this. Mr. Slipper here doesn't recall your reciting gospel to him while you were assaulting him. Don't you remember his pleas, begging that you not hurt him, and your statement, "Die mother, die," as you repeatedly struck him with your gun?

LEECH: No. It's been quite a while.

J.W.: When is the last time you held a job?

LEECH: You mean before I devoted my life to the Church of the Sing-a-Song? Well, a long time ago. I delivered clothes in the garment district.

J.W.: That was over ten years ago, wasn't it?

LEECH: Something like that.

J.W.: How have you made a living since then?

LEECH: State's been feeding me, mostly. I've been in prison a lot.

J.W.: Looks like they've been feeding you pretty well. Did you take a vow of poverty?

LEECH: Not exactly. You don't need to when you're in prison.

J.W.: But what about during those brief interludes when the state made the colossal mistake of freeing you? What did you do then to make a living?

CON LAW

LEECH: You know. The other me, before being reborn into the Church of the Sing-a-Song, did bad things. Things the Lord has forgiven. But before that, in prison, I majored in con law, you might say, and came out worse than I went in.

J.W.: Okay. Tell us what He has forgiven.

LEECH: I stole in my former life.

J.W.: Right. When you wanted something, you just took it from people. You robbed people at gunpoint of their belongings 'cause you wanted it and they had it.

LEECH: Sometimes.

J.W.: You're a professional thief, right, a guy who makes his living at it?

LEECH: Never stole professionally. A pro wouldn't get caught as frequently as me. I think it was all part of the Lord's plan for me to do wicked things, to be a sinner, and then be saved by the grace of God.

J.W.: And I suppose it's just a coincidence that for taking this confession and mouthing the liturgy of the Church of the Sing-a-Song to these jurors, the prosecutor's gonna give you freedom? Miles Landish is really your savior, right? The D.A. is the god you worship because he converts liars like you from inmates to outmates?

LEECH: [To Judge] Isn't the D.A. going to object to that? That ain't a question.

LANDISH: I object! That ain't a question.

COURT: Mr. Wilkes, that's about it. Come up here. That question or statement will be stricken. Ladies and gentleman, as I told you several dozen times by now, when I strike one of the criminal defense lawyer's gratuitous comments, you are to ignore them entirely and you may take into consideration his resort to such improper tactics in weighing his presentation. [To Wilkes, now at sidebar] You're asking for immediate sanctions right here, Wilkes. And I mean in the tank.

J.W.: I move for a mistrial based on this blatant perjury.

COURT: I'm listening, but all I hear is misconduct.

J.W.: Judge, with all due respect, have you had your hearing checked recently?

LANDISH: Contempt! Contempt! Bucket him, Judge! Do it now!

COURT: Yes, it is contempt, but I will not allow Mr. Wilkes to cause a mistrial. The comments are noted and we shall take them up following today's testimony. Now get out there and try this case. [Parties return to their respective counsel tables]

EPISTLE TO SAINT LANDISH

J.W.: [Showing witness letter] Father Leech, did you write this letter to the prosecutor?

LEECH: Is that my epistle to Mr. Landish? The one where I tell him about your client's confession? The one where I applauded Mr. Scribner's bravery in making a full confession to relieve his guilt? I hope I was able to give him some comfort in this time of need.

DEFENDANT: OOOOOOAUUGH!

J.W.: And in return for your offer of testifying, you make a list of your demands in your so-called epistle to Saint Landish, right? For example, you ask for the dropping of all charges against you?

LEECH: They didn't do it, but I wanted to be able to leave prison and continue my ministry in the free world.

J.W.: And geographic relocation to Miami Beach for the winter, right?

LEECH: Right. I did. They didn't.

J.W.: A new identity? A job? Cash?

LEECH: Right. I did. They didn't.

WILKES: A guaranteed annual income? A limousine with a chauffeur for transportation to and from court, and mileage?

LEECH: Right. All that. I did ask. They didn't respond.

J.W.: And even witness fees?

LEECH: As I have said, I did. They didn't. No harm in asking, Mr. Wilkes. After all, it is better to give than receive.

J.W.: Expert witness fees perhaps?

LEECH: Huh?

J.W.: For being a professional perjurer?

COURT: The jury will ignore the last comment. Mr. Wilkes, that's tonight's lodgings for you. You know what I mean.

J.W.: Conditions are not too good in the Tombs or at Riker's, are they?

LEECH: No.

J.W.: Answer me this. Your religion was created in prison, right?

LEECH: The Founder was a prisoner, yes.

J.W.: And the special dietetic requirement of the Church of the

Sing-a-Song is filet mignon for dinner every night, right?

LEECH: Yes, and if you'll just read the cases, you'll see that the courts have recognized us as a religion. Filet mignon is part of our special dietetic need, for, as it is written, "Every man should eat and drink, and enjoy the good of all his labor, it is the gift of God." Ecclesiastes, 3:13.

WILKES: Why do you look at the jurors, Mr. Leech? Did your Lord and master [points to Mr. Landish] tell you to do that too?

LEECH: No.

J.W.: Just sizing up future victims, eh?

LANDISH: I object!

COURT: Sustained. That's another night on the house, Mr. Wilkes.

WILKES: You know that if you just make up a story and offer it to the D.A., one he wants to hear, you can cut a deal and get out of jail?

LEECH: You have to tell the truth. "My lips shall not speak wickedness, nor my tongue utter deceit." Job 27:4.

J.W.: This is all a game to you, isn't it, Mr. Leech?

LEECH: No game. It's life.

J.W.: You just come in here, say a few words that the prosecutor wants to hear, and you're free, right?

LEECH: No.

J.W.: Do you always sweat so much when you lie under oath?

LEECH: "The beginning of strife is as when one letteth out water." Proverbs 17:1.

READING MODERN SCRIPTURE

J.W.: Let's talk about my client's so-called statement to you. You read the papers about this case?

LEECH: I read the Scriptures, "Seek ye out of the book of the Lord, and read." Isaiah 34:16.

J.W.: So if another inmate came in here and testified that you kept a file of clippings on this case, he'd be a liar?

LEECH: I clip only the religious section of the newspaper, for I always do as John said: "Search the Scriptures; for in them ye think ye have eternal life: and they are they which testify of me." John 5:39. I read nothing of this case.

J.W.: You smile when you read that, Mr. Leech. "One may smile, and smile, and be a villain." Hamlet, Act One, Scene Five.

LEECH: Mr. Wilkes, somebody's lying to you about me reading about this case, and if I have a pleasant expression on my face, it is only because "God loveth a cheerful giver." 2 Corinthians 9:7.

J.W.: Leech, if lying strikes you as funny, your testimony could be dangerous to your health.

LEECH: Huh?

J.W.: You could die laughing.

LANDISH: I object! Time for more sanctions! Contempt!

COURT: Yes, yes, yes. Same admonition to the jury about the comments of the criminal defense lawyer. Three nights on the house now. How much longer with the witness, Mr. Wilkes?

J.W.: Oh, about ten pounds more. Father Leech, the term "snitches." You are familiar with it?

LEECH: It's a fellow who relates the confession of another inmate.

J.W.: For a reward, right? For something in return.

LEECH: One good turn deserves another.

J.W.: You're smiling again, Mr. Leech. Now, do some inmates keep files on highly publicized cases in order to know the details of the case, and then lie about a confession from the defendant?

LEECH: That has been said to happen, although not in this case. I took an oath, Mr. Wilkes. "When thou shalt vow a vow unto the Lord thy God, thou shalt not slack to pay it: for the Lord thy God will surely require it of thee." Deuteronomy 23:21.

J.W.: Give me a break. Now, you kept such files on this case, didn't you?

LEECH: As I testified, my interest in newspapers is pretty much limited to the religion section.

J.W.: How about answering my question? Did you cut out, or look at, or keep, or store, or otherwise come into contact with any news clipping on this case? Answer yes or no.

LEECH: Based upon your rather prolix question, as presently formulated in its detailed yet compound state, I can only answer, not to my knowledge.

J.W.: How many guys have you snitched-off in your illustrious snitching career?

LEECH: You mean, you want me to count the number of times I have taken confession? That's my job as a priest in the Church of the Sing-a-Song. I haven't counted.

J.W.: What about the priest-penitent privilege? How come you always reveal to the D.A. the confessions you take? It's because the D.A. is the true Lord of your church, right? [Pause] You're looking at Landish, Leech.

LEECH: Mr. Landish is not the Lord, and the priest-penitent privilege does not apply because we have not been able to maintain the confidences given us by our inmate parishioners.

J.W.: Have you resisted? Have you refused to reveal them? Has a court forced them from you?

LEECH: No. We render unto Caesar what is Caesar's.

J.W.: Don't you just. Now, Father Leech, when did you see my client in the Tombs?

LEECH: Only time I saw him was once. He was going to court and so was I, and we got to talking while we waited.

J.W.: Why do you think he chose to confess to you, a crook whom he'd never seen before?

LEECH: Honest face, I guess.

J.W.: *That* face?

LEECH: He asked me about general matters. You know, like what was gonna happen that day in court. And we got to talking, and he told me all about what he had done.

J.W.: Mr. Leech, who else was in the tank with you that morning?

LEECH: Lots of guys, but they probably didn't hear anything because we were in a corner talking rather low.

J.W.: And why did you wait a month before you wrote the D.A., telling him about the confession?

LEECH: No reason. It was a routine confession. Just didn't get around to it.

J.W.: [Hands exhibits to witness] Mr. Leech, these are the newspaper articles which appeared on the case before you allegedly talked to my client. I want you to tell me if there is one fact in your letter to the D.A. that isn't in the news articles.

LEECH: [Pause. Witness reads articles] I also told the D.A. the victim begged for his life as he was being killed. I don't see that in these articles.

DEFENDANT: OOOAAAUUUUHHH!

J.W.: Having tried to kill so many people before, it wouldn't be too tough for you to make that up, would it? Didn't all of your victims plead for their lives before you cracked their skulls?

LEECH: It's not in the papers. That's what he told me.

J.W.: Everything else you wrote the D.A. could have been taken from the papers or TV news, right?

LEECH: Could have, but wasn't.

PEPPERONI TRAP

J.W.: Now sir, read this part of the *Times* article where it starts, "John Wilkes, lawyer for the accused, says . . .

LEECH: [Reading] ". . . on the afternoon in question his client and Judge Knott had just finished a late snack they had called in from NYPD Pizza." Yes, Mr. Wilkes, he also told me that. Pepperoni and mushrooms, I think. That's what I wrote to the D.A.

J.W.: No, I don't think so. You should not believe what you read in the papers, Leech. I made that up.

LANDISH: HE'S TESTIFYING NOW. OBJECTION!

COURT: Sust—

J.W.: Just hold it, Judge. Just hold on one stinking minute. Let me get some truth out. It might be refreshing. I will testify right now. I told the reporter about the pizza to plant a false fact for the perjuring snitches like Leech to fall for. And he did.

LANDISH: HE'S STILL TESTIFYING. OBJECTION!

COURT: SUSTAINED! The jury will disregard the comment of Mr. Wilkes. He will have the opportunity to call his witnesses later, ladies and gentlemen. For now, disregard his comments except as they may reflect the lengths to which he will go. Four nights' lodgings now, Mr. Wilkes.

J.W.: [To judge] So be it. [To witness] But let me put it to you this way, Father Leech. If you were to hear the reporter testify that I told that little fib about the pizza so as to plant a phony fact so that my client would be protected from perjuring pukes like you who use the papers as scripts for perjury, how would you explain that?

D.A.: Same objection, Your Honor.

J.W.: I'm trying to save a lot of time here, Your Excellency.

COURT: Not by testifying.

LEECH: Mr. Wilkes, I have the answer. I can only suggest that Mr. Scribner also lied to me about the pizza, as you did to the reporter, when he stated that he and the judge ate Italian that afternoon.

J.W.: Leech, you're smiling again. They never ordered pizza. They never ate pizza. No pizza was found in chambers or in the judge during the autopsy. I made that up and you bought it hook, line, and sinker. You bought the whole thing, you lousy snake.

LEECH: It wasn't me. It was the Lord.

J.W.: Yes, well, why don't we see if Lord Landish wants any more singing out of you . . .

LANDISH: OB—

J.W.: . . . and if not, you can roll off the stand and . . .

LANDISH: —JECTION!

J.W.: . . . slither back to jail . . .

LANDISH: OBJECTION! MISCON—

J.W.: . . . where I'm sure your filet mignon awaits you. You've sung for your supper. [Mr. Wilkes is seated]

COURT: SUSTAINED. The jury will disregard that. Mr. Landish, any questions of Father Leech?

LANDISH: Just one. Did you tell the truth here?

J.W.: [Standing and yelling] OBJECTION! THIS WITNESS IS INCOMPETENT TO ANSWER THAT QUESTION!

COURT: The jurors will be the judge of that. Overruled. Sit down.

LEECH: Yes, "I have chosen the way of truth." Psalms 119:30.

NIGHTY NIGHT

And so, the perjurer left the stand after bearing false witness for two days. I thought Wilkes tore Leech up, especially when the planted pizza story came to light, but what difference did it make? The confession was going to take its toll. The jury could think Leech was the perjuring slime-bucket that he was, but they would also think, "You know, that guy may be a jerk and a liar, but with all the evidence we've heard, the confession could well be true." And the damage would be done.

After Leech oozed out of the courtroom, Landish announced, "The People of the Great State of New York, having proved their case beyond a shadow of a doubt, rest."

Junior replied that it was late and time to adjourn. He dismissed the jurors for the night. After they left, he added, "Bailiff, seize Mr. Wilkes and take him away. He will spend his next four nights in jail."

Wilkes was not too distressed at this order. As the bailiff approached, he said, "Your Honor, you do me great honor in punishing me, albeit unfairly, for my defense of my client against the lies of the State. However, despite the honor bestowed, I must at this time make a motion for mistrial given that you are incapacitating me and thus depriving me of any ability to mount the defense of Mr. Scribner. If you do this to me, if I am jailed, I warn you that I will rest tomorrow based solely on the fact of my inability to prepare my witnesses, to consult with my client, and to do all the important and multitudinous things a trial lawyer does in the midst of trial. I can cite you, right now off the top of my head, Supreme Court cases reversing convictions for judges handicapping defense lawyers far less egregiously, if you'd care to hear them."

HORNS OF A DILEMMA

The motion was audacious. We had no defense witnesses worthy of the name. Scribner could be called, of course, if we wanted to hear our man moan under oath for a couple of hours. But actually, it was a terrific motion. If the judge bucketed Wilkes, we'd have a dandy issue for appeal, an insurance policy guaranteeing trial number two. And Wilkes being in jail wouldn't hamper the defense. There wasn't any defense to hamper.

Everyone looked at Junior. He seemed on the verge of saying something, but was blocked by verbal constipation. As the wheels spun, he thought: If Wilkes is right, and the bastard might well be, this case would never withstand appeal after Scribner's convicted, as he surely will be. And there may be cases on point, like that bastard says. I dunno. I haven't read a Supreme Court case for years. Who's got time to read that crap! But a reversal would be disaster! They'd blame me! My appeals court appointment would be gone for sure, thanks to that devil. On the other hand, putting him in jail now might be worth it all!

After pondering the matter, Junior finally moved his lips. "Upon reflection, I am going to stay the service of the four nights in jail until the defendant Scribner is found guil— I mean, er, until the jury verdict is read. Scribner deserves a full opportunity to defend himself, although I fully believe, Mr. Wilkes, that if you were incarcerated, Mr. Schoonblower could handle matters of preparation. But until the verdict, Wilkes, you are on bail to the court, revocable if we have another series of outbursts of unprofessional conduct like we've had these past two days. We are adjourned until tomorrow."

—17—

Suicide Is a Pain in the Ass

"Truth like stab of cruel knife."
CHARLIE CHAN

"One thing about the Guadalajara Café. When you leave here, you know you've swallowed something."
JOHN WILKES

If you want to know how things are going in an airplane, look to the flight attendants. Through most turbulence, they stroll down the cabin serving food and drinks as calmly as if they were walking through their own homes. Very reassuring. But when you see fear leap on their faces, you know there's trouble.

It's no different in the criminal courts. The demeanor and reactions of the court personnel—the bailiff, the court reporter, the court clerk—tell a lot about how things are going. Usually, their looks of boredom telegraph that it's litigation as usual, even in the most sensational of trials. But when they start looking at you with pity, or anxiety, or downright dread, you begin to feel as out of place as a pregnant leper at a swimsuit contest.

Such were the stares Wilkes and I received as we entered the court to begin our so-called defense of our client. We didn't need the looks of the court personnel to tell us of the powerful case put on by the D.A. Wilkes was desperate. This morning he carried a huge leather-bound book—almost two feet square and one foot in width. Giant gold letters were emblazoned on the cover and the spine so that a near-blind man could read the title—WRONGFUL CONVICTIONS— from any seat in the courtroom. Maybe jurors might think twice before snuffing out poor Alvin's liberty if they thought that they were making a mistake.

Like I say, Wilkes was desperate.

SURPRISE

We took our places at counsel table. Wilkes put the book down so that the spine faced the jurors, and we waited for our client to weep his way into the courtroom. The place was packed as usual, but the mood was far different than when we began almost two weeks previous. In the beginning there was the heightened feeling of expectancy like before a heavyweight fight where the lightly regarded challenger is given little chance, but a chance nevertheless. The chance of the lucky punch. Court watchers thought Wilkes, in his inimitable way, might rope-a-dope his way through the early rounds and then maybe beat the case with a last-second sucker punch.

But now the mood was more like—how much worse can this thing get?

Answer: Worse. Much worse.

When Junior assaulted the bench, I noted an unusual spring in his step. He seemed positively enthusiastic. "Counsel will approach the bench," he trumpeted.

We gathered beneath the shadow of the throne and looked up at Junior's ghostly, whitewashed face. "Gentlemen, there's good news and, I am afraid, bad news also. The bad news I must report to you is that the defendant attempted to hang himself in his cell during the late evening hours. A guard found him unconsciousness and cut him down in time, and I am told that the infirmary reports him to be in good condition, although somewhat depressed."

Wilkes and I were stunned at this news. Alvin had been having a hard time of it to be sure, but we never thought it was that bad. "Thank God he's okay," I said to Wilkes. "That's good news."

Junior corrected me. "Yes, very fortunate, but the good news I was referring to is that the doctors say he can be back in court tomorrow. I propose to excuse the jury for the day and we can work on jury instructions so as not to waste precious court time. Any objections?"

"The poor bastard," mumbled Wilkes.

"No objection from the People," said Landish. "But upon hearing this, Your Honor, I think we will wish to reopen our case tomorrow to put on evidence of the defendant's attempted suicide."

Wilkes's face reddened. He looked at Landish. "The man's almost dead, and the first thing you want to do is put it on as evidence?"

"Now, now, Mr. Wilkes," said Junior. "Mr. Landish raises an interesting evidentiary question which I hadn't considered. I take it quite seriously, and anyway, he's just doing his job."

"Yeah, he's a regular professional human being."

Encouraged by Junior, Landish expanded upon his ridiculous point. "Yeah, the defendant's attempt at suicide is the same as if he were running from the scene of a crime. It's something from which the jury can infer a guilty mind."

Wilkes looked at Landish. "Are you nuts? Have you lost your mind? This is irrelevant," said Wilkes. "And whatever minimal probative value it has would be outweighed by the prejudice to the defense and to the defendant personally. It could only further depress my client and possibly bring on another attempt."

"Since when is an attempt by an accused murderer to flee from the arms of the law irrelevant?" said Landish to Junior. "That is the clearest demonstration of consciousness of guilt."

Wilkes thought the argument so morbid and silly, he just gave Landish the raspberries in rebuttal, "THPHPPHPHPHPHPHPH-PHPHPHPHPH." All of the jurors, save for the ever-dozing Wyatt Wonderlick, turned their heads in wonderment at the loud sound, curious at what was going on at the throne.

Junior, as he said, was taking this seriously. He looked lost in contemplation over the weighty legal issue as he tapped a gold ballpoint pen on the desk. Quickly noting that the raspberries did not convince the judge, Wilkes verbalized, "But he was unconscious."

"Well, then perhaps it shows an unconsciousness of guilt," said Junior after a moment of additional thought. "Okay, I have decided. I'll ask you both to research the matter overnight and present your respective positions to me tomorrow."

MUMBO JUMBO

Junior excused the jurors for the day without telling them why, and we spent the next hours haggling endlessly over jury instructions— the incomprehensible, monotonous litany of legal mumbo jumbo read by the judge to a totally bewildered jury at the close of the case. Jury instructions are that special part of the trial liturgy. Constructed in isolated law temples by appellate high priests, written in the mystic juridical argot, and handed down to earthly mortals in sacred unread tomes, they decree the metes and bounds of the law's mighty reach. No one understands them and they are impossible to communicate in a comprehensible fashion. Yet the inviolable dictates from on high ordain that they must be read exactly as written by the high priests on penalty of a judgment reversed. So resentful trial judges read them to juries exactly as penned by the appellate high priests and with all the enthusiasm of a man paying taxes.

Unfathomable as they are, jury instructions are the rules by which men and women on trial will be awarded their freedom or be consigned to life in a cage.

Because we had no defense, we asked for instructions which would allow the jury to imagine one: self-defense, defense of property, alibi, claim-of-right, entrapment, outrageous government misconduct, duress, consent, impossibility, and insanity. Junior rejected them all. He did agree to give a reasonable doubt instruction, but only because he knew the appellate high priests commanded it be given in every criminal trial no matter how strong the evidence against the accused.

When we finally finished arguing with Junior and Landish about the instructions, we had a typical set which were complex enough to baffle a convention of linguists. Wilkes and I then went to pay our respects to our poor client in the jail infirmary.

MULRANEY

Mike "the Hanky" Mulraney was busy reading a new homicide report written by Jaime Perez, about a drive-by drug shooting in Spanish Harlem, when he got the call from Chief Lorton to come to his office. When he got there, he stood in front of the chief's desk and announced his presence with a sneeze. The chief looked up and handed him a subpoena. "You are going to be called by the defense tomorrow."

Mulraney was not surprised. After Alice Knott testified that she had told him during their interviews that she had seen a spot of blood on Alvin's sleeve before he touched the body of her husband, he expected to be called. His notes of his interview reflected no such statement by Alice and he was sure she had not said it. The first he heard of the spot was when she testified.

"Oh yeah, no big deal. It's going to be about Alice and the blood spot on the sleeve."

"Yeah, yeah," said the chief. "But how are you gonna handle it?"

Mulraney looked puzzled. "Whad'ya mean? I'm gonna say that I have no recall of her ever saying that to me. And the defense will ask me if I would have found that fact significant, and I will say yes, 'cause it was."

The chief was not happy with Mulraney's response. He wanted him to shade his testimony, as in the traditional police fashion, to support the star prosecution witness. "Why, Mike? Why say that? Can't you just say that she could have said it? I mean, she could have, couldn't she? Maybe she said it while you were sneezing and you just missed it. Coulda happened."

Mulraney wiped his runny nose, miffed that the chief was putting on this pressure. He began walking out of Lorton's office, and with his back to the chief said, "I don't think so, Chief." Walking down the hallway he heard the chief's voice following him, "Ahh-hah! See, you don't THINK so! Those sneezes are pretty loud, Hanky. You're not certain in your mind. All those medications. It's a possibility still, SHE COULD HAVE SAID IT. . . ."

TO STAND OR NOT TO STAND

The next morning, Alvin appeared, looking much the same as he did last night when we saw him in the infirmary—drugged to the hilt on antidepressants and almost catatonic. He sat down between Wilkes and me and stared straight ahead. Actually, today was an improvement. Sure, he looked like a drugged-out zombie sitting there staring vacantly into space, but at least he had his head up and wasn't weeping.

Junior called us up to the throne. "I note the defendant is present and looking no worse for wear. Now, I've decided in the interests of fairness and expedition not to let the People reopen their case to introduce evidence of the suicide attempt. However, if the defendant testifies, it may well become a relevant subject of inquiry and I may allow Mr. Landish to explore it on cross-examination. You may proceed with your case, Mr. Wilkes."

Junior's ruling was geared for one purpose—to frighten our client off the stand. What he didn't know was that long before the suicide attempt, we knew Alvin could not testify. He was so shamed and fragile, and he looked so guilty what with the head down and the constant moaning, he would have cracked on the stand and confessed to anything Landish asked.

OUT DAMNED SPOT

Wilkes called our first witness, Detective Mike Mulraney. Mulraney testified just as he told the chief he would the evening before: Alice had said nothing about the bloody spot to him. Predictably, Landish asked him on cross, "She COULD have said that, right? You just don't remember, right? Maybe you missed it during one of your sneezes." But Mulraney was resolute and said she did not mention the blood spot on the sleeve.

As Mulraney answered, Landish looked back at Lorton, who was sitting in the front row of the gallery, and turned back to the witness to press the point. "You were very sick that day. Asthma, sneezing, head stuffed and aching, runny nose, the whole nine yards, right?

"That's pretty normal for me," said the Hanky. "It doesn't impact on my work."

"And you were taking your usual medications, right? The nose and eyes drops, the inhalers, the antihistamines, the decongestants, the espresso coffee and aspirin, right?"

Mulraney looked at Lorton. The bastard had primed Landish with these questions. This was the first time anyone had used his allergy-asthma condition against him in a courtroom. And his own boss was behind it!

"Yes," said Mulraney, still glaring at Lorton, "the usual."

"So you cannot sit there and tell this jury that she did not say anything about the spot, given your disabled condition, can you?"

"I said I heard what she told me. The subject of the spot didn't come up."

"That you recall?" stated Landish, attempting to end on at least an ambiguous note. "Between coughs, nose-blowings, and sneezes."

"Obviously, I'm testifying to what I recall, which is all the significant aspects of my interview with Mrs. Knott. A bloody spot would have been significant. She didn't say it."

Wilkes, amused by the prosecution cross of its own case agent, sat and watched. When Landish finished, he had no questions for Mulraney, who left the stand, gave Landish a dirty look, and moved his chair as far away from the prosecutor as he could and still be sitting at the prosecution table.

WILKES CALLS WILKES

Wilkes then called our next witness. "I now call John Wilkes to the stand." With that he strode to the stand and sat down. He looked to Junior and announced, "I could do my own questioning of the witness, but I have decided to have my associate, Mr. Schoonover, examine me."

Landish rose and objected. Out of his melon head came the usual thunder: "Objection! Objection, Your Honor! It's against the rules for an advocate to be a witness in a case he's defending."

To which Junior replied, "What's new? He's broken every other rule of this court so far."

To which Wilkes retorted, "Surely I must have inadvertently obeyed one or two."

I delayed no longer and fired away with the first question. "Mr. Wilkes, in the *New York Times* on the morning following the arrest of Mr. Scribner, you are reported to have said that Mr. Scribner and Judge Knott ate a pepperoni and mushroom pizza on the afternoon of the murder. Did you say that?"

Wilkes looked at the jurors. Most of them avoided his eyes, except for Wyatt Wonderlick, whose eyes were closed. "I did. I told the reporter that I was informed of this by my client. But in reality, the bit about the pizza was made up entirely by me. As I said when cross-examining the perjurer, this was a trap to prove that Harry Leech got all his information about the case from the papers. Alvin never told Leech that or anything else. I know."

"Are you suggesting then that Harry Leech lied when he was testifying before this jury."

"OBJECTION!" yelled Landish.

"ABSOLUTELY," yelled Wilkes.

"SUSTAINED," yelled Junior.

"Thank you, Your Honor," said I, hoping the jurors would still not understand the difference between "sustained" and "overruled." I then introduced the newspaper article into evidence and sat down.

Landish could not let the moment go without asking Wilkes a question. I prayed he wouldn't ask the right question. "So you lied to that *Times* reporter, Adell Loomis?" he asked. That was the wrong question. The right question would have been, "How often do you lie with Adell Loomis—in bed?" Fortunately, he didn't know that Adell and Wilkes were an item.

Wilkes smiled at Landish. "I didn't lie. I like to think of it as entrapping a perjurer," he snapped. "It's an effective and time-honored technique, as you know, Mr. Landish. The cops do it all the time."

That answer led to more yelling objections by Landish, who claimed the answer was nonresponsive, with me responding by yelling legal rationalizations to preserve Wilkes's nonresponsive answer ("Landish opened the door to the answer"). Junior sustained Landish's objection. I said, "Thank you, Your Honor." And so ended Wilkes's brief stint as a witness for the defense.

PARADE REST

With Wilkes, our short parade of witnesses concluded and we rested. Final arguments to the jury began. Landish started. He gave a repeat performance of his opening statement. It was like a symphony. He began quietly going over the evidence he had produced, then gradually, as he began urging damning deductions of guilt from the facts, he grew louder, until finally, by the end, he was gesticulating wildly, spraying the jury with spittle mist and madly screaming for a verdict of guilt. He characterized our defense as based upon two puny points: (a) whether or not Alice Knott told Mulraney about the blood spot on Alvin's sleeve, and (b) how Harry Leech came to testify that Alvin and Judge Knott ate pizza. He dismissed them both with, "So what? Even if Wilkes is right on those points, and I don't for a moment concede that he is, they don't make his client innocent. He's still bloody guilty and you will find him guilty! The evidence is overwhelming and, this is important, VIRTUALLY UNCON-TESTED!"

Then he ended with a moist call to arms: "Let justice be done!"

As he sat down, the jurors wiped their faces. Wilkes whispered to me a response to the "let justice be done" comment: "We'll appeal."

Now Wilkes rose to argue. He went over to the jury rail and started quietly pacing in front of the jury. I had no idea of what he would say given that there wasn't a whole lot he could say.

"Ladies and gentlemen. First off, I want to get one thing clear. The judge and I have been at odds throughout this trial. I've tried to do my job in putting before you ALL the evidence at my command to show you that Alvin is innocent. And he has cited me for contempt several times for it. Apparently I must go to jail after the trial concludes."

Junior interrupted. "Mr. Wilkes, this is improper argument. Carry on with it and I'll have to add another citation. The jury will disregard it. Continue."

Wilkes continued as if Junior had said nothing. "With jail awaiting me at trial's end, perhaps I should make this argument the longest in recorded history. At least then I can postpone the dismal fate which awaits me. Maybe the judge will relent or retire or pass—or something else. But I won't do that to you ladies and gentlemen. All I want to say to you is that if you are disenchanted with me, John Wilkes, this old country lawyer, well then, please don't hold it against my client.

"I rise to talk to you about truth. Truth. Truth is the secret of any trial, and it's going to be your job to find it. It's not an easy job. Like Robert Frost said, 'We stand in a circle and suppose while the secret sits in the middle and knows.' You think you know the truth of this case? I'm telling you that the truth is sitting here with us in the well of the court, invisible like Harvey the Rabbit, wondering if he's ever going to be recognized.

"Now let me tell you the tool you must use to find the truth of this case. We are going to talk about reasonable doubt. You didn't hear Mr. Landish say much about that, even though it is the most important constitutional rule of American procedure; it is your guide to the evidence in this case. What does it mean? Let's see if I can help you with examples of reasonable doubt.

"Perhaps you have wondered what areas I would have explored if allowed to by the judge. THAT concern of yours, THAT is reasonable doubt! Perhaps you have wondered why the prosecutor never even mentioned the reasonable doubt rule in his argument. THAT wonderment, that is reasonable doubt! And perhaps you have noticed my client sitting there at counsel table racked with the excruciating pain of being falsely accused. That pain, so visible to you, THAT IS reasonable doubt! And what about me? You've seen my commitment to this case and to Alvin. You know my personal standards would never let me defend a person I knew to be—"

THREE SOBS

At this point Wilkes abruptly stopped arguing. He knew if he said the next word—GUILTY—Junior would contempt him. Instead, Wilkes did the damnedest thing. He came over to counsel table, sat on it and began crying. I mean really crying. He pulled out his hanky and spread it over his face to catch the tears that fell like a monsoon cloudburst. At this development our catatonic client, hearing his own lawyer's loud sobs, came out of his mute spell and started bawling himself. I was so overcome by the weeping duet, I put my arm around Alvin and joined him and Wilkes in sobbing. We wept for the ugly fate that awaited us. At the moment, it seemed like the right thing to do.

Miles Landish was befuddled. He rose to object, but could not figure out what to say. He looked to Junior, who returned the stare in equal befuddlement. They both looked at defense counsel table to see three grown men uncontrollably crying their eyes out. The diversion caused both to miss the opportunity to strike from the record everything Wilkes had said so far as improper jury argument. After listening to the three of us bawl our heads off for thirty seconds, Junior said, "Counsel, please approach the bench."

Wilkes composed himself, stood, pulled a piece of paper from his coat and went forward to the throne. I joined him there.

Junior was not pleased. Wilkes's argument was not only improper, but by crying tears-a-plenty, it was far too sincere. That made it dangerous. A juror might believe that Wilkes actually believed in his client's innocence. Jurors know that defense attorneys usually know. The belief might rub off. Junior looked down at us. "Wilkes, I shall not allow you to weep during argument. It is not professional; it is not advocacy; it is a cheap attempt to draw sympathy untethered to any fact in this case."

"With all due respect, Your Honor," said a dry-eyed Wilkes, who had made a miraculous recovery from his emotional outpouring. "I have some familiarity with the rules in this area. Allow me to read to you from a court of appeals decision written by a distinguished relative of mine, the late Justice Wilkes of the appellate court of Tennessee. He wrote—brilliantly, I might add—what is still the leading case on the subject, *Ferguson* v. *Moore,* in volume ninety-eight of the *Tennessee Reports* at pages 351 to 352."

Wilkes started reading from the Xerox of the case he held:

> "Tears have always been considered legitimate arguments before a jury, and while the question has never arisen out of any such behavior in this court, we know of no rule or jurisdiction in the court below to check them. It would appear to be one of the natural rights of counsel, which no court or constitution could take away. It is certainly, if no more, a matter of the highest personal privilege. Indeed, if counsel has them at command, it may be seriously questioned whether it is not his professional duty to shed them whenever proper occasion arises."

"I'm just exercising my right of personal privilege here, Judge. If the innocence of my client drives me to tears, well, there's nothing wrong with that, and in fact, as my beloved ancestor writes, it may be my professional duty not to obstruct my natural glandular excretion, but rather to let the tears flow. I don't mind if Mr. Landish cries during his rebuttal argument, although I would prefer to see his tears when the verdict comes in. I'm sure the jurors prefer seeing his tears rather than being sprayed with his spittle."

Landish had no case authority to counter that of Wilkes's celebrated ancestor. He shot back, "For all I care, you and your client can float all the way to Sing Sing on your crocodile tears. No one's gonna buy that bull."

Junior was not so ready to agree with Landish. He knew the risks of Wilkes's watery-eyed peroration. "The law of the state of Tennessee has no application in New York. Mr. Wilkes, you may cry all you want when the jury is gone, but not through your argument."

"So you are ordering me not to feel the deep emotion of the

moment? Are you ordering me to control the involuntary aspects of my physiology?"

"Precisely," and with that and a wave of his hand, he dismissed us. As we walked back to our respective corners, he told the jury: "Ladies and gentlemen. The issue has arisen as to the use of tears by counsel during final argument. I have decided that both counsel should try to refrain from crying their hearts out before you. It undermines their delivery. Proceed, Mr. Wilkes."

A dry-eyed Wilkes began again, but he kept his hanky in his hand just to remind the jury of his feelings. "We were talking about reasonable doubt—in other words, about Alvin's innocence—before my feelings overcame me. You may be wondering about that. Well, THAT WONDERMENT about my feelings, THAT is reasonable doubt!"

And so it went. Wilkes gave the jury about five hundred other examples of reasonable doubt, all of which, if compiled in a text book, could be used for a college course in bad logic.

After he finished, Landish spit and yelled his way through his rebuttal argument. "The evidence can't be any stronger," he roared, "and now the ball is in your court. The world is watching you and expecting you to do your duty as you swore to God almighty that you would at the beginning of trial. He is watching too. So do your duty. Do it quickly. Find him what he is. A miserable, stinking little cowardly murderer!"

Landish made finding Alvin guilty sound like one of the Ten Commandments. He was like a tent evangelist threatening non-believers with eternal damnation. For the preacher, true faith is measured by the donations put in the offering basket. For Landish, a juror's true faith was to find Alvin Scribner guilty. Fast.

As Landish sat down, Junior read the incomprehensible instructions to the uncomprehending jurors. He may as well have been speaking in tongues.

. . .

WAITING

At about four P.M. the jury went out to deliberate. "I expect a quick verdict," said Junior as soon as they departed. "I'm going to excuse the alternate jurors at this time with the thanks of the court and order that counsel not leave the building for the balance of the afternoon. We should, er, we could have a verdict within the hour."

Waiting for a verdict is the worst of times. Wilkes nervously paced the courthouse hallway as I sat on a bench and watched him tromp back and forth like a man awaiting his execution. At five we went back to the courtroom half expecting the bad news to be delivered to us by the jury. It was a surprise that they weren't back already, a delay caused perhaps by a spirited contest among the jurors in electing their foreperson. Or maybe they were just making it look fair by taking their time. Wilkes, Alvin, and I watched the jurors march back in the box. They were relaxed and cheerful—too cheerful.

Junior asked if they had reached a verdict and if they had a foreperson—in that order. A woman juror announced she was the designated leader and that no, they hadn't reached a verdict as yet. Junior's face showed disappointment. But then she added, "But we've made excellent progress already."

"Excellent news," said Junior. "We'll see you then tomorrow, and you may resume and hopefully complete your deliberations. We are adjourned."

As soon as the jury left, Wilkes made a motion for a mistrial. "Your Honor has already begun to coerce the jury by giving them a false deadline for a verdict. I move for a mistrial."

Junior was unmoved. The jury's great news of progress made him positively serene. "Denied," he said. "And because of the nearness to a verdict, I must require both counsel to be in this courthouse tomorrow to take the verdict when it comes in."

.   .   .

THE LONG WALK

We left the court and did our usual speed-walk to the Woolworth. Wilkes was extremely agitated. All the way back he cursed himself. "Damn. Damn me. I should have tried the case differently. I shouldn't have let Junior contempt me so many times in front of the jury. Hell, maybe I should have put Alvin on the stand. He's so innocent, maybe it would have shone through even if he got badgered into confessing on the stand. God! I can't stand it."

Such bitter self-criticism was extremely un-Wilkesian. As he castigated himself, Wilkes kicked at every piece of garbage in his path. Beer and pop cans, styrofoam cups and containers, newspapers, gum wrappers, used hypodermic needles and rubbers, cigarette and cigar butts, even that rarest of objects on the sidewalks of New York, a rock, flew off Wilkes's foot like balls at a soccer-kicking contest. His strange attitude got me wondering again about just how much Wilkes knew about the death of Yulburton Abraham Knott.

My worry was heightened by even more un-Wilkesian conduct on our walk back to the office. As we walked over or around the omnipresent homeless, Wilkes threw his paper money at them whether or not they begged for it. By the time we got back to the foot of the Woolworth, we had a small army of them following us, hollering for more and vacuuming up ones, fives, tens, and twenties until Wilkes ran out. Then he borrowed what little I had and threw it all into the crowd. At the entrance to the building he said, "I can't just go up to the office and wait around with nothing to do. I'm going to walk for a while."

With that, he took off down Broadway with the battalion of the ragtag homeless following, many calling out to him to "throw the dough." I stayed at the office all night waiting, except for the breaks when I went looking for him around the building, on the benches at City Hall Park, and in the local dives. He was taking this case *so* personally. The thought kept coming up, the one I hated thinking about, the one I tried to suppress, the one that would not go away.

It was like a hundred-point headline in my mind which read: MAYBE HE'S ACTING LIKE HE'S RESPONSIBLE BECAUSE HE IS.

MUD SLINGING

I woke up from my catnap at about seven in the morning and recommenced the search for Wilkes. I found him in the most unlikely of places—across from the Woolworth Building asleep on one of the pews in St. Peter's Cathedral. Or more accurately, dead drunk. I half carried him to the Guadalajara Café to pour as much of Lunko's mud coffee down him as I could. After the third cup, I thought he was coherent enough to tell him of the phone call I got late last night from our investigator, Uriah Condo.

"He found the Hacker-Cracker. Didn't say where and I didn't really care to know, but he wants to know what to do. The Hacker's requiring a guarantee that you'll represent him for free on his escape charge in return for any cooperation with us. It's dicey. The guy's a flake and a fugitive from justice."

Wilkes's bloodshot eyes seemed to focus for the first time. The look of a shit-faced drunk quickly disappeared. He pulled out his wallet, fingered through an assortment of cards and papers, and extracted a ticket which he gave to me. "Call Condo. Tell him to tell the Hacker to go to the address on the backside of that ticket, where he'll get his instructions."

I looked at the ticket he handed me. It read:

FREE PASS

FOR ONE BLISTERING JACUZZI AT THE LOVE TUB TUMBLE

ADMINISTERED BY THE HOUSE MASSEUSE AND PROPRIETOR

MS. BECKY BUTTERMILK

Won't you please come?

It was one of the passes for a free, watery orgasm given us by our former client, the bosomy Becky Buttermilk. I looked to my rejuvenated friend, who was now ordering one of Lunko's famous grease-filled doughnuts and another cup of mud. My small bit of news was bringing on a miraculous recovery. He smiled at me as he picked up the stale, heavy glazed pastry in his hand, drowned it in the java, and then pushed the sopping mess into his mouth. "One thing about the Guadalajara," he said happily, with his mouth full of mud and glaze, "when you leave here, you know you've swallowed something."

"Wilkes, are you thinking what I think you're thinking—of having Becky—"

Wilkes accurately completed my thought: "Suck the information out of the little bastard? You're damned right I am."

— 18 —

End Games

"Neque enim lex aequior ulla,
Quam necis artifices arte perire sua."

["For there is no law more just than for the
plotters of murder to perish by their own designs."]
OVID

"Good idea not to accept gold medal
until race is won."
CHARLIE CHAN

". . . he's so wickedwy wondaful. I can't bewieve I just met him. It's wove at foist bite. He woves me too. Thank Mr. Wilkes so much for sending him to me. It's weally wove, Mr. Schoonwover. Twue wove, you know wad I mean?"

"Yeah, I do, Becky." And I did. It was Becky Buttermilk on the phone telling me that based upon one Love Tub Tumble (albeit at the all-inclusive blistering level), the horn-rimmed, greasy-haired, pimply, gangly, teenage computer genius with the sociopathic personality—known to his adoring public as the Hacker-Cracker—had fallen in "wove" with the floridly painted madam and sole employee of a health emporium known as the Love Tub Tumble. Of course, what teenage computer hacker wouldn't fall for a self-sufficient woman who spoke like a cartoon character and looked like a gaudy centerfold from an adult bookstore magazine? They were meant for each other.

"We're gonna be mawwied and, oh yeah, Jethwo's gonna help Mr. Wilkie too. He's already gotta idea for him."

Becky was eager to help. "I'll pump him for information," she had told Wilkes in her characteristic way. "I'll scwutinize and pwobe and quewy till I get to da bottom of it for youse guys. I still owe youse for your wictowy in my owal sod-on-me case."

OUT OF COURT

I went back to the office while Wilkes waited it out at the courthouse for the jury verdict. He said he'd call in for progress reports.

It was just before noon when Becky called. She had come through sensationally. "He's gotta weal hot tip; a weal good idea on your case, Schoony. And he even wote me a poem," she said proudly. "A wove poem."

"In the Jacuzzi?" I asked, wondering how the Hacker could have found the time that morning to Jacuzzi, make every form of love imaginable, fall in love, propose marriage, write a love poem, and give Becky a hot tip on Alvin's case.

"No, siwwy. On his wap-top. And he's gonna put all my weceivables in a coded computer accounting system which will pwotect wegular customer pwivacy. Ain't he tewwific?"

"Tewwific," I said. "Now, what's the hot tip?"

BAD NEWS

As soon as I hung up, Wilkes called, sounding like a man who just had been prematurely pronounced dead. "They've got a verdict."

"Don't let Junior take the verdict!" I said. "Stall! Do anything! Go to jail! Get sick! Becky got a hot tip!"

"Her business is getting hot tips."

"No, I mean she's come through for us." I told him the tip she got from the Hacker, and Wilkes simultaneously translated my news into an assignment to Uriah Condo, who was there with him. Then he told me to get to the court ASAP.

I ran to court and arrived within fifteen minutes of Wilkes's call. The court was filled with people buzzing with anticipation for the certain guilty verdict. Alvin was evidently off the psychotropics because he was sitting at the defense table with his head in his arms again, trembling and moaning softly. All the players were in court except Wilkes and Junior. As soon as Junior's clerk saw me, he motioned to me to come forward to his desk. "Wilkes has been in the bathroom for the last twenty minutes. We've been waiting and waiting for him to come out. The judge is gonna send in the bailiffs to haul him out so we can take the verdict. I suggest you get him in here immediately or take the verdict yourself."

STALL IN THE PAIN PARLOR

I wasn't about to take the verdict, so I went to the bathroom, an experience to be avoided in the Criminal Courts Building excepting for the most urgent and extreme calls of nature. The first thing to hit you in the courthouse bathroom, if you're lucky, is the searing stink. If you're unlucky, it's a mugger's fist. Then there's the filth, or what you can see of it in the darkness. Light bulbs don't last a day, and what fixtures haven't been ripped out, don't work. The floor is awash in a sea of urine and water and scum. What remained of the toilet tissue and paper towels was afloat on it. The walls are dark and worn from kicking, head-bashing, graffiti, and chiseling. They are beyond redemption by painting. Now they are the playground of the roaches.

A few people, the ignorant first-time visitors to the Temple of Doom, enter to use the facility for its intended purpose. Others come to smoke weed, or shoot up, or consummate a drug deal, or have sex, or vandalize what's left to destroy, or coerce a witness's testimony, or commit a robbery or sometimes a murder. The bathroom in the Temple of Doom is one of the most dangerous places in the city.

Wilkes was not using it for its intended purpose. He was in a stall. Literally. The door to the stall had been ripped off long ago and he was sitting on the commode holding the remains of a torn newspaper someone had left behind which he couldn't possibly read in the dim light.

He heard me come in and jumped up into a combat posture. "Oh, it's you, Schoon, good to see you. I didn't know how much longer I could last in here." We quickly left the bathroom, proceeded into the courtroom and went straight for the clerk's desk.

"Tell the judge we must have a chambers conference immediately," commanded Wilkes. We had to see Junior if there was to be any chance of stalling the return of the verdict.

The clerk looked at us defiantly. "He's not going to like that. I'm sure he wants to take the verdict first. I know that. Better tell me what this is about." So said the clerk, praetorian guard of the judge's chambers.

"You tell him it's about moving into evidence a couple of exhibits. Tell him it's urgent. Tell him the fate of the entire trial depends on this." Wilkes knew he had to pour it on strong just to get an audience with His Excellency, who was at that moment back in chambers coveting the prospect of unsealing the guilty verdict this jury surely had returned and then sending Wilkes to jail on his contempts.

"Okay, I'll go and tell him," said the clerk, rising to leave, "but I doubt he'll talk to you before we announce the verdicts."

Wilkes looked at me the second the clerk disappeared into chambers. "You know, the clerk's right. Junior won't go for it. Let's go in." With that, Wilkes followed the clerk into chambers pursued by a bouncing Miles Landish and your humble servant.

THE AUDIENCE

The clerk had only got the words out of his mouth that Wilkes wanted a chambers conference when we all barged in like invited guests. Junior was seated in a high-back leather swivel chair and looked surprised by the invasion as he swiveled in our direction.

Junior's chambers were a surprise to me. I expected a perfectly neat and tidy office to match Junior's anal-retentive personality, but this place looked like a paper-recycling plant. Law books, manila case files, a Barbara Cartland novel, lots of the supermarket tabloids, *Sports Illustrated*, the *Post*, sandwich wrappers, yellow Post-Its, Kleenex, law magazines, racing track forms, candy wrappers, empty pop cans, pink phone messages, bills, personal correspondence, fast food flyers, legal pads, and miscellaneous crumpled pieces of paper were among the debris piled on his desk. The mountain range extended off the desk onto the floor and then up to each of the three chairs in front of the desk. What a dump.

As we all stood before His Majesty's desk, Junior said sharply to Wilkes, "What's this nonsense about moving exhibits into evidence? You got all your evidence in. What there was of it. You've got a lot of nerve coming in here with a request like that."

"All I want is a half-day continuance," said Wilkes in as sincere a servile tone as he could fake. "I want to reopen my case based upon new evidence we've uncovered. It's been subpoenaed and will be here tomorrow at nine in the morning along with the witness through whom we'll introduce it. Now, if you'll ask that the court reporter come in, I'll make my offer of proof and tell you what it's all about."

A huge, sickening smile appeared on Junior's ivory face as Wilkes supplicated. It was not a smile of happiness; it was the sadist's elongated cheek-to-cheek sneer, the monster's smirk just before the victim's disembowelment. "This is an act of pure desperation," said Junior. "I've seen too much of this already in this trial. Whatever it is that you have subpoenaed could have been presented days ago when you had your opportunity. The motion for a continuance and to reopen is denied as being dilatory. And I suspect purposely so. You can bring it all up in your motion for new trial prior to sentencing. Perhaps you will argue that you were incompetent in not coming up in a timely fashion with whatever it is you've supposedly now obtained. Now, get out there and we'll take the guilty verdict we all know awaits us."

Miles Landish added a meaningless, "For the record, the People strenuously oppose the defense motions."

Wilkes stood at the front and center of Junior's huge, paper-covered desk and leaned forward in Junior's face. "But, Your Honor, I must beg the court . . ."

"No! Enough!" said Junior. He motioned us out with his backhand.

". . . in the name of justice and all that is right . . ."

"No! Out of here at once!" He pointed to the door.

" . . . please let me put on this brief bit of . . ."

"I'll hear no more! Mr. Clerk, call in the bailiffs at once!" The praetorian ran out to fetch the constabulary.

". . . evidence which will clear my—say, what's this? HEY! WHAT THE HELL! WHAT THE BLOODY HELL IS THIS?" Wilkes's face was looking down at the midsection of Mount Rubbish, the highest peak on Junior's desk. My friend's eyes bulged at whatever he had spotted. He put his finger on a small note from the foot of the paper mountain, slid it to a bit of open space, and read it to himself. Then he starting kissing the note and jumping up and down hollering, "HOLY MOTHER OF GOD! MAY THE BLESSINGS OF BABY JESUS BE UPON YOU! IT'S A MIRACLE! IT'S A MIRACLE!"

A NOTABLE NOTE

"WHAT? WHAT?" I yelled as I watched Wilkes jumping around the judge's chambers like a priest on a pogo stick. I could barely contain my excitement. This was going to be good.

"WHAT? WHAT?" yelled a concerned Miles Landish. From Wilkes's reaction, he knew this was going to be bad.

"WHAT? WHAT?" yelled an alarmed Junior. His ivory cheeks turned to pink chalk. From Wilkes's reaction, he knew this was going to be terrible.

Wilkes finally stopped jumping and calmed himself a bit, but guarded the small note so carefully it might have been a Dead Sea scroll, or a winning Lotto ticket, or a not guilty verdict. Wilkes was triumphant. He said to me, "Schoon, I hold in my hand a short handwritten note from juror number eleven, Ruby's pick, the tight-assed urban cowboy, Wyatt Wonderlick. It was written just after the jurors went out at four P.M. yesterday and it's my guess it has not been acted upon." He looked to a cringing Junior, who seemed to become smaller before our very eyes.

Wilkes then read the note aloud. Here is what it said:

> *Judge Throckton,*
> *Sir, my methadone is*
> *wearing off. What should*
> *I do? Sincerely,*
> *Wyatt Wonderlick (Juror No. 11)*

This was truly a note from Heaven. I had thought throughout the trial that there was something peculiar about Wyatt. He appeared to be a fellow taking too much medication. In reality, he wasn't taking enough.

Junior looked like a shelf of books had just fallen on his head. "What's that? What's that you say?" He reached out with a tremulous hand for the note, but Wilkes caressed it protectively to his chest.

"Not just yet, Judge. We have a juror who has been blotto on drugs and you kept it from us. I assume you know what this means. Whether or not you purposely ignored this note thinking you could squeeze out a quick guilty verdict, it was an enormous blunder only exceeded by your fatal mistake in dismissing all the alternate jurors. You can't replace Wonderlick with anybody. That makes the error uncorrectable. So either the drug fiend, Mr. Wonderlick, is with us for the duration or we don't have twelve to rack in the box anymore. If I move to disqualify him, that means relief for my client. And I spell relief M-I-S-T-R-I-A-L. You know, if I want a mistrial right now, I'm absolutely entitled. You know that! God! I love this!"

THE WORM TURNS

Just then two bailiffs and the clerk hurried into chambers and roughly grabbed Wilkes and me. "You three, get the hell out of here.

Now!" hollered Junior to the four arms of the law and the clerk. The clerk was stunned. A minute ago Junior wanted Wilkes and me bodily tossed out. Now he was angrily evicting the would-be tossers. Ah! How the judicial worm can turn! Two confused bailiffs and one befuddled clerk turned and marched out of chambers.

Wilkes continued working the excellent turn of events for everything it was worth. "In a high profile case like this, these judicial errors are the type which tend to draw extended media attention for weeks and months to come. Oh, I don't mean the predictable giant *Post* headlines like 'Throckton Blunder Blows Scribner Case.' No, I'm talking about the endless analysis in the editorials questioning whether your bias against me and for the victim in this case led to this regrettable situation. And you know how the press can be with those unflattering psychological profiles. Perhaps there'll be an official inquiry as well. Then, of course, there'll be the very nasty professional gossip which, however unfair, tends to frustrate, if not kill, ambitions for higher office."

A mortified Junior continued to shrink in his high-backed chair. Wilkes's words were causing him to dissolve before our very eyes. The back of his hand went up to his mouth and he began chewing it. Wilkes continued, "I could take the mistrial now, but Judge, it's you're lucky day. I'm feeling charitable. None of us want to have to try this case a second time. Right, Miles?"

Wilkes turned to the bewildered hulk standing next to him. Landish knew enough to grasp his dilemma. If Landish moved for a mistrial, things could not get better for his case than they were at the moment, especially given Wilkes's information that he had new defense evidence; and, after all, this jury had just reached a guilty verdict. Yet he instinctively knew that agreeing with anything Wilkes suggested had to be a bad idea. So he said nothing.

"Yes, Judge," I added in the exuberance of the moment and to fill the void brought on by Landish's mental constipation. "Meet the kinder, gentler John Wilkes." Who'd rip your spleen out through your left nostril if it would work to his client's advantage.

•   •   •

A MODEST PROPOSAL

"What's your suggestion?" whispered His Mortification.

"I want my one-half day continuance so I can reopen the case tomorrow. You tell the jurors to tear up their verdict because after the evidence comes in tomorrow they'll have to recommence deliberations. And, by the way, I know you've been rethinking those contempt citations."

"Oh yes," said Junior. Having just received a reprieve from intense embarrassment, investigation, and professional suicide, it was time to be magnanimous. One good turn deserves another. "I've decided that they were adversarial excesses propelled by the heat of battle, and I'm going to discharge all of them as soon as we go on the record."

Amazing what sweet reason can accomplish.

Wilkes added, "And we'd better let Mr. Wonderlick get his methadone this afternoon so we can have a jury of twelve good and true for tomorrow."

Junior grabbed a pen on his desk and hastily wrote a note that told Wyatt to use that afternoon "looking after his personal health needs and be ready for duty tomorrow morning." Wilkes approved. A struck dumb Miles Landish didn't know what to say. We didn't wait, and quickly stepped out of chambers. It was the most amazing turnabout I've ever experienced in a court of law. We went from ruin to running the show within a few seconds. Our case had risen from the dead. We had a chance.

And all because Wyatt Wonderlick ran out of dope.

SUBPOENAED

The next morning a sedated but awake Wyatt Wonderlick took his position as a juror as Junior announced that Wilkes was being given permission to reopen his case for one witness. He told the jurors and the assembled multitudes in the gallery, "This is a bit unusual, ladies and gentlemen, but when the cause of justice demands extraordinary procedures to guarantee fundamental fairness, we can all rejoice that the American system of justice is flexible enough to accommodate. Call your witness, Mr. Wilkes."

Wilkes stood and said, "I recall to the stand Mrs. Judge Yulburton Abraham Knott." At the announcement of her name, into the courtroom stormed Alice Knott, subpoena in hand, mad as hell, and tailed by three three-piece suits, the last two carrying huge brief-cases. Her lawyers. She wore no fur this day, just an off-white business suit probably made out of silk, plenty of makeup and per-fume, and the usual poundage of gold jewelry. She looked like a dowdy, middle-aged Eva Braun. She took the oath and carefully sat down in the witness seat.

Before Wilkes could pop a question, the leader of the three-piece suits addressed the court. "I am, as the court knows, William Pence Fosworth of the firm of Fosworth, Scott, Morrow, and White. We represent Mrs. Knott. May we please approach the bench?"

RULE OF THREES

Junior knew Bill Fosworth from his work before the civil bench where Junior had been holed up for years. Fosworth and his firm represented only the rich and infamous whose troubles, even when labeled "civil fraud and conspiracy," for some reason always ended in civil instead of the criminal courts. And there the firm of Fos-worth, Scott, Morrow, and White was ready to defend them—for a price. All of the partners of the firm were world-class billers, the fee policy of the firm being the notorious Rule of Threes: "Why have one attorney bill time on a client's case when three can do it at thrice the rate?" Bill Fosworth, creator of the rule, was reputed to be the highest billing lawyer in the city. He was known as "Born to Bill" Fosworth, the gold-medal biller who ran out front in the silk-stocking race to seize a pirate's fortune from his clients' treasure chests.

Junior waved everyone to the bench, where Fosworth, followed closely by his two briefcase-carrying toadies, stated, "Your Honor, we received word late yesterday afternoon that the medical files of Mrs. Knott and her late husband have been subpoenaed here by the defense. I see the custodian of the records seated in the first row with the files. Of course, we protest any invasion of the sacred doctor-patient privilege by the defense in this court and move to quash the subpoenaed materials."

Miles Landish finally found something to say. "Yeah, the People of the State of New York join in that."

"Of course," added Fosworth, "my staff worked diligently through the night to research the issue, and we have a short memorandum of the applicable state authorities." One of Fosworth's flunkies opened his briefcase and passed to Fosworth an inch-thick pleading which Fosworth gave to Junior. The second toady handed one to Landish and me.

Junior looked to Wilkes. He was distressed that the little matter of taking new evidence had taken such a turn. He was being placed in the position of having to disappoint a rich and powerful law firm, a potentially influential supporter for higher office. But then there would be no quest for higher office if his faux pas over Wyatt Wonderlick surfaced, as it surely would if he crossed Wilkes.

Wilkes responded, "My reply is threefold. First, the doctor-patient privilege is a mere creature of state statute, riddled with many exceptions which I won't bother to discuss save to say that they make Mr. Fosworth's research irrelevant. The privilege is not guaranteed by the United States Constitution, whereas the defense right to produce relevant evidence in a criminal case is constitutionally guaranteed. When they conflict, there's not much question which right prevails. It's really just a matter of natural selection, the law of the legal jungle, the supremacy clause of the U.S. Constitution. My entire staff has also worked diligently through the night and we have Xeroxed several court cases for your review, if you like, where medical material was required to be divulged under similar circumstances. I invite the court to take the subpoenaed materials into chambers, as the cases suggest, and look at them to determine their relevance before making a ruling."

The entire staff of Wilkes's office, me, handed copies of the cases all around. Wilkes continued. "Second, neither Mr. Fosworth nor his client may move to quash the late Judge Knott's medical records as they have no standing. Finally, I would just invoke the call to justice I made to the court yesterday in chambers."

Junior didn't know what to do. His pale blue eyes darted right to left, looking at Fosworth, then to Landish, and then, but only for an instant, to Wilkes. Finding no direction there, he looked down at his desk at the papers he had just been given. "Born to Bill" Fosworth came to the rescue. Having been lied to by his client, Fosworth had not looked at the medical records and had no idea of their relevance to the proceedings. In fact, nobody knew the relevance of the files except Wilkes, Alice Knott, and me. And the Hacker-Cracker. It still amazes me the wealth of material one can obtain with the use of a computer modem and a telephone line. //

FAMOUS LAST WORDS

Fosworth said he thought an in-chambers view of the medical files by Junior not a bad way to resolve the issue of relevance without conceding the issue of privilege. As he told Junior, "From what my client has told me, there is absolutely nothing that could be of any assistance to the defense in those records. And that should settle the matter."

Junior jumped at the idea of getting out of making a decision on the spot. He told the jury to stand at ease in the jury box while he went off to chambers to read the files. He didn't keep us waiting long. He returned to the bench within five minutes looking like he had just seen another note from Wyatt Wonderlick. "I have reviewed the documents," he said softly to the lawyers gathered beneath him at the throne. "Mr. Fosworth, your objection, which I take it comes to me in the form of an oral motion to quash the subpoenaed materials based upon privilege and relevance, are denied for reasons . . ."

Fosworth interrupted: "But Judge, the privilege."

". . . which I am sure will become very apparent in the next few minutes. The privilege must give way to the United States Constitution. I am sorry. Let's proceed."

· · ·

TO THE POINT

Wilkes wasted no time getting to the point. "Mrs. Knott, let me show you these medical records of yours we've subpoenaed."

An aura of toxicity surrounded Alice. Hatred oozed from every perfumed and powdered pore of her body. Wilkes would need a chair and whip to contain her fury. Alice looked to "Born to Bill" Fosworth. "I object to this," she said bitterly. "Born to Bill" was now standing next to her. Not being privy to the judge's ruling at the bench conference, Alice looked at Fosworth as if he had just betrayed her. "Born to Bill" moved close and whispered in her ear, but she jerked her head away and turned to Junior. "Surely this cannot be relevant, Your Honor. It's an invasion of my privacy. Haven't I suffered enough?"

To which Miles Landish added, "Objection, Your Honor. Invasion of her privacy. She's suffered enough."

Junior, still reeling from the trauma of yesterday, was not about to cross Wilkes. Fosworth might be a supporter in the future, but Wilkes could destroy him today. He looked to Alice and said coolly, "I've talked to your lawyer about this and overruled his objections. You'll have to answer these questions."

Wilkes didn't wait for more debate. "Madam, I note you saw your doctor the morning of Judge Knott's murder. That's the day you found out, isn't it?"

"I refuse to answer any questions about my personal health." A thin band of sweat began to appear on Alice's forehead above the eyebrows. She fidgeted in the witness seat against imaginary restraints, as if she were strapped into the electric chair.

"I wonder if I could impose upon the good offices of the court to suggest that the witness answer the question," asked Wilkes ever so politely. Junior was gazing at the tranquilized but conscious Wyatt Wonderlick at the moment. He told Alice to answer. Fosworth moved in again and whispered expensive advice in her ear.

"I saw my doctor. Maybe it was that morning. I don't recall. So what?"

•   •   •

REFRESHMENT

"Perhaps this will refresh your recollection." Wilkes approached her and pointed to a page in her medical file as well as her late husband's. She picked them up as if they were asps. "That's the morning you were shocked to learn that your husband had given you a dread disease, a fatal sexually transmitted disease, which, in addition to imposing a death sentence on you, meant he was sleeping with someone else." To make this accusatory speech into a question, Wilkes added what all good lawyers add at this moment: "Right?"

Alice thought for a few moments. With her sleeve, she wiped the sweat from her eyebrows and said, "I refuse to answer that odious question."

As Alice was proving unresponsive, Wilkes continued with his own explanation—just like in the movies. "You came to chambers a little early that afternoon, making sure you weren't seen by anyone, at least not the first time. You wanted to confront him on his treachery. While you waited for him in chambers you noted his love poem on his computer screen, which you knew wasn't meant for you. More treason."

"How do you know it was not meant for me?" interrupted Alice. "I think it was."

"Because you told Detective Mulraney during one of his interviews that you never saw it before and that he'd never written you a poem in all the time of your marriage—or would you like to tell this jury that this is another time he got it wrong?" Wilkes pointed to Mulraney sitting at the end of the prosecutor's table. Mulraney waved his hanky.

"Y.A. could have been working on it as a surprise gift to me."

"If one looks at the date of that file in the computer, it was created over a year ago." Another hot tip from the Hacker. "You knew from the text it wasn't meant for you. And when he got off the bench and came into chambers, you showed him your medical records because I note the records reflect you got a copy that very day."

"Drop dead," testified Alice.

"A little louder. We can't hear you," said Wilkes. "Tell us the words you said to your faithless husband before plunging the letter opener in his back."

Fosworth was now whispering loudly in Alice's ear. She pushed his head away and said, "I don't believe Y.A. was sleeping around."

"Do you visit the grave site?"

"What? Of course I do."

"Now you know where he sleeps at night."

"Drop dead."

"Tell us, Alice Knott. Do a good deed today and free an innocent man. Tell us the truth. In a fit of jealous rage, you picked up the expensive Italian letter opener on Y.A.'s desk and stuck your husband in the back. Right?"

THOSE MAGIC WORDS

"I refuse to answer any more insulting questions. They are too disgusting and—and—uh, illegal."

"Well, if you want to refuse to answer, you'll have to say the magic words. You can't just refuse."

Alice motioned for more of Fosworth's whispered advice, but she did not like what she got. She sat silent. Wilkes repeated the advice her attorney had just given her. "You can refuse to answer only if you refuse to answer because the answer might tend to . . ." Wilkes paused here for jury effect, and then continued, "INCRIMINATE YOU!"

"That is true, Mrs. Knott," said Junior helpfully.

Alice looked at Junior, then to Fosworth, who nodded. Juror Wyatt Wonderlick also nodded—off. Alice had trouble choking out the words, "I refuse to answer . . . I refuse to answer because the answer might . . . might . . . might tend to . . . incrim— No! I'll not say that, damn you all! I DID NOT KILL Y.A. THERE, YOU HAVE AN ANSWER TO YOUR FILTHY QUESTION! SWINE!" She folded her arms together in front of her, slammed them into her midriff, and scowled at Wilkes.

"Mrs. Knott. Mrs. Knott. One may sometimes tell a lie, but the grimace with which one accompanies it tells the truth," said Wilkes, quoting Nietzsche.

"Drop dead," grimaced Alice.

"No further questions. I move into evidence the medical files."

END GAMES

With that, Junior called a brief recess to figure out what to do next. As the jury filed out, Wilkes picked Alvin up by the shoulders and took him over to Landish's table. "Landish, I think it would be appropriate for you to dismiss at this point. You don't want to be responsible for convicting an innocent man of murder."

Landish was apparently unmoved by Mrs. Knott's grimaces. "You're quite a showman, Wilkes, but in the words of the last witness, drop dead. I'm going to investigate just how you came across those medical files. I smell criminal conduct."

Wilkes put Alvin in front of Landish. "Look this man in the eyes before this jury comes back. Tell him this is no game. Tell him that after what you just heard you actually believe he's guilty."

Alvin Scribner looked at Landish; it was an innocent look which Landish did not recognize. Landish picked up some files and looked at Wilkes. "You know my motto, Wilkes—it takes a smart prosecutor to convict the guilty, but a genius to convict the innocent. I'm not worried." He stuck his index finger in Wilkes's chest. "You, buster, you should be worried. You wanna tell me how you got into her med files or should I give you your rights first?"

"Drop dead, jerk," said Alvin. He slapped Landish's hand away from Wilkes's chest and looked ready to make war on the hulking persecutor. Wilkes quickly drove Alvin back to his seat.

BURGER KING CASE

After that exchange, the jury came back and the attorneys reargued. This time Wilkes had all kinds of logical examples of reasonable doubt to talk to the jury about. The most memorable moment came when he told the jury, "Miles Landish served you folks what we call a Burger King case—a big Whopper. The main course was perjury—and you almost swallowed it. Now it's time to throw it back in his face."

"Yeah, ladies and gentlemen, and the bastard just told me and Mr. Wilkes while you were out that he didn't care if he convicted an innocent man in the process!" A renewed Alvin Scribner, standing ramrod straight, uttered his first words to the jury. They brought on an eruptive exchange of hostilities between Landish and Wilkes.

"Objection! Move to strike. This was staged! Move for sanctions against the defendant and his counsel!" yelled a wounded Landish.

"Would you care to deny to this jury," said Wilkes acidly to Landish, "that you just told us privately precisely what Mr. Scribner just said to the jury? Or will you continue feeding the jury the big Whopper?" Wilkes looked back to the amused jurors. Even Wyatt Wonderlick was now listening as intently as someone could who had overdosed on methadone. "Mr. Landish reminds me of the man who wakes up one morning and says to his wife, 'I just had a nightmare. I dreamed I was reincarnated as a no-good lying piece of skunk-slime.' To which his wife replies, 'Oh, don't worry. God wouldn't do that to anyone twice in a row.'"

"Why you dirty, no-good sonova—" Landish got up from his chair and began to move toward Wilkes, but Detective Mulraney grabbed him and put him back in his seat. Junior called for calm and told Alvin to be quiet. Alvin smiled and sat down.

Wilkes then ended his argument with a quote from Mark Twain. "Ladies and gentlemen, the facts didn't come to you until late in the case, but that's because a lie travels around the world before the truth gets out of bed. Now Lady Truth is up and she is angry. She stands before you. Listen to what she says. She says she has been defiled. She says the case is a plate of perjury served up by the master chef of manufactured evidence." Wilkes pointed his finger at Miles Landish. "She says, 'Free Alvin Scribner.'"

Landish was apoplectic, what with Wilkes's personal attack. He gave a long-winded, self-serving speech on what a great guy he was, a model of ethics and professional responsibility who was honestly doing his job to prosecute the guilty. He came off like the guy Emerson had in mind when he said, "The louder he talked of his honor, the faster we counted the spoons." He got so caught up in defending himself, he hardly touched upon the new evidence except to say that Mrs. Knott's testimony added nothing. He said, "She quite properly refused to talk about her personal medical problems, which is none of our business. That don't prove diddly squat."

The jury thought it proved diddly squat and took less than ten minutes to acquit Alvin.

EPILOGUE

The trouble with indicting and trying the wrong man for murder is that it makes it difficult after the acquittal to point the finger at the person who really did it. Belatedly charging someone else also makes the D.A. look stupid, like he made a little mistake in trying to put the wrong man in prison forever. So Alice Knott was never charged for the murder of her husband by the D.A.'s office. Anyway, she had enough problems.

Wyatt Wonderlick washed police cars in Queens for a few weeks following the trial but was fired for falling asleep on the job. He now is a drug counselor at the Nancy Reagan Center for Artists in New Addictions, a drug and alcohol rehabilitation program catering to dropouts from the Betty Ford Center.

Becky and the Hacker got married a week after the trial. Services were held at the Love Tub Tumble, and Wilkes was best man and I was a witness. Their wedding announcement carried with it the "wove poem" the Hacker wrote to Becky the day they met in blistering Jacuzzi waters.

A few weeks after the wedding, we got another attorney to handle the Hacker's surrender to the NYPD after explaining to Jethro that it might not look so good for Wilkes to represent him. Anyway, he was only a fugitive a couple of weeks, and after explaining he only left the hotel because he was lovesick for his girlfriend, whom he had just made his bride, all was well. He got his sentence reduced to a few months because the cops and prosecution told the court that his "technical assistance and cooperation in *People* versus *Scribner* helped crack open the case." Little do they know.

Today, the Hacker runs the new computerized customer accounts system at the Love Tub Tumble, where business is said to be hot and better than ever. He is also vice-president in charge of sales, which means he runs the cash register.

We took a financial bath defending Alvin, and I was still worried about Wilkes. The last two cases he took for either a reduced rate (Becky's) or for nothing (Alvin's). So when our next prospective client came in, I listened with great interest to the fee talk.

The first promising client was a millionairess named Mrs. Stephanie Bowman who was suspected in the death of her husband of twenty-five years. She was telling Wilkes, "It was a horrible mistake. We had separate bedrooms, you see, and there'd been reports of break-ins in our neighborhood. I didn't know it was him, Mr. Wilkes. Really. It was self-defense. He came at me in the dark in the middle of the night. I saw a flash of something metallic-looking in the man's hand. How was I to know he was bringing me a glass of hot chocolate in a pewter cup? Can you believe it?"

"Yes, quite tragic."

"No, I mean putting hot chocolate in a pewter cup!"

"Yes, yes. Very peculiar. How many shots did you fire?"

"Just two, Mr. Wilkes. Both hit the target—I mean, Eddie, my poor husband, unfortunately—in the body, well, to the heart and between the eyes. I'm quite a good shot."

"So it seems. It might interest you to know that you violated the Warning Shot Rule of the French Foreign Legion. It says that when shooting someone, always fire two shots, the first in his chest, the second in the air. When explaining later, remember them in reverse order. But let's not worry about that right now. We need to talk about fees. Let's see here."

Wilkes made a big production out of doing complicated mental calculations in his head—"let's see, so many hundred hours of this, and for that, and investigation, and the forensic experts, and so on"—and then wrote a large number upon his legal pad. Without saying a word, he pushed it toward Mrs. Bowman. These were always moments of truth for both Wilkes and the client. If the amount on the pad was too much, the clients would, after recovering their wind, walk out. If it was too little—a rare event—well then, the Wilkesian estimate was obviously grossly undervalued.

Mrs. Bowman looked at the figure and reacted as if she had just read the menu at the Four Seasons. "Oh, that's no problem, Mr. Wilkes. Very reasonable. Shall I write you a check?"

She reached into her purse. Wilkes didn't hesitate a second before replying, "By all means, Mrs. Bowman. But please understand that the amount I've written there is not my fee; it's my price per shot."

Wilkes was back.